BAD
COMPANY

ALSO BY VIRGINIA SWIFT

Brown-Eyed Girl

BAD
COMPANY

VIRGINIA
SWIFT

HarperCollins*Publishers*

This is a work of fiction. The characters, incidents, and dialogues are products of the author's imagination and are not to be construed as real. Any resemblance to actual persons, living or dead, is entirely coincidental.

HarperCollins books may be purchased for educational, business, or sales promotional use. For information, please write: Special Markets Department, HarperCollins Publishers Inc., 10 East 53rd Street, New York, NY 10022.

FIRST EDITION

Printed on acid-free paper

Library of Congress Cataloging-in-Publication Data

Swift, Virginia.
   Bad Company / Virginia Swift.— 1st ed.
      p. cm.
   ISBN 0-06-019554-1 (alk. paper)
   1. Laramie (Wyo.)—Fiction. I. Title.
   PS3569.W516 B33 2002
   813'.54—dc21   2001046494

02 03 04 05 06 ❖/RRD 10 9 8 7 6 5 4 3 2 1

For Vi and Bunk

THANKS

THIS WORK OF FICTION would not have been possible without the expert advice, generous support, and all-around kindness of many friends. In Cody, thanks to Officer Darrell Steward of the Cody Police Department, for an introduction to police procedure; Mary Ackerman and Marty Coe, Wyoming businesswomen and early morning risers; Paul Fees, Lillian Turner, and all the good people at the Buffalo Bill Historical Center; Doug Hart and Harriet Corbett, hospitable ranchers. In Sheridan, Officer Trevor Martin patiently answered my very basic questions. Katie Curtiss and Hal Corbett have, as always, provided endless insight, guided tours of the big country, put me up, and even bought the wine. In Laramie, Kathy Jensen and Audie Blevins make me feel at home even when they're planning the next trek to, yes, Kathmandu.

Thanks to new friends who help me navigate the writer's world: authors Fred Harris and Stephen White; my incredible agent, Elaine Koster; my amazing editor, Carolyn Marino.

For keeping the music alive, thanks to Steve Ballou, Tom Baumgartel, Michael Davis, Henry Fountain, Catherine Kleiner,

Colin Keeney, Joe Massey, Jon Myers, Craig Pinto, Bev Seckinger, and Joe Vinikow.

Here in Albuquerque, I'm grateful to Dr. Mike Crossey, for cheerfully answering my impertinent questions about matters of pathology; Dr. Beth Morgan, for other medical expertise; Kay Marcotte and the fine folks at Page One; patient readers and dear companions Beth Bailey and Melissa Bokovoy; number one consumer Karen Marcotte; the Gators and their parents; and the First Friday group. As always, Peter Swift has been my most excellent editor, audience, and beloved partner, and Sam and Annie Swift have fed my heart. Other Swift family members have sustained us all, even though we're far away.

Finally, thank you to Violette and Henry Levkoff, who have had faith in me from the beginning. Not just for the gourmet wines and black-tie guests at the Black Orchid bookshop, or even the haute cuisine barbecues in Manhattan, but for (egad) almost half a century of love, this is for you.

MONDAY

CHAPTER 1
THE DEATH TRAP

SALLY ALDER had never been all that big on the notion that the two sexes were, in some fundamental way, opposites. She tended to believe that men and women had a lot more in common than, say, palm trees and golden retrievers, and she'd always held that any woman had the potential to be as big a jerk as any man.

But she was beginning to think that there might be some differences between the genders that were hardwired. Take, for example, the inability of male drivers to navigate supermarket parking lots. Every time you came within a hair of a head-on with some flea brain evidently unaware of the fact that all the parked cars were pointing in one (i.e., the other) direction, you just knew there'd be a guy behind the wheel. Even Hawk Green, a man who could find his way through the densest forest and navigate across the most trackless desert with the confidence of a man getting in an elevator, seemed to have a brain freeze every time he had to tackle the grocery store lot.

On this lovely Wyoming summer morning, the parking lot of
the Laramie Lifeway was terrifyingly full of them, in big rusting
pickups and behemoth RVs and SUVs, half of them hauling horse
trailers, scaring the hell out of the regular shoppers and the mild-
mannered tourist families who had the lack of imagination to be
headed down the aisles in the normal way. Sally'd decided to play
it safe and park halfway down an empty row, far from the store,
when a long-bed king-cab Ford swerved ass-backward into the
space right next to her. Just as she was opening the door of her
mint-condition, 1964 1/2 Mustang and stepping out, three happy
cowpokes in plaid shirts and brand-new straw hats leaped out of
the Ford in a clatter of empty beer cans, hauled a giant Coleman
cooler out of the bed of the pickup, pulled the plug on the bottom,
and started draining cooler water all over her new Italian sandals.
She looked down into the open cooler. A ballooning plastic bag
containing a loaf of Wonder bread and a half-open pack of bologna
floated in two inches of cloudy fluid.

Bologna water on her new shoes.

She gave the pokes a murderous look, but they were too busy
deciding that their lunch looked good enough to go another day.
Fine. Maybe they'd get botulism.

To be fair, the pokes weren't the only source of congestion.
Threading her way to the store, Sally first ran afoul of a Winneba-
go with Nebraska plates unloading an oversize couple, tempers
inflamed by raging red sunburns, fighting about whose idea it had
been to spend Sunday by the pool at the Little America campground, and who had forgotten that the sun was stronger at high
altitude. Then she was nearly run down by a pair of spandex-clad
mountain bikers who were treating the parking lot like the rad-
most slickrock at Moab. And finally, wonder of wonders, a vintage
Volkswagen van sat blocking the handicapped access ramp. The
van had disgorged a tribe of pierced and tattooed dreadheads in tie-
dyed T-shirts and jeans, panhandling shoppers for grub money.

Jubilee Days. Every July, for one week, it was the same. Here it
was only Monday morning, and already the multitude was gathering for the feast. Laramie locals had three choices: party down,
hunker down, or get out.

Long experience had taught Sally to plan a combination of the three, starting with getting out. She and Hawk were taking the afternoon off and heading up to the mountains for a hike. The Laramie Range, east of town on the way to Cheyenne, wasn't as high or as breathtaking as the Snowies, but it was a shorter drive. Hawk could get some work done in the morning, and she figured she'd get in a bout of grocery shopping. Pulling a cart out from the line of them nested together, she nearly collided with the red-faced Nebraskans. Yep, "bout" was the word.

Laramie had four supermarkets, and Sally had shopped them all and settled on the Lifeway. It was closest to her house, she knew where everything was, and now and then she could even find a piece of fish that didn't look like it had been forced to crawl all the way from the ocean to Wyoming. Ordinarily she found the store well enough stocked, spacious, and clean. The employees, if not uniformly friendly and helpful, were at least not generally surly and incompetent. A model consumer experience, even though she and Hawk had the habit of referring to the place as "the Death Trap."

Today the place was nearing overload. The aisles were jammed. The shelves had already been denuded of high-demand items like hot dogs and Oreos and Velveeta, and the stock clerks were having a hard time keeping up. Sally was rushing through her own shopping and trying to get the hell out of there when, as was inevitable, she ran into someone she knew, who wanted to yak. Amber McCloskey, a University of Wyoming student who was house-sitting for Sally's friends Edna McCaffrey and Tom Youngblood, was bearing down on her with a cartload of trail mix, instant oatmeal, and macaroni and cheese. "Hey, Dr. Alder! How you doin'?" she said cheerfully, the metal stud in her tongue flapping up and down in a hypnotic little dance.

"Hey, Amber," Sally returned weakly, registering two facial piercings (lip and eyebrow) she wasn't sure she'd seen before. "How's Edna's house?"

"Great! Gosh, I can't believe how big it is compared to my apartment. I don't know how they keep it clean all the time!"

Bad sign.

"And all those plants they've got—inside, outside, upstairs, downstairs, jeez, it's practically a jungle. The water bills must be, like, gigantic! Of course, you don't really need to water as much as they told me to," Amber said with a laugh. "Most of what's out there will survive or it won't. If I was going off to do my fieldwork in Kathmandu for the summer, like Dean McCaffrey is, I sure wouldn't have bothered planting that big vegetable garden."

They probably shouldn't have, Sally thought. She imagined that by the time Amber was done ignoring the garden, Edna and Tom's yard would be a scale model of the surface of Mars. Edna wasn't all that good at unpleasant surprises, and despite having a sterling character and excellent manners, Edna knew subtle techniques for passing the unpleasantness along. Not only was she one of Sally's best friends, but she was also the dean of arts and sciences, and Sally was a history professor. On just about every level, Sally figured, it paid to keep Edna happy.

"Maybe I should come by and take a look at the garden," Sally offered. "I love to weed and water—I do it to relax. You'd be doing me a favor."

"Yeah, well, whatever. Actually, I'm glad I ran into you. The dean told me to call you if anything came up, and as it turns out, my boyfriend just asked me to go camping in Canada for a couple of weeks. We're heading out tomorrow, so I won't be around. I felt kind of bad about leaving the house, being as how I told Dean McCaffrey and Mr. Youngblood I'd hang around and all."

And, er, "being as how" Edna and Tom were paying Amber for the hanging. Sally gave the girl her best professorial stare. "You're just leaving Edna and Tom's house for two weeks?" she asked.

"Oh, don't worry, Dr. Alder. I was kind of freaked about taking this little trip, but everything's all worked out. This guy called yesterday to say he was an old friend of the dean's from Princeton, and was planning to drop by for a visit on his way out to the West Coast. He said he'd be in tomorrow, and since he didn't have a tight timetable, he'd be glad to stick around and keep an eye on things. How about that?" Amber said.

An old friend of Edna's from Princeton? An academic with two weeks of slack in his schedule? "Oh really? What's the guy's name?" Sally asked.

Amber's face scrunched up in thought. Her facial jewelry quivered. "Something to do with an appliance, I think. Oh yeah! Stover. Sheldon Stover. He said they were colleagues at the institute."

Sally knew that Edna had been a fellow at Princeton's Institute for Advanced Study, so that made sense. But she'd never heard of this Sheldon Stover. "You say he'll be here tomorrow? Do you plan to stick around to meet him?"

Now Amber was frowning. This perfect solution to her house-sitting dilemma might have its drawbacks. "Well, actually, no. We want to get an early start, so I told this Stover guy I'd just leave a key in the mailbox. He said he was driving in from Omaha or someplace, and he'd be in around three in the afternoon. Said he was really sorry to miss Dean McCaffrey and all, but he was glad to be able to stay at her house."

Shit. Sally figured she'd better make a point of getting over to Edna's and check out this Stover guy. He might easily turn out to be a substantially better house-sitter than Amber McCloskey (could hardly be worse, from the sound of it), but at the very least she thought Edna would want her to show Sheldon Stover how to turn on a hose. "Well, don't you worry about it, Amber. I'll get over there tomorrow afternoon and meet him, give him the house and garden tour. You just have a great camping trip."

Sally would email Edna in Kathmandu and let her know what was up. Since Edna was out in the villages much of the time, the email connection was unreliable, but at least Sally would have made the effort. And duly notified, Edna could decide herself whether to fire Amber's ass and have Sally get somebody else to stay in the house. Meanwhile, Sally'd better keep an eye on things over at the McCaffrey-Youngblood abode.

By now, people were bumping into each other's carts in their haste to grab the last tube of Crest or package of Charmin. Sally hustled to the checkout counter, only to find herself dangling at the back of a tediously long line. The new issues of the check stand tabloids didn't come out until Tuesday, and she'd already caught up with last week's scandals from Hollywood and Washington. She'd have to fall back on *Martha Stewart Living*, which at least offered the amusing possibility of trying to imagine anyone in

Laramie taking a shine to Edwardian silver teapots or water lilies.

But she knew why the line was moving so slowly. Checker trainee. That was bad enough—they always had trouble with the scanner, and had to look up the codes for fruits and vegetables—but to compound the delays, the trainee in question was one Monette Bandy, recently promoted from shelf stocking, a kid who might already be stretching her peak career potential.

As it happened, Sally knew a little more about the new checker than she might have wished, because Monette was the niece of Sally's good friends Dickie and Mary Langham. Dickie was the sheriff of Albany County, a man with a past that didn't bear much scrutiny. Dickie's wife, Mary, had at one time been the crunchiest young earth mother in Laramie, raising her three children on buckwheat groats and spaghetti squash, and wondering why the kids always seemed to have Dorito breath when they came home from parties. Mary's sister Tanya, a woman famous for her lack of common sense even in the judgment-challenged 1970s, had run off with a bad-news roughneck by the name of Pettibone "Bone" Bandy, and Monette was the result. Sally had met Monette a couple of times at barbecues at Dickie and Mary's.

From the looks of things there in the checkout line, Monette had inherited her mother's unerring predilection for scumbags. Just now she was flirting awkwardly with an evil-smelling fat guy in a sweaty cowboy shirt that gaped open between the snaps, barely covering a barrel belly that was slopping over a belt that didn't manage to keep his jeans from riding down unpalatably in the back. When the guy smiled at Monette it made Sally think of medieval dentistry, but Monette was simpering and smiling back as if he was frigging Mel Gibson or something.

Then again, Monette wasn't exactly Julia Roberts. Her mother, Tanya, and her aunt Mary had been what Sally's family had always called "zaftig," and Monette had added a few Twinkies to the package. She'd dyed her hair the color of number two pencils, and her teeth were a fair match for those of the guy who was hitting on her. In fact, if there was a Hollywood star Monette could be said to resemble, it would be Gene Hackman. But he would probably have gotten those teeth fixed.

"I get off in an hour," Monette was saying to the guy. "Maybe we could go get a beer or something. I know all the good places."

"I'd sure enough like to get a little something," said the guy, "but I reckon my old lady would kill my ass. She's out in the truck right now, waiting for her carton of Kools. We drove down from Worland and she ran out of cigs fifty miles back, and then the baby started screaming her head off. The wife's ready to tear the fucking truck apart, but she's gotta breast-feed the brat so I get to come in here and get her butts for her."

What a prince.

"Well, if you're in town for the rodeo, maybe later this week you can sneak off and you and me can party somewhere," Monette suggested.

What, Sally wondered, could the girl possibly be thinking?

The guy just chuckled, leered at Monette's chest, took a minute to give Sally an unwelcome once-over, pocketed his change, and swaggered away.

"Hey, Monette," Sally said, loading her stuff onto the conveyor belt. "Insane in here today."

"Yeah, it'll be busy all week," the girl mumbled, not looking Sally in the eye. "Jubilee Days. What do you expect? What're these things?" she asked, holding up a plastic bag full of vegetables.

"Artichokes," said Sally. "They're really good."

"Never heard of 'em." Monette looked up the code, punched it in, went back to scanning bar codes.

"Think you'll get out to the rodeo?" Sally asked, passing the time.

"Yeah, I'll get there," said Monette, eyeballing a tin of anchovies with suspicion, but passing it across the scanning glass, "if they let me out of this puke hole." She looked wistfully out at the parking lot, where the man she'd just hit on was firing up a particularly noisy Chevy pickup and—what else—heading the wrong way down the aisle. "Everybody's in town lookin' for fun, and I'm stuck working afternoons and nights almost the whole week. Today's about my only day to get it on. I got things to do."

"Well, I guess as the newest checker in the place, everybody else must have seniority, huh?" Sally said.

Monette said, "Whatever."

Thinking about the exchange she'd just seen, it might be a good thing for Monette to be confined to the Lifeway during prime party time. Rocky Mountain rodeos always brought in more than enough of the kind of men who were looking, as the fat guy had so poetically put it, to "get a little something" from a girl witless enough to make eye contact in a bar. Monette might try to act streetwise, but Sally knew that she was only twenty-one, new in town, obviously desperate for attention, and not the brightest pixel on the screen. Sally had found the conversation she'd just witnessed disturbing, and she said nothing as Monette bagged her groceries.

As Monette handed Sally the receipt, her eyes wandered away to the man next in line, a skinny dude with stingy eyes, sporting biker colors. "Hi there," Monette said throatily. "Nice leather." And then, remembering the Lifeway training manual, she turned to Sally and said, "Have a nice day."

"Yeah, you too," Sally replied. And then on impulse touched Monette on the wrist and said, "And a nice week. Take care, okay?"

But Monette had already moved on to the biker.

Shaking her head, Sally wheeled her cartful of bags out the door. How was it possible that a girl like Monette Bandy had gotten to adulthood without developing any sense of self-protection at all? Maybe Tanya had never gotten around to telling her not to take candy from strangers. Or, as happened in too many families, maybe strangers looked like a good bet, compared to what Monette had to deal with at home. Sally didn't really want to think about it. But she figured that next time she saw Mary and Dickie, she'd better let them know that Monette could use a little more friendly guidance from the loving auntie and uncle.

Sally was pulling into the driveway of the house on Eighth Street just as Hawk was swinging down the front walk, his daypack bulging at the bottom, full of rocks and notebooks. College professors were supposed to have the summers off from teaching to do their own research. Sally herself had just turned in a book manuscript to her publisher, and she had the whole summer to catch up on a backlog of reading so mountainous it was nearly driving her out of her office. But Hawk Green was a geologist, so for him, summer meant spending at least half his time shepherding his grad students through the fieldwork they had to do for their theses and dissertations. Mostly he liked it, but it did mean hauling around other people's rocks.

Ah well, he had the back for it. On the far side of forty, Hawk was long-legged and lean-hipped, carrying most of his weight in his shoulders. As long as Sally had known him, he'd never seemed to care enough about his physical appearance to change it. He wore jeans and T-shirts and boots or basketball shoes, and the same round John Lennon glasses he'd favored since she'd first laid eyes on him, more than twenty years ago. He'd never bothered to cut his hair, but tied it back in a thick ponytail that fell, black streaked with silver now, halfway down his back. His face had developed some seams and crags over the years, and she considered that all to the good. The two of them were the same age, and they both looked it. It worked for them, especially when they were naked.

The thought of Hawk naked made her smile as she opened the trunk to get the groceries, and he smiled too as he came over and picked up a couple of bags. "How was the Death Trap?" he asked.

"Lethal," she said. "I got hosed with bologna water before I got halfway out of my car."

"Bologna water?" Hawk asked.

"Never mind. You'd know it if you saw it," she said, following him in the door and into the kitchen–dining room to put down the bags. "It's the liquid generally found in the bottom of a cowboy's cooler."

"Got it," said Hawk. "Ick."

"Yeah, that's about how it was. The parking lot was a madhouse and the lines were starting to creep back into the aisles. I ran into Amber McCloskey, that student who's supposedly house-sitting for Edna and Tom. It sounds like she's already filthied up the place and killed all their plants, and now she's taking off on a camping trip for two weeks. But she told me not to worry, because some guy named Sheldon Stover had called up saying he was a friend of Edna's from Princeton, headed this way, and he offered to stay in the house for a couple of weeks."

"You've got to be kidding," Hawk said.

Sally shook her head. "This Stover shows up tomorrow. I'll go over there and give him the holy word. Jesus, just what this town needs this week, one more damn flatlander. The Jubilee-ers have arrived."

"You make it sound like an invading army," Hawk said, shrugging off his pack and starting to unload a grocery bag, frowning at the tin of anchovies.

"They say an army marches on its stomach," she replied. "And if that's so, I saw some well-armed people doing their marching. You know Monette?" she asked him.

"The one who's Dickie and Mary's niece, who works down there? Vaguely. Why?"

"They promoted her to checker trainee, and I ended up in her endless line. When I finally got to unloading my stuff on the check stand, she was making goo-goo eyes at a real horror-show redneck specimen, and by the time she'd checked me out, she'd already started chatting up a ratty little biker with a face like a pocket gopher. Looking for trouble. Hell of a week for it."

Hawk tilted his head, thought a minute. "Maybe she's just clueless. Either way, you might want to say something to Dickie and Mary. Monette's an orphan or something, isn't she?"

"Or something," said Sally. "Her mother's dead, and from what I hear, she'd be better off if her father were."

"Family values," said Hawk. "Every time a politician starts in on the subject, it makes me want to check my wallet." He pulled a jar of pepperoncini and a bottle of cooking marsala out of the bag he was unloading. "Didn't you buy any real food?"

Sally laughed. He ate pretty much anything anybody served him, but when it was Hawk's turn to cook, he liked it straight and simple. "Yeah yeah. I've got the peanut butter and jelly."

"Good," he said. "I thought maybe being in mortal danger left you too shell-shocked to shop. Why don't you make us a lunch and I'll gas up the truck and we can get going."

One of the great things about Laramie was that even at the moment when the town was filling up for the annual week of hell-raising, it took only about five minutes to get out of town, and get into the mountains or the prairie or the desert. And nothing beat being out in the boonies in Wyoming on a July afternoon. After lunch Sally and Hawk headed east on I-80, up into the Laramie Range, aiming for the pink granite hills the locals called Vedauwoo, a word they pronounced "Vee-da-voo," sort of rhyming with "peekaboo." Rock climbers loved the rugged cliffs, and hikers could follow a hundred different little-traveled trails, or simply head off along streambeds or across meadows toward high places, looking for a view. They'd decided to try a place neither of them had been, identified on Hawk's topo map as the Devil's Playground. From the Death Trap to the Devil's Playground in one day? Playing with fire there, darlin', Sally thought.

But the weather was perfect—cloudless big sky, balmy and not too windy, wildflowers everywhere. They walked for hours, mixing easy strolls across the rolling grasslands with scrambles up and down tumbled piles of boulders, catching endless views large and small. Part of the way, to catch some shade, they'd followed the path of a creek, marveling at the delicacy of tiny wood violets and moss. And then, wanting views, they'd hiked up to a sweeping meadow between two jutting granite outcrops. Carpets of tall blue lupines flourished, mixed with delicate fleabane and purple asters, buttery yellow thermopsis and little sawtooth prairie stars. The Indian paintbrush, the state flower and Sally's favorite, was abundant. There was something impudent and sexy about those clusters of flaming spikes, something that had her shooting a certain kind of look at the man she'd loved twice in her life, including this time. But he was too busy watching birds to catch her drift.

She looked up. A red-tailed hawk swooped, looking for prey. Over the outcrop they were headed toward, a half-dozen vultures swung lazily overhead, circling lower and lower.

"Something dead over there," said Hawk.

"Probably a cow. Maybe we should turn around," said Sally. "I have no desire to hike out there only to end up looking at cattle remains."

Hawk shook his head. "I don't know. I don't think they're grazing up here. Not that much good grass, and we haven't seen any cow pies. I think we should take a look."

"Why?" said Sally. "It could be anything. This is where the

deer and the antelope play. What's the big deal?" The hair on the back of her neck was standing on end. For no reason at all, she had that big-deal feeling too, but wondered why they'd walk toward death rather than run away from it.

But Hawk was already walking, his hand on the sheath of the knife he took hiking, fingering the snap, determined to get to whatever they were looking at on the ground. She had a hard time keeping up, half running, panting as she reached the place where the grass began to be broken up with rocks, the terrain turning into flat nooks of grass and dirt ringed by boulders, at the edge of the outcrop. Sally decided this place must be familiar to people who liked to get out in the country to do some of their partying. The grass had been well-trampled, the ground dusty. There was an old fire ring, full of cold ashes and burned beer cans, and a lot more litter than Sally cared to see. Empty Coors cans and the cardboard twelve-pack box. Cigarette butts, empty cigarette packs. An old tin of Skoal chewing tobacco.

Hawk was already on his way up, making his way over the rocks. When he crawled between two upended boulders and disappeared behind them, she doubled her pace to catch up.

And then wished she hadn't.

There was a sickening, rotten-sweet odor in the air. Hawk stood there, rock-still. Sally's whole body turned to granite, looking at what he was seeing. Sticking out of a crevice between a jumble of rocks, just below, was the arm of a woman. There was some kind of cord wrapped around her wrist, one long end dangling down.

"Don't get any closer," Hawk finally said.

It shook her out of her paralysis. "What? We have to. There might be a chance she's still alive."

Hawk cleared his throat. "Sally, she's not alive. Buzzards have a real good feel for that."

But Sally was a woman spellbound. Slowly, carefully, she crawled over the scrambled rocks to the crevice and looked down. At hair the color of a number two pencil, matted with blood.

CHAPTER 2
IT'S JUST A SHOT AWAY

SALLY STRAIGHTENED UP, the peanut butter sandwich she'd had for lunch a new and unpleasant return visitor. Hawk, using his own personal mojo combination of Yankee self-control and desert survivor stillness, had managed to keep from throwing up, but he was white-faced and wide-eyed.

She knelt down, took off her daypack, and balanced it on a rock. Rooting around, she found a bottle of water. She twisted off the top, took a big swallow, and spat to get rid of the sour taste. No help there. She drank some, then poured half the rest over her head.

Shit, Monette. Why?

"We've gotta call Dickie," Sally said at last.

"Call?" asked Hawk.

She dug back in the pack and pulled out a cellular phone. She'd given it to Hawk for his birthday, hoping he'd take it with him when he went out in the field, but he'd so far refused to have anything to do with it. He liked being where nobody could reach him. Cell phones, he said, were wrecking the world, cluttering up the landscape with cell towers, making every place the same as every other.

"Handy to have that," he conceded, "but it probably won't work up here."

"Maybe not. It's worth a try," she told him. "Every day you see them putting up more towers. We could be in range." She stuck the phone in the pocket of her shorts and climbed up out of the dip, back through the gap between the two upended rocks, hoping to pick up a relay.

She turned on the phone, and was relieved to see the icon for the cell tower appear. Punched in 911. A dispatcher answered.

"My name is S-Sally Alder," she stammered. "I'm up in Vedauwoo, somewhere around the Devil's Playground, and, uh, I've f-found a body. That is, we've found a b-body." She took a deep gulp of air, exhaled. "Ah, you'd better tell Sheriff Langham to get up here."

"Calm down, ma'am," said the dispatcher. "Can you give me your exact location?"

That was too much for Sally. About all she knew was that she was in the Laramie Range. When it came to knowing where the hell she was, she usually just looked at the scenery and left the locating to Hawk.

"Just a minute," she said, as he came out of the declivity and she handed him the phone.

While Hawk was unfolding his map, talking to the dispatcher, giving directions to the nearest Forest Service road, Sally entertained a series of irrational thoughts. She should have made a point of talking to Monette right that morning, as she'd watched the girl deal with those guys in the line. Should have warned her. Or she and Hawk should be running around, seeing if they could find whoever had put Monette in the crevice. Or maybe she should pick up all the litter. She stooped down and scooped up an empty cigarette package, shoving it in her knapsack.

But this was a crime scene. Sally realized suddenly that she shouldn't mess with anything. She could already see the prints of her hiking boots and Hawk's on ground scuffed by other shoes, including somebody's pointy-toed cowboy boots. The cops would want to see those tracks. She'd better sit down.

Moving toward rational thought, anyhow. And then a rational question occurred to her: What were she and Hawk doing hanging around someplace way out in the outback, with the cops at least an hour away, where one person had already been murdered? How freaking brilliant was that?

She ran to Hawk, just ending the call with the dispatcher, yanking his arm. "We have to get out of here! What if whoever did this is still around? Come on, hurry—we've got to run!"

Trust Hawk to be reasonable at a time like this. "Run where? We've just been calling the cops. They'll be here in half an hour. If I'd done that"—he tossed his head back in the direction of Monette's body—"I'd get the hell out, fast. And if, for some reason, I was still hanging around when a couple of hikers showed up, and then heard them phoning for the police, I'd figure it was high time to split."

"What do you mean, the cops will be here in half an hour?" Sally demanded. "We've been walking all afternoon. How could they get here that quickly?"

"Sal, we parked all the way back at the Lincoln Summit and set out for a summer stroll. You can get here a lot faster by pulling off the highway at the Vedauwoo exit and then coming up the dirt roads. Trust me, they'll be here before you know it. And meanwhile, we're supposed to sit tight."

By now she was shivering. He peeled her hand off his arm, so that he could hold her. Dickie Langham and two deputies found them still wrapped together, not quite forty minutes later.

The outcrop where they stood was only a few hundred yards from the road, but Dickie was huffing and puffing as he walked toward them. That's what came of being forty pounds over your game weight and smoking two packs of Marlboros a day. Sally had tried to get him to quit smoking, and Dickie's sister Delice was constantly on his case about losing weight. He always responded that he'd give up smoking when they invented a way where he didn't have to wear a stupid patch or enter an insane asylum to do it. And as for being overweight, he didn't see how Delice could put him on the kind of diet where he couldn't eat the burgers and fries and cattlemen's coronary breakfasts she was so glad to serve everybody else who came into the Wrangler Bar and Grill, the dance hall and grease haven that Langham women had been running for more than half a century. The fancy food they served at the Yippie I O café, the restaurant in which Delice was a partner with their cousin Burt and his chef boyfriend, was a little healthier than the stuff at the Wrangler, and Delice often claimed it was too wholesome for her taste. So Dickie said he'd rather be fat than a hypocrite like Delice, and that usually shut her up for a while.

It wasn't like he was trying to destroy himself. Dickie had done that years ago, when he'd been a beanpole of a coke-dealing bartender who got a little too fond of the merchandise. He'd ended up on the run, gone missing for eleven years, come back to Mary and the kids fatter and wiser and sober and ready, at last, to settle down. He'd never been convicted of a crime, but that fact was more a product of police neglect and incompetence and his own skill at evasion, than of model citizenship. Not everyone would have thought of a law enforcement career under those circumstances, but Dickie had always had an original mind.

And a warm heart. Maybe that was why the good citizens of Albany County had seen fit to elect him sheriff. He took one look at Sally and Hawk and folded them both into one of his patented I'm-big-but-I'm-gentle Dickie Langham hugs. Then he beckoned to a deputy holding a giant travel mug of extra-strength coffee from the Kum 'n' Go Gas and Convenience Store. "Brought you some coffee," he said. "Have a jolt while we have a look around, and then we'll talk."

Sally took a swig of the coffee. It was bitter and muddy, but from a chemical standpoint, it worked. She could speak. "You know, don't you? You know who . . ."

"Yeah," said Dickie, his face unreadable, coplike. He'd shifted from friend to pro. "Hawk told the dispatcher. Monette."

"We weren't completely sure," Hawk explained. "We couldn't actually see the face. She's all jammed up in that crack . . . but from the hair, and what we could see of her body, and, well, the uniform."

Dickie didn't say anything, but his eyes shifted. His deputy had clambered up over the rocks and was calling for him. "We'll take it from here. Stick around. We're going to want a statement."

He turned to the deputy. "Did you call the county attorney?"

"Yeah," the deputy replied, "but he wasn't in the office. I called his house and his wife said he went fishing and he won't be back until tomorrow."

"Goddamn it," said Dickie. "I guess that'll have to be soon enough. If we need a warrant before then, we can manage. What about Scotty?"

"He's on the way," the deputy answered. "So's the coroner. And I called the crime lab in Cheyenne."

"Good," said Dickie, turning back to Sally and Hawk. "Detective Scotty Atkins is our investigator. He'll be here any minute, and he'll want you guys to answer some questions. If you don't mind, I'll listen in."

"Thanks," said Sally.

"Nothing to it," Dickie replied. "Where're you parked?"

"We left the truck back at the summit," Hawk said.

"Okay," Dickie said. "We'll give you a lift back there when we're finished with you."

By the time they were all done, it was well past dark. Sally and Hawk sat on rocks and watched as the police did their thing. In a perfectly gruesome way, it was fascinating. The state crime lab van arrived from Cheyenne, not long after Dickie and his deputies. They took about a million photographs and drew sketches, then searched the surrounding area, looking for footprints and taking more pictures. They cast latex impressions of the best footprints, including the waffle tread of Sally and Hawk's boots and the cowboy boot print Sally had noticed, along with an imprint of a square-toed platform shoe. From Sally's point of view, the cops weren't adding to the scenic beauty of the place. The few straggling wildflowers left in the glen leaned at angles, trampled and half broken at the stems. Even the ants didn't want to hang around. Sally watched as a stream of them marched off to their hole, carrying a yellowed and dried stalk of grass, straight and thin as straw.

The techs put on surgical gloves and went around picking up every beer can and cigarette butt, putting the refuse in plastic baggies and tagging each bag with the location of the contents. They took particular care with the Skoal tin. It had been crushed, and the techs speculated about whether they'd get any decent prints off it.

And now here came another man, tall and spare with thinning sandy hair, taking the same hill that had gotten Dickie winded, in long, easy strides. He wore Dockers, running shoes, and a button-down shirt with a pony on the pocket. As he came closer, Sally saw his eyes, sharp and very light green, sweeping over the scene and lighting on her briefly, then on Hawk.

"Hey, Scotty," said Hawk.

"H'lo, Joe," the man replied.

Most people in Laramie knew Professor Josiah Hawkins Green not by his college nickname but as Joe, the given name he used professionally. This guy—Detective Atkins, presumably—must be a recent acquaintance, Sally surmised.

"We play basketball three times a week," Hawk explained, reading her mind, offering an introduction. "This is Professor Sally Alder."

"Professor Alder," said the man, shaking her hand with both of his. "I'm Scott Atkins. Sorry about this." He let go of her hand. "I'm handling the investigation for the Sheriff's Department. I understand that you two found the body. In a little bit, I'll be needing to ask you some questions."

"We'll tell you what we can," said Hawk, but Atkins had already turned away, getting out a notebook and walking toward the body.

This Atkins didn't waste time. "How's he on the basketball court?" Sally asked Hawk.

"Hell on defense, great jumper from the top of the key. I guess he was a hero at Laramie High in his youth, but blew out his knee his freshman year at UW," Hawk answered.

Sally waited for more.

"Good teammate, bad opponent," Hawk said.

The Albany County coroner showed up just as the sun was slipping below the horizon. He and Dickie talked briefly, then he

went over and took a look down at the body in the crevice. The
coroner took some pictures and made some notes of his own.

And then it was time to get Monette out of there. Sally didn't
want to watch, but some flaw in her personality made her climb
back into the declivity to get a view anyway. Hawk, it seemed, had
the same character weakness. He was right behind her.

It wasn't pretty. Monette's body had stiffened up with death,
and the rocks she was stuck between were way too big to move.
The crime lab techs were as careful as they could be, trying to preserve the body in the condition it had been left, but they had to get
the deputies to help them pull and haul for minutes that seemed like
hours, cursing and sweating. Dickie, the coroner, and the detective
stood to one side, talking in low voices, watching intently, their
faces blank. Sally could hardly believe how calm they all were.
Once she thought she heard the crunch of breaking bone, but it
might have been nothing more than the sound of her own senses
stretching to the snapping point. Suddenly she was aware of sitting
spraddle-legged on a hard lumpy rock, elbows on her thighs, the
almost empty Kum 'n' Go mug dangling from her forefinger. She
drank the dregs of the cold coffee and nearly barfed all over her
hiking boots.

Hawk must have been watching her. The next thing she knew,
he had his hand on the back of her neck and she had her head
between her knees and he was saying, "Deep breaths. Come on,
Mustang. They've got her out of there now. They'll be talking to us
soon. Don't mess up the second pair of shoes in one day."

She finally looked up again. Couldn't help herself. She'd never
looked at a corpse before.

In the waning daylight, the coroner had set up battery-powered
lamps, aimed at what was left of Monette Bandy. And then he started handling the body, making more notes, mumbling into a tape
recorder. The crime lab techs set to work beside him, but Sally
couldn't quite see what they were doing. The coroner's body par-
tially blocked her view.

But she could see that Monette's uniform shirt was torn and
bloody. Sally searched her memory. The Lifeway checkers wore a
uniform polo shirt with whatever pants they favored. That morn-

ing Monette had been wearing black jeans, a little too tight. The coroner got up from where he was squatting and went around to work from another angle, giving Sally a better (was that the word?) view. Monette wasn't wearing jeans, or anything else on the lower half of her body, now, and there was a lot more blood, dried grass sticking to her legs, and between them. She'd been shot. God.

One of the crime lab techs had gone down into the crevice and pulled out the jeans. Now Sally saw them draped over a rock, the techs looking in their kit for a bigger plastic bag to put them in. "Hunh," said the tech. "No blood. The guy must've got these off her before he shot her." That was about as much as Sally could stand. She turned away.

And registered, distinctly, for the first time, what the coroner had been saying in his soft voice. "Shot twice at point-blank range with what appears to be a small caliber weapon . . . head, abdomen . . . likelihood of sexual assault . . ."

Only that morning, Sally, thought, she'd talked with a living human being, somebody she'd pitied more than liked, but a person nonetheless. Sally couldn't remember exactly where Monette Bandy had grown up—one of the energy boomtowns, Newcastle or Gillette? She'd come to Laramie to widen her horizons, a young woman, probably damaged by a girlhood that hadn't offered much in the way of comfort or encouragement or pleasure. (Sally could see her holding up that bag of artichokes: "What're these?") Monette had just been looking, as she'd said, to "get it on." Rape murder, it's just a shot away.

"Pull it together, girl," said Hawk, putting out a hand to help Sally up from her seat on the rock. "The detective and the sheriff want to talk."

"Sorry to keep you waiting," Atkins said, all business.

"I didn't expect we'd have such a tough time getting the body out of that crack," Dickie added. "Wish you hadn't had to watch that."

"I assume that was where you found her?" Atkins asked.

"Yes," Hawk said. "We were headed up this way, and saw vultures overhead. We figured something was wrong. Came up to take a look. I got here first, but Sally was right behind me."

Atkins just nodded, taking notes. "And you didn't disturb anything? Didn't pick up any beer cans or kick things around?"

"No," said Sally. "Oh, wait a minute. Yeah, I did. Here." She dug the cigarette pack out of her knapsack and noticed, for the first time, that somebody had torn the foil on top into strips, like the fringe on Buffalo Bill's jacket. She handed the pack to Atkins, who gave her a look that said, "Real bozo move, girl," and then handed it to a tech, who bagged it.

"Sorry. I guess you'll find my prints on that one. But that was all I touched. We were careful. Still, when I saw her arm, I did go over there and look down into the crevice. That's how we knew who it was." Sally shook her head, fighting a small wave of nausea. "What was that cord on her wrist?"

Dickie looked up, his eyes grim, revealing nothing. "A piggin' string. The calf ropers use them to tie animals down. There were rope burns on both her wrists."

"That's not for public consumption," said Atkins, giving Dickie a quick glance. "I reckon we'll ask the questions, Professor Alder."

But Sally wasn't really listening. The shock had fallen away, and anger was taking over. "Some fuckhead cowboy brought her out here for a party, tied her up, attacked her, shot her? Is that what you think happened here?"

"We don't have any idea," said Dickie. "We're just collecting evidence."

"Not our job to jump to conclusions," Atkins added.

"Bullshit," said Sally. "Tell me that isn't what it looks like. Beer cans, butts, even a can of chew? Cowboy boot prints in the dirt? A piggin' string?"

"We know what it looks like," Dickie told her, with labored patience. "But at this point, that's all we know. Lot of work to do on this yet, Sally." He looked over at the crime lab guys and the coroner, getting ready to put Monette into a body bag. "We're just beginning."

And there was no time to waste. If Monette had been killed by some kinked-up bastard who'd come in Monday morning just for the rodeo and started his week off with a bang, Sally knew he might be gone already. Might stick around for the week, wreaking more havoc. Potential witnesses might only be passing through. Dickie and his people would have to work fast to get their man before the week was out. After that, the trail would get colder than a fence post in February.

Cold bloody murder and hot brutal rape. They just had to find the guy who did it and make him pay and pay. But what could Sally do?

Hawk was a step ahead of her. "You saw Monette this morning at the Lifeway, didn't you?" he asked her.

"Yes. She checked me out this morning," Sally told Dickie and the detective.

Poor Dickie. For a moment the wretched man leaked through and showed in the eyes of the dispassionate cop.

"Yeah. She got promoted this week. Mary was real proud of her." He looked down at the ground, swallowed, got possession of himself. When he looked up, the man had gone back inside, and all that showed was the cop. "So did you talk to her?"

"Yeah, I did. Small talk. She was pissed off that she'd have to work nights most of the week and would miss the fun."

Atkins, the investigator, wrote it all down. Dickie stared off into the distance, at something that had him swallowing hard again. "Monette had a fucked-up idea of fun," he said.

And just the way he said it made Sally forget her own mad and sad, and remember that Dickie was the dead girl's uncle, and a man who'd had, and paid for, more than a few wrongheaded notions about fun in his day. "I know what you mean. So when I was checking out, I was in line between a couple of guys who looked like the human versions of a sloth and a salamander—or maybe that's not fair to the animals. Maybe they were lower species. A blob and a virus. Anyway, Monette hit on both of them. Told one guy she knew 'all the best places' in town to get a beer. Seemed like she was determined to hook up with a man, any man, the nastier and rastier the better."

"Did the men act interested?" Atkins asked.

"The guy in front of me did. Said he'd love to 'get a little something.' He was a real wit, a regular Bob fucking Hope. He bought a carton of Kools for his wife."

"Did you happen to notice whether he smoked them himself?"

"Couldn't say. He acted like it was his wife who needed them, but she couldn't come in and get them herself, because their baby was acting up, so she was out in the truck nursing. Great, huh—nursing and smoking? You ought to arrest her." Sally was a real prohibitionist when it came to cigarettes. "Did you find any Kools butts?"

"I don't know. We'll see about that when we get things over to the lab. What about the guy in back of you?" Atkins asked.

"I don't know. By the time I left, he hadn't said much of anything. Just stood there looking stupid and revolting."

Atkins glanced up from his notes and gave her a wisp of what almost looked like a smile. "Do you think you could give us a more precise description of these guys than that?"

She narrowed her eyes, trying to get the clearest possible mental picture of the two men. "Sure. I can even tell you what the first guy's truck looked like. An old white Chevy pickup, maybe a ton and a half, rusty and dented. I didn't notice the plates, but he said he was from Worland. And, of course, he was traveling with a woman and a baby."

"That's good. Let's get down to details."

"Okay," Sally agreed. "The second guy was a biker, kind of scrawny and squinty-eyed, had that worked-over, windburned look." But then she hesitated. She put her hand on Dickie's arm, gave it a squeeze, and then said, "Look. I hate to say this, but the way Monette was going, there's no telling how many guys she flirted with before she found Mr. Wrong. It's not like she was being discriminating."

As Scott Atkins recorded what Sally was saying, Dickie worked his lips, like a man who'd taken a drink of milk that had gone off. When he raised his eyes, they were glittering. "I'm not sure Monette Bandy ever had the luxury of being discriminating," he said.

TUESDAY

CHAPTER 3
SWEETHEARTS
OF THE RODEO

THE RINGING PHONE woke Sally before seven on Tuesday morning. She fumbled for the cordless beside the bed, mumbled a hello.

"God, Sally. You and Hawk. You found Monette."

It was Delice, and she was barely keeping it together.

"Yes," Sally said. "It was horrible. I'm so sorry, honey. How's Mary doing?"

"About as bad as you'd expect. She lost Tanya just last year, and now this happens to Monette. Her parents are dead. She's pretty much down to Langhams."

Sally knew what that was like. She was an orphan herself, her brothers far off in St. Louis, the rest of her family even more distant and scattered. More than twenty years ago she had been a bootless California country-rock singer, out on the road, looking for a place to land. The Langhams of Laramie had taken her in.

Dwayne Langham had been behind the counter at the Axe Attack music store when she'd stopped in, her head still full of white noise from a marathon drive east from Berkeley to anywhere on I–80. She'd been looking to buy guitar picks and strings, and mentioned that she sang and wrote songs, might even be in the market for a gig. Dwayne had smiled and sent her to see his sister, Delice, who had hired Sally on the spot to play happy hours at the Wrangler. Given her then pathetic financial state, that job had looked to Sally like the opening of King Tut's tomb.

Dickie Langham had followed suit, booking her into the "lounge" at Dr. Mudflaps, the phony gourmet restaurant where he tended bar and dealt dope. Almost before she knew it, she'd rented an apartment in Laramie. By the end of that summer she was gigging with Dwayne's band, a sub-legendary group that went by the name of Branchwater, fronted by another of Laramie's purveyors of illegal substances, the amoral Sam Branch. That had led to several years of making a hair-raising living in clubs and bars all over the Northern Rockies, and dragging her ass into the Wrangler for Monday morning hash browns and eggs with Dickie and Delice.

Sally had enrolled in grad school in history at UW, just to have something legitimate to do, and found that she'd accidentally discovered her calling. She'd ended up heading back to California, gotten a Ph.D. at Cal, taught women's history at UCLA. It was a good enough life, but she'd known some lonesome times in the big city.

So when she'd gotten the offer to return to Laramie and the University of Wyoming sixteen years later, as the holder of the Margaret Dunwoodie Endowed Chair and head of the Dunwoodie Center for Women's History, she'd jumped on it. To her infinite delight, not only had she and Hawk found each other again, but the Langhams took up with her exactly where they'd left off. Of course, Langhams knew how to welcome their prodigals home.

So Sally played a little music with Dwayne, hung out a lot with Delice, and cadged dinner at Dickie and Mary's at least once a week. She'd come to think of herself as an aunt to their nearly grown kids, especially Mary and Dickie's daughter Brit. Gorgeous, amusingly sulky, and bright as a golden Sacagawea dollar, Brit had worked for Sally when she was writing Meg Dunwoodie's biography. Indeed, Brit had played a big part in solving that particular human puzzle. The Langhams were as much family to Sally now as her own.

And when she thought about it, they'd been Monette's only family too. Her mother was dead, and her father—well, nobody ever had a good word to say about him.

Sally could only begin to conceive of what the Langhams were going through. "What can I do to help out?" she asked Delice.

On the other end of the line, Delice swallowed, sniffled, blew her nose. "We're going to get together this morning at nine, over at Mary and Dickie's. The coroner hasn't released her body yet, but we're going to plan the funeral, all that stuff. You could come over and hold everybody's hand if you feel like it."

"Sure," Sally said, "if you don't think it would be an intrusion."

"We need you around. Brit's here, but with the other kids gone, Mary's feeling a little bereft."

"I'll be happy to help Mary any way I can," Sally said. She knew that Brit's sister was in London with the university's summer abroad program, and her little brother was up in the Wind River mountains with some survival school where they gave you a box of matches and a sharp stick and sent you out to live on snowmelt and lichens. Mothers needed their children at times like this, but in a pinch, friends helped.

"Hell, if nothing else, it'll be good to have you there to give Nattie somebody to whine at," Delice said. Natalie Charlay Langham was Delice's sister-in-law, Dwayne's wife. Nattie had started out adulthood as a bartender at the Gallery, a low-rent watering hole that specialized in good bands, bad bathrooms, and steamy Saturday nights. By marrying Dwayne, who'd done very nicely in banking, Nattie had risen to become a Realtor, known for her garish ways of spending Dwayne's money and her rather too obvious predilection for screwing around on her husband. Delice had remarked on many public occasions that she hoped Nattie would one day fuck herself into a divorce.

Sally wasn't much on Nattie either, but she sometimes found

entertainment in trying to piss her off. "If it helps you to have me deal with her, I'm willing. I should probably eat some yogurt or something first, so that my stomach's well-lined. Should Hawk come?"

"Hawk's welcome to come too, but if he's got something else going on, you can tell him that there'll be plenty of stuff he can do for us later."

"Okay. I think he'd been planning a day in the field with one of his grad students. How's Dickie?"

"He's already gone to work, down at the Lifeway talking to the other employees." Delice paused, and when she started talking again, sounded more like her normal feisty self. "Jesus, I hope he finds the guy quick. You should have heard my cocktail waitresses going wacko last night when they heard the news. By the time we closed up, they were all demanding that somebody had to walk them to their cars. They were sure they'd be dragged off by a homicidal rapist. Imagine what the supermarket checkers are saying today."

Sally could. Tell the truth, she was feeling a little shaky herself. But then, she had the right. What she'd seen the day before was finally beginning to sink in. "I guess you can't blame them," she allowed.

"I don't blame anybody for anything, except the bastard that killed Monette. But I hate to think that tonight I'll be walking my customers to their cars too. By tomorrow night people could be deciding to stay home behind locked doors and watch *Walker, Texas Ranger* on TV, or go back to wherever they came from and skip the rodeo, or just move along down the road. You know how rumors spread in this town. The paranoia could get out of hand pretty easy."

No kidding. Laramie had its share of bar fights, domestic incidents, drunk and disorderlies, traffic accidents, and small-time property crimes, but as in most small towns, citizens hardly questioned their safety. People didn't much bother to lock their houses or their cars. With a population of twenty-six thousand, you'd never go more than ten minutes in public without running into somebody you knew. It might be some annoying person (Sally thought of Amber McCloskey and remembered, with vexation, that she had to go take care of things at Edna's that afternoon). Still, there was something reassuring about living in such a neighborly place. Delice liked to tell the story of how her son, Jerry Jeff, had once left his bicycle at Washington Park after a soccer game, and two days later, not only was the bike still there, but a neighbor out for a morning walk recognized it, knew who it belonged to, and wheeled it back to Delice's house.

Rape was uncommon, or at least hardly ever reported. Murder was rare. Rape and murder, in combination, was almost unheard of. And it was, Sally thought with a rush of fury, unacceptable.

"You're right," she said. "I'm sure that this is all people are talking about."

Sally had her first demonstration of that fact when the phone rang only seconds after she'd hung up from talking to Delice. She picked up the phone. "Have you seen the paper?" said a soft steely voice.

"Not yet, Maude. I haven't even had a cup of coffee."

"Well go get your coffee and your *Boomerang* and call me back. Something's happened, and we've got to take action."

"Action?" said Sally.

"A girl's been raped and murdered—Monette Bandy. She works down at the Lifeway."

"Yeah, I know, Maude," said Sally. "She's Dickie and Mary's niece. I'm going over there later to be with them. I'm sure they'll be grateful for your concern."

"They're next on my list," said Maude. "I didn't want to call them too early."

Maude Stark, chairperson of the Dunwoodie Foundation, was a six-foot, sixty-something pistol, who wore T-shirts with slogans like "Get Your Laws Off My Body." She was also the richest former housekeeper in Wyoming, a stalwart friend of womankind who baked like an angel, benefactor to a passel of causes, and a person who knew exactly what to do with a shotgun. She had a little farm outside Laramie and had probably been up since four, feeding her chickens and working in her garden and greenhouse. She'd never scrupled about early morning phone calls to Sally. She was showing restraint.

"That's good, Maude," said Sally, not sure what else was expected.

"I really think the community needs to get together to talk about how to fight this kind of violence," Maude insisted. "Maybe some public expression of outrage is in order. This kind of thing should not be happening in our town."

Sally tried to focus on what Maude was saying. "Like some kind of demonstration or something?" she asked. "I sympathize with your point, but in the middle of Jubilee Days? I don't know about that. A lot of people aren't going to be too thrilled about the idea of focusing on this murder during the biggest business week of the year."

In her younger years Sally would have been rushing to the barricades too. Like Maude, she was horrified, but she was more realistic nowadays. Thousands of people were coming to Laramie to watch cowboys do battle with large, unruly mammals, to drink rivers of beer and boogie until their shoes melted, maybe try to get laid. If instead, you laid a Take Back the Night rally on them, how many would just close up their wallets and say adios?

"I know there'll be people worrying about their bank accounts instead of our women, but for me it's a matter of honor," said Maude. "Let's keep in touch. I've got some more calls to make," she finished, and hung up.

And so Sally's day began. Hawk, always an early riser, was already up and gone. He'd left a note—"At the gym. Back soon. Here's your newspaper. Love, Fido." He was off to his early morning basketball game at the university gym. Sally wondered if Detective Atkins was there too, keeping to the routine. Such a normal thing to do, on such a strange day.

Do normal things, she told herself. It helps.

She began the elaborate but familiar ritual of morning coffee making, a consumer ceremony that was, Sally had to admit, threatening to get out of hand. She'd thought her coffee obsession bad enough when she'd insisted on mail-ordering coffee beans from Peet's in California, to Laramie. But it turned out there was another level of fetishization she had yet to achieve. When Hawk gave her a cappuccino maker for Christmas, she reached that new plateau.

It was an elaborate rite that bordered on excessive: meting out beans and grinding them, measuring water, watching every second while the coffee dripped to just the right level in the glass carafe, pouring just enough milk into a stainless steel pitcher, getting the amount of steam and foam just right. The results were pleasing, but were they worth the damn fuss? When it came right down to it, you could get just as good a caffeine buzz by drinking four or five cups of the translucent horse dung extract Delice served up at the Wrangler.

Well, Sally thought, at least I know the difference between shit and shinola.

Good thing. More shit was on the way. She sat down at the table and unfolded the *Laramie Daily Boomerang*. The story of Monette's murder appeared on the second page, below the fold— the top story on the front page was, of course, about the Jubilee Days rodeo queen and her court. There were large photographs of five carefully coiffed and made-up girls, smiling in spangled Western wear, with accompanying stories about their hobbies, studies, religious beliefs, missions in life, and favorite rodeo events. Young and pretty, full of fire and piety and promise, sweethearts of the rodeo.

The murder didn't even lead the second page. That honor was reserved for a piece about a rancher who'd found himself compelled to "put down" a calf that had been attacked, and grievously chewed up, by a coyote. Wyoming newspapers could be hell on predators, at least the four-legged kind. A color picture of the mutilated calf took up a quarter of the page, roughly five times the space allotted to the murder of Monette Bandy.

Way down below, a small headline read, "Newcastle Girl Slain Near Cheyenne." True, Sally thought, Monette had moved to Laramie only six months or so earlier, but she had been, after all, a resident of the community, gainfully employed at a local business, related by blood to one of Laramie's really solid families. Saying she was a "Newcastle girl" was a little like stripping off her epaulets and tossing her out of the fort.

And saying she'd been killed "near Cheyenne" was a bit of a

stretch—Vedauwoo was between Laramie and Cheyenne, if anything a little closer to the former than the latter. Mentioning Cheyenne was a time-honored way of getting Laramie people to think that the story was about someplace else, a town full of politicians that was nearly in Nebraska.

The story itself was brief and to the point—Monette Bandy, twenty-one, a Newcastle resident who had recently relocated to Laramie, had been found murdered at the Devil's Playground in the Laramie Range. She'd been employed at the Lifeway. The Albany County Sheriff's Department was investigating. Sexual assault was suspected. The police had, at this point, no leads.

Obviously the *Boomerang* didn't think it was in the best interest of the town, of the good citizens who survived through the long, dark winter and looked forward to the annual summer party, to play up the murder. Tourists wouldn't be pleased. And that meant bad news for the many Laramie folk who waited all year not only for long, warm days, but for the sound of ringing cash registers.

She understood self-interest, but could people really be this callous? Maybe Maude had a point. Sally took a sip of cappuccino, and tasted rage. Poor Monette. She'd been nothing but a transient and a loser, and her death was barely a blip on the screen. If the *Boomerang* was any evidence of anything, the town's boosters were more worried about maintaining the festival atmosphere, and the accompanying profit potential, than about the brutal snuffing out of a fellow human, a pathetically exploitable young woman, a neighbor. It was disgusting. What if, instead of Monette, one of the rodeo princesses had been raped and murdered? Sally bet the *Boomer* would've paid attention.

Boy howdy.

If she had anything to say about it, she vowed as she drank the last, rich, dreg-free swallow from her cup, they wouldn't bury Monette Bandy so damn deep and easy.

CHAPTER 4
WORKING PEOPLE

JUST HER LUCK. Sally arrived at Dickie and Mary's at the very moment that Nattie Langham was pulling up in front, taking up two parking spaces with her big, shiny four-wheel-drive Cadillac Escalade, an automobile name that always gave Sally the appalled giggles. Sally had been known to covet a fully loaded off-road unit or two, but down deep, she held it as an article of faith that the luxury sport utility vehicle was a multiple oxymoron, designed chiefly to swill gasoline and impress other people who had more money than sense. She could just imagine what would happen to Nattie's deep pile carpet and leather upholstery if she were ever compelled to actually take that Escalade on a Wyoming dirt road in the rain. How much good would the satellite navigation system be, wallowing down a gully-rutted track fast turning bottomless, ending up hub-deep in red gumbo? Then again, how much good would Nattie's stiletto heels be when she had to walk out for help?

But today Nattie had put aside the spike pumps for bright

turquoise lizard cowboy boots, with toes pointy enough to skewer the most active cockroach scurrying into the least accessible corner. The boots matched a new turquoise cowboy hat festooned with a whole pheasant's worth of feathers, a sleeveless Western shirt in the same color with white silk fringe dangling fetchingly from the front and back yokes, white jeans tight enough to leave no doubt about what Nattie wasn't wearing underneath, cinched up with a black leather belt with a solid gold reproduction of a championship rodeo buckle. She was also wearing a button bearing the message, "We're the Real Deal, Podner"—the company slogan for Branch Homes on the Range. Just your typical cowgirl drag.

Nattie was giving the seams of her jeans a stress test, trying to haul an industrial-size coffee urn out of the back of the Escalade. The coffeepot had gotten jumbled up with all the other junk she kept in the car. Most Wyomingites did, of course, keep emergency equipment in their vehicles. Every fall Sally outfitted the trunk of her Mustang with a winter supply box that held tire chains, a quart of antifreeze, a scraper, window de-icer, a whisk broom for sweeping snow off the windows, a flashlight with spare batteries, a sleeping bag, some highway flares, and a first aid kit. Year-round she carried water (frozen solid all winter, of course), a shovel, a couple of boards, and jumper cables. The toolbox in the back of Hawk's old Ford pickup contained a slightly more elaborate set of gear since he did so much off-road driving, out in the field. It made sense to be prepared.

Hawk, like most people in the state, also kept a loaded gun in his vehicle; in his case a Smith and Wesson .38 in the glove box. Sally made a point of not keeping a gun of any kind, anywhere. Those of her Wyoming friends who knew about her eccentric weaponlessness considered it a delusional vestige of sixties liberalism.

The stuff in the back of Nattie's Escalade was, well, the escalated version of anybody's emergency kit. Three gallons of antifreeze. A propane torch. A Coleman lantern. An assortment of different-size boards, a sawed-off broom, and not one but two shovels. Not just tire chains, but a tow chain, a saw, and enough rope to pitch a circus tent. If the visible stuff was any indication,

Nattie probably had a howitzer in her glove compartment. Judging by everything she'd accumulated in the back, you'd think Nattie was a maniac lumberjack, heading out to pull stumps in the dead of winter. But in fact, in an automotive crisis, Sally couldn't imagine Nattie hefting anything much heavier than a cell phone to call the Triple A. She'd never risk one of her famous fingernails.

Today, Sally noticed as she parked and went to help, the nails were bright orange with white diagonal pinstripes. The orange matched Nattie's hair, which would probably never be permitted to develop either stripes or whiteness. Knowing that the day would go worse for them all if Nattie experienced so much as a chip in her manicure, Sally dislodged the spigot of the coffeepot from under the broom handle, found the big lid wedged between the torch and a leaky five-gallon water jug, retrieved the innards of the pot from the tangle of shovels and broom and damp, muddy ropes and chains. "You ought to clean out for the summer, Nat, or at least hose this shit down," Sally said, surprised to find evidence that somebody had actually had the Escalade out on the dirt, sometime since the day it had rolled off an assembly line in Mexico or Canada (buy American!).

"Oh crap, that's Dwayne's problem," said Nattie, picking up the coffeepot without bothering to thank Sally for helping. "He's the one that said he wanted me to get the Escalade, for safety reasons. He's so worried about me, afraid I'll be out in some new development or showing a ranch sometime and end up in the ditch. He just loads the back up with everything he thinks I could possibly need. I think there's a case of Spam buried in there somewhere, if I'm stuck for a month and need survival rations. Or at least that's what he tells me. Then he borrows it all the time to go fishing, and I end up having to drive around in his little-bitty Beamer—like, how safe is that if I'm broadsided by some goombah in a monster truck?"

Sally shook her head. "Yeah. That really does suck."

Nattie missed the irony. "I guess!" she said, sighing as they walked up to the door and rang the bell. "I really hope this Monette thing doesn't mess up Jubilee Days."

Sally chose to act as if she hadn't heard. With what the Lang-

hams had to face in the next few days, it wouldn't be fair to anyone to have to open the door this morning and find Sally socking
Nattie on the nose.

Brit Langham answered the door, and Sally half wished she'd
gone ahead and done the clobbering. Brit would have appreciated
it, for one thing. For another, Sally liked the idea of doing something that might get a reaction out of the Langham family's most
blasé member. Sally would never have predicted that she'd have to
come to Wyoming to understand the meaning of "sangfroid," but
the term must have been invented for Brittany Langham. In the two
years that Sally had been back in Laramie, she'd often amused herself watching Brit fail to react to things that turned other people
into hysterics. On those occasions Sally recalled Dorothy Parker's
famous remark about Katharine Hepburn's acting running the
gamut of emotions from A to B. Sally had once seen Brit moved
nearly to C, but that was a life and death matter.

At twenty-three, Brit was blessed with a supermodel body, ash-
blond hair and aquamarine eyes, and the kind of lips that made a
disinterested pout a weapon of mass destruction. Men tended to
assume that anyone that beautiful must be stupid, and Brit always
used their pathetically false assumptions to her advantage. She was
headed for law school at the University of Wyoming in the fall, and
Sally got positively gleeful contemplating what would happen to
the first fool who faced Brit across a courtroom.

"I'll take that," Brit said, relieving Nattie of the coffee urn and
holding the door open. "Looks like we're gonna need it. We've had,
like, sixty calls already, maybe half of them from people who say
they'll be bringing a coffee cake by. Maude says she's already baked
four loaves of pumpkin bread and a plum kuchen. Now all we need
is ten pounds of coffee."

"Somebody else can do that," said Nattie, sweeping past Brit.
"I've done my part."

"I'd be glad to get coffee and whatever you all need, later,"
Sally said. "I don't mind."

"She borrowed the pot from her office," Brit whispered to
Sally. "Big deal."

"You might want to run some water and baking soda through

it," Sally advised, making a face. "I saw the inside, and I'd bet that nobody at Branch Homes on the Range has washed that sucker out since private property was invented."

"I'd better get to it, then," Brit said. "We've been telling people not to come until later this afternoon, but it hasn't been easy fighting them off. A lot of them aren't even really friends of Mom's. I don't know why the hell they think they should barge in."

Sally narrowed her eyes. "Most of 'em are well-intentioned. But then again, some people in Laramie would have been great in Victorian London. They'd have made a point out of getting to public executions early so they'd get a front row seat for the hanging."

Sally entered to the sound of the ringing telephone. So far, however, only the family had arrived. Mary, eyes red but dry, sat on the couch, next to Delice. Neither of them was dressed for mourning. Mary wore loose black-and-white print pants with a matching short-sleeved tunic top, the kind of outfit she'd wear to her job as a secretary in the College of Education, comfortable but presentable daywear for a middle-aged woman who'd given up on the battle of the bulge. Delice was attired for business too, but her job had a different dress code, especially this week. She wore a cream-and-brown Western shirt, a pair of form-fitting Levi's, her thousand-dollar Charlie Dunn boots, and enough silver jewelry to keep the Navajo economy afloat on her purchases alone. She looked distressed but great as she always had, trim and wiry, long black hair in a fat braid fastened with a carved silver clip. Obviously, she was planning to go from Dickie and Mary's straight to work at the Wrangler.

Mary probably didn't plan to go in to work today, but everybody else was obviously taking the morning off from their jobs. Sally herself had planned to catch up on some of that backlog of scholarly reading, and was feeling secretly guilty for having put the work aside. Brit, who'd sworn that, as God was her witness, she'd never waitress again, was wearing a long flowered skirt and tailored white shirt—Sally surmised that she must have been pressed into service as an extra hostess at the Yippie I O. Nattie's costume, ridiculous as it was, was supposed to make her a walking billboard for Branch Homes on the Range. She was already on her cell phone, calling into her office to check for messages, rescheduling appointments, chatting up clients. Dwayne walked in, making a concession to the rodeo in a Western-cut jacket instead of his usual banker's pinstripes. Delice's son, Jerry Jeff, who at not quite fifteen seemed to have grown a foot since Sally had seen him a month ago, followed, with grass stains on his pants and green dirt under his fingernails from his summer yard work business. Sally told herself she'd never seen such a hardworking bunch.

With the exception of Dickie, whose job it was to find Monette's killer, and Brit's brother and sister, who were away for the week, the Langhams were there for Mary. Much more than for Monette. Nobody, as far as Sally knew, had been close enough to the girl to really grieve for her.

Sally went over to the couch. Mary stood up. As they hugged, Sally felt the sorrow and fatigue radiate from Mary's warm, soft body.

"Thanks for coming, Mustang," Mary said. "I guess the hordes are going to start descending this afternoon, and we might need you to do a little steppin' and fetchin'. I don't know if this could have come at a worse time. Everybody's so busy."

"There's no good time with something like this," Sally said. "It's just senseless and sad. But Dickie'll find the guy who did it, I know."

There was a bleak expression on Mary's round, pretty face. "You think so? There are a couple thousand people a day passing through town this week, not to mention all the highway traffic all summer long, or all the local garbage a girl like Monette could have picked up since she moved here. And the guy who killed her could be way long gone, just some piece of poisoned trash rollin' down the highway. I really wish I felt more optimistic about that."

Brit came in the room, bringing a can of Diet Coke for her mother and one for herself. She flopped down in an overstuffed chair, and Mary sat back down on the couch, making room for Sally beside her.

"You'd be surprised what the cops can do," Sally said, trying to sound reassuring. "Dickie's got a great team. It's amazing to watch them work. Far as I could tell, they collected every single conceivable piece of anything that was lying around up there, and I guarantee, in the next couple of days they'll be talking to everyone in Laramie who even saw Monette in the last week. I bet that if Dickie has his way, his guys'll talk to anybody who ever bought a box of cereal at the Lifeway. And that Detective Atkins guy, jeez. By the time he was done asking me questions, I was looking at my arm to see how deep the teeth marks were. They'll find a trail."

"Yeah, that Scotty's a real bloodhound. But with Monette, there's liable to be a whole bunch of trails. She took after my sister. She never met a jerk she didn't want to take home and beg to abuse her."

"Bummer to admit it, but it's true," Brit put in. "Monette was sitting at the bar at the Wrangler last weekend, pounding down White Russians and doing her damndest to pick up the worst-lookin' men in the place. She ended up leaving with an ugly little guy who had about three teeth in his whole head, none of which met."

"Did she have a thing for guys with bad teeth?" Sally wondered, thinking that might be a clue to who had lured her out to Vedauwoo.

"Nope," said Brit. "She went for all kinds, as long as they were gross. This particular one wasn't a regular, just some skank passing through, and from the look of it she was planning to take him home with her that night, or go to his motel, or whatever."

Nattie, punching "end" on one call, pressing more buttons and getting ready for "send" on another, chimed in. "Dwayne and I were down there too, and it was downright embarrassing. She was making a spectacle of herself. Disgusting."

Sally heard Delice mutter something about pots and kettles, and Sally said, "So what do you think, Dee?"

"Yeah, I saw her," Delice admitted. "And it wasn't the first time. Sometimes when I was bartending I had to cut her off when I thought she was getting too wasted for her own good. It never seemed to help. She'd get surly, or she'd get all baby-faced and hurt, but one way or the other, it seemed like the whole purpose was to hook on to some loser for the night. It was like Russian roulette."

Sally had run women's centers, had volunteered for rape crisis hotlines. She knew something about that kind of sexual compulsiveness in women. She tried to put the question delicately. "Mary," she said, holding both of her friend's hands, looking straight into her eyes, "is there any suggestion that when she was a kid, some man may have messed with her?"

And now Mary looked truly wretched. "I've thought about it." She swallowed. "But maybe she was just looking for somebody to be nice to her. It wasn't like she had it easy at home, no matter what my sister tried to do. That Bone Bandy is one nasty-ass motherfucker. Pardon my French, but that's the God's honest truth. He's little, but he's mean as a rattlesnake and twice as twisty. Tanya stayed with him more than twenty years, and I'll never understand why, as long as I live.

"Before they were ever even married, when they were still just going out, she came to the apartment Dickie and I were renting, with a black eye and a bloody lip. Said that time he'd accused her of going around on him, and just lost it. Tanya claimed she was through with him, but he showed up maybe an hour later with a bunch of roses, swearing never to do it again, and she fell for it. The next time he'd hit her hard enough to knock out a couple of teeth. After that they left town, and I barely heard from her at all."

"They say that women who stay with abusive men get to be, like, prisoners in their house," Brit said. "Like in *The Burning Bed*."

"The guys scare the life out of them," Delice said. "You can always tell those shitheads. I've seen couples come in my bar, and they have a few pops, and maybe get into an argument, and the man will grab the woman's arm and squeeze it, or maybe give her a little slap. The worst ones are the quiet ones, the ones who twist a finger or think they're causing pain in a way nobody can see."

"It takes a hell of a lot of guts to leave," Sally said. "When you're living with that, and you think the alternative might be that he'll just kill you.

"Did Monette's father beat up on her?" Sally asked.

"I don't know," Mary admitted. "One of the few times I talked to Tanya, she told me she'd decided she could take whatever he dished out, as long as she could protect Monette. But that was a few years ago. And then the last time we spoke she'd called to tell me that Monette was thinking about moving down here, and asked me to keep an eye on her. I asked her how it was going, and she said about as good as could be expected. I shouldn't have left it at that, but I did." Mary teared up.

"What could you do? She was up there, and you were down here," Delice said. "What Mary hasn't told you, Sal, is that she went up to Newcastle half a dozen times after they moved up there, and tried to convince Tanya to leave the son of a bitch and come back home with her. Tanya wouldn't leave, and it wasn't just because she was protecting Monette. Whatever the sick fucking reason, she was sticking it out."

Mary fought down the tears, but her voice shook. "I guess when Tanya finally did get it up to run, it was just too much. Bone had gotten drunk and beaten her up good, then passed out. She drank the rest of the bottle, then got the keys out of his pocket and took his truck. And then drove it off an overpass. I kept thinking there was something I should have done . . . When Monette moved down here, I figured, well, now at least I could keep an eye on her for Tanya. But she was so hostile. Dickie said maybe it would just take a little time until she trusted us. Just a little more time . . ." Mary began sobbing.

"Come on, Mom," said Brit, rising and pulling Mary up off the couch. "Why don't you go lie down for a while." The telephone began ringing, and everyone glared at it. "You ought to get some rest before other people get here." She took her mother's arm and led her off.

Sally looked around. Nattie was finishing up another call, and Dwayne had answered the ringing phone. Jerry Jeff sat silent, looking at the floor. "It's Dickie," Dwayne said to no one in particular. "He says he's on his way down to the courthouse, then he'll be back home."

"If he's coming soon," said Delice, "we'd better get out and pick up some donuts." Sally gave her a quizzical look, and Delice admitted, "I'm not in the mood to nag today. We can get the coffee too, and anything else you all think we need. Come with me, Sal."

Sally didn't have to be asked twice, even if she wasn't wild about returning to the Lifeway.

The scene was familiar, a crazy parking lot, hollering cowboys, befuddled tourists, even the panhandling hippies; this time, they said, they wanted gas money. Delice gave them five bucks, telling Sally that maybe it would get them out of town. But in other ways the Lifeway was an eerily new place, transfigured in the last twenty-four hours. Two Sheriff's Department cruisers were parked in the no parking zone out front. People who passed the cop cars on the way to the entrance gave one another quizzical looks: *Why the police? Is there some reason why we ought to be buying our Hamburger Helper someplace else?*

The differences didn't stop at the front door. Over the years, as a musician and a songwriter who'd done her fair share of recording, Sally had learned something about room tone, the sound a place has when there's no foreground noise and everything is supposedly quiet. The background hum, a blend of muted small noises, was indiscernible unless you were listening for it. Sally had an excellent memory for sounds, and she knew that the previous morning, the room tone of the Lifeway had been lively, clattering, full of snippets of conversation, the rumble of wheeled pallets stacked with food, the frequent announcements over the loudspeaker: frozen catfish fillets on special at the seafood counter, baggers wanted at the check stands.

Today the place had a kind of anxious hush. The shelf stockers, usually brazen as they careened around corners pushing racks of canned soda or laundry detergent, were moving slowly and silently. In the front of the store, Scott Atkins stood in conversation with a man in a white shirt and name tag, whom Sally recognized from the smiling picture over the store entrance: the manager. Two deputies were talking to a couple of the regular checkers, who kept casting anxious eyes on the lines building up at the three open registers.

"This place feels weird," Sally told Delice. "Like she'd died right in here."

"It's a damn good thing she didn't. And if they don't get rid of the weird feeling real fast," Delice retorted, "it'll start costing them big money. I'm sorry if that sounds unsentimental," she added, reading disapproval on Sally's face, "but that's the way it goes. You can't just let business go to hell because of something like this."

Evidently one of the checkers talking to the cops agreed. They'd finished up with her, and she went into the office, got her cash drawer, and walked over to open up another register. Her name was Charlene, and she was a friendly, motherly looking woman with hair like a poodle and inch-long red fingernails (how did she run a cash register?), known to regular shoppers as something of a check stand comic. She picked up the phone next to the register, pushed the intercom button, and said, "Check stand five of the formerly demonic but now fully exorcised Lifeway now open for your shopping pleasure. We live to serve," she added, and finished with a long, diabolical laugh: hooooohahahahahahahaha.

Laughter broke out here and there in the store, and Sally and Delice joined in. Sally grabbed a hand basket. "You take the cart and go get the donuts," she told Delice. "I'll go pick up some fruit. It's always nice to have something to munch on that isn't fried. I'll catch up with you."

Sally loved the fruits of summer—fat grapes and juicy peaches, sweet melons and plump berries. And it was high fruit season in America. She began loading the basket, figuring she'd quit when it got almost too heavy to carry. Just as she was zoning out over the strawberries, trying to decide if their season was really over, she found herself unintentionally (and then deliberately) eavesdropping on a whispered conversation between two produce clerks, one a pimply-faced kid, the other a middle-aged man who smelled like a carton of presmoked cigarettes, stacking a gigantic pile of watermelons.

"You gotta tell 'em," the older man was saying. "They're gonna find out anyhow. It looks better if you come forward with the information, instead of them having to nose around and then weasel it out of you. If you clam up, it makes it look like you're guilty or something."

Trying for nonchalance, Sally sidled over to inspect a display of cut watermelon, where she'd hear better but they wouldn't notice, since they had their backs to her.

"Guilty!" said the kid, his voice breaking. "They can't do anything to me—I was here at work all day yesterday, just like you, and I didn't do nothin' wrong. Fer chrissake, all I did was let the bitch give me a hand job now and then. Well, maybe a little more than that, but it don't exactly count as true love. I was careful. We'd go off where nobody ever saw us."

"Listen, I don't care if she gave you blow jobs on the dark side of the moon. Sooner or later, with all the questions they're askin', the cops will dig it out, Adolph."

Adolph? What kind of parent would name a kid Adolph? Sally winced. But then, this was Wyoming. She knew a couple who'd named their baby Buster.

"The sheriff already talked to me this morning," Adolph said. "I told them I knew her, of course—hell, we all know each other—but that we weren't close friends. And that's the truth. Monette wasn't the kind of girl you had to be friends with. Shit, Eddie, I bet she even offered to do you. Did you tell the cops about that?"

Out of the corner of her eye, Sally saw that the question surprised the one named Eddie.

"Why the hell should I? Nothin' ever happened. But you, now, you're different. You say nobody knew, but shit, man, you bragged to me about how she wanted it all the time. Who else did you tell?" Eddie asked.

"No-fuckin'-body. I swear it. I'm counting on you to help me out here, Eddie."

Suddenly the two turned around, as if they'd sensed somebody listening. Sally got very busy trying to load half a watermelon into her already groaning basket, and humming along with the muzak. The young guy—Adolph—scowled at her and stalked away. The older one—Eddie—said, "Looks like you need a bigger basket, ma'am."

"Heh-heh, yeah," said Sally, blushing fiercely and tucking the watermelon under the arm that wasn't carrying the basket. "Silly me. I'd better go get a cart." And she was off like a shot.

She caught up with Delice in the paper goods aisle. With a grunt, she put the watermelon in the top of the cart and dumped the heavy basket between an economy-size can of Folger's and a large plastic sack of nested Styrofoam cups. Her first impulse was to say, "You'll never believe what I just heard." Her second, and more mature reaction, was to say nothing, for the moment. Delice was her best friend, but this was the kind of news that Dickie ought to hear first.

So Monette had been having—was it an affair? Sex, anyhow—with this Adolph, an odious and interesting thought. Then again, if he really had been at work all day Monday, he had an ironclad alibi. He was a scumbag, but maybe even he was entitled to privacy. Sally had to think about it.

They got in Charlene's checkout line, knowing it would move fastest. "Hey, Delice," said Charlene, who knew everybody, "how are you all doing?"

Delice bobbed a shoulder. "Mary's taking it hard. Everybody else is coping. And my brother you've seen, I take it."

"Seen, and heard. He rounded up all the employees this morning and gave us one hell of an introduction to police procedure. I guess ol' Scotty Atkins is running the investigation. Boy, he's one cool piece of stuff, isn't he?" Charlene wiggled her eyebrows.

"Has been ever since high school," Delice said. She could never resist a little gossip, and turned to Sally to explain. "Half the girls at Laramie High were trying to get into his jeans. The other half already had. The basketball coach said he had a fifteen-inch vertical jump, and from what I heard, he was even better horizontal. But he doesn't let on much, does he?"

Charlene grinned. "Makes you want to see what you could do to loosen up his tongue."

Hmm.

"I don't know as anybody's managed that since he got back in town," Delice said, explaining to Sally, "He went off to police academy after college, worked for the Department of Criminal Investigations in Casper, and married some girl from up there. They got divorced last year and he came back here to work for the Sheriff's Department. From what I hear, he does nothing these days but work out and eat bullets for breakfast. He's a real cop's cop."

Right on cue, Scotty Atkins turned and looked straight at them. So he was the kind of man who had a sixth sense about when women were discussing his, er, attributes. Sally looked away, not quite fast enough.

"I guess it'll be a regular policeman's ball around here. Dickie made it clear that we'd be seeing all we cared to of him too," Charlene told Delice. "He said we should all try to remember and tell them anything we could think of about this place, or Monette, or yesterday, or the rodeo, or the last time we had the creepin' heebie-jeebies, anything that might help them find the killer. Then they started in with everybody who worked yesterday. Monette went off duty at ten, and I guess she was found by some hikers at five or so."

Five-seventeen. Sally knew precisely. Hawk had mentioned the time as he gave the dispatcher directions. But the police had chosen not to release the identities of the hikers who'd made the horrid discovery.

"Anyhow," said Charlene, bagging their purchases and making change, "they asked everybody a whole bunch of questions, and then when they were done, asked all the same questions all over again in slightly different ways, five or six more times each. Then they said they'd want fingerprints, and we all gave them. We're only just now getting back to normal."

"Sounds like you're all cooperating," Sally said, wondering about Adolph the produce clerk. Probably he wasn't the only person in the store, or in town, who wouldn't be telling the police everything he knew about Monette Bandy.

"Of course we're cooperating!" said Charlene. "Nobody here wants to be next. If this guy's got some kind of thing for supermarket checkers, we want him found, and now!"

Sally had to ask. "So what do her friends think, Charlene? Who could have done such a thing?"

Pity flashed across the checker's face. "Her friends? Now who would that be, I wonder? You could say that we all knew her, but I wouldn't call anybody at the store exactly a friend of hers. It's such a shame. Maybe if somebody here had been looking out after her, this wouldn't have happened."

"Maybe," said Delice. "I guess there's a lot of that feeling going around. I know there's a lot of us who'd like to see the guy who did it fry in hell." Sally and Charlene nodded hard.

As they wheeled their groceries out to Delice's Ford Explorer, Sally asked, "Do you think anybody could have done something to prevent this happening to Monette?"

Delice took her time answering. "I've never been a fan of second guesses. Even if I were, I'd say no. Monette was young, and in some strange ways incredibly naive. Maybe Dickie and Mary could have done more, but they really did try. Monette blew them off. She was hell-bent, and the world's too full of devils. Whatever made her that way started a long time before she showed up here."

Sally thought about that. "You know, Dee, it doesn't really matter what kind of demons were driving her. She didn't deserve to die that way. She shouldn't just be thrown away because everybody's got places to go and things to do. Her death has to mean something." And we'll never know what it means until we know what she did, and why she did it, Sally told herself.

Delice said nothing. But as they drove down Third Street, past the Loose Caboose bar and package store, Delice gasped, swerved, and nearly hit the car in the oncoming lane.

"What the hell!" Sally shouted, reaching over to grab the wheel. "Are you having a heart attack or something?"

"No! Goddamn it, take your hands off the wheel. I'm fine," shouted Delice, pulling off the road into a vacant dirt lot. "Look over there, at the drive-up window of the Loose Caboose."

Sally looked. All she saw was a beat and dusty old Dodge truck with Wyoming plates, a man with a cowboy hat leaning out the driver's window as the liquor store clerk handed over a twelve-pack of Old Milwaukee and a bottle in a brown paper bag.

All Wyomingites knew that the state's license plates began with a number that indicated the county in which the vehicle had been registered. Real license plate cognoscenti knew which numbers stood for which county. The state had twenty-three counties, and Sally, no connoisseur, knew only about five by number. "What's county twenty?" she asked, knowing that Delice, a Wyoming native and lover of the state's history and geography, would have the answer.

"That's Weston County. Newcastle's the county seat. Guess we were speakin' of the devil. That there truck," she said, taking a deep breath and glaring hard, "is being driven by none other than Pettibone Bandy. And it looks like the son of a bitch is stocking up for a party."

CHAPTER 5
DIFFERENCES OF OPINION

SO THIS WAS what it was like for the astronauts at liftoff. Before Sally had time to do more than squeak, Delice had peeled out across four lanes of traffic, fishtailed into the Loose Caboose parking lot, and screamed to a rubber-burning halt with the Explorer pointed at an angle, between the exit of the drive-up and the entrance to the street.

The driver's door of the Chevy flew open, and Bone Bandy popped out, face red as a beefsteak tomato. Sally's first thought: rabies. He was, it seemed, mad enough to be literally foaming at the mouth. But then, as she caught sight of the big bulge in his cheek, she realized why there was a big stringy gob of saliva hanging out of the side of his mouth. Like so many Wyoming men, Bone was a user of smokeless tobacco. He must have been getting ready to spit when Delice pulled in front of him, and ended up with his wad all over his face.

He was cussing some, too, damning Delice in ways that made

Sally's own use of questionable language look like *A Child's Garden of Verses*. The words he was using, in the particular combination in which he was using them, brought back strong memories of dozens of guys like him, and reminded her why she'd quit making her living singing in bars.

Way back then, nothing had mattered more than the music. In return for the chance to get paid for singing, for doing something she'd have been doing anyway, she'd logged thousands of hard miles of road, spent way too many nights on rump-sprung mattresses in cheap motels, dealt with too many men whose intentions were not good. Five years of following the music and the money all over the Rockies had given her a substantially more pessimistic view of human nature in general, and of the character of the average American male in particular.

Sally had never really known Bone Bandy, but she'd known who he was, having encountered him in the Gallery bar, twenty long years ago. The first time he'd come in with a drilling crew working out by Elk Mountain, a bunch who'd drawn her attention because none of them had bothered to clean up after work, but come straight to town to party on a Friday night. Sally had been sitting at a table with Delice, Mary, and, now that she recalled it, Mary's sister, Tanya Nagy, minding their own business but getting fairly happy at the hour of the same name. Bone and his friends had started sending drinks over to their table. Delice had wanted to send them back, but Tanya had said she never looked a free drink in the mouth, and then Delice had insisted that it was a better policy never to take a free drink from a horse's ass.

Delice, Sally, and Mary had left at the end of happy hour. Tanya had stayed.

No second-guessing that one.

Now Bone was leaning in the driver's window of the Explorer, wiping the dark brown clump of spit away with the back of one hand and grabbing Delice's shirt with the other. "Just what the fuck do you think you're doing?" he asked, red-rimmed blue eyes squinting back and forth between Delice and Sally in a hard flickering glance that made Sally hope that he wasn't packing.

Delice was too furious to be scared. "Surprised to see you here

so quick, Bone," she said, all frost. "I realize it's customary to noti-
fy the next of kin in case of death, but I'd never have believed
they'd find you in whatever rat burrow you're living in now, let
alone that you'd come. Picking up a little something to contribute
to the wake?"

Bone actually laughed. "Contribute? To a wake for Monette? I
don't know why in holy hell I should. My darling daughter let me
know just last week, she didn't need a goddamn thing from her old
man," he said, leaning in the truck window and spitting a stream
of dark juice onto Delice's left boot. "Called her up to tell her I was
between jobs and comin' in for the rodeo, and she told me—let's
see, what were her exact words—that she was in 'tall cotton,' and
I better not come around wanting a loan or a place to crash, and I
should just stay the fuck away. Kids these days got no respect."

Delice was obviously using every ounce of self-control she possessed not to look down at her gooked-up Charlie Dunn, and
instead to stare Bone down. "So what'd you do, decide to grab her
and teach her some respect, like you did with Tanya?"

For a very long moment Bone glared at Delice, saying nothing.
And then, in a low, flat voice, he said, "Maybe somebody oughta
teach you a little respect, Delice. You've got a habit of getting up
on your high horse and pissing people off, and that's the kind of
thing that can put people in mind to learn you a lesson. I know two
or three guys who've given it some thought, over the years." He
moved closer, dribbling more tobacco juice down his chin, twisting
his fist in Delice's shirt and pulling her face close. "Might be they're
in town and in an educatin' mood."

Sally was very unhappy with the trend of the conversation. She
glanced at the glove compartment. Delice was a staunch Second
Amendment person who believed that antique weapons were a
form of poetry, and who kept a couple of long-barrel Colt .45s,
locked and loaded, by the cash registers in her restaurants, just in
case there was a need for poetic justice. Sally felt certain that Delice
would also have a gun in her truck. Sally could see her hand inch-
ing toward the glove box, could visualize Delice taking the gun out
and pointing it at Bone, just to give him the hint that it was time to
go away. To Sally, that seemed like a precipitous choice.

There was a large, heavy, chrome-plated flashlight mounted on a bracket on the roof of the Explorer, just over the passenger's door. Sally snapped the flashlight out of the holder, brandished it in what she hoped was an intimidating manner. "That'll be enough!" she commanded in an arrogant voice she'd practiced, in case she ever had to deliver a lecture at Heidelberg, or some university where they had professors who specialized in bullying. "Delice, we've got to get back to Mary and Dickie's. Bone, if you like your knuckles the way they are, you'd better let go of Delice's shirt, right now."

Bone looked at Sally as if seeing her clearly for the first time. "Well, I'll be. Is that the famous washed-up guitar whore, Mustang Sally Alder, wavin' a flashlight around in there? I believe that it is. Just terrifying, Mustang. 'Course, just lookin' at you two is all that." He whistled between his teeth. "Ain't you girls worried that both of you ridin' in this truck will be so much ugly it'll crack the windshield?"

But he let go of Delice and backed off. Score one for Fraulein Dr. Professor Alder.

Delice gave him a narrow-eyed scowl. "I'll let Dickie know you're in town, Bone. I expect he'll be wanting to have a word with you."

He was climbing back in his pickup but stopped, one leg still hanging out, and leaned out of the truck. "Don't fuck with me, girls," he said, his face a blank. "You really don't wanna fuck with me."

"Don't mess with us!" Sally found herself yelling back, shaking the flashlight for emphasis, even as it occurred to her that this was the kind of conversation that ended up in the Laramie newspaper. One minute people were talking, and the next somebody was whacking somebody with a flashlight. It didn't take much to get in the *Boomerang* police report; Sally had once chuckled over the story of a man who filed a complaint that he'd been out with some friends, drinking on the prairie, and somebody had punched his truck. Then again, with damn near everyone in the state carrying firearms, it didn't take a whole lot for a routine truck punching to turn into deadlier stuff.

"Come on, Delice," she said, hoping Delice wouldn't decide to get out and try to beat up Bone Bandy. "Let's leave him to Dickie." She put the flashlight back up in the bracket.

Delice fumed all the way back to Dickie and Mary's, muttering about how Bone didn't scare her, about how curious it was that he happened to be in town just now, about what kinds of rotten business he'd done or was doing.

Sally only half listened. Of all the things that Bone Bandy had said in that short, unfortunate exchange, she'd gotten hung up on only one.

What had Monette meant when she said she was "in tall cotton"?

She could have been referring to her promotion. Checkers made good money, more than Monette could have expected to make in any other job. Bone had evidently told her he was unemployed. In what they called "the Oilpatch," layoffs were like flat tires—never convenient, but something you came to expect on a rocky road. Maybe Monette had just been lording it over her dear old deadbeat dad. Did Bone know any more about it?

Or maybe it was something else. Did Monette think she'd finally caught a rich boyfriend? Sally knew that plenty of rodeo cowboys spent it when they had it. Sure, some of them were God-fearing Christian lads who lifted weights and toted along tiny house trailers instead of paying motel bills, and saved every penny they earned, knowing that they were making their living courting spinal injury. But lots of them were young enough to want to raise hell, and old enough to do it. They rolled along and rode for the purse every night, never knowing whether a saddle bronc would buck them into a traction bed in some dusty cowtown clinic, or open the door to a fine steak dinner or new tires for the pickup or just a wild night in a strange place.

If Monette had been willing to settle for the two pathetic specimens Sally had seen in the Lifeway checkout line, what would she have thought if some tight-butt bull-riding boy had paid one second's worth of attention to her?

Over the years Sally had seen her share of relatively sane, judicious, intelligent women lose their marbles over the swagger between the hat and the boots. Take Delice, for example. There had been a time when Sally and Delice had gone through their share of the eligible men of Laramie (and in truth, some who weren't legally eligible), but they'd agreed on many a penitent Monday morning that at least they weren't marrying the fools. And then Delice had suddenly gone crazy and ended up hitched to, of all people, Walker Davis, a half-bright piece of range-fed beefcake whose annual income, when he was having his best years as a team roper, almost approached that of, well, a supermarket checker. Most times Walker kept it together stretching fences and herding cows and getting part of his wages in room and board in somebody's bunkhouse, and, of course, sponging off besotted females like Delice. When Walker had finally lived up to his name and strolled off into the sunset with a blond barrel racer from Belle Fourche, Delice had little Jerry Jeff Walker Davis to remember him by. JJ was every bit as handsome as his big gray-eyed daddy had been, and already starting to wreak havoc with the ladies.

If even somebody as hardheaded as Delice could fall victim to cowboy sex voodoo, what of a bleeding bag of need like Monette?

Sally would have to get Delice's expert opinion on the matter, but by now they were pulling up in front of Dickie and Mary's, and the front door of the house was open. They could hear the argument all the way out in the yard. Delice slammed the truck into the driveway, turned off the engine, grabbed the watermelon, and rushed into the house, with Sally hard on her heels, toting grocery bags.

"I don't know why you want to go and have some big public memorial thing for some girl who never amounted to anything, who nobody liked, who wasn't even *from* here," Nattie was saying. "It wasn't like she was your daughter or something. Your sister made her bed a long time ago, when she went off with Bone Bandy. Have a little consideration for those of us who are still trying to make a living. Jubilee Days only comes around once a year. Besides, I'd have thought you'd rather have a quiet family service. It's so much more tasteful," Nattie added.

Nattie Langham talking about tastefulness was about as plausible as Bill Gates talking about business competition. Sally looked at Delice to see if she was appreciating the irony, but Delice was in no mood for either appreciation or irony. Her encounter with Bone had gotten her black powder primed, and Nattie had lit the fuse.

"Shut the hell up, Nattie," Delice hissed between her teeth. "When we want advice from you on good taste, we'll stop gagging and ask for it. What's going on here?"

Dickie took the bags from Sally, reached in, and began his quest for the perfect jelly donut as he said, in a calming voice, "We're just discussing the funeral arrangements. There seem to be some differences of opinion."

"What differences?" Delice snarled, darting glances around at everyone.

Sally took in the scene. Mary Langham was back on the couch, wan and miserable, with Brit beside her, holding her hand. Jerry Jeff hunkered down on the brick hearth in front of the fireplace, waiting for Dickie, standing next to him, to hand him the donuts. Dwayne and Nattie sat in the overstuffed chairs facing the couch. Nattie was flushed, obviously angry. Dwayne's face revealed nothing more than mild concern, but that was more emotion than Sally had seen him show in more than twenty years. Hawk occasionally played poker with Dwayne, and he reported that the best you could hope for was that Dwayne would win somebody else's money.

Brit answered Delice's question. "We've had, like, a hundred phone calls already this morning. Some of 'em are from people who just want to get in on the action, but some are from people who're shocked and sorry, and outraged. That priest from the university and the Unitarian minister both called to offer to say something at the funeral, and Maude Stark wants to call a big community meeting about how to prevent violence against women. We even had one lady call and ask when the protest rally will be held."

Sally wondered if the protest rally person would like being called a "lady."

Nattie huffed out a disgusted sigh. "Protest rally. Classic. Of course it's horrible what happened, but think about it. Some little slut who's no better than she oughta be gets exactly the trouble she's been looking for, and all the PC types come out of the woodwork."

Nobody said anything. Finally Sally found enough control to

offer the mildest version of what she was feeling, voice shaking. "That seems somewhat insensitive to me, Nattie. Monette didn't deserve to be beaten and raped and killed, and everyone in this town ought to know they've got good reason to hope the killer's caught, and to see that things like this don't happen again."

"Anyone with a shred of decency would have figured that right out," Delice added.

Nattie knew she'd gone too far. Sally watched as she came close to biting a fingernail, recalled her fresh manicure, and got hold of herself. Nattie was regrouping, but couldn't back all the way down.

"Sorry, but you can't deny that Monette did have a way of running after trash," she said, tossing her head, as if it was okay to say anything, no matter how revolting, as long as there was some truth to it. The manners bus must have skipped the stop at Nattie's house. "It's too bad, but if you want my opinion, I hope we can get this behind us as quick as possible," Nattie continued. She looked around for help and settled on her husband. "You all may want a big to-do, but Dwayne and me have a real busy week. I'm handling my first make-or-break land swap deal. The investors are coming in this weekend, from California, and we've had this ecologist guy in town for the last few days checking out the properties. The whole thing has me so worked up I'm like to bust."

"Take a Valium," mumbled Delice. "Take ten."

"Sam Branch has turned over a big land deal to you?" Sally asked, shocked. Sam Branch, the CEO of Branch Homes on the Range, was Nattie's boss, and a man who made a point of calculating and maximizing his advantages. Sally knew Sam, all too well, and if the deal was any good, she couldn't imagine him sharing the wealth.

"Nope," said Nattie, who'd known Sam every which way too. "I'm putting this one together on my own, with a little help on the financing end from my banker over there."

"So what are you swapping?" Sally wanted to know.

Nattie inspected her nails, which had fortunately survived her moment of discomfiture. "I've been negotiating with Mary Louise Wood to get her to trade her place in the Centennial Valley for an inholding parcel in the national forest, up in the Laramies, which these California people have optioned."

Land in the Laramies? Sally gulped, thinking of what she and Hawk had seen, only yesterday. "Your land swap isn't near—" she started to ask, and stopped. It was a mountain range, for God's sake, not a neighborhood. That land swap property was probably miles from the Devil's Playground.

Brit looked up, sighing as if it was a tremendous effort to open her mouth, and then asked Nattie, "So your Californians want to trade some shut-in piece of mountain property for Wood's Hole?"

"Wood's Hole?" Jerry Jeff looked up. This was something he could understand. "That ranch where we used to go to ride? Why would Mrs. Wood want to sell? I thought she loved that place. She used to come out to the corral with her pockets full of apples for us to feed to the horses, and then she'd get all excited showing us the birds and antelope and stuff." Realizing that he sounded like a little kid, he added, in sullen teenager mode, "Like it was some big deal or something."

Surprisingly, it was Dwayne who answered, in a voice that sounded a little too much like Mr. Rogers having a soothing chat with the four-year-olds of America. "Well, JJ, part of the problem is that Mrs. Wood isn't making a living raising horses or running cattle or much of anything anymore. She's decided it's more important to save the earth than pay the bills, and she's sitting on a prime piece of real estate. Face it—pretty soon Laramie is going to be the next Jackson or Cody—heck, Wyoming's going to be the next Montana. The reality is that people want fifteen-acre ranchettes, and ranchers can sell their property at top dollar to developers who'll do a quality job subdividing."

Sally hated it when people used the word "quality" without an adjective. Anybody who forked over real money for something called "quality goods" deserved, in her opinion, to learn too late that "quality" could be piss-poor too.

"I can't imagine Molly Wood wants to sell Wood's Hole," Delice said. "She's damn near made that place into a nature preserve. She hasn't had a cow out there in ten years—says she's resting the grass—and won't let her horses near the pond or even the creek. Claims she's trying to do riparian restoration."

"Oh, *that* Molly Wood," said Sally. "I read a piece about her in *High Country News*. She got some kind of award from the Nature Conservancy for ecologically sensitive range management."

"Yeah, so sensitive, she's liable to end up out on her fanny," Nattie put in. "She's in a pickle—ranchers generally are, but she's even worse at business than most. What we're trying to do is help her out—the Laramie Range property isn't a tenth the size of Wood's Hole, but it's up off the Happy Jack Road, surrounded by national forest, which won't ever be developed."

Happy Jack was, as Sally had thought, miles from Vedauwoo and the Devil's Playground. It was idiotic to imagine that there was any connection between the two places. "I still don't see why Mrs. Wood would want to move," she told Nattie.

"Nobody ever accused you of being a financial wizard, Sally," Nattie tossed back. "Molly Wood could build a little house, watch birds to her heart's content, *and* get a nice chunk of change out of the deal—plenty to live on, even something to pass on to her heirs."

"Something for her heirs?" Delice asked, exchanging a skeptical look with Sally, then with Brit. All three of them had excellent bullshit detectors.

"In other words, her greedhead kids are trying to get their hands on some cash before their mommy runs their inheritance into the ground," Brit offered. "Obviously they're pressuring her to sell."

Brit liked to cut to the chase.

"And you're 'helping her out'?" Delice said. "Boy, Nattie, I'd never pegged you as such a philanthropist. Next thing you know, you'll be serving lunches at the senior center and driving the bookmobile."

A quiet voice came from the couch. "Please, you guys. Do we have to do this? I thought we were just trying to get the, um, arrangements for Monette squared away. We couldn't seem to do anything else for her, so I guess we can handle this much. Then everybody can get on with business, and rodeo, and partying, and whatever."

Everyone looked guiltily at Mary. She was right. It wasn't the time to argue.

Dickie knew it too. "Let's get on it. Something for the family. Something for the community." A look at Nattie and Dwayne. "Nothing that'll take too much away from the goddamn celebration of Jubilee Days." And then, taking his wife's hand, "Most of all, something for Monette."

CHAPTER 6
LIKE A GOOD NEIGHBOR

SALLY NEVER GOT the chance to tell Dickie what she'd overheard at the Lifeway, or even to mention their encounter with Bone Bandy. First there was the matter of what to do about Monette's body. The state crime lab had it, and wouldn't be releasing it until after they'd done a whole lot of forensic stuff, along with an autopsy by the Albany County coroner. In any event, there wouldn't ever be a burial—Monette's mother had been cremated, her ashes scattered to the wind up Ninth Street Canyon. The same, Mary thought, should be done for Monette eventually. So they had to figure out a different approach. They had managed to agree on a Thursday morning memorial service, followed by a reception at the Ivinson Community Center, when Dickie got a call on his cell phone.

There was a fight down at the Torch Tavern, where the noontime drinkers tended to gather, and a few too many of the patrons had gotten involved. A bronc rider reported that his truck had been broken into, and several thousand dollars' worth of gloves and chaps and boots and rigging were missing, along with all his CDs. South of town, on Route 287, a deputy had been kicked in the shins by a woman who claimed that by no means had she been doing ninety miles an hour when he put the radar gun on her, and then she'd pulled a gun of her own to emphasize her point.

"And this is just diddly-shit, on top of our usual traffic violations, domestic assaults, and wicked meth heads," said Dickie, working hard at not moaning. "By tomorrow night there'll be an extra five thousand people in town. By this weekend, if the weather holds, there could be twenty thousand more. If you combine my department and the city cops, we have a total of twenty-five people, including secretaries, dispatchers, and the motor pool guys. Even with everyone working around the clock, policing fifty thousand souls, a good half of them drunk and stupid, well, it's a bitch."

"So all this diddly on top of Monette's murder," said Sally. "How the hell can you cope?"

Dickie made a wry face and shook his head. "How can I not? It's crazy, if you think about it. I figure I've got just this week to try to get some evidence and crack this mother of a case. And to be honest, I don't know which is worse—the killer still walking around Laramie, or long gone. I will say I don't mind having the community be upset. Maybe it'll shake loose some information we might not get otherwise."

"Information—oh yeah! Dickie, I—"

But he was already putting on his hat. "Sally, I gotta go. Maybe I'll catch you later tonight. Figure I'll drop by the Wrangler after I get done talking to people."

Gone, like a cool breeze.

Dwayne and Nattie used Dickie's departure as their ticket out too. Nattie was already getting into her Escalade before Dickie had finished holding and murmuring to his wife, but Dwayne took a moment to talk to Sally. "Hey, Mustang. Don't forget about band practice tonight at seven, my place, as usual."

"Oh yeah, of course," she said. Band practice? Of all things. She'd forgotten completely. The Millionaires, the hobby band she was in, along with Dwayne, Sam Branch, and some other aging but unrepentant bar musicians. They were scheduled to play the benefit party that Delice threw, every year, on the Saturday night of Jubilee Days. It was one of those bands that never quite practiced enough, but usually managed to pull a few decent sets together by rehearsing their butts off the week before the gig. Sally turned to Delice. "What's the benefit for this year?"

Delice loved historic preservation, so the Albany County Historical Society was a frequent beneficiary. She also gave money to the Ivinson Memorial Hospital, a couple of environmental groups, and, Sally and few others knew, to pro-choice organizations. Sally suspected that Delice also donated to one or two libertarian political organizations she preferred not to talk about with her knee-jerk big-government lefty friends.

Delice watched as Dwayne walked out to his BMW, and kept staring as Nattie's Escalade pulled away, pursing her lips, narrowing her eyes. "I think this year we'll donate the proceeds to the women's shelter," she said quietly.

With Dwayne and Nattie gone, it was possible to talk about whether there was something they ought to do about all the people who thought that Monette's murder deserved some kind of community remembrance. Listlessly they batted around a few ideas, but by now they were feeling stale and tired, the phone was ringing again, and people had started trickling in. Delice told Sally to drop by the Wrangler later on, and they could talk about it. And then she turned to greet women bearing tuna casseroles and pea salad. Time, Sally thought, for the neighbors to take over.

And time, she realized with exasperation, to do a little good neighboring of her own. It was after two in the afternoon. She'd better get over to Edna's and greet the uninvited houseguest.

As she was about to leave, Delice pulled Sally and Brit aside and said, "Can I get you guys to do me a favor? I'm collecting stuff for the Historical Society white elephant sale we're having Saturday morning, right before the parade. I rented a U-Haul trailer, and I'm going to do a run tomorrow. Would you two come along and help me lug furniture?"

"Sure," said Sally. "You know me. Anything for history, and a little extra aerobic exercise."

Brit said she had some time too. "I've got to work tomorrow night at the Yippie I O, but I can do anything during the day."

"Great," said Delice. "I'll call Molly Wood and let her know we'll be out there about ten tomorrow morning."

"Molly Wood?" Sally asked, eyebrows raised. "We're going to get furniture at Wood's Hole? What a funny world it is."

"Yeah," said Delice Langham, one of the nosier, more interfering people on planet Earth, clearly up to something. "Hilarious."

"But very neighborly," Sally allowed. "Nice of Mrs. Wood to help out the Historical Society."

"One good turn deserves another," Delice said.

That was something Sally Alder actually believed. She didn't deem it wise to make too many rules of conduct, and she had certainly never been that good at upholding most people's idea of public morality.

But Sally had a rock-bottom belief in the idea that friends had to be honest and loyal to each other. Wyoming—all one hundred thousand square miles of it—was in some ways a village, dependent on honor and trust, on the idea that the person you screwed today, you'd have to face at a Rotary luncheon tomorrow. Obviously, too many people went ahead and did the screwing anyway, but the face-to-face reckoning probably prevented at least a few lapses in judgment.

If Nattie and Dwayne were really trying to work a deal that would help this Mrs. Wood while they helped themselves, then it wouldn't hurt for Sally, Brit, and Delice to have a little more information about the land swap. If nothing else, it would give Sally something to think about besides Monette. And if, as Delice obviously suspected, her brother and sister-in-law were running a scam on a hapless ranch woman, then somebody had to warn the old lady about what she was getting herself into.

Besides, maybe there'd be some cool white elephants. Sally was looking for a desk chair for Hawk. Always a pleasure to be able to combine altruism and acquisitiveness. Was this how young State Farm agents felt when they sold tornado insurance in Wichita Falls, Texas?

The pleasure bloomed, then faded as Sally pulled up in front of

Edna McCaffrey and Tom Youngblood's house. At this time of
year, the neighborhoods in the tree district surrounding the university turned into gardeners' paradise. The citizens of Laramie had
the whole long winter to salivate over seed catalogues, start cut-
tings in bay windows, wait and wait for the ground to thaw enough
to break up and turn. Sally had lived in Berkeley and L.A., where
unspeakably fragrant flowers—jasmine and nasturtiums and even,
in the south, gardenias—grew, well, promiscuously, with or without the commitment of some human to horticulture. But gardening
in Wyoming had something in common with marriage. Hardy
perennials—daffodils and tulips and irises, delphiniums and
columbines, asparagus, strawberries—were invisible for nine
months of the year. They sent out pale green shoots in May and
reached glory in the weeks to come. Carefully tended annuals—
peas and beans and lettuce and squash, marigolds and zinnias and
petunias and pansies—thrived while they lasted, and it was always
too soon when the first frost came to blast and blacken. Then you
stuck it out, all over again, devoted and waiting for renewal.

Edna and Tom loved gardening. Alas.

Where Edna's columbines ought to be, a few wisps of crackling
dried stalks stood. Where her pansy and petunia bed had been, lov-
ingly planted in a rush the week before she left, was parched dirt
strewn with straggling stiff threads. The front lawn, which Tom
kept lush and velvety, was overgrown in spots and clots, and dead
in others. The window boxes where Edna liked to put fat red geraniums bore no sign of recent planting. How could plants the size of
Edna's geraniums simply disappear? Sally came up the front walk,
looked into the window boxes, and had her answer. The planters
were, it appeared, being used as bathrooms by the neighborhood
cats.

She didn't even want to think about the backyard. It was too
late to replant the little vegetable garden, unless Edna preferred her
green beans prefrozen.

Better have a look at the house. Good thing this Sheldon Stover
hadn't shown up yet. She'd have the chance to see the place as
Amber McCloskey, geranium murderer, had left it.

Sally took the key out of the mailbox and opened the front

door. The place, as she'd expected, smelled like unemptied garbage and dead houseplants, but also . . . like cat. She heard a thump and a crash, coming from the direction of Edna's home office. Yep, she thought, as something furry twined around her ankle and went *mrowwrr*: definitely cat. Kitten, to be precise. A very skinny, sorry-looking piece of baby catwork.

Amber had left a note on the dining room table. "Hey there, Dr. Stover. Thanks for filling in for us." (Us? Of course, the boyfriend had been living there too. Why not?) "We didn't have time to clean up much, so we hope it's okay. We adopted a kitty—please feed him. His name is Mr. Skittles and he doesn't need any kind of special cat food. There are some cornflakes in the pantry, and he'll eat them with water or anything. Kitties love home-cooked meals!"

A sodden saucer of cornflakes was slowly turning to cement in the corner of the kitchen floor. Poor Mr. Skittles. Sally was, to put it mildly, not a cat person, but she'd be damned if the sad little fur ball at her feet would go another hour without something decent to eat. She couldn't leave the cat there, either—Edna was very allergic to cats. The whole house would have to be detoxed.

Amber's note continued. "We'll be back in two weeks. Please water the yard if you think of it. When you leave, just put the key back in the mailbox. Have fun!" The last exclamation point was dotted with a happy face.

Sally went into the kitchen, looking, without surprise, at the sink piled high with crusted dishes, the overflowing garbage can, dirty counters, dirty table. She decided she'd better see if there was something for Mr. Skittles to eat. She found a small can of imported, oil-packed Italian tuna, opened it, dumped it out on a plate, and set it outside by the back door, next to a bowl of water. As Mr. Skittles set to devouring what must be his first reasonable meal in days, Sally caught a glimpse of the shriveled wreckage of Edna McCaffrey's vegetable garden. Members of the University of Wyoming College of Arts and Sciences would be paying for that, one way or another, all year long.

Then she returned to the kitchen, hauled the garbage out to the alley, came back in and tackled the mess. It wasn't that bad—inside half an hour, she'd done the dishes and scrubbed the place down. She shared a silent thought with the benighted Bone Bandy: Kids these days.

Now Sally remembered the crash that had first alerted her to Mr. Skittles's presence. With a gallows feeling in her heart, she went into Edna's office. It was a pleasant, well-organized space, full of afternoon sunlight from a great, tall window sectioned off with wooden shelves that held Edna's Pueblo pottery collection. One shelf must also have recently held Mr. Skittles, nestled among the pots for a sunny snooze. And when he'd been startled awake and come to investigate, he'd knocked off a black-glazed pot. Sally knew that Edna had one small, glossy black pot made by the Michelangelo of Pueblo pottery, María Martínez of San Ildefonso. Heaven help them all if that was the one.

Sally stooped down to pick up the fragments of the pot, lying desolate on the wood floor next to an Oriental rug that might have cushioned the impact if Mr. Skittles and Sally had been luckier. Praise Jesus, it was signed by some potter from Santa Clara (probably the Botticelli of the Pueblos, but still). She squatted there, picking up pieces, and wondered if she should give it to Hawk to get him to glue it back together. He was a genius with superglue.

"Hello!" came a voice from the doorway of the office. "Are you a housebreaker or a cleaning lady?"

She looked up at the man who'd asked the question: a long, thin face with a brushy mustache, wavy brown hair, a T-shirt and fishing vest above cargo shorts that hung straight down in back, as if God had forgotten to equip him behind. Black socks and walking shoes, skinny white legs. And he was staring at her like she must be retarded.

"Does a cleaning service come with the house?" he asked.

Cleaning service? Sally looked down at her Italian sandals, her Ann Taylor trousers, her black silk T-shirt. The gold jewelry she'd put on to dress up a bit more, out of respect for the morning's somber errand.

This moron went to Princeton?

She rose slowly, holding in her hands the obsidian shards of what had once been art, and was now archaeology. "No. I'm not the cleaning woman. I'm Sally Alder, a friend of Edna's from the university."

"The university?" he asked.

"Of Wyoming," she said. "I run the Dunwoodie Center for Women's History."

"Of Wyoming," he repeated, as if trying to place the name. "Mmm. Well."

Obviously the Dunwoodie Center and UW were too low-flying to register on the man's Ivy League radar. Time to give this guy a clue whose turf he was on. "You must be Sheldon Stover. Edna and Tom's house-sitter told me you were coming. I understand you're a friend of Edna's from back East?"

"Yes," said Stover, "we were at the institute together." Like there was only one institute in the world.

"Was Edna expecting a visit from you?" Sally inquired.

Stover gave her a look that asked what business it was of hers. "As a matter of fact, no. I don't have a fixed itinerary, so I can't commit to being anyplace in particular at any given time. But as it happened, a California colleague I've been planning to hook up with is here this week, so I thought I'd drop in. Edna told me in Princeton that I should look her up if I ever got out West. When I called and the girl asked if I'd be willing to fill in as house-sitter, it just seemed like it was meant to be."

Weird. "So it doesn't matter to you whether Edna's here or not?"

"Naturally," said Stover, "I'd like to see her. I was hoping to talk with her about my current project."

Now Sally was supposed to ask him about his work. "Your project?" she inquired obligingly.

"I'm an experimental ethnographer," he said, as if he were saying, "I'm a farmer." "I'm part of the Insurgency."

First an institute; now an insurgency. "Yes?" Sally prodded.

"Surely you've heard of the Insurgency?"

"Something to do with Central American revolutions?" Sally tried.

Stover chuckled maddeningly. "Only as intellectual fellow traveling," he said, illuminating nothing and obviously talking for his own benefit. He looked as if he didn't think she understood a word he said, and cared not a bit whether she did. "This summer I'm developing a concept that will destroy, once and for all, the confining canons of ethnographic fieldwork."

"Destroying the canons?" Sally asked. With guys like Sheldon Stover, you could appear to make conversation simply by repeating combinations of words they'd just said, but phrasing them as questions. The tactic had gotten her through more academic cocktail parties than she cared to remember. Edna too was a master of getting through cocktail parties, but she wasn't known for her easy sufferance of blockheads. Sheldon Stover could not actually be a friend of hers.

"Exactly," said Stover, shifting into lecture mode. "Consider the phrase 'ethnographic fieldwork.' 'Ethno'—having to do with a folk or tribe or culture, all terms we've come to hold in disrepute. 'Graphic'—asking questions and writing down answers and observations about folk life or culture. But as postmodernists have proven, nobody ever gives answers to questions that the questioner can really understand. And writing down oral traditions, or trying to describe visual or material symbols or objects, simply deadens living things. 'Field'—it implies that there's something 'out there,' as opposed to the observer's perspective. A highly suspect notion. And, of course, 'work.' Here in the modern, industrialized world, we've divided the undifferentiated flux of experience into artificial categories—'work' and 'play' for example."

"Or day and night," Sally offered.

"Yes, that's right," Stover nodded indulgently. "Stark dichotomies. Utterly Western and arbitrary. My summer project is to reveal the subjectivities at work in all these canonical notions."

Was he knave as well as fool? "So, if I get this straight, this summer you're just rambling around wherever and whenever you please, not observing, not asking questions, not writing, and above all, not working. Very insurgent."

"Why yes," said Stover. "Have you read Roland Barthes?"

Sally'd had enough. "How long are you planning to stay?" she asked, knowing and dreading the answer.

Stover looked skyward, his patience taxed. "I guess you don't really get it."

"Get this," said Sally. "I am hereby asserting my authority as Wyoming agent for Edna McCaffrey and Tom Youngblood, who own what we literal-minded souls would refer to as 'this house.' I could kick you out. In fact, I probably should kick you out. But by now every motel between Cheyenne and Rawlins is probably booked solid. Maybe you should just ease on down the road, huh?"

"Actually," said Stover, "I need to be in town a few more days. It's not just that I want to see this colleague. I'm having my last fellowship check forwarded to general delivery in Laramie."

"You're broke?" Sally asked, unnecessarily.

"Just a little cash flow problem," Stover explained cheerfully. "I'm sure it'll be solved shortly."

Uh-huh. Sally sighed. "All right. You can stay, for the moment. I'll email Edna and let her know you're here, but if I don't hear from her by this weekend indicating otherwise, I'll expect you to leave. And you stay only on the conditions that you keep the place clean, water the yard, and don't have any guests of your own."

She put the potsherds down on Edna's desk, found a piece of paper and a pen, and wrote down her phone number. "Call me if you need anything, and be sure to let me know before you take off. I'll drop by from time to time, just to make sure things are going okay. And you leave absolutely no later than Sunday, unless Edna writes and tells me to let you stay. Understand, Mr. Stover?"

"It's Dr. Stover, but you can call me Sheldon, Susie," he said. "I don't believe in hierarchical designations of rank."

"It's Sally, but you can call me Dr. Alder," she said. "I do."

CHAPTER 7
BUSTED BREAKS
AND BAD RHYTHM

SALLY LEFT EDNA AND TOM'S and stopped by the house to pick up her guitar, leaving Mr. Skittles to explore the inside of her Mustang and assuring herself that he wouldn't pee on the floor. Then she headed over to Delice's in the hope that Jerry Jeff would be there. JJ was in some regards a typically feckless teenage boy, but he was known to be a sucker for animals. Sally figured that by the time Delice got home from work, Mr. Skittles would be fully installed as JJ's buddy. She found Jerry Jeff out front with his lariat, roping the mailbox, and as she'd predicted, he was happy to help out a cat in need. She said she'd return with some food for the critter.

Then she'd gone downtown to a florist, where she'd spent more than an hour trying to figure out what kind of flowers to send Mary. Nearly brainless by now, she went to Albertson's (couldn't face the Lifeway, not so soon again), spent several minutes baffled by the array of choices in animal feed, and settled, finally, on Little Friskies. When she caught herself thinking that the tuna-flavored kibble sounded pretty good, it dawned on her that all she'd had to eat that day was four pieces of fruit. She might be a little smarter if she ingested some calories, but she couldn't handle cooking for herself. Hawk wasn't due home until nine or ten, so she decided that she'd just grab dinner somewhere. She took the cat food back to Jerry Jeff, and after vacillating over which of Laramie's fine dining establishments she would patronize, driving all over town, and deciding she didn't feel like sitting in some restaurant and eating by herself, she'd ended up, uninspired, grabbing a burrito at Taco John's.

By now self-pity was kicking in hard. Nobody should have to cope with Nattie Langham, Bone Bandy, Sheldon Stover, *and* fast food in a single Tuesday.

The burrito did seem to wake up a few brain cells. With some hope of improving her spirits, she'd gone by the Wrangler and spent another hour drinking iced tea and listening to a happy hour act called "Horse Sense" (a fiddler and guitarist who sang and played old-time cowboy songs), watching the place fill up with cowboys and tourists and local folks. Delice was rushing around, bossing the employees, caught up in the frenzy. The fiddler had a sweet tenor voice and an even sweeter face, but the party mood still eluded Sally.

By the time she got to Dwayne and Nattie's huge, hideous house in a fifteen-year-old, windswept suburb of similar outsize, ostentatious domiciles, Sally was in the kind of foul humor that had once inspired Delice to ask, "So who shot your dog, hagbody?" She figured she was entitled to her shitty mood, and the pretentious setting wasn't helping. In a mammoth "great room" faced with flagstone on one wall, nothing but glass on another, and a couple dozen badly executed cowboy-and-Indian paintings on the other two, the band and all its gear, including drums and amps, took up scarcely a corner.

The drummer, fiddler, and guitarist-bass player gave her a wave and went back to talking about some disaster movie Sally hadn't

and would never see. Dwayne Langham, seated behind his pedal
steel guitar, was tuning the instrument. Wearing hiking shorts, a
Grateful Dead T-shirt and Teva sandals, he'd made the transition
from pillar of the community to vehicle of musical divinity. In her
life, Sally had known many adequate, and several very good, but
only a few terrific musicians. Dwayne was one. Though he was as
bland as Pillsbury dough in his banker life, angels and demons
seemed to swirl around him when he stepped onto a stage. He
could play pretty much anything, but in the Millionaires, he alter-
nated between bass and steel.

Sam Branch, the Realtor, a man with whom Sally had played a
lot of music and been unwise several times, years ago, was tuning
up his electric guitar, chatting with Dwayne. Sam nodded, heavy-
lidded, as he saw her come in. They weren't pals, exactly, and that
bothered her. Sally liked to think she was the kind of higher life
form who knew how to stay friendly with old lovers. In some cases,
often involving men of the guitar-playing persuasion, the best she'd
been able to do was turn sex into music.

Well, what could you do with Sam Branch? There had been a
time when Sam and Dickie Langham, between them, conducted
most of the traffic in smokable and snortable substances in the
town, but like Dickie, Sam had gotten into a putatively straight
racket. Unlike Dickie, there was something permanently repro-
bate about Sam. Sometimes Sally enjoyed that. Sometimes she
didn't.

Sam leaned down and reached into the cooler at his feet, and
pulled out a cold can of Budweiser, handing it to Sally. She popped
the top, took a swig, set the can on top of an amplifier, and then
got out her guitar and electronic tuner. As she tuned her instrument, she couldn't help listening to Sam and Dwayne.

"So is the old lady getting cold feet?" Sam asked.

"No," Dwayne answered. "I wouldn't say that. She's concerned that this be the right kind of deal for her. She's a conserva-
tionist. We're pretty sure we can avoid having to do a full-scale
environmental impact statement, but we've had a consultant in
here the last few days, looking things over, and he'll write up a
report for her, if that's the hitch. Nattie thinks we should have the

guy give it to her in person. Seems he's the kind who can charm little old ladies out of big ranches."

"Does that really happen anymore?" Sally didn't really want them to know she'd been eavesdropping (and it wasn't, she thought guiltily, the first time that day). But on the other hand, this was obviously a conversation about the Wood's Hole land swap. The way they were going on about Mrs. Wood chapped her butt. "Little old ladies have big old lawyers these days."

Dwayne chuckled. "'Course they do. But human nature's human nature. This guy looks like Robert Redford's younger brother. He's got a killer résumé—he's done ecological consulting for everybody from agribiz multinationals to the Vernal, Utah, Friends of Dinosaur Bones. I was at a Sierra Club picnic with him in Boulder last month, and by the time they were handing out the ice cream cones, he had half the people writing big checks to save the grizzly bear, and just about everybody palming his business card and promising to give him a call."

"What's this paragon's name?" Sally asked, frowning at a high E string that had gone flatter than it ought have, cranking the tuning peg.

"Marsh Carhart," said Dwayne, and the string snapped.

"Dwayne," said Sally, digging in her case for a new E string, but not pausing to consider her words, "are you aware that this guy is one of the biggest pigs in the universe?"

Sam grinned. "I thought you only said that about me, darlin'," he told her. "What'd he do—tell you that you give a lousy—"

"He wouldn't have had any way of knowing," Sally interrupted. "I knew him back when I was in grad school in Berkeley. He was getting a Ph.D. in biology and writing for *Evolved Earth Quarterly*. Leching after every little coed from San Jose to Santa Rosa. *And* half the high school girls. And claiming it was his duty to the species, as an 'alpha male,' to get his genes around as widely as possible."

"Now there's a line I've never thought of," said Sam. "Why do I sense that it didn't work on you?"

"Because I considered it my duty to the species to pray, every night, that his sperm motility was lower than worm squeezin's," Sally said. "He got a little bit famous recently—wrote a book called

Man, the Rapist, made quite a stir. He was on *Larry King Live* and *Rush Limbaugh*, explaining how men are biologically programmed to rape, and women are designed to incite them to rape. Very scientific. What a shithead."

"I don't pay attention to controversy," Dwayne said. "From what I hear, when it comes to ecological consulting, he's good at his job." As if that settled that.

"Dwayne," she said, "this is a real big deal for you and Nattie, huh?"

"Could be," Dwayne allowed, his face expressionless. "Let's play some tunes."

Sally had to admit, it wasn't the Millionaires' best practice. Frankly, it sucked. The drummer had clearly spent much of the afternoon down at the Buckhorn bar, celebrating Jubilee Days, and he was at the point where he couldn't tell a twelve-bar shuffle from a Texas two-step. Sam's cell phone kept ringing, and he kept answering it. Dwayne, whose performances ordinarily varied from rock-solid to brilliant, was on some other planet, and Sally's own mind wasn't on the music. Screwed-up solos, flat harmonies, busted breaks, and bad rhythm—a hell of a musical mess. If she'd been a rookie, she'd have thought they could never be ready for a Saturday night gig. But she'd done her time, and she knew that some nights, the gods of song were playing on the other side of town.

Finally Dwayne called a halt. "Boy," he said. "We're really bad tonight."

"Maybe this gig isn't meant to be," said Sally. "Maybe we ought to cancel. After the murder and everything, I'm not feeling exactly inspired."

"Nobody's expecting inspiration," said Sam. "Just do the job. Besides, didn't you say Delice is going to donate the proceeds to the women's shelter? That oughta fire you up."

Could Sam Branch actually be showing some sensitivity? Implausible. He probably thought Delice ought to give the money to a shelter for real estate taxes.

"Look, I've gotta go," Dwayne said. "I told this Carhart guy I'd meet him at the Wrangler ten minutes from now."

Sally was meeting Hawk there, er, ten minutes ago. And looking for Dickie, and for Delice. And for trouble, it would seem.

The Wrangler bar was packed and rocking. During Jubilee Days they had live music every night, and the band, imported from Austin, Texas, expressly for rodeo week, was doing a right lively cover of "Beyond These Walls," one of Sally's favorite tunes about love and jail. For the first time all day, she was off-duty.

She remembered how she'd come to love this time of year, the weather idyllic, the town full of people looking for a good time, the rodeo season bringing in the green for any musician good enough to get a gig. The cowboys and cowgirls hauled their rigs and their horses from town to town in search of fortune and enough fame to get laid on demand. It hadn't been much different for the pickers and the singers, although they kept slightly different hours. Instead of having to get up mornings and tend to animals, the musicians stayed up nights and arose in the afternoon to minister to their own wasted carcasses.

Cowboys had their riding and roping, and God knew, that could beat up a body. But Sally'd had her own brutal schedule, sometimes doing as many as four performances a day—pancake breakfast jams, fairground tent nooners, happy hours, and then three or four sets, deep into the night. She'd done it for the money, and the exposure, and because she loved it.

Love, as the sainted Gram Parsons had pointed out, hurts. She recalled any number of afternoons, lounging around some motel pool in the darkest possible sunglasses, eating a plate of Tabasco-drenched eggs and swilling translucent coffee that never quite cut the fog. By happy hour she'd had to be ready to get up on some stage and do it all over again. It had taken her years to realize that there could be any other way to live.

But now she approached the Wrangler without having to sing for her supper. It felt good. Hawk was sitting at the bar, drinking a longneck Budweiser and chatting with Delice. Most of the people in the place were wearing cowboy hats, but Hawk was barehead-ed. He had a battered, sweaty straw Resistol he wore in the field, and since he'd come straight to the bar after work, the hat was probably out in his truck. Refused to wear his hat in bars because, he said, it wasn't polite. A fastidious man, Hawk Green.

"Hello, darlin'," she said, kissing him and plopping down on the bar stool next to him, requesting a beer of her own. "Good day at the office?"

"About average," he replied, leaving his hand in the middle of her back, producing a nice tingle. "We took two vehicles out of the university motor pool, and on the way out to the fossil sand dunes the grad student drivers managed to stick one in the ditch and get two flat tires on the other one. Cost us most of the day and half the evening. Maybe sometime we'll get to do some geology. I ended up having dinner in the truck at Taco John's."

"I had the burrito," Sally commiserated. "You must have just missed me there."

By mutual consent, it seemed, neither of them asked how the other was feeling, one day after finding that body.

"Life's a bitch," said Delice, completely unsympathetic. "For one thing, somebody came over and foisted a cat off on my son this afternoon."

Sally smiled brightly. "I know how Jerry Jeff loves animals. Mr. Skittles is such a cutie too."

"Yeah. Thanks a lot. You can tell Edna McCaffrey she owes me one."

"I'll do that. And thank you for being a one-woman humane society," Sally said.

"Don't push it. It's not that big a deal. What really ruined my day was that two of my waitresses quit. One said she didn't like having cowboys hit on her, and the other said she did, and she could make more money at the Torch."

"How so?" asked Sally.

"Let's just say that the Wrangler isn't the kind of place where the waitresses who are willing to let the 'pokes live up to their names can book their dance cards," Delice explained. "The Torch is kind of their headquarters."

Ah. One more way of cashing in on rodeo time.

"You're telling me you don't hire hookers?" Hawk asked Delice.

She wiped down the bar, thinking about it. "Let's just say I prefer to have my help focus on making money doing what I'm paying them to do. And let's say I also like to know that when some ass-hole starts pawing one of my girls, and she objects, there's no mis-understanding about what kind of business we're in. We got enough problems with boys hassling the paying customers."

"I tell you," said Hawk, "Jubilee Days certainly does ring in a festive atmosphere."

"Actually, Sal," Delice said, "I've been thinking about the Jubilee Days thing, and about Monette and all."

Sally drank a little beer, pondering. "I'm not sure what you're driving at."

"I believe there's a way we can all have what we want."

Delice was a businesswoman. People in business specialized in the idea that everyone got pretty much what they wanted, or at least what they deserved. "Which is?" Sally asked.

"Some kind of public event commemorating what happened to Monette, but not disrupting this week."

All kinds of pictures came into Sally's mind, many absurd, some obscene, some downright horrifying. None remotely tourist-friendly. "I'm waiting."

"The Jubilee Days parade," said Delice. "A float in memory of Monette, and in favor of the community taking care of its girls. Banners, stuff like that. We can put it all together in the parking lot behind the bar. Anybody who wants to can march along. Hell, this is supposed to be the Equality State, right? It could be a celebration of being a Wyoming woman, and a kind of 'I'm entitled to make my own rules' deal at the same time. Accentuate the positive, and make everybody see what's at stake."

Sally looked at Hawk, who looked back. "Damn," he said. "I like that."

So did Sally. "It's good. It gives us until Saturday, and between now and then, we can work on the design, and all kinds of people will see it getting built."

"And they can help out if they feel like it," said Delice, pour-ing herself a shot of Cuervo Gold, downing it without benefit of salt or lime. "It was Brit's idea. She and Maude Stark are already signing up volunteers. I've talked to a few people about it tonight, myself."

If building a float satisfied Maude, it was one more point for Brit being a genius. "Count me in," said Sally.

Suddenly Delice's bar-owner radar pricked up. Out on the dance floor a stocky young cowboy in a mattress-striped shirt and a black hat was just about to take a swing at a tall, blond man. A little redhead was hanging on to the cowboy's arm, her face an obvious plea to cool down. In a wink Delice was stepping between them, swinging a bank deposit bag of rolls of quarters in one hand.

"Remind me not to mess with Delice," Hawk told Sally. "Ever."

The cowboy backed away and stomped off to sulk at a table, the girl following with outstretched hands, mouth moving. Men fighting, women supplicating. Just another night in the barroom. And now Dwayne Langham had gone over to tap the blond man on the arm. They turned and walked toward the bar.

Sally might have known. Marsh Carhart, making a move on somebody maybe thirty years younger than he was. At least he'd nearly gotten his ass kicked this time. Maybe the next tavern keeper wouldn't be quite as efficient as Delice.

Maybe the cowboy and the three friends he was sitting with would be waiting in the parking lot when Marsh went home.

Carhart had his hands on Delice's shoulders, approaching the bar. "I swear," he was telling her, "all I did was ask that girl to dance." He smiled his most ingratiating, boyish smile. "Thanks for rescuing me, lady. I love a woman who runs with the wolves. Wanna buy me a drink?"

Maybe Delice would disembowel him.

"Amazing coincidence," said Delice, peeling his hands off her shoulders. "We sell drinks. What'll you have?"

"Stoli on the rocks with a twist," he told her, looking over his shoulder at the cowboy, still glowering away. "Around here, looks like a man has to keep his strength up."

Delice looked Carhart up and down, plainly assessing his state of inebriation, and evidently decided he was good for one more. "Yeah. I'll let you know when I think you're strong enough. That's four bucks."

"Some trouble around here?" said Dickie Langham, casting a

sideways glance at the cowboy and the redhead as he stepped up to the bar.

"Nothing an experienced barkeep can't handle. The cowpoke over there didn't like the idea of his date dancing with somebody else." Delice set a Coca-Cola in front of her brother. Dickie, in his sheriff's khakis, had come in with Scotty Atkins, who was wearing the prepster plainclothes he'd had on at the Lifeway that morning. Atkins ordered a club soda.

"On the meter?" Sally asked him.

"Longish day," said Scotty.

Sally wanted information. "Doing what?" she asked.

He regarded her over his club soda, pale eyes narrowed. "Our job."

Dickie threw her a bone. "As it happens, Scotty and I and the county coroner spent a good hunk of the day over in Cheyenne. In our line of work, we often enjoy passing a few hours watching an autopsy."

"So what did you learn?"

"Sheriff . . ." said Atkins.

"What the hell, Scotty—I'm not going to give away any trade secrets. We'll get the preliminary report by Friday, but won't have the results of the tricky lab stuff for a couple of weeks anyway. And by then, well . . ."

"It could be too late," Sally filled in. "The killer could be long gone. So how do you guys go about solving something like this?"

"We hope the bad guy dropped his wallet, so we can go return it to him," Atkins said sourly, scowling into his drink. "Christ, I wish this was a scotch."

"Be my guest," said Dickie. "I won't tell your boss."

"I don't want to dull my razor-sharp powers of observation," Atkins told him.

"So there's no physical evidence?" Sally asked.

Scotty whistled. "Boy, you sure sound like you know what you're talking about, Sally."

"Not really, but just from what I could see, there was plenty of litter around. And," she swallowed, looking down, "Monette's body was in such horrible shape."

Atkins patted her hand. "Let's put it this way. I didn't see anything today I feel like talking about with a nice lady like you."

"I'm not that nice," Sally told him, looking up.

"No? Hmm," said Atkins, catching her eyes and making them go very wide.

"Nice fake, Scotty," Hawk said, softly. "You managed to distract her. But risky. Guys get shot for trying that twice."

"Hawk's a crazy man," Delice explained to Scotty.

"He'd die for love," Dickie added.

Hoo boy. Sally was getting a glimpse of what Charlene, the Lifeway checker, had been talking about. This guy Scotty had the flat-out je ne sais quoi. The hell with that. "So you guys went from the morgue to the bars?" she resumed.

"In my experience, it's sometimes hard to tell the difference," Dickie said.

"Yeah. We've been making the rounds. You know, you meet so many interesting people in bars," Atkins answered.

Sally wasn't sure if he was making fun of her celebrated sordid past. "I understand that Eleanor and Franklin Roosevelt met in a bar," she said.

Atkins shocked her by laughing out loud. "At least it wasn't the morgue," he said.

"So come on, did you guys find out anything useful?" She really wasn't giving up.

Dickie acted like he hadn't heard the question. He'd spent years bartending right in front of bands whose idea of amplified sound was to attempt to deafen everybody in the place, so he had the perfect excuse. The best ears of Sally's generation were two-thirds impaired.

Scotty Atkins, politely curbing the je ne sais quoi, gave her his best nonanswer. "We've got a lot of questions, and a lot of asking to do. It's sort of like being a historian, only the people are alive."

"Not all of 'em," Hawk put in, and Scotty nodded thoughtfully, draining his club soda.

"That's not very informative." Sally stated the obvious. "I know you can't say much, you guys, but seriously, I want to help."

This time Scotty did the deaf boy thing, and it was Dickie's turn to answer. "You're a helpful sort of person," said Dickie, smiling faintly at her. "But leave the driving to us."

Sally decided on a strategic retreat. She could hassle Dickie anytime, and maybe work on Scotty sometime when Hawk wasn't around. So they all looked around for a new subject, and found it just down the bar. Marsh Carhart was still hustling Delice. "Who's your friend, little brother?" Dickie asked Dwayne.

Carhart stuck out his hand and gave Dickie a big smile, aimed mostly at his badge. "You must be Sheriff Langham," he said.

"What was your first clue?" Dickie inquired.

"Hello, Marsh," said Sally.

And now he turned and looked at her, squinting. "Do I know you?" he asked.

"Sally Alder," she said. "Remember me?"

Carhart took a sip of his drink and the boyishness fled from his face. Busted. "Sally . . . Mustang Sally? Jesus. I'd never have recognized you. What happened—did you have a face lift or something?"

So much for winsome charm. Sally, Dickie, Delice, and Hawk exchanged glances. "Am I crazy, or does everybody in this place sooner or later want to take a swing at this guy?" Hawk asked.

"This is Dr. Marsh Carhart," said Sally, "world-famous author of *Man, the Rapist*. Maybe you saw him on *Sally Jessy*, telling all the girls not to wear short skirts or they'd be asking for it."

"Call me Marsh," he said, "and it wasn't *Sally Jessy*, it was *20/20*."

"*Man, the Rapist?*" Hawk said. "And all this time I'd believed all those ecstatic women who were yelling, 'It's you, only you, oh my God, yes yes yes!' And they were nothing more than robots, programmed to serve the master race. I'll never live it down."

"What the hell are you doing in Laramie, Sally?" Carhart asked, pointedly ignoring Hawk.

"I teach at UW," she told him.

"A Berkeley Ph.D. and that's the best you could do? I thought you were at UCLA," he said.

"I decided I could do better," she replied.

But Carhart was distracted. A very young-looking cocktail waitress had come up to the bar to place an order. She stood between the rails of the server station, rattling off a long list of drinks to Delice, and Carhart was fully engaged with gulping his vodka and ogling the waitress's butt.

"I'd consider relocating my eyeballs back into my head if I were you," Scotty Atkins told him.

Carhart favored Scotty with a condescending stare. "What are you, her bodyguard?"

"Nope," said Scotty. "But you could be her daddy."

"Maybe her granddaddy," said Hawk.

Even Dwayne snickered.

"What are you guys?" Carhart shouted, "the Wyoming sex police?"

"I think he's strong enough," Sally told Delice. This was the charisma that was going to get Molly Wood to roll over? Maybe some people found the combination of arrogance, ignorance, and Stolichnaya alluring. Maybe Carhart had a multiple personality.

And maybe he was drunk enough to play loose with information. "So I hear you're giving rape a rest, doing ecological stuff. Working for Dwayne here on the Wood's Hole land swap," she told him. The whole deal creeped her out. His involvement was just one more reason to be suspicious.

"No," he said, "I work for myself. I do independent consulting, evaluating environmentally sensitive areas. I'm doing a study of a parcel up in the Laramie Range, at Mr. and Mrs. Langham's request. When I work on cases where private property transfers are involved, I focus on the science and stay away from the transaction part."

Not drunk enough, damn it. The bureaucratic squirm language must come naturally.

"You wouldn't want even an appearance of conflict of interest, of course," Hawk said genially, his words for Carhart but his eyes on Sally's.

"Are you an attorney?" Carhart asked.

"Nope," said Hawk. "I don't even know what you're talking about. I'm just a longtime friend of the land."

"It's a friendly town," said Sally, smiling at Hawk.

It seemed likely to get even more sociable. Sally and Hawk

drove home in their separate vehicles. She pulled the Mustang into the garage, and he parked the truck in the driveway just behind her. Before she knew it, he'd pulled her out of the car and wrapped her up and was kissing her lips off.

"I can't help it. I've been thinking about this all day," he said finally, close to her ear, in a voice that clenched several of her intimate muscles and melted several others. "Feel like being love slave to the master race tonight?"

"If you beg me," she replied against his neck, using her tongue and what was left of her lips in the way of persuasion.

When they finally managed to leave the garage, they saw that their front door was standing wide open. She hadn't bothered to lock up after she'd stopped off to get her guitar. Nobody did; after all, this was Laramie. But she hadn't left the door open.

An uninvited visitor. They checked the stereo and television, which were still there. Hawk's laptop computer was still on his desk, undisturbed. No robbery.

Then Sally went into the bedroom. Somebody had dumped out her underwear drawer and taken a knife to her nightgowns and her fanciest lingerie. Shredded silk and lace littered the bedroom floor. And presumably the same somebody had taken Sally's reddest lipstick and written a message on the mirror in the bathroom.

IT WASN'T GOD WHO MADE HONKY-TONK ANGELS.

Very original, thought Sally. Then the trembling began.

WEDNESDAY

CHAPTER 8
STUDS AND DUDS

ALL THOSE MOTHERS who reminded their daughters to wear clean underwear in case they were ever in a car accident would have appreciated Sally's distress at having Dickie Langham and Scotty Atkins come into her bedroom and examine her shredded undergarments. The sight of Atkins putting on rubber gloves and picking up the tatters of what had once been a fetching cherry-red silk teddy trimmed with cream lace nearly did her in, and that was before the crime scene deputies showed up.

Dickie had tried to convince Sally to talk to the department's victim counselor, but she had refused. She couldn't explain quite why, but she didn't want to make a big deal of this. It was embarrassing to have a bunch of cops pawing through your lingerie, and of course somebody else had been doing the same at some point between the late afternoon, when she'd stopped by with Mr. Skittles, and about midnight, when she and Hawk had come home. But Sally hadn't been physically present. The intruder had slashed up half a dozen garments and stomped all over the rest, but she could go to a store and buy new underwear. Nothing was missing.

It had been a long, insane day. Two days, come to think of it. Yesterday a body, today this. Maybe she was just too done in to know how scared she ought to be. Too numb. Or maybe it was just that she refused to put what had happened to her side by side with what had been done to Monette Bandy.

She did take the opportunity to tell Dickie and Scotty about the conversation she'd overheard at the Lifeway, between Adolph and Eddie, the produce clerks. And she told them about her and Delice's encounter with Bone Bandy. They both took notes.

"So what do you make of the message on the mirror?" Atkins asked her.

"I don't know. It's got to be some kind of reference to Monette, right? She spent plenty of time in the dives trying to pick up guys—hell, she even treated the Lifeway like a singles bar. What else could it be?"

Atkins looked up from his little spiral notebook, narrow-eyed. "I'd say the most obvious interpretation is that it refers specifically to you."

"We'll check it out," said Dickie. "There might be a connection."

Scotty added matter-of-factly, "In the last two days you've found a body, talked with maybe a couple dozen people about the death, been seen and heard talking about it in several places. We didn't release the information that you and Joe—you call him Hawk?—found the body. But in a town like this, with a crime like this, rumors tend to spread, and that Dunwoodie case last year does make you something of a public figure. Not to mention the fact that you're well known for your, er, colorful past."

"I was a professional," Sally objected. "I got paid to hang out in the honky-tonks."

"As you like," Atkins allowed. "It's also possible that whoever killed Monette was still around when you two showed up. There are plenty of ways in and out of the Devil's Playground."

Sally was beginning to feel like she'd found too many ways in, and not enough out.

"Or"—Atkins looked straight into her eyes—"it's conceivable

that there's somebody who's got a slightly larger problem with women he thinks aren't behaving properly."

"Great. So you're saying there's no telling who it was."

"We're saying," Dickie said, "that we'll find out. Trust us. And keep a low profile for a few days, if that's possible."

Her first act of keeping a low profile was to refrain from telling her friend Dickie and his ace detective that she was not simply exhausted, but also as angry as she'd ever been. A sex maniac in Sally's own house? Maybe the same guy who'd savaged and killed Monette? Maybe getting ready to terrorize or hurt more women? Wasted and scared, yes, but infuriated too.

"If you don't mind," Dickie said, "I think we won't release the details of this particular home invasion. We'll put it in the *Boomerang* as a reported prowler at this address."

"That suits me," said Sally. "I'll just tell anybody who asks that somebody came in while we weren't home, and made a little mess, but they must have gotten spooked and split before they could take anything." Yeah. Like she was going to feel like having a hundred conversations about this nightmare.

Scotty Atkins looked like he was using the last ounce of alertness left in a tired body. He took out a business card and wrote a number on the back. "My home and work numbers. You call me anytime," he said, putting the card into Sally's hand. "Anything you think of, anything that makes you edgy."

"Edgy?" said Hawk, putting an arm around Sally. "You'll be on the phone day and night."

Atkins looked at them both, smiled a little. "I suspect edgy works for you, Joe—er, Hawk."

Hawk had no comment.

"And if either of you two get the urge to try to conduct your own investigation," Atkins said, with an edge of his own. "Don't."

"Ditto don't," said Dickie. "I meant that, Mustang, Hawk. I know you're pissed. But seriously, don't put yourself in the line of fire." Dickie went with tough love. "We don't know what we're dealing with here. If we've got some guy who thinks it's his job to purify the town of honky-tonk angels, Laramie could look like Waco before he's through."

It was nearly two in the morning by the time they'd finished, leaving behind the residue of black fingerprint powder along with the mess and the obscene aftertaste of violation. Hawk insisted that Sally go out into the living room and sit on the couch while he cleaned up the bedroom and bathroom. He asked what of her underwear she wanted to save, and she told him to throw away everything that had been in the drawer. All of it.

She'd have to go down to the mall in Fort Collins to buy new bras. Laramie was not exactly the bra capital of the West. The thought made her giggle, and then guffaw. Before long she was in full-fledged hysterics. Hawk emerged with the broom and took a bulging black garbage bag out to the trash, and returned to sit with her, arm around her, until she'd cried herself out.

"You need to sleep, Sal," he said. "It's all too much." He led her into the bedroom, neat and tidy now, the empty bureau drawer back in place, and offered to loan her a T-shirt to sleep in. She took the T-shirt, but slept only fitfully. They lay curled up together, Hawk cradling her with his body, and he felt warm and good and safe. But she was way too wired to relax.

By six A.M. the birds were singing and Sally had just about had it with insomnia. Maybe if she got up and worked out, she could come back and catch an hour or two of rest before she had to go out to Wood's Hole with Delice. She knew she was too fatigued to go for a run, but she had a free pass to try out Iron Man and Woman, a new upscale gym that had opened up on Second Street, downtown. She could spend half an hour on an exercise bike, then flog some machines, pretending to be a buff yuppie.

Good thing she kept her exercise bras in a different drawer.

Iron Man and Woman wasn't really Sally's type of gym. Of course, there'd never been an athletic club that wasn't in the business of cashing in on human narcissism, but in some places the clientele seemed to take vanity to the next level. This was the kind of facility where the tanning beds did a big business, and pumped young men fondled their own muscles when they got done with a set of biceps curls. There was a glass wall between the crowded weight room and a large aerobic studio, where a couple of dozen people were punching and grunting their way through a kickboxing workout led by a woman about half the size of an Olympic gymnast.

Morning in America, thought Sally. Amber waves of grain and wet spandex.

Up a flight of stairs, even more fitness freaks were flailing away on treadmills and elliptical trainers, Nordic ski machines, and rowing contraptions. All the stationary cycles were in use, so she got on a stair climber and began trudging up the hill to nowhere, feeling like the women on the bikes behind her were evaluating every spare ounce on her thighs. In the effort to block out their critical thought waves, Sally turned on her Walkman, closed her eyes, and stepped harder. Soon she was working on a nice little fantasy about going to Carolina with Mr. James Taylor.

Three minutes later she opened her eyes to find Nattie Langham pumping along on the machine next to her.

She had to hand it to Nattie. Not even seven in the morning, and her makeup was perfect. Sally had dressed in her usual hideous workout ensemble of black tights and ancient faded T-shirt (this one commemorating Los Lasers, a great, long-gone bar band) but Nattie was sporting the latest high-tech synthetic shorts and stretch top. You never knew when you'd run into somebody who'd buy real estate only from a perfectly groomed saleswoman.

Seeing that Sally had come out of her trance, Nattie swung her attention away from a television that was silently broadcasting a Janet Jackson music video. "Jesus, Mustang, what happened to you? You look like you've been rode hard and put up wet," Nattie shouted, looking shocked at the sight of her.

Actually, underneath the powder and paint, Nattie didn't look so great herself. But Sally was too weary for a war of words. She took off her headphones. "Tough day yesterday."

"Yeah, me too," said Nattie. As usual, she was more interested in her own life than anyone else's, but Sally was, for once, glad of it. The less said about Sally's previous day, the better. "By the time I got done answering my voice mail it was after ten and I'd had it. I was supposed to meet Dwayne and our ecologist guy at the Wrangler, but I decided Dwayne could entertain him for one night. Not that it's much of a chore."

Maybe it was a good thing that Nattie had showed up this morning. The mixed music tape she'd brought had moved from Mr. Taylor to Janis Joplin, and it was too early for "Piece of My Heart." Sally was in the mood for a little sparring. "I've known Marsh Carhart for years. I acknowledge that it's possible that you could consider him good-looking, but he's so frigging conceited that I'm completely mystified that anyone, anywhere, could find him even excusable." Even you, Nattie, Sally added silently.

"I don't know. Arrogance isn't that bad in a man," said Nattie. "In Marsh's case, it's made him very rich. He's head of one of the biggest environmental consulting firms in the country, and a lot of people think he's a visionary. Maybe arrogance is just another word for self-confidence."

"And maybe it's just not giving a damn about anybody except yourself. Visionary—jeez."

"Hey, I heard he bought Microsoft the day they went public," Nattie told her. "Tell me that's not visionary."

"It's good, but it's not exactly being the Dalai Lama. You always did have a weakness for greedheads with big egos, Nattie," Sally said, legs pounding faster, working up a nice sweat.

"What about you?" Nattie shot back. "I wasn't the only one boinking Sam Branch back in the day," she pointed out.

"Fair enough," said Sally, "but at least I haven't done him since Carter was president. Goes to show it's possible to learn something in this life." If lifelong learning could be measured in terms of the men Sally Alder had stopped sleeping with, they ought to give her another Ph.D. But then, complicated as they were, the old days had in some ways been simpler. "You've got to admit, Nat, we did have the luxury of making mistakes in those days. No AIDS, for example. Seemed like the summer of love went on for eight or nine years."

"Or at least the golden age of sex," Nattie said, sighing a little.

"Golden age? Probably just because we were too loaded half the time to care whether the guys were studs or duds," Sally admitted. "Remember that little assistant football coach with the Napoleon complex? That night I walked into the Alibi bar and found you making out with him I nearly busted a gut. He was so short that you practically had to kneel on the floor to sit on his lap."

"Yeah, well, he might have been short, but he was built," Nattie shot back. "Jesus, but he had a wicked temper on him. You wouldn't have known it, watching him glad-handing around town, schmoozing up the boosters and all, but he couldn't handle his liquor. I stopped going out with him when he came into the Gallery one night when I was tending bar, and he was already shit-faced. When I spilled a little of his shot he busted the glass and tried to cut me. I hate to think what would have happened if he'd gotten that mad sometime when we were alone." A shiver ran through her, and Nattie stepped faster at the thought.

Sally considered Nattie's story. "You know, we were pretty lucky—Delice, you, me, Mary even. We let ourselves get in some damn dangerous situations. One night when I was playing a rodeo in Rawlins, I had a couple bourbons too many and ended up in a trailer with a cowboy. We were messing around, and two of his buddies came in for a piece of the action. Lucky for me, they were drunker than I was and I got out of there. Could have been a really ugly scene." She blew out a big breath, pushing the machine harder.

"We used to have a saying," Nattie recalled. "If you mess with the bull, you get the horns. It's a miracle none of us were gored to death."

"What about Tanya Nagy? I mean, there were plenty of lowlifes to choose from, but why run away with a textbook hard case like Bone Bandy?" Sally shook her head, baffled and sorry, sweat streaming into her eyes, sliding off the tip of her nose.

"Who knows?" Nattie shrugged. "Maybe she thought he was Clint Eastwood. Maybe he had a lot of cocaine. Maybe he's hung like a giraffe."

"My money's on the dope," Sally decided. Cocaine had never been her own drug of choice—it made her jittery. But in the seventies it had been everywhere. People who should have known much better, Dickie Langham, for instance, had succumbed.

"Probably dope," Nattie agreed. "Tanya was really into freebasing."

Freebasing: the coke-smoking technique that had turned David Crosby into an animal and blasted Ricky Nelson into the next garden party.

"Remember those freight yard hobo guys, Shannon and Jack-straw? The ones who showed up in town one winter, and crashed in that abandoned hotel behind the Ivinson Street Senior Center, down by the tracks?" Nattie asked.

"Yeah. They tore up the original oak floor to start a fire and smoked out about fifty old people having a hot lunch."

"As I recall, their fingernails were so dirty they could write their names on a bar napkin without a pen," Nattie said, grimacing. "Scary. Somehow they had a whole lot of money sometimes, and they'd go get a big bunch of blow and party it all away as fast as they could."

Sally didn't admit it, but she'd once—very briefly—visited the hobos' crash pad with Dickie, who'd been making a delivery. What was left of the floor was littered with paraphernalia, including a syringe. They were getting set to shoot up. Sally had fled at a run at the sight of the needle.

"Well, Tanya liked to hang out with them. So you see, maybe she could have done worse than Bone Bandy. At least he wasn't a junkie, and at that time he had a job. Probably she thought he was the best she could do. Tanya wasn't exactly the queen of the prom at Laramie High."

Since Sally, unlike Nattie and Delice and Mary and Tanya, hadn't grown up in Laramie, this was news to her. "Did she have a tough time?"

"Let's put it this way," said Nattie, "she was famous for being ugly, but putting out. You know all those high school awards—'Miss Congeniality' and 'Best Dressed' and all that?"

"Sure," said Sally, who had, in fact, been voted "Most Likely to Succeed" but had never admitted the fact to anyone, ever. At the time, she had thought that success would mean getting into a good enough college to latch on to the richest possible husband. Talk about your lifelong learning.

Nattie shot Sally a deadpan look. "Tanya was voted 'Miss Barnyard.'"

Horrible. "Were they actually rotten enough to put it in the yearbook?" Sally asked, dreading the answer.

"Of course not—it wasn't official or anything. They

announced the real awards at the spring formal. Tanya got hers afterward. One of the football players lived out west of town, on a little hay farm. There was a party out there, and the story was that Tanya took the whole team on, out behind the barn, that night."

Hot as she was, Sally shivered. "What a world for women."

The thought of her lingerie cut to ribbons, of the terrifying note on the mirror, intruded. IT WASN'T GOD WHO MADE HONKY-TONK ANGELS. She shuddered again.

And then she looked at Nattie. "If you think about it," she said, "you and Delice and I weren't that different from Tanya, or Monette, for that matter. We took a million drugs, drank our nights away, slept with losers, killed half the brain cells God gave us, and thought we'd live forever. You're right. It's a damn wonder most of us made it. If ever there were a bunch of pathetic sinners begging for their just deserts, it's us."

No! Get a grip, Mustang old thing. There were differences too. For example, Sally had lost her taste for drugs (except Jim Beam, Budweiser, snooty California wine, and Peet's coffee, but nobody was perfect). She had long stopped believing that snagging some guy was the answer to everything. Not that she was against marriage, and in fact she would have loved a kid or two. She liked a good romance as much as the next woman, and as it had happened, her taste ran to men. But during the years in which she might have thought about settling down, she hadn't come across a man she wanted to marry and have babies with.

She felt a hard pang of regret for all those years Hawk had been out of her life. That long summer of love had an even longer winter of discontent.

Still. She was pretty pleased with what she had managed to achieve. She'd made a life for herself in her chosen profession, and done work she was proud of. She loved her friends and tried to be worthy of them. She'd kept her music alive. And after all that time, when she'd made her bones on her own, fate or the Force or whatever had brought Hawk back to her. He was her partner, not her master or her meal ticket. "Sometimes I think the women's movement saved my soul," she mused.

For a fraction of a moment Nattie looked thoughtful—troubled, even. But then her usual sulky, self-important expression returned. "Just like you to come up with some feminist moral-of-the-story. You know something, Sally?" she asked. "You've got your problems, I've got mine. Life bites. But I figure on some level, we all make our own chances. I grew up with nothing—a mother who worked all the time, a father who didn't give a good goddamn if my brothers and I were dead or alive. I'm making something of myself, and I don't owe anybody one fucking thing. Everything I've got, I earned with hard work and planning."

So much for their moment of sisterly bonding. This was, after all, Nattie Langham she was talking to, state champion at the game of studs and duds. If sleazing around anything in pants, hooking a rich husband, and then cheating on said husband counted as hard work and planning, Nattie was a regular Andrew Carnegie.

Nothing pissed Sally Alder off more than canting hypocrisy. "Well, if I were you, Nattie, I wouldn't be planning on working too hard on Marsh Carhart. He's not half the man Dwayne Langham is." Jesus, now who was Miss Self-Righteous of the Millennium?

"If I were you, I'd mind my own damn business," Nattie replied, and that was it for conversation. They climbed on in silence, the sweat pouring off them. Eventually Sally put her headphones back on, cranked up the volume, and let Janis, the queen of the honky-tonky angels, obliterate all thought.

CHAPTER 9
THE SCHOOLMARM

WHEN SHE GOT BACK HOME, feeling somewhat the better for the sweat if not for the conversation, she found Hawk sitting at the kitchen table, reading the *Boomerang* and drinking his coffee. She could hear the washer and dryer running, out in the mudroom off the back porch. He looked up with a piece of a smile. "You know, Sal, you need to work on your laundry habits. You're a real washer hog. I went to do a load and found you'd left your wash in the machine yesterday. I moved it over to the dryer."

Her wash? She had underwear? "You didn't put my bras in the dryer, did you?" Speaking of sin.

He was offended. "What do you take me for? I hung the flimsy stuff out on the line."

She looked out the window. Bras and underpants, even a nightie, flapping happily in the morning breeze. She'd never seen a prettier sight.

"Have I mentioned that you're the ideal man?" she told him,

wrapping her arms around him and giving him a kiss on the ear.

"Get away from me, you're all sweaty," he said, swatting her off with the newspaper. "But don't forget about the love slave thing. So what're your plans today?" he asked.

"I told Delice I'd go out to Centennial to help her pick up stuff for the white elephant sale on Saturday."

"Are you really up for this?" He looked worried.

"Yes, I am really up for this," she said. "I'm not going to lock the doors and hunker down in the house, Hawk. Life has to go on."

"Where in Centennial?" Hawk asked, hearing something in her voice.

"Wood's Hole. Actually, we are going to get things for the sale, but Delice thinks it might be a good idea to have a little talk with Mrs. Wood about that land swap Nattie and Dwayne are trying to get her to do."

"Land swap? Is that the one your Carhart guy's working on?" Hawk put the paper down. "Is this really any of your business?"

"He's not 'my' Carhart guy, and it's probably not my business," she admitted. "But look at it this way. You're always complaining about all those deals around Tucson, where the developers trade a parking lot for some mountain range, and then they scrape off all the saguaros and ocotillos and turn it into Levittown in the Desert. Your father's ready to run off to Mexico to get away from the ranchette crowd in the Tortolitas. Could you just let the same thing happen in the Centennial Valley?"

Hawk thought about it. "Maybe you guys need a hand with the more elephantine white elephants," he said at last.

"We're taking Brit along," said Sally. "We can probably manage."

"Yeah, Brit's a real Charles Atlas."

"Don't you have work to do?" she asked.

"Hey, I'm a college professor. Everyone knows we sit around all summer long and eat bonbons." Now his eyes turned serious. "Look, I know I'm not supposed to act like this," he said, "but after what happened last night, I just feel like keeping an eye on you for a while. It'll wear off soon enough, but for the moment, that's the way it is."

She swallowed once, twice. And finally managed, "Oh well. If that's the way it is."

Delice was happy to have Hawk's help. If he was willing to drive his truck, between that and her Explorer, everything would fit. She could cancel the U-Haul trailer she'd rented and save twenty-five bucks. She insisted that Sally ride with her, and Hawk follow along with Brit. They had, she said, things to discuss. "Tell me about Mr. Personality," Delice demanded, before they'd even gotten out of the driveway.

"Carhart?" Sally asked. "You got a good demonstration. He's insensitive, boorish, egotistical, sexist, and pompous."

"The hell of it is," said Delice, "he's tolerable on the eyes."

"And agony on the brain," Sally retorted.

"Maybe I could just stuff a sock in his mouth," Delice mused.

"Oh shit," Sally exclaimed, "don't tell me . . ."

"You have to admit, he does bear a resemblance to Robert Redford," Delice persisted.

"Which has served him well over the years. I'm all for Robert Redford of course, but don't be deceived. Marsh Carhart makes me puke."

"And he's had that effect since when?" Delice asked.

"Always. Back in Berkeley, there were a bunch of young hotwires who were going to prevent environmental meltdown with something they called 'appropriate technology.' Everything from solar food dryers and composting toilets to personal computers and bioengineering.

"He was one of them. Marsh is a sociobiologist, which means he's one step away from just making things up as he goes along. He did his dissertation work on birds—sooty terns, to be precise. Evidently, everybody thought these terns mated for life, but Marsh watched them go at it for about six months and then wrote a paper saying that the males snuck off and 'committed adultery' with younger females. He concluded that adultery was adaptive behavior for males of all species—those who were most successful at getting their sperm around were improving the gene pool and doing the species a favor."

"Huh? Adultery?" said Delice. "Do the girl sooty terns go out and get nasty little birdie divorce lawyers? This sounds like total bullshit."

"Ten-four. At the time his then-wife was booting him out after catching him in the back of their VW van with one of the girls who scooped ice cream at Swensen's," Sally said.

"He gets away with this stuff?" Delice was confused.

"What can I say? But he's the king of headlines. The Redford thing doesn't hurt when it comes to media coverage, or the fact that he's marketed himself as a defender of the earth."

"While porking everything in sight?" Delice asked.

"Especially the young ones, but of course, anything for the species. And then, of course, there's that stupid book on rape. I hate to think what kind of participant-observer research he did on that one."

Delice's eyes went cold. "I doubt that what happened to Monette was a matter of natural selection. Okay, the guy's a slimeball. He sounds like he and Nattie were made for each other. But my brother will put up with him, if he's good for their business. I'm just amazed that people aren't on to him. From what I saw last night it doesn't take a lot of Stoli to get him talking."

"Not about business. On the land thing, he was very coy. It's not that surprising. He's made some money. He bet large on Microsoft when it was just a couple of dudes with two tin cans and a string, so he must know a good thing when he sees it. I don't care what kind of crap he slings about not getting involved in the financial end of these deals. If Nattie and Dwayne stand to make some bucks, Marsh probably has a piece of the action somewhere."

"Maybe he just wasn't interested in talking to you," Delice said.

"And with good reason. Trust me, Dee, he does his talking with his wanger."

"Oh, I believe it. He thinks I 'run with the wolves.' Maybe I can use that." Delice fancied herself a Mata Hari when she needed to be.

"And if that fails," said Sally, "you've got that bag of quarters."

They fell silent as they passed the West Laramie Fly Store,

heading out for the Snowy Range Road. The valley opened up before them, the Snowies looming ahead under the huge blue sky. Black-eyed susans nodded by the roadside, and Sally spotted half a dozen antelope, scattered over a hill. The windows were open, and the smell of sage and clean air enveloped them. The tension of the previous two days began, somehow, to fade. There were so many beautiful spots in Wyoming. It was a sad and amazing thing that somebody like Monette Bandy could have spent her whole life in such a place, and never learned to see or to care. "You know," said Sally, "this is one of my favorite places in the whole world. If I had a piece of this, I'd never, ever let it go."

"I'm with you," said Delice. "And from what I've heard, Molly Wood is of the same opinion. That's why I can't understand how this deal's gotten this far. Wood's Hole is just about the biggest ranch in the valley. There can't be a piece of property up in the Laramies that's even close to the size, so there's gotta be a bunch of cash involved. She must be under heavy pressure to be even considering this swap. And she's the type to handle pressure. Wait until you meet her."

As they neared the picturesque town of Centennial, nestled at the foot of the Snowy Range, Delice turned right on a gravel road, Hawk's truck following behind her. Horned larks shot up out of the ditches as they rolled past. They took the road until it forked, bore left over a rise, and swept down, on a dirt driveway now, curving along the contour of the hill. A row of cottonwoods at the bottom marked a winding creek. Not far from the streambed, a grove of trees sheltered a cluster of weathered outbuildings and a sprawling white clapboard house with green shutters.

"A little bit of New England in the Rockies," Sally remarked.

"That'd be Molly's doing," said Delice. "She's not from here originally—came out from the East during World War II, to teach school."

"How'd she come by the ranch?" Sally asked.

"Married money. Zeke Wood was a builder who got a nice chunk of the government contracts that turned Fort Warren, over in Cheyenne, into F. E. Warren Air Force Base, during World War II. And after that, well, let's say they invested wisely."

As Sally knew, FDR and his boys hadn't been too scrupulous about cost overruns in the service of whipping Hitler and Hirohito. But then federal boondoggles during wartime were a time-honored way of getting rich in America. You didn't have to be a corrupt profiteer to end up seeing some nice returns from government work. Westerners loved to bash Washington and then cash the checks.

Delice parked next to a brand-new Ford Expedition, in a turnaround between the barn and the house. Hawk pulled in beside her and jumped out. "Pretty place," he said. "I like the house." Hawk had spent his earliest years in Connecticut, with his grandparents, before his father and stepmother claimed him and took him to Tucson. He'd gone to college at Yale. He had a love-hate thing with New England. After all those years in Arizona, the ancient architecture still called to his Yankee blood.

"When I phoned this morning to tell her we'd be coming, she said she'd be down by the stock pond. I guess she's a regular with the bird count for the Audubon Society, and she's putting in a morning down there."

"Cool," said Hawk. He'd once confided to Sally that the finest thing his grandparents had ever given him was his first pair of binoculars. The Venerables, as he called them, hadn't been much for showing affection, but they'd shown him how to look at birds, how to read field guides, how to use his eyes and his head to see the world more clearly. With his mother dead and his father gone, the birds of the Connecticut woodlands had provided little Josiah Green with a lot of company.

Hawk headed around to the toolbox in the back of his truck and pulled out his binocular case. "Check out those redwings and yellow-headed blackbirds, staking out their territory in the willows along the creek. Maybe I can become her assistant. I should have brought a six-pack."

"She'd probably have appreciated it. Come on," Delice told them.

They walked along the watercourse, on a path beaten through tall grass, weaving through sagebrush and trees to the pond. Not far along the shoreline, a small, compact woman in a straw hat sat in a folding lawn chair, leaning over a large bird-spotting telescope, mounted on a tripod. As they approached, she straightened, put on reading glasses that hung from a chain around her neck, wrote something in a notebook, took the glasses off and let them dangle, and turned on them a gaze so penetrating, Sally suddenly knew how those long-ago students of Molly Wood's must have felt when they'd done something to call the teacher's attention to themselves. Ahem.

Her expression wasn't unfriendly. It was alert. Her eyes, strikingly blue, were relentless even as she smiled. Straight, short, silver-white hair framed her sturdy, beautiful face. She wore a button-down oxford shirt, pressed to crisp perfection, a pair of equally immaculate cotton pants, and a combination Sally had seldom seen since her fifties childhood: Keds with peds. "Hello there," she drawled, the music of autumn, and apple cider, and sleigh rides in her voice. Sally instantly wished she could hear Molly Wood reading aloud. Edward Lear, or Thoreau, or *Goodnight Moon*. "So awfully nice of you to come and pick up all my old stuff."

"I brought some folks to help," said Delice, introducing them.

"Oh yes," said Molly Wood. "I knew Meg Dunwoodie, Dr. Alder—may I call you Sally? I look forward to your biography. And in fact, Dr. Green—did you say Hawk, Delice? I'd thought it was Josiah—I attended your lecture last fall on southern Wyoming mineral deposits. A fascinating subject."

"Glad to hear you think so," said Hawk. "Most people don't." He swung his eyes to the edge of the pond, where birds with long, slim necks and stilt legs, red heads, white chests, and black and white wings pecked about in the tules. "Avocets," he said. "Nice. What have you got out there in the way of ducks?"

"Take a look for yourself," said Molly, gesturing at the scope.

Hawk leaned down and peered in the angled eyepiece. "Mallards, teal, a couple of pintails," he chanted. "Coots. Eared grebes. Long-billed curlews. White-faced ibises." He swung the scope over to look at the tules again. "Some yellowlegs over there too." He stood a moment and listened, silently. Now Sally was aware of the rustling of the wind in the leaves, the twittering of birds. "Do I hear a chestnut-collared longspur?"

Now Molly smiled broadly. "There's a Wilson's phalarope nest over there too. Come back this fall. We get great ducks here then."

Hawk looked at her and grinned back. "If my grandmother were here, she'd have me down in the rushes, stomping around trying to flush rails."

"I'm hardly old enough to be your grandmother!" Molly sniffed.

"I never exactly had a mother," Hawk told her.

"Oh," she said, taken aback. "Well then."

"I should've brought Jerry Jeff." Delice tried a diversionary tactic. "He's very good at stomping."

"He's a teenager, yes? I'm sure he is. Teenage boys have feet of lead." Molly seemed grateful for the shift, but she couldn't help one sympathetic glance at Hawk. "I'm pretty much done here," said Molly. "I'll just pack up my stuff and come up to the house with you."

"Let me help." Hawk was trying to put her at ease too. He ran a finger over the aluminum body of the scope. "I don't mind toting a Swarovski," he told her.

"A what?" Sally asked.

"This fine piece of Austrian optical engineering. Mrs. Wood here has the Cadillac of spotting scopes." He turned to Molly. "I'll wager you take some pictures with this thing from time to time."

"Not me," she said. "My husband was the photographer in the family. I never even took snapshots of my children at their birthday parties. I probably should have," she finished on a mumble, as Hawk stowed scope and eyepiece in their cases, broke down the tripod, and shouldered all the equipment.

"Don't worry about it," said Sally. "I'd be just as happy if my mom hadn't taken a million embarrassing pictures of me in some dress with puffy sleeves that cut off the circulation in my arms, with chocolate cake smeared all over my face and a stupid party hat." All this talk about parents and children seemed to be making everyone nervous.

Hawk was still looking at the pond, searching for another subject. "You know, Mrs. Wood, for a stock pond, I'd say this one's in great shape. The tules look good, there are cottonwood saplings, the water's even clear. How do you do it?"

"Do you see any cows around here?" Molly Wood asked him. "Any cow pies even? I haven't let them anywhere near this part of the place in almost ten years. We started out back then, just fencing them away from the pond and keeping them downstream. I've been reducing the herd steadily over the years, and by next year I'll be ready to give up on cattle altogether."

A ranch with no cattle? Not exactly a paying concern, Sally realized. How did Molly Wood make the mortgage? Jerry Jeff had said she'd stabled horses—could that possibly pay the bills? Obviously it would be rude to ask, but after all, they'd come out in part to find out what was up with Molly's property.

"I was so sorry to read in the paper about your brother's niece," Molly said to Delice. "I don't know what things are coming to around here. I understand that the memorial will be held tomorrow. I expect to be able to get there, but I have some appointments. If I'm delayed, please offer my condolences."

Delice looked startled. "There's no need to make a special trip. And thanks, I'll pass on your thoughts to Mary and Dickie."

"Don't be so shocked that I'd attend," Molly said acidly. "What happened to that poor Monette Bandy is just unconscionable, and I wouldn't be surprised if you have a big turnout. People haven't talked of anything else. Maude Stark called me up yesterday to tell me that she was thinking about organizing a demonstration. I don't know about that, but I certainly believe in paying my respects."

"Molly's a Republican," said Delice. "Republicans don't demonstrate."

"At least the ones who have any sense of decorum," Molly acknowledged.

They'd gotten to the house, and were standing at the front door, when Brit turned an appraising eye on the creek, and the cottonwoods, and the carpet of wildflowers in the ungrazed pasture beyond.

"What are you looking at?" Hawk asked her.

Brit's expression was halfway between blank and bleak. "I'm trying to imagine a bunch of condos by the creek, and those meadows all full of trophy vacation homes nobody lives in."

Molly's eyes flicked to Brit. "I beg your pardon?" she said.

"I understand that my Uncle Dwayne and Aunt Nattie are putting together a deal to get you to swap this place to some California developers, for some acreage up in the Laramie Range," she said. "People haven't talked of anything else."

Molly Wood just stared at Brit. Brit returned the glare. Neither one blinked. A real Wyoming moment.

Molly's eyes shifted and scanned them all. Nobody said anything. "Well," she said at last, breaking the silence but smiling pleasantly, as if the conversation had just begun. "Why don't you come in?"

Walking into her living room, Sally could imagine Ralph Waldo Emerson holding forth to sea captains and Harvard divines and Margaret Fuller. It smelled like lemon furniture polish and lavender sachets. Homey, but not precisely comfortable. Clean plank floor, mahogany chairs, stiff upholstered sofas, gleaming tables, a curio cabinet full of fossils and arrowheads, old coins and tintypes. Rich, red, Persian rugs that somebody's great-randfather had probably brought back from the Orient on a clipper ship. Not a single speck of dust, anywhere. The walls held a pair of heavily framed oil portraits, a man and a woman in somber clothes. The woman had blue eyes and Molly's jaw line. There was a seventeenth-century map of a Connecticut land grant, in remarkably good condition, and a couple of what looked like excellent Japanese prints.

Hawk walked up to the map, squinting. "Walling Plantation?" he said. "I was born five miles from there."

"And I was born right in the middle of that grant," said Molly. "In Wallingtown. First person in eleven generations of my family to leave."

Hawk took the opening. "I wasn't. You've been out here in Wyoming a long time, haven't you?"

Once again she examined them all. "You are a nosy bunch, aren't you? Oh, all right!" she exclaimed, exasperated. "I might have known that like everybody else in the county, you want to know what's going on with my ranch. Maude pumped me for a good half hour. I suppose it makes as much sense to let people hear the truth as to feed the Laramie rumor mill. The things for the rummage sale are in the spare room. Why don't you load them up, and then we can have some lunch and I'll explain."

"We wouldn't want you to go to any trouble, Molly. It's nice enough of you to donate to the Historical Society," Delice said.

"It's no bother. I've got some very good frozen pizzas and some beer," she announced firmly. "I don't mind the company, and I'd just as soon have a civilized meal and a conversation as have you try to worm things out of me so deviously."

"It appears," said Hawk, "that we're not so clever after all."

Molly got lunch ready while they worked. Her white elephants filled the back of Hawk's truck and most of Delice's Explorer. She had already wrapped dishes and small objects in movers' paper and packed them in neatly labeled cardboard cartons. They hauled the boxes out, along with a chrome and vinyl kitchen table set and some other furniture. If you liked Early American stuff, there were some real treasures. Sally had her eye on a captain's chair and was giving some thought to a drop-leaf Governor Winthrop desk she'd seen Hawk linger over. It was time, she thought, for them to think about acquiring some decent furniture. They lived like grad students.

And besides, she'd been touched by the instant connection between Hawk and Molly Wood. She knew Hawk as a man who took his time getting to know people, and she suspected that Molly Wood didn't warm quickly. But they'd clicked in a heartbeat.

At last they were all settled on a redwood deck overlooking the creek, sitting at a wrought-iron table eating pepperoni pizza and drinking—what else?—Budweiser. It must be the beer that made New Haven famous.

Hawk watched the redwing blackbirds dart at each other, squabbling over their turf, but returning, finally, to their original perches. "So how far can we see to the edge of your place?" he asked.

"I suspect that's your polite way of asking how much land I have. About five thousand acres," Molly replied. "Seven and a half sections. And it's mine, outright. Most ranchers lease public land for grazing, but Ezekiel didn't like the idea of having to rely on the government," she said.

Another Wyoming moment. Oy veh.

"We had a thirty-year mortgage. Paid it off in 1988."

"Land of the free and the home of the brave," Sally couldn't help saying.

Molly was somewhat amused.

"So it doesn't cost you anything to live here," Brit said. "Then why would you sell?"

Boy, Brit was really rolling today. She'd either slay them in court or end up looking at a shootout at high noon.

"I don't need the money myself," Molly explained. "I'm somewhat choosy about my gear, as you've noticed, Josiah. But my needs aren't extravagant, and the stock market's done fine for me. I'm not piling up a fortune, but I have no problem living on dividends."

They waited while she ate her pizza, took a swallow of beer. And then Delice ran out of patience. "Come on, Molly. Why sell paradise? It can't be that you've gotten tired of the winters. It'll be colder and snowier and windier up in the Laramies."

Molly took some more time, chewing, sipping before answering. "The land I'd swap for is a seventy-acre tract off the Happy Jack Road. It's quite private, and it's exceptionally pretty up there too," she said at last. "The property has power and well water not too far down, a creek of its own, even a beaver pond. I've already seen crossbills and goldfinches up there, and there's a nice aspen grove that will be heavenly in the fall. It's an in-holding in the Medicine Bow National Forest, so the land around me would never be developed. I could build a nice, new, small house where everything would work, and I wouldn't have to deal with constant upkeep and updating."

"Could you show it to me on a map?" Hawk asked.

"Of course. In a while," Molly told him. She gazed out at the creek, and continued. "Look around the valley," she told them. "Out here, the landholders are under so much pressure to sell or subdivide, half my neighbors are saying that it's not a matter of whether, but when. Right now people are getting an excellent price for their land. But we all know that the booms don't last forever. A year from now the bottom could drop out of the market, and I'd have let my best opportunity pass me by."

They all nodded thoughtfully. But here came Brit again. "You have kids, don't you?"

"Yes. A son and a daughter," Molly said, without much expression. "And five grandchildren." There she perked up some.

"Doesn't it bother them that you're thinking of selling this place?" Hawk asked, with what Sally considered an uncharacteristic lack of finesse. It bothered him, that was for sure.

Molly thought about it. "They say they understand why it's tempting."

And now Delice gave up on subtlety. "Dwayne said something about the deal giving you a nice legacy to pass on."

Molly laughed cheerlessly. "I could pass on an even better legacy by simply giving Wood's Hole to a land trust that would protect the place." She'd finished her pizza, wiped her hands on her paper napkin, and folded it carefully, along the original creases. "My children are, shall we say, not as attached to this place as I am. In fact, they couldn't wait to get out of here. My son, Philip, went off to college in Boulder, and it took him about eight years to graduate. Drugs had something to do with it. Then he got born-again and joined that football coach thing—the Promise Keepers—and cleaned up his act. Now he lives in Colorado Springs, with his wife and three children, and works for some company that markets what he calls 'Christian products.' I confess, I've never quite understood how a product could be Christian. But I know that his church tithes. A good percentage of any money I leave him will probably end up with them. I'm not too sure how I feel about that."

Molly folded her hands in her lap now, as carefully as the napkin. "At least I see Philip from time to time," she said evenly. "He brings the kids for a visit once a year or so. He's very worried about my immortal soul. That's what comes of being a descendant of Jonathan Edwards."

"The guy who sang 'Sunshine, Go Away Today'?" Delice wondered.

"The minister who wrote the sermon 'Sinners in the Hands of an Angry God,'" said Hawk. "Mighty scary stuff. Better than Stephen King."

"Indeed. Philip is certain I'm not prepared to meet my maker.

I keep telling him I'm in better shape than most people in this world and the next."

Sally didn't doubt it. "What about your daughter?" she asked.

"Alice hasn't been back here in twelve years. Partly it's because she hates Wyoming. She left for school when she was eighteen, telling me it was the happiest day of her life. Now I hardly ever hear from her, and she claims that her work just doesn't leave time for a visit where she has to change planes three times just to get here."

Sally felt a minor pang of guilt. Her own parents were dead, but she hadn't been back to St. Louis to see her brothers in a couple years. She should at least call. "So what does your daughter do for a living?" she asked.

"I suppose you'd call it e-commerce," Molly explained. "Five years ago she and a couple of partners started a website. It's called Alice's Restaurant. They started with organic food products, but now they specialize in selling personal services, whatever that means."

"I can guess," said Sally. "You can get anything you want."

"Yes. They've gotten very big. She must have made a ton of money, but all she does is work. My grandchildren go to boarding school and to camp in the summer. I doubt she sees them for two weeks put together at a time. Her husband left her last year, so when the kids have free time, they're with him. I don't blame him for walking out—she never had a minute for him either."

"So Alice is too busy to care whether you sell or not?" Sally asked.

Molly raised her eyebrows. "Not quite. When I called her to tell her I might have an offer on the place, suddenly she was very interested. Not only does she think I should do it, but she's urged me to simply give her and Philip the cash from the sale, right now. She's pointed out that I've always intended to leave them everything in my will, and I don't need the money to live on. Giving it to them now will avoid inheritance taxes. It's a lot of money, so of course the taxes would be considerable."

"Excuse me?" Brit said. "Oh yeah. It's about taxes, not about greed."

"Perhaps," said Molly. "Philip assures me that Alice is simply thinking about what will be there for her own children, and he agrees with her. Alice says she could invest the money now, and in short order it would be worth ten times the current value of my land." Molly sighed. "They're probably right. And I'd still have a lovely piece of Wyoming to call my home."

Hawk tilted his head and looked Molly in the eye. "Why not just sell off part of this place? Why the whole thing?"

"I suppose it might be possible. I don't particularly wish to live here to watch them build condominiums on my creek," she said, aiming one of her schoolmarm looks at Brit. "In any case, the offer that the California investors have put forward is for the whole ranch, conditional on the swap. Nattie tells me that they want an answer by this weekend. My kids say I should think about it. So I'm thinking about it."

But Sally was thinking about all those websites blowing up on a wing and a prayer. Hadn't she read somewhere that most of them operated on three or four days' cash reserves? Maybe Alice's Restaurant was one of those undercapitalized high flyers, and Alice Wood needed the dough more than she was letting on, for boarding school tuitions and summer camps and lawyers. And what about Nattie and Dwayne's investors? Sally wanted to know a lot more about what they were offering, and why. The idea of Nattie Langham and Marsh Carhart out there on one side of the deal almost made her hope that Jonathan Edwards, the minister, had been right about what happened to sinners when they ticked the Big Guy off.

CHAPTER 10
YOU CAN GET
ANYTHING YOU WANT

"THIS IS DRIVING me nuts!" Sally said at last, as they headed back to Laramie.

"Huh?" said Hawk, who'd been silent the whole way, keeping his own company. Delice had been ready to leave just when Molly got out the map to show Hawk. Sally had stayed and ridden back with him, thinking thoughts of her own.

But thinking had led her along a picaresque path, as so often it did. "I can't get the song 'Alice's Restaurant' out of my head." She sang a couple of bars.

"Thanks a lot," said Hawk. "Now you've given it to me."

"The only antidote," Sally declared, "is to get another song in there immediately."

"But the cure can be even worse," Hawk allowed. "Consider 'Bad, Bad Leroy Brown.'"

Sally shuddered as the toxic song slithered into her brain. "Give me some help here. Tell me what's on your mind."

It took him a minute. He darted a quick glance at her as they rounded a curve by a tree-shaded house where Sally had always been amused to see horses wearing sweaters, nearly to West Laramie.

"I've been thinking about that land up at Happy Jack," he said, trouble in his eyes. "I've been giving some consideration to heading up there this week and walking around."

"Up to the Laramies?" she squeaked.

"Come on, Sal. You can't declare a whole mountain range off-limits. That property is miles from the Devil's Playground. There's absolutely nothing connecting the two places, so don't worry. I'm just not sure whether I should go up there or not."

"Why not?" Sally asked.

"Because I've got plenty of work of my own to do. Because Molly Wood's affairs are none of my goddamn business." Hawk snapped off the words.

"What do you mean? I bet Molly would value your opinion." He and Molly had pored over the topo map of the property for a good half hour. She'd pointed out nearby private areas in the national forest (all far enough away to be reassuring), shown him where she'd had good birding, located the beaver pond.

"My opinion? Sure. I guess you think everybody ought to solicit quickie impressions on life-changing decisions from people they just met. Not everybody operates that way," Hawk sneered.

What was up here? "Hey Groucho, chill out," she said. "After all, she did open up to us, and I had the distinct impression that one reason she was so forthcoming was because she took a liking to you."

Hawk kept his face blank. "She's got a beautiful spread. What she does with it is no nevermind to me."

"Right. Like you're completely indifferent to seeing that ranch busted up and sold off, with her shut up in the trees, listening to the wind howl while her kids siphon off the ill-gotten gains. Anybody could tell it'll break her heart. You ought to watch it, Hawk. Your white knight is showing."

"I don't give a damn," he muttered.

"No? You never let *anyone* call you Josiah."

"Hmph," he said.

"Well, at least somebody who knows something about the country might want to check out the acreage Nattie and Dwayne's people want to trade. I mean, of course Marsh Carhart will offer his expert and impartial evaluation . . ."

Hawk glared at her.

"Look, sweetheart. I know that part of what's bugging you is that you think you have to keep an eye on me. But I'll be okay. I promise not to do anything stupid," she assured him. That is, nothing stupider than talking to a few more people about Monette, asking some questions here and there, bugging Dickie Langham and Scotty Atkins, stuff like that. And maybe, just for the diversion of sticking her own nose into Molly Wood's business, doing a little web surfing in the area of personal services. Whoops—she was in danger of getting that song stuck again. "If you do decide to check things out up at Happy Jack," she said, controlling the urge to smirk at him, "I'd be so impressed with your chivalry, I'd probably be inspired to nibble on your knees."

"My knees?" he said.

"Or perhaps you'd prefer higher ground," she said.

"Possibly." Now he was working on a straight face. "Over the years I've been pretty partial to the higher elevations." He paused. "So, would you like to come along?"

Sally told herself to ease up. No need to feel like screaming at the thought of going back up there. It's wasn't like she was planning a trip to the scene of the crime to look for bloodstains or lipstick messages or something. "Maybe," she heard herself say. "When do you want to go?"

Hawk thought about it. "Too late this afternoon—you still want to go to the rodeo tonight, right? Tomorrow's a possibility. After the memorial service."

"Let's see what happens there," said Sally. "There could be things to do for the parade on Saturday. I might have to go buy a case of crepe paper or something." Or see if old Dickie, or, er, old Scotty had time for lunch. But she wasn't mentioning that. How many ways could she actually be a chickenshit at once? This was really terrible.

She decided not to brood on it, so to speak. They had to get Molly Wood's things unloaded. Delice had persuaded the fire department (more precisely, the fire chief, a sometime boyfriend) to donate some garage space for the white elephants, so they stopped off, unpacked the goods, and went on home.

Where, just to screw things up a little more, Sheldon Stover was sitting on their front stoop.

Sally leaped out of Hawk's truck and showed Stover why some people believed that in Wyoming, there was some confusion between "hospitality" and "hostility." "What are you doing here?" she asked. "I don't recall giving you my address."

"Edna's Rolodex," he said cheerfully. "You said to get in touch if there were any problems. I called and left a bunch of messages on your machine, but after a while I decided to go out and figured I'd just stop by here and wait until you got home. There seems to be some trouble with the plumbing."

"What kind of trouble?" Hawk asked, coming up behind. "Who the hell is this?"

"This is Sheldon Stover," said Sally. "The one who's over at Edna and Tom's. He's the experimental ethnographer."

"That does sound like trouble," Hawk observed.

Stover chuckled. "You'd be surprised," he said, cheerfully oblivious to the insult. "But the problem is that the drains at the house have backed up. It's getting yucky. I figured you'd want to come over and clean up and call a plumber."

"Sheldon," Sally was really trying to be patient, "I thought we'd cleared up the misunderstanding about me being the cleaning lady."

"Oh. Oh yeah," he said. "But I thought you were kind of in charge of the place. And really, somebody ought to do something about the mess, and get the pipes cleared out. It's not very pleasant."

Sally could easily imagine. "Here's a crazy idea," she said. "What if *you* got out a mop and a bucket, and took a stab at it?"

"Me?" Stover inquired. "Why?"

"Well, Sheldon, while you're waiting for that check in the mail, you're supposed to be house-sitting, aren't you? And it's just barely possible you had something to do with clogging up Edna's plumbing, isn't it?"

Stover thought it over. "I guess you could see it that way. I hadn't really thought about it."

Could this guy possibly be this clueless? Sally was ready to put him to the test by blasting his ass to Nebraska, but Hawk evidently decided the conversation wasn't going anywhere. "I'll come take a look at it," he said. He went in the house and before Sally knew it, returned with a plunger, a bottle of Drano, and a plumber's snake. "Let's go," he said.

The kitchen sink spilled over with dirty dishes and slimy water. In the downstairs bathroom, the toilet had overflowed, and there were two inches of definitely yucky liquid in the tub. While Sheldon Stover stood staring (now Sally knew where the word "dumbfounded" had come from), Sally found some towels to soak up the water on the floors. Hawk went to work emptying the dishes out of the sink, sending the snake down the drain, and finally pouring in the Drano. As the water began to bubble, and at last to recede, he looked around and saw the scummy frying pan, sitting on the stove. "So . . . what'd you do, Stover? Put bacon grease down the sink and bung up the whole house?"

Stover had disappeared. They found him in the backyard, seated at Edna's picnic table, eating pâté de foie gras straight out of a tin Edna had brought back from Zabar's, last time she was in New York, and had been saving, Sally knew, for a special occasion. Happy Plumbing Day.

"You're unclogged," Hawk said. "Now go clean up."

"Yeah, okay," said Stover, globs of goose liver sticking in the crevices between his teeth.

"Here's your equipment," said Sally, brandishing a mop and a bucket and a bottle of Mr. Clean. "I'll explain the procedure. You squirt some Mr. Clean in the bucket, then you fill it with hot water. You scrub out the bathtub, and then you mop the kitchen and bathroom floors. I did the dishes in the kitchen and put the dirty towels in the washing machine. When the washer's done, you put them in the dryer and turn it on." She thought a minute. Back in the distant past, she'd lived in communal houses with men so ignorant of housekeeping that they sat in their bedrooms and threw their beer cans in the hallway, believing that the beer can fairy would make them disappear. Best to be explicit. "That is to say, push the button that says 'dry.' "

"Dry," he repeated carefully.

Hawk squinted at him. "Do you have a nanny or something?"

"I'm not really into domesticity," Stover said. "My needs are simple. I like to live lightly on the earth. Never stay in one place too long."

Sally imagined a string of eviction notices bumping along behind Sheldon Stover like the cans and streamers on a "Just Married" car. "Where do you live?"

Stover stuck a finger in the pâté tin, pulled out a big fingerful, licked it off. Mr. Light Living. "I've moved around. Been mostly on soft money since I finished up at Harvard. Last year I was in Stuttgart studying consumerism and folk syncretism among immigrant Pakistani punk rockers. This fall I'll be out in California on a fellowship at the Center for Postdisciplinarity."

"That sounds right up your alley, Shel," said Sally. "You wouldn't want anybody to mistake you for a person who had retrograde attachments to discipline."

"Exactly," nodded Stover. "Discipline is over."

Hawk couldn't help asking, "What is it that you fellows do out there at that center?"

Stover blinked. "Look at the big picture," he answered. "Engage in collective problem-solving process, although, of course, I'm skeptical that any problem could ever actually be, well, solved. But some of the fellows remain committed to certain forms of empiricism and pragmatism. The environmental consultants are especially task-oriented, I'd say. My colleague Marsh Carhart, for example, the guy I'm getting together with while I'm here. He was one of the founders. A very holistic dude."

Holistic? Maybe if you thought of the word in terms of "hole." Sally contained her surprise. "You're connected to Marsh Carhart?"

Stover scooped up the last of the pâté, licking his lips. "Sure.

We've talked about the idea of me being hired as a consultant to his firm, on ethnographic issues."

Sally had a hard time imagining that Marsh would pay good spot cash money for Sheldon Stover's multisyllabic horseshit. Then again, a little horseshit here, a little horseshit there, and pretty soon you were looking at enough fertilizer to start a green revolution, of one kind or another. "Gosh, wouldn't that mean you'd have to, like, do some actual work?" Sally inquired.

He thought it over. "I'd prefer to think of it in terms of offering my impressions of particular predicaments," he said. "Which he could choose to take, or maybe not. Either way."

"Either way," Hawk echoed faintly, and then realized what Stover was saying. "Do you happen to be sharing impressions with Carhart on a particular parcel of land in the Laramie Range?"

"Not precisely as such," said Stover.

Sally waited, vainly, for explanation. "Well, then, as what?"

Carhart thought it over some more. "As part of a more complex exchange, involving a traditional, or neo-traditional cultural grouping at a crossroads, with its customs, rituals, and subsistence practices buffeted by the forces of postmodern multinational capital."

Hawk nodded slowly. "You mean, you're here to see how ranchers handle it when somebody from out of town offers them a pile of money for their land."

"In a reductive sense, I suppose so. But as I've tried to explain," he continued with elaborate patience, "I try to operate at a greater level of both detail and abstraction, knowing that my presence modifies what goes on around me, but trying to minimize that effect as far as possible."

"No point in falling victim to the curse of task orientation," Hawk allowed.

"Actually, I do try to avoid that. It may strike you as—what shall we say—effete, but I've seen enough situations where scholars succumb to the temptation to influence the outcomes of their research. Bad things can happen, man." Stover shook his head.

"What about Carhart?" Hawk pursued the matter. "Does he try to affect outcomes?"

Stover wagged his head from side to side, evidently moving thoughts around inside. "I don't really know how to answer that. Marsh takes a different approach. As a sociobiologist, he's not much concerned with action at the scale of most individual interventions. He's more interested in the long-term, large-scale processes that determine human activity."

"In other words," said Sally, "no matter what he or anybody else does at any given moment, it's not a question of choice, or even consciousness, or certainly not conscience. It's all part of a larger process of natural selection."

Stover did the head-wagging thing again, frowning. "I guess, on the highest plane. Not very appealing in some regards, huh?"

"Makes me not sorry to be down here on earth," Sally said, thrusting the mop at him. "Offering you the choice of cleaning up Edna's bathroom."

On the way back home, Hawk started to laugh, and kept it up until the tears rolled down his face. "Soft money!" and "Postdisciplinarity!" and "T-t-t-t-task-oriented!" he exclaimed between gasps and guffaws. "Boy, whoever bankrolls that guy really gets what they pay for. On the other hand, why Carhart? He's a jerk, but not a fool. He must have some use for that little twit. I'm damned if I can figure out what it is." And now he was laughing again. "If it weren't for academia," he finally managed to say, "Sheldon Stover would have been dead years ago. It makes you wonder why we ever abandoned the survival of the fittest. The war of all against all. Nature red in tooth and claw . . ."

"It makes me wonder how I'm going to replace Edna's foie gras," Sally moaned.

Hawk, still trying to get himself under control, giggled once, inhaled deeply, exhaled with a "whew." "Go online," he said, "www.goose guts."

"But of course," said Sally. "The Internet."

"In this world of consumerism and folk syncretism," Hawk declared, "you can get anything you want."

CHAPTER 11
GO RODEO!

BY THE TIME SALLY got done deleting all the messages from Sheldon Stover, Hawk had contracted a case of hiccups from repeated fits of giggling, and Sally was ready to throw the answering machine against a wall. But the last message on the machine was from Brit, saying that her cousin Jerry Jeff was entered in the calf roping that night. That summer Jerry Jeff had started winning decent prize money roping, and everybody thought he'd qualify for the National High School Rodeo. In honor of Jerry Jeff, Uncle Dwayne had invited everybody to be his guests that night at the rodeo. Alice's Restaurant would have to wait.

Dwayne, as Sally knew, was a member of the Jubilee Days Committee, a bunch of beef-eating boosters who made sure there were plenty of posters around town, an abundance of ads in the program, lots of free publicity on local radio, and most importantly, big prize money for the PRCA circuit cowboys and cowgirls who came to compete. It was good that amateur ranch hands and local kids like Jerry Jeff came out to try their luck in a non-PRCA event, but the crowds came to see bull riders and barrel racers who had made (and broken) their bones touring, riding, and roping for a living.

To Sally, Dwayne had always been something of an enigma. Where Dickie wore his heart like an open wound, and Delice masked hers with a cynical toughness that didn't fool her friends for a minute, as long as Sally had known him, Dwayne had never displayed a whisper of passion for anything, except music. Everyone in town knew that his wife fooled around on him, but Sally had never heard him say a jealous word, or show the least bit of concern. As a couple, Nattie and Dwayne kept a busy social schedule, and Dwayne was unfailingly pleasant and polite and even sweet to Nattie, praising her business skills, and even her fashion sense (not all that surprising in a man whose idea of sharp dressing ran to brown suits). Nattie liked big baubles, and Dwayne had, in the years since he'd gotten her out of the Gallery bar and into the Escalade, given her plenty of what Hawk called "hog jewelry"—bracelets big as bagels, necklaces that resembled horse collars, earrings so pendulous her head looked like a chandelier, all studded with gemstones in every color of the rainbow. But as devoted as Dwayne appeared, Sally had to wonder about that marriage. Fleetingly she considered their sex life, and quickly squelched a mental image of Nattie with a whip in her hand.

Well, hell, you never knew about people. Maybe Dwayne was the one with the whip. Maybe he had a little whippersnapper on the side, and that was why he was so tolerant of Nattie's shenanigans. For all Sally knew, he attended meetings of a group sex cult once a week, when everyone thought he was just having bowling night. He was a banker. A trained specialist in discretion.

Dwayne and Nattie had never had kids, and they never talked about it. But if Dwayne wasn't anybody's father, he and Dickie had long acted as surrogate daddies to Delice's boy, Jerry Jeff. They took JJ trout fishing and duck hunting, showed up at his football and baseball games, watched him try his hand at calf roping and saddle broncs, did what they could to make up for his own father's conspicuous absence. JJ's love of sports and indifference to school was a constant source of frustration to Delice, but Dwayne had quietly let it be known that if the kid ever did shape up and manage to get himself into college somewhere, Dwayne would be happy to foot the bill. The way it was looking, JJ was pushing to go to UW on a rodeo scholarship. The rodeo part didn't please Delice, but she figured that maybe he'd get an education by accident.

Dwayne had left guest passes for Hawk and Sally at the gate to the VIP parking area. They parked and went to the rodeo committee lounge to meet the Langhams. The lounge was in a low cinderblock building behind the arena, next to a big dusty lot where the contestants hung out before and between events, having a smoke, or communing with their horses, or flirting with the buckle bunnies who always managed to find their way into the restricted area. Sally spotted Dickie Langham, talking to Jerry Jeff and another cowboy.

The lounge itself was decorated in early chamber of commerce—linoleum floor, fake wood-grain Formica meeting table, beige folding metal chairs, and walls lined with photographs of the members of the rodeo committees for each year. Row after row of head shots of white men in gray Stetsons wearing business smiles. Dwayne was sitting in a chair, feet up on the table, sporting the Stetson and a brown and gold satin baseball jacket that had "Jubilee Days Committee" emblazoned on the back, and his name embroidered over the breast pocket. Brit was there too, slouching on a beat-up couch in faded jeans and well-worn cowboy boots. In honor of her cousin, she wore a Western shirt, black twill. She wouldn't wear a hat, and that was probably unfair to the cowboys. Her shiny blond hair was like a lust-triggering death ray that drew them close and laid them out, before they even knew what hit them. Marsh Carhart was there, resembling an ad out of the *Sundance* catalogue, standing in a corner talking quietly with Nattie. She was decked out in yellow this time, from hat to boots, looking a little like a character out of *Curious George Meets Cat Ballou*. If she really wanted men to pay attention to her, she'd better stay away from Brit.

Everybody was drinking out of plastic cups, making small talk. Dwayne asked Sally and Hawk if they felt like a beverage, and they said sure. He opened a refrigerator stocked with soda and beer and jugs of wine and booze, poured them each a big slug of Jim Beam, and added some Cuervo to his own cup. "We can't take these out of here," he said, "so drink up, Shriners."

It had been a long time since Sally had tossed down four fingers of Beam in under two minutes, but she did her duty. A fireball slid down her throat and detonated in her gut, and little white sparks exploded behind her eyelids. Yee hah—go rodeo!

And not a moment too soon. Outside, dusk had fallen, the first stars were coming out, the moon was rising fast, big and bright as a searchlight. The rodeo announcer finished reading a list of sponsors, and now he was asking everyone to rise for the national anthem, to be played by the Casper Troopers Drum and Bugle Corps. The noisy waiting area, crowded now with chattering contestants, restless horses, fans, and officials, fell first to a murmur, and then to a hush as the contestants reined their mounts to a standstill, the dust settled, and everyone faced the flag. Some of the cowboys and cowgirls put their hands over their hearts. More than half the people sang along.

Maybe it was the bourbon. Sally felt tears come into her eyes and cursed herself for a sentimental idiot. For God's sake, this was the country that had reduced Vietnam to a cinder, savaged its own black citizens, paved paradise and put up a parking lot. She didn't believe in countries. She didn't even believe in borders. Jim Beam and Laramie, Wyoming, had weakened her mind.

But damn, there was something about the moment that shocked her out of herself. About the silvery-dark light, the cooling air, the smell of horses and popcorn and drifting dust, the earnest faces, young and old, the kids holding their parents' hands. Some sense of order, repose, well-being, gratitude for the simplest things. A ritual of communion, reminding everyone there that they were part of something larger, if not always noble, at least worth a minute of recognition. A community. She looked at Hawk. His hands were at his side, and he wasn't singing. (He never sang. Ever. Except, rarely, late at night, out on the lone highway, in the deep privacy of his truck, if a Merle Haggard song came on the radio.) He was silent and still, looking at her, a warming glance. He smiled. Peace and harmony.

But then, for some reason, her skin began to crawl, a chill starting at the base of her spine, traveling up as a shiver, all the way to the top of her head. Maybe another side effect of that honking hunk of Jim Beam? She turned, saw Bone Bandy lolling against a fence, staring at her, and the peaceful night shattered.

Bone looked like he might have had a few himself. His arms were draped over the top rail of the fence, maybe all that was keeping him standing. He looked her up and down, his expression somewhere between a sneer and a leer, then leaned over and spat a stream of tobacco juice between his beat-up cowboy boots. Looked up again, narrowing his mean eyes, a silent warning. And then, as if he'd seen enough and satisfied himself, he turned and walked away.

Hawk had turned to say something to Brit. Sally looked around for Dickie. He was still talking to Jerry Jeff and his friend. She ran over and said, "Hey—did you see? Bone Bandy's over there—hurry, you're gonna lose him!"

Dickie said, "Excuse me, boys," and put his arm around Sally, leading her away. "Listen, Mustang," he half whispered. "I'd appreciate it if you wouldn't go around running your mouth while I'm investigating a homicide."

"What do you mean?" she asked. "You were just talking to JJ."

"Lower your voice," he hissed, then smiled and waved at some Langham or other. "Sure I was talking to him—he's a calf roper, and so's his buddy over there. As you'll recall, Monette's hands had been tied with a piggin' string. It might be useful to know if any of the ropers are missing one."

"Can't you just buy them in any ranch supply store?" she asked.

"Sure," said Dickie. "But from what I've been able to piece together in the last couple of days, only two were sold in Laramie in the past week, both to local cowboys. Obviously, if any of these kids killed her, he's not going to up and admit a damn thing. But there's also the possibility that the perpetrator stole the rope."

"Or maybe just bought himself a piggin' string in Cheyenne, or Rock Springs, or Denver . . ." Sally said.

Dickie sighed. "Or Amarillo, Texas. Or Paris, France. Isn't police work great?"

"What about Bone?" she asked, looking around. "I don't see him. He's getting away!"

Another sigh, this one heavier, very weary. "I've already talked to him, Sal. He's got his trailer out at the KOA. Went out and paid him a visit this afternoon. I wish there were some reason we could hold him for questioning, but at this point we don't have jack shit. He says he don't know nothin' about nothin'. He admits he came into town Saturday, and he's mostly been hanging out at the KOA and the Torch Tavern since then. Several witnesses at both places corroborate that."

"Did he see Monette?" she asked.

Dickie pursed his lips. "Sally," he said very patiently. "Have I mentioned that this is a police matter?"

"He did see her. You're not saying he didn't, so he must have. Did he go to the Lifeway? Did somebody see them there? Did he go to her house? I know what his truck looks like . . ."

"Easy, easy," Dickie said, steering her farther away from people. "Okay, yeah. We have information to put him at the Lifeway on Sunday afternoon. They talked. We're looking into it. Will that satisfy you?"

She put on her fierce face. "What about my house? Can you put him there?"

Dickie looked heavenward, then back at her. "No. He claims he was at the Torch all last night. A bartender and a cocktail waitress say he was there from at least eight to closing time. He could have come by earlier, of course—but at this point, we don't know."

Sally thought it over. "If it was him, you'd think he'd have done something to Delice too. We were together when we saw him at the Loose Caboose."

"That occurred to me," Dickie said. "I asked her if she'd had any weird encounters around town this week, and she said no. Doesn't look like anybody bothered her house. But then, Jerry Jeff told me he was there watching TV all evening. Their television's in the living room, and they never bother to pull down the shades. You can see people in there watching, right from the street. Whoever busted into your place probably wouldn't have wanted to tangle with a big galoot like him."

"Did you tell Delice about what happened to me?" Sally asked.

"Er, not exactly," he said. "She was suspicious enough about why I was asking her if she'd had any problems. I just told her that we'd gotten some calls about prowlers, since the murder and all. I don't know if I convinced her. And by tomorrow morning, she'll see the report of a robber at your house in the *Boomerang*."

"Shit. I'd better tell her about it. She'll be really pissed at me for not saying anything this afternoon. Delice thinks my business is her business."

"Well," said Dickie, "hold off if you can. All I need is for her to get the same bug up her ass about this case that you have. Thank God she's too busy this week to do anything except serve beer and burgers and beat up drunks."

He didn't know that Delice was not too busy to meddle in the Wood's Hole land swap. No reason to bother him with it—nothing illegal there, as far as Sally knew, and of course, Dickie had his hands full with the murder. And whatever else was going on.

Despite Dickie's big arm around her, Sally felt the chill slide up her back again. She looked around quickly for Bone, but he wasn't there. Instead she found herself looking into the light green eyes of Scotty Atkins. Scotty raised his eyebrows but didn't smile.

Dickie saw Scotty too. "I gotta go. Now you just have a good time at the rodeo and leave things to Scotty and me. We don't need you playing detective. Monette doesn't either. And it won't do you any good yourself, come to that," he added, for emphasis, giving her shoulders a squeeze and then striding off in Atkins's direction.

Sally felt a little ashamed. Scotty probably took a dim view of the likelihood that Sally was pumping Dickie for privileged information. Dickie didn't need the added stress. Maybe she was just indulging herself, and getting in the cops' way. Curiosity and fury weren't reasons enough for her to interfere in police business. And the fact that she and Hawk had found the body, and then somebody had walked into her house and shredded her underwear and left that message on her mirror, didn't mean she had some special stake in this thing. Right?

Yeah. Right.

"Hey, we were looking for you," said Hawk, who'd walked over with Brit. "Dwayne says we can go down by the chutes. The bareback bronc riding is about to start, any minute."

"Oh boy," said Sally weakly.

"Brit! Brit Langham!" came a loud voice. "How you doin'?"

Suddenly a horse and rider loomed over them, skidding to a halt in a clatter of hoofbeats. Sally felt her heart leap in her chest, slammed down on the panic. The cowboy, a broad-backed, narrow-faced young man with skin that bore the scars of recently conquered teenage acne, was beaming the kind of idiot grin that Brit tended to bring out in human males.

Brit looked up and for once actually smiled back. Cowboy sex voodoo in action? "Hey, Herman! How's life in the big time?" she asked.

"Can't complain," he said. "Makin' enough to keep me and McGuinn here in Top Ramen and oats." He stroked the horse, a glossy chestnut mare, on the neck.

"This is Herman Schwink," Brit said, introducing them. "We went to high school together. He's a big star on the PRCA circuit. Team roper."

Herman Schwink? Weren't rodeo cowboys supposed to have names like Ty Travis and Boot Bodine?

"How about that," said Hawk. "Roping steers for a living? Hell of a hard way to earn a paycheck."

"Yeah, but it's a pretty good paycheck for a guy who never went to college," said Schwink.

"Herman finished in the top ten on the circuit last year," Brit explained. "He can probably afford chicken pot pies by now."

"Even a T-bone now and then," he said. "I could see my way to buyin' you one, honey, if you've got the time." He hesitated a moment, then took off his hat. "Hey Brit. I was real sorry to hear about your cousin," Schwink said. "Terrible, terrible thing. Tell your mom I send my condolences. I'm gonna try to make it to that memorial service tomorrow."

"Thanks," said Brit. "Did you read about it in the paper?"

"Naw," said Schwink. "Heard all about it from my brother. I

guess the police have been all over the Lifeway, giving the employees the third degree. Adolph said the detective kept him for over
two hours."

Adolph? Mmm-hmm. That was it. Herman was bigger and
sweeter, but the skin and the shape of the face made the connection.

"Was your brother Adolph a friend of Monette's?" Sally asked.

"Naw—not as I know of," said Herman. "Just a coworker.
Barely knew her. But you know how it is. Cops gotta question
everybody that might have seen anything."

Barely knew her? Sally thought back to the conversation over
the melons. What was young Adolph Schwink trying to hide?

Herman Schwink's mare shuffled nervously, snorted, tossed her
head, rolled her eyes. Sally took a little hop backward. The cowboy
tugged tight on the reins, whispered "Whoa, McGuinn," and the
horse stood still. It was probably her imagination, but Sally was
sure that horse was giving her a threatening look.

Sally had done plenty of time around rodeos, but generally
didn't get closer to the livestock than the grandstands or the beer
tent, and she'd chiefly experienced the festivities from a stage or
bar stool in some honky-tonk. Hawk had bought her a forty-dol-
lar Stetson hat, twenty years back in Moab, Utah, as a lovestruck
present. She'd come by her battered old cowboy boots honestly,
one long-ago night in Ennis, Montana, winning them off a ranch
hand who'd been confident that his pair of queens would assure
the sight of Mustang Sally Alder topless at the table. Sally had
bet her three sixes, unwisely perhaps, but well. The boots had
even fit.

But Sally was no cowgirl. Nobody, not even Hawk Green,
knew that Sally Alder was terrified of horses.

"Come on," said Hawk, tugging on her hand. "I want to see
them let those barebacks out."

"Don't forget about the steak, Brit," Herman Schwink pulled
a business card out of his wallet and pressed it in her hand. "Call
me on my cell phone. Name the night."

"A cowboy with a cell phone," said Hawk. "What would they
say out on the Chisholm Trail?"

"Probably just punch in their GPS location and try to find out what cattle futures are going for in Kansas City," Brit muttered, pocketing the card. "He's a nice guy. What the hell."

The first bareback riders were getting mounted up by the time Sally, Hawk, and Brit got to the chutes, and the place was crowded with contestants waiting for their turn to ride and stock handlers and spectators. The cowboys wore big black hats and gorgeously fringed and spangled chaps in brilliant colors, strapped around the backs of their thighs leaving the butts of their jeans exposed in fetching fashion. They swaggered around, taping their hands and arms, tightening their gloves, flexing their hands. Those next in line sat up on the high rail of the aluminum chute enclosure, psyching up, focusing silently on some inward third eye of bareback riding, or talking to themselves. "You're the Man!" affirmed a boy in turquoise chaps trimmed in iridescent green fringe, with sequined red roses on the thighs, as he threw his leg over a snorting black gelding. The horse reared, nearly leaping out of the chute, its hooves clashing against the stall fence, its big body crashing the secured chute gate, the handlers grabbing the straps of the rigging that was all that kept the cowboy sunnyside-up on the horse. "That sumbitch is one hell of a high roller," said someone nearby.

The cowboy might be the Man, but Sally was sure that the horse was the Horse, and it wasn't happy being in the chute. Her breath came in shallow pants, and sweat trickled down her back. If she didn't get hold of herself soon, she'd never make it to see Herman Schwink wrestle a steer, let alone be around at the end for the bull riding.

Jostled by the milling crowd, Sally found herself separated from Hawk, closer than ever to the bucking chute, standing next to Dwayne. "These guys are incredible," Dwayne said, and pointed at the man in the turquoise chaps. "Look at how that kid works his rigging. He's gotta get it just tight enough around his mount—too tight and the horse won't buck. Too loose and he'll slide around like hot bologna in red-eye gravy. Every bareback rider has his rigging custom-made. The handhold's the real art—it's got to be just the right length, width, and thickness to fit the rider's hand. Using somebody else's rigging would be like wearing somebody else's boots."

Sally had happily been wearing the Montana ranch hand's

boots for many years now, without visible harmful effects, but maybe that was because she'd kept strictly clear of horses. And now, at this moment, as the throng of spectators lunged forward for a better look, she was pushed up against the back rails of the chute.

All at once the cowboy whooped and gave a signal and the front of the chute slammed open. That was almost the last thing Sally remembered. The very last was the sensation of being shoved hard in the back, her head snapping into the big space between the second and top rails, just as the bucking gelding plunged out of the chute, its huge hooves slashing out behind.

CHAPTER 12
SMILE WHEN YOU
CALL ME THAT

"COMIN' AROUND THERE. All right. Okay. Take it easy, miss. Here—hold her head. Easy, easy, that's it. All right. Can you sit up now?"

Ugh. She struggled to a seated position, hands pushing from behind.

"You gonna lose your cookies there, lady?" someone asked.

Sally's stomach lurched, but didn't actually do a somersault. "No. Thanks. Could I have a drink of water?"

Someone handed her a Dixie cup half full of warm water. She drank it down.

Someone else sponged off her face with a wet paper towel. It was Hawk. "Hi, honey," he said, his eyes searching her face. "You okay?"

It took her a minute to answer. "Yeah, I'm fine. I think," she said. "What happened?"

"You fainted and almost fell into the bucking chute," said Dwayne. "Scared the heck out of me, Mustang."

"Didn't know you were the fainting type," said Marsh Carhart, who was also in the room.

She was damned if she'd tell them how she felt about horses. "I'm not," she said shortly. "What are you doing here, Marsh?"

"I helped Dickie and your boyfriend carry you in," he said. "You were dead weight."

She was sitting on a metal examining table in a room with white-painted cinder-block walls. "Where am I?"

A middle-aged woman in a white shirt and jeans, wearing a MEDIC armband, explained. "This is the emergency medical assistance room. This is where we bring the contestants when they get smashed up. We're right behind the chutes." She shone a penlight in Sally's eyes, while another medic wrapped a blood pressure cuff on Sally's arm. "We got you right in here when you fainted. We thought at first that bronc had kicked you in the head. That wouldn't have been good."

Hawk was still wiping her cheeks with the cool towel. The thought of the close call with the demon horse almost had her passing out again. "How long was I out?"

"Just a couple of minutes. We work fast," said the medic woman. "Do you have a history of fainting or a medical condition that gives you seizures?"

"No. This is the first time I've ever fainted."

"Any idea why?"

"I'm not sure," said Sally. "Maybe the crowd. Maybe the heat. I got shoved into the fence and all I could see was that bucking horse's hooves coming at my head."

"That'd make me faint," said Dickie sympathetically, patting her hand.

The medic finished up the examination, testing Sally's reflexes, making her count backward from ten to one, getting her to answer simple questions. "You look okay to me—no shock, even. Nothing serious going on. Did you have dinner?"

"Salad," Sally answered. With a bourbon chaser.

"Maybe you should think about getting something to eat,"

said the medic. "And see your doctor. Maybe you're a little hypo-glycemic."

"Smile when you call me that," said Sally.

"All right. Get out of here," said the medic.

It was a little more difficult than she'd thought. People began to filter out of the room. Nattie had shown up to commandeer Dwayne, and he gave Sally a little pat on the back before he left. Carhart went with them. Jerry Jeff stuck his head in, waved, and said he had to go get ready to rope. Brit, who'd been hovering in a corner, nodded at her, reassured, and took off after JJ. The medics were next, finished with Sally and going back on alert for more serious contusions and concussions.

Sally wobbled when she put her feet down on the floor, and had to put a hand on Hawk's shoulder to get her balance. But at last she walked out on her own, Dickie and Hawk at her heels, and ran smack into Scotty Atkins.

"Okay, what happened?" said Atkins. "Can't you keep out of trouble for twenty-four hours?"

"What?" she said. Annoyance cleared her head. "What the hell's your problem, Scotty?"

"I turn my back for one minute, and the next thing I know there's commotion over by the bucking chutes, and then people saying some woman got kicked by a horse, and by the time I get over here, of course, I find you lying on a steel table. What are you, Calamity Jane?"

"What are you, John Wayne? Give me a break, Scotty. I got squashed up against that fence, and the next thing I know, some-body gave me a shot from behind and I was on my way to La La Land."

Hawk took her by the shoulders. "Somebody gave you a shot?" he said through his teeth.

"Ouch, quit squeezing. Yeah. Somebody shoved me. Hard. My head went right between the rails, right into kicking range of that fucking bucking bronco. I hate rodeo!" she fumed.

"Can you tell me," said Atkins, very evenly, "exactly what you remember? Details are important."

"Details? Okay—Hawk and I went over to the chutes. It was

crowded back there, and by the time they got ready to ride, the crowd had gotten pretty packed. I got separated from Hawk and ended up next to Dwayne, right by the chute. He was explaining all about the cowboys' rigging and all that, and the rider was having serious problems controlling that horse. But then again, I guess they breed 'em to be hard to handle, right? I mean, if the horses just came out all nice and trotted around the ring, who'd pay fifteen bucks to watch? Certainly not me! When it comes to watching guys ride horses, I want to see the riders nearly get killed every time! Or at least a good maiming, right? That's my idea of a good time, yessirree . . ."

"You said you wanted details," Hawk told Atkins.

"We'll get 'em, eventually," Atkins said impassively. "She seems a little upset at the moment."

Dickie put his face close to Sally's but kept his voice warm and sweet. "Do you have any idea who might have pushed you?"

"Jesus!" she said, flailing her arms to knock Hawk's hands off her shoulders, pushing Dickie in the chest to get him out of her face, waving her hands to keep Scotty Atkins from coming any closer. "Don't you think that if I knew who did it, I'd be telling you? Boy, I swear, you guys are some ace investigators. That's the kind of police interrogation that usually requires rubber hoses, huh?"

"Sally . . ." said Dickie, half warning, half pleading.

Hawk put up a hand of his own. "That's enough. She's out of her mind. I'm going to take her home and feed her and put her to bed."

"I've already eaten," Sally insisted. "We had a big salad for dinner, as you'll recall."

"More details," said Atkins to himself. "Great."

"Salad," said Hawk, "isn't dinner."

"Sure it is," Sally shot back. "That salad had plenty of stuff in it. I could put a porterhouse steak in a salad, and you'd say it wasn't dinner."

"The lettuce contaminates it," said Hawk.

"That's a known fact," Dickie agreed.

"Much as I enjoy discussing nutrition," said Atkins, "this is a waste of time. I want to ask you some questions, Sally. You're not up for it now, but tomorrow for sure. After the service for Monette. You," he said, pointing at Hawk, "see if you can keep an eye on her for one night. And you"—he rounded on Sally—"put me on your busy schedule."

"I think I can work you in," she said, mustering her dignity.

"I'll bring the rubber hose," he said with a scowl, and turned and walked away.

Hawk was silent and thin-lipped as they drove home.

"Salad," he said at last, each syllable raspy with exasperation.

Sally stared straight ahead until he pulled into the driveway and turned off the truck. Then, still not looking at him, she said, "You're mad at me."

"No! I'm in a dazzling mood. I'm filled with joy and amusement. I love the life we're living—rape, murder, some kind of deviant sex lingerie attack, now a real assault." His voice rose. "What's next, Sally? What's tomorrow's crime? Arson? Grand theft auto? Shit!" he said, smacking the steering wheel with the flat of his hand, hard. *Whump.* "Shit, shit, shit!" he repeated, whacking the wheel in time: *whump, whump, whump.* Seventeen times in all. She counted. He'd be lucky if he hadn't broken a bone in his hand.

Finally he slumped back against the seat, breathing hard, and said, "No. I am not mad at you. I'm out of my mind with worry and frustration and rage. I'd like to think I can protect you. I don't think I can."

She turned to him, took his face in her hands, and turned his head until he was looking in her eyes. "Listen to me very carefully," she said then. "I did not pass out because you weren't protecting me, or because I had salad for dinner and went into a hypoglycemic swoon. I fainted because somebody pushed me into that fence, right next to a big, bucking piece of horsemeat, and horses scare the bloody hell out of me."

Hawk took her face in his own hands. "I know about the horses. In all the years we've been doing fun things together in cowboy country, you've never once mentioned the idea of horseback riding. You've never shown the least curiosity about farm animals. I've thought about planning trail ride treks now and then, and decided that you'd have brought it up if you had any interest in going."

"I admit it. I think horses are goddamn intimidating big beasts, I don't like *anything* that has its eyes on the sides of its head, and I want nothing to do with them, now or ever." She blew out a breath of her own. "I'm getting a little tired of being frightened. For three days I've been alternately terrified, disgusted, mortified and pissed off. I need a more satisfying emotional palette. And I don't need to eat."

They were still holding each other's faces, looking in each other's eyes.

"I'm tired of being scared too," Hawk told her, moving closer, his mouth now slipping across hers. "And I don't need to eat either."

He was kissing her sweet and gentle, and underneath, she could feel another kind of hunger. "Tell me what you want," he whispered in her ear, a little breathless, fingers massaging the back of her neck. "You've been through a lot. I don't want to push you."

She brought his mouth back to her own and tasted his lips, and traced them with her tongue. "I don't know," she said. "Having things go this crazy, I'm actually kind of flexible. Go ahead and push me."

By now they were lying down on the bench seat of the truck, kissing deep and starting to mess with each other's clothes. "Are you flexible enough to fuck in my truck?" Hawk asked.

They made an earnest effort, but between deciding not to put their feet out the window and arouse neighborhood curiosity, and bumping their heads and various extremities on the steering wheel, the gearshift, and the glove compartment latch, they opted for the bed.

It was a good strategy. It had been hot and horny, banging around in the truck, but the necessity of rearranging their clothes, getting out into the night air, unlocking (sigh) the house, and going in started the fun all over again.

"This might be an unhealthy idea," she said, "but I could use a brandy."

They'd bought a bottle of Courvoisier the previous Christmas, and hadn't opened it since.

"Not a bad idea at all," said Hawk, heading for the kitchen cupboards. "Since you didn't have an actual head injury, I suppose it's okay."

The bottle had come with two balloon glasses, and Hawk poured them each a temperate shot. His hands, Sally noticed, weren't as rock-steady as usual. "Let's take these in the bedroom," he said, unnecessarily. She was already halfway there. He followed with the glasses.

By the time he got there, she was sitting on the bed, trying to get her boots off. He put the glasses down on the bedside table. "Let me," he said, sitting beside her, putting her leg in his lap, pulling the boot off by the heel, and slipping off her sock. He kneaded the arch of her foot, a bit of bliss. "Now if you want me to do the other one, better give me a sip of that stuff." She held the glass for him while he sipped, then picked up her other leg and pulled the other boot free.

"Now yours," she said, putting his glass on the table. Sally pulled up a small needlepoint footstool, an incongruously delicate heirloom from the Venerable Grandmother Green, and sat down in front of Hawk. She ran her hands all the way up the sides of his leg and down before settling them around his heel, and dealing with the boot and sock. "I get a sip too," she said, and he obliged her, but found he had to put his hands in her hair and kiss her for quite some time before she went to work on the other leg.

The brandy and the kisses were warming her up nicely. He put her glass down and pulled her up onto the bed, and rolled over on top of her, their mouths fierce and open to each other. "Isn't this a stroke of luck," he said, raising his head and noticing the metal snaps that fastened her denim shirt, and ripping them open, then moving quickly to unsnap the front closure of her bra. "I have to admit, Mustang, I do admire the fact that you believe in efficiency in garment engineering."

"You've always said you thought underwear was overrated," she observed.

But he wasn't saying anything, because his lips and tongue had gotten very busy.

"Wait a minute there, son," she gasped, her fingers numb,

knowing that most of her available blood supply had risen to meet the explorations of Hawk's accomplished mouth. "Don't I get my turn?" She worked at the buttons of his shirt while he reached for the brandy, and had it mostly unbuttoned when he dipped his fingers in the glass and shook a few droplets on her breasts, then bent down to lick them off.

He sighed and rolled on his back. "My woman tastes like fine French cognac. Must be a sign of maturity."

But now she was working on dragging his jeans off. "Two can play at that game," she said.

Much later: "Boy, these sheets have gotten pretty sticky."

"Just a part of the effort to keep you from going hypoglycemic."

"Smile when you call me that."

"I am."

THURSDAY

CHAPTER 13
CLOSE ENCOUNTERS

HAWK WOKE SALLY up in the middle of the night, his body hard and heavy on top of her. "I have to use you," was all he said, and there was nothing tender or gentle about it, or about her response.

And it scared her, that craving to be dragged over rough ground, to a jagged place. This kind of coupling wasn't about warm sensuality, or about their respect and affection for each other, or about the depth of their mutual understanding. It wasn't about having the ability to write true stories, or read maps, or conduct sparkling conversations regarding the events of the day. This pounding need clawed at her somewhere far beyond and below the brain or the heart. Not the kind of impulse Sally liked to own up to.

But if she was honest, she'd known a long time that she liked to walk the edge of the dark side. Over the years she'd teetered over the brink a time or two and plunged in. The hot threat appealed to some pulse in her, like the mean-ass sandpaper twang of Steve

Earle's singing, or Eric Clapton's guitar screaming when he was strung out on pain and God only knew what else.

She had the luxury of waking up in the morning knowing that whatever went on between her and Hawk in the black night, she wanted as much as he did. If they used each other hard, the act was surrounded and cushioned by everything else they were to each other. But she hadn't always been that noble, or that lucky. She'd had some bad close calls along the road. Mercifully, she had never paid too high a price for dallying with danger.

Some women got way more than their share of misfortune. Tanya Nagy's luck had been so excessively bad that she'd passed it on to her daughter.

Hadn't there once been a bestselling self-help book about smart women making stupid choices? But this wasn't just a matter of stupidity. This was a wicked dive into the volcano.

On some level, she thought as she went through her coffee-making ritual, you couldn't get away from the fact that humans were animals. Animals with giant frontal lobes, whose survival depended on making complicated choices: tinker, tailor, soldier, spy? Baseball, football, or basketball? Caf or decaf? People were hard-wired for wide-open possibility, and capable of pledging their lives, their fortunes, and their sacred honor for high-minded purposes. Cows and catfish, wasps and wombats didn't know jack shit about sacred honor. But still the beast lurked.

The espresso machine growled and hissed. Dark liquid dripped down. Hot steam shot into cold milk. Sally watched the white froth in the steel milk pitcher rise.

The search for Monette's killer had made it onto the *Boomerang*'s front page, a small story below the fold. The sheriff said the investigation was ongoing. According to the medical examiner's preliminary report, it did indeed appear that the victim had been raped. The head of the Jubilee Days Committee told the paper that the crime was deplorable, but blessedly rare for Laramie, and thank the good Lord they didn't live in New York City or Miami or someplace where such things happened all the time.

That added a reassuring and typically xenophobic Laramie note. A plague of locusts could descend on Wyoming, and people

would say that at least it wasn't Chicago or San Francisco or someplace so overpopulated, they didn't even *have* locusts.

The locusts were swarming in her head today. Sally always
counted on the first cup of coffee to focus her brain and energize
her body. This morning she got the usual spark of physical igni-
tion, but she couldn't get her thoughts to fall in line. She barely
registered the *Boomerang* police report notice of the "unlawful
entry" at her address on Tuesday night. Hell, she was having
enough trouble assimilating what had happened to her very own
self the night before. She needed to face it, though.

A hard tremor went through her. Too much for now. Follow
Hawk's example, she told herself. Keep on doing those normal
things. He'd headed out early, as usual, for Thursday morning
hoops with the annoyingly fascinating Scotty Atkins. She'd go for
a jog. Just another dulcet summer day in the Gem City of the
Plains. But as she laced up her running shoes, picked up her Walkman, and headed out the door, she felt as if she was steering into
her street, her town, and her life, at an oblique angle, and all the
things she took for granted had slid down to the bottom of the
world. Everything was out of kilter, unfamiliar, and she was waft-
ing in the fog.

Even the music didn't help. Looking to touch the wordless
place where beauty lived, she'd foregone her usual assortment of
rock 'n' roll, folk, and country tunes, and picked out a tape of
Mozart piano concertos. But even as she found her stride and tried
to let the pianist's remarkable fingers massage her mind, she was
seriously creeped. Was somebody following her? Lying in wait? As
she ran up Sheridan Avenue, headed for Washington Park, she
found herself looking at every parked car, at every driver in every
vehicle that passed by, and bracing for another attack.

Ridiculous. Give it up. Turn up the concerto and get out of the
funk. She was approaching the park band shell when she saw the
Dodge pickup with the county twenty plates, parked at the curb. It
took a moment for her brain to record the sight, and with her ear-
phones on and her head still full of Mozart, she didn't register the
rapid footsteps coming out of the band shell, didn't know a thing
until he yanked her by the forearm and spun her around.

"I wanna talk to you, Mustang," Bone said. "Let's get in the truck."

Sally rammed into him with her shoulder, throwing him off balance. But he held on to her arm, and they crashed, tangled up, onto the hard-packed dirt of the jogging track.

In an instant he was sitting on top of her, his thighs straddling her legs, his hands pinning her arms to the ground, giving her a close-up view of the broken veins in his eyes and on his nose, and far too good an acquaintance with a set of teeth that might not have been that great to begin with, and had not been improved by years of tobacco chewing. He smelled like a man riding a hard binge, sweating stale beer and cheap whiskey. He coughed in her face and she nearly gagged, kicking her feet wildly, without effect.

"Goddamn it to hell, stop struggling!" he hollered. "Or I'll give you something to struggle about!"

"Leave me alone!" Sally hollered back. "Help! Somebody, help!"

"Shut up!" he hissed in her ear, lying flat on top of her to hold her down, and letting go of one arm to put his hand over her mouth. "I oughta beat the shit out of you, but that's not why I'm here. Just shut up and listen a minute. I wanna talk to you."

"Talk?" she said against his hard, damp palm, thinking about whether she should try to bite his hand.

"Yeah. Use your head, dumbass. Don't you think if I really wanted to hurt you, I could?"

He had a point. She nodded.

"Now, I'm gonna let you up in a minute, and when I do, you're gonna answer my questions, understand?"

Disoriented by the unprecedented experience of being assaulted in a public park, Sally didn't understand much of anything, but she nodded anyway.

By the time he rolled off her, two elderly women in large straw walking hats, a young mother pushing a sleeping baby in a stroller, a muscle-bound male jogger, and a kid with a soccer ball had gathered to see what was wrong.

"Just a friendly little tussle," Bone told them, getting to his feet and slapping dust off his jeans. "Just showing my old pal Sally here a few wrestling holds." He patted the kid on the head and kicked the soccer ball away, like he was the chief counselor at Camp Hell playing every game at the camp—wrestling, soccer, you name it.

The kid ran after his ball. The walking ladies looked worried. The jogger looked suspicious. The baby kept sleeping. The mother pulled a cell phone out of her diaper bag and said to Sally, "Should I call nine-one-one?"

The man was drunk, and maybe half crazy, but by now Sally was considering the encounter as a golden chance to ask Bone some questions of her own. "Nope. No problem, everything's fine here. Old Bone is a great kidder, aren't you, Bone?" She couldn't resist jabbing him in the ribs with her elbow.

"Unh. Yeah." He put his arm around her and pinched her biceps hard. She'd have a nice bruise. "Just kidding. You folks'll excuse us, now, won't you?"

The little crowd dispersed.

"Not in the truck, Bone," Sally told him through clenched teeth. "If you want to talk, we can sit on a bench and talk. If you don't mind, I'd just as soon we had our conversation in a nice, public place."

He appeared to consider his options. "Okay. This won't take long."

They found a bench. Bone was sweat-soaked, plum-colored, and wheezing hard from their encounter, but as soon as they sat down, he reached in his shirt pocket, found a crumpled pack of Camel Lights, and lit up.

"I thought you chewed," she said.

"Lotta places these days where you can't smoke," he explained. "I like to have options."

Mr. Pro-Choice. Sally had been running, lifting weights, watching her nutrition, and taking long, stress-reducing baths for ten years, and with all that, she'd been unable to overpower an alcoholic smoker who probably lived on canned beef stew and TV dinners, whose tongue would one day rot right out of his head. That really pissed her off. "Okay, Bone," she snapped. "What gives?"

He took a hard drag on his cigarette, double-inhaled through his nose (just to make sure he didn't miss any carcinogens), blew out a stream of smoke long enough to document for a class action suit. And finally he said, "Who killed my daughter?"

That was a curveball. "Why would you think I'd know?"

Bone considered the glowing end of his cigarette. "I been keeping an eye on you and Delice ever since you hassled me at the Loose Caboose. The both of you always did think you got the right to stick your faces in everybody's business. You're even worse than she is, and that's sayin' a whole lot. You probably don't remember giving me a raft of shit one night when Tanya and me had a disagreement at the Gallery. You got me thrown right out of that place. I been a little annoyed with you ever since."

He was right. She didn't remember.

He narrowed his eyes and stared her down. "Nobody likes a busybody. Last night at the rodeo, somebody let you know that, didn't they, Sally?"

"You saw me get pushed into the bucking chute?" she asked, matching him stare for stare.

Bone looked back at her, silent.

"Did you push me?"

He took another drag of his smoke, crushed it out on the bench, very deliberately. "Reckoned you mighta had some idea about who did."

She squinted at him. "And what if I do?"

He looked down, then back up. "Way I figure, you've probably mouthed off enough in your time that half the guys in town'd just as soon kill you as hose you. Then again, you're the one found Monette, and you been stirrin' the pot ever since."

Sally was aghast. "Found her? What the hell are you talking about?"

Bone sighed. "That brilliant lawman Dickie Langham had me in for questioning Tuesday. In the middle of our little chat, one of his deputies came into the interview room and asked him something, and he got up and went over to talk to the guy. He'd been looking at the file on the murder and left it open, and I just read a little of it. When you been hauled in by the cops as many times as I have, you get real good at reading upside down. I know you saw her at the Lifeway Monday morning too."

Reading upside down. One more skill Sally hadn't yet thought about mastering. "What if I did?"

"I ain't the only one talkin' to Dickie these days. And that detective of his looks at you like he wants to slap you in jail a few days to keep you out of trouble."

Bone had seen a lot more of her than she had of him, at the Wrangler as well as the rodeo, and where else? Wood's Hole? Taco John's? Was he stalking her? Had he taken the opportunity to slip out Tuesday night and pay a visit to her house while she was watching Marsh Carhart display his bad barroom manners? "Why are you following me around?"

"Let's say I got an interest in finding out anything anybody knows about Monette. And let's put it this way—if I seen what you're up to, and me not half lookin', whoever pushed you into that chute must be at least a step ahead of me."

Gosh, that was a comforting thought.

Sally considered her options. Bone was vile, but he wasn't stupid. Right now he was trying to convince her, in his weird way, that he wasn't the murderer. If this whole conversation was a bluff, and he'd killed Monette, there was no point accusing him. It could lead to Sally ending up prematurely dead. If he hadn't murdered his daughter, somebody else, a person who meant Sally no good, had. She had nothing to lose by talking to him. "An interest. What kind of interest?"

Bone turned his head and gazed at the sky. When he looked back at her, his eyes were as mean and crafty as ever. "Maybe one I could take to the bank."

"Are you saying that you think Monette had some money stashed somewhere? Why would you think that?"

"I told you before. When I called her, she told me to get lost and said she was in tall cotton. I got to thinkin' about that, and last Sunday I went down to the Lifeway and let her know she better tell me what she thought she was doin', blowin' off her old man that way."

"Yeah, Bone. I bet you let her know."

"Damn right. And what she said was, she didn't need nothin' from me no more. She'd got herself into something sweet and she didn't want me comin' around, tryin' to get a piece of it," Bone said bitterly. He fished for another cigarette.

"Do you have any idea what she was talking about?" Sally asked.

A pause while Bone replenished his supply of toxic gases, noxious chemicals, and heavy metals. He scratched his scalp, shook his head. "Monette always thought she'd get herself a cowboy one day, and ride away."

"You think she had a boyfriend?" It couldn't be Adolph Schwink. Nobody would ever consider a produce clerk a one-man gold mine.

"Hell no," said Bone. "Can you imagine any guy with eyes in his head wanting a sloppy little dog-face piece like Monette for anything more than a quickie behind the barn?"

Nothing like paternal affection. Or spousal devotion. Nope: nothing at all. Imagine being Tanya Nagy Bandy, or Monette Bandy, and living with that. Sally closed her eyes and sighed. "Okay, Bone. What are you trying to tell me?"

Bone looked exasperated. "I'll just tell you what she said. She told me, 'Daddy, I roped me a good one, and this week I'm gonna ride this sucker down hard and then get the hell out of town."

"So you think she was shaking somebody down?" Sally asked him.

"I think she knew something, and she thought somebody'd pay her to forget all about it. If that somebody was a stud hoss cowboy, and I know Monette, she'd offer to take part of her payoff in nookie. You know what they used to say about Will Rogers. Monette was the hoochie version of him. When she was twelve years old I caught her with the propane delivery man. Near took her hide off, *and* his, but it didn't do no good. That gal never met a man she wasn't ready to drop her panties for."

Everything in the world really had slid to the bottom.

Bone looked her up and down. Really. "So now it's your turn, Mustang Sally. Did Monette tell you anything?"

She was too disgusted to be afraid of him anymore. "Why in the world would I tell you if she had?"

Bone drew himself up. He ruined the attempt at dignity by

leaving the cigarette hanging out of the corner of his mouth, but something winsome cracked through the nasty façade. "Well after all, I am her daddy. Leastways, that's what her ma claimed."

And at that moment, sitting on that bench, watching him sweat and smoke, Sally couldn't help seeing Bone Bandy for the pathetic loser he surely was. "I'm sorry, Bone," she said. "All Monette told me, Monday morning, was that she had things to do. She didn't say anything more than that. I don't have any idea what she was up to." Sally sat a minute, and then asked very softly, "What do you intend to do if you find the guy?"

Whatever vulnerability she'd glimpsed in him, Bone shut it away instantly. "I raised her, didn't I? Let's just say as the surviving next of kin, I reckon I got payback comin' to me."

CHAPTER 14
FRITO PIE

SO MANY PEOPLE jammed the Ivinson Community Center for the memorial service for Monette Bandy that they had to leave the doors open and let people stand out on the lawn. The soft-voiced Unitarian minister, unaccustomed to evangelical cadences, had to yell to make himself heard. He'd kept it brief, ecumenical, simple, and familiar. "We've got to stop hurting and hating each other, people!" he'd exhorted. "Everybody get together. Try to love one another. Not next week, not tomorrow, but now, right now. Right now. Right now!"

Sally had believed in that message from the first time she'd heard it, going on thirty years ago. But she'd wondered, even in those bead and bell-bottom days, how in the world human beings would ever put it into practice. As the minister finished, she turned to look at the crowd and saw Bone Bandy slip out the door. She was still wondering.

After the service the crowd flowed outside, under the trees,

talking and waiting and setting up folding tables and chairs while
the ladies got out the food. To be fair, not quite all ladies. Burt
Langham and John Boy Walton, partners in the marvelous Yippie I
O café, had brought a whole poached salmon, glistening in aspic
and garnished with cunningly carved vegetable flowers. Dwayne
Langham, ever the gentleman, had picked up a Sara Lee pound
cake.

If calories were horses, everybody in Wyoming could have ridden to Mexico on the spread for Monette's funeral reception.
Molded salads and covered dishes, stiff with mayonnaise and
cream of mushroom soup. Half a dozen casseroles and platters
courtesy of the Wyoming Cowbelles, the ranch women's group, fea-
turing the state's favorite ingredient (Enjoy Beef Daily). Cold cuts
and sliced cheese, iced tea and lemonade, pies and cakes, and five
kinds of pickles. Sally saw Dickie Langham pile his plate with short
ribs and crock pot meatballs and potato salad and then head for the
desserts, stoking up for another tough day of crime fighting.

There were a lot of folks she'd expected to see. The Langham
clan, of course, this time dressed for the occasion in dark suits and
sober dresses, and a contingent from the Lifeway, most of them
wearing their uniforms, getting ready to head back to work. The
feminist types—women who ran the shelter and the rape crisis center, the orthodontist and the university's lawyer (the town's lesbian
power couple), Maude Stark, looking unusually formal in a tailored
powder-blue skirt with matching short-sleeved jacket, her steel-gray
hair in a sleek ponytail. Polite old-timers like Molly Wood.

And then there were people who came representing groups—
contingents of firefighters and police officers paying their respects.
They too were all in uniform, even Scotty Atkins in his Sheriff's
Department khakis, which made him look, er, taller. Local civic
groups like the Cowbelles and the Sunshine Nellies (Laramie's gay
and lesbian barbershop quartet). Some rodeo cowboys had showed
up too, Herman Schwink among them, with serious faces and
slicked-down hair and creases pressed in their starched shirts. Some
people surprised the hell out of her by being there—Sam Branch
and Marsh Carhart, for two. It occurred to her that it was the second time that week she'd seen vultures circling.

Most of all, there was an extraordinary number of humans she just plain didn't know. Some of them she recognized by sight, the way you'd have some impression of a person who might have been sitting next to you in the doctor's waiting room. But others she felt she'd never laid eyes on. Incredible that Laramie was that big. More amazing still that so many had turned out.

Carhart was making his way down the buffet line just ahead of Sally, smiling and introducing himself, taking little bits of this and that and chatting up the ladies who'd brought the dishes. "You know," she heard him tell one middle-aged woman sporting helmet-sprayed hair, a bad-fitting brown dress, and a giant diamond ring, "it's a real treat to find Frito pie anymore. This is some of the best I've ever had."

The woman blushed and grinned and explained, "A lot of people just go ahead and make it with canned chili and American cheese and whatever ol' corn chips they got on special down at the store. You just throw all that stuff into a dish and call it real Frito pie. I don't mind using canned beans," she admitted, "but the secret"—and here she beckoned him toward her, and lowered her voice—"is browning your own meat, and using real Fritos, and Cracker Barrel cheddar."

"You can always tell when somebody's given it their own personal touch," Carhart said, smiling, his face still close to the Frito pie lady's.

"And garlic powder," she replied, and introduced him to her daughter. That Frito pie did look tempting, but Sally was determined to be moderate. Browning your own meat, indeed. Sally had bought one of the Cowbelles' beef cookbooks at the county fair last year. You didn't often see that many recipes calling for suet.

She saw Hawk edge Marsh Carhart out for a seat at a crowded table, next to Molly Wood. In black jeans, a white shirt, and a silk tweed sport coat that some rich former girlfriend had talked him into buying, Hawk looked comfortable and elegant, at ease and alert. Sally wasn't eager to join him. They'd had, well, a little disagreement about whether he ought to go ahead with his plan to look over the land swap property later in the day. He'd been just getting his breakfast when Sally had returned and told him about

her skirmish with Bone at Washington Park. Hawk had slammed
his cereal bowl on the table so hard that the bowl cracked and
Cheerios and milk flew all over the room. She'd spent the next half
hour watching him rage and clean up spilled milk.

Then, of course, they'd had an adult discussion of their plans
for the day ("I am damn well not letting you out of my sight!" "You
damn well are! I'm not a baby!" "Oh yeah?" "Shit!") Sally wasn't
sure why it seemed so important to her that Hawk proceed with his
plan to go up to the Laramies. Maybe she liked seeing what the connection with Molly Wood did for him. Or maybe she just didn't
want him around when she got together with Scotty Atkins. Her
intentions, as usual, were probably purer than her motives.

But at last she'd managed to convince him not to keep her
locked up in the house while he stood guard with the Remington
over-under shotgun he never used for hunting anymore. He was
planning to head up to the mountains right after the reception, and
for now Sally was giving him some room. Neither one of them was
exactly him or herself today.

She turned and saw Delice sitting at a card table, along with
Brit, Maude, and Charlene from the Lifeway. "Can I squeeze in with
you guys?" she asked, pulling up a metal chair to perch at a corner
of the table.

"Hey, you took some of the ambrosia salad," said Charlene. "I
brought that from the deli at the store. Can't go wrong with pineap-
ple, mini-marshmallows, and maraschino cherries, can you?"

"Yeah, but it's the whipped topping that really makes the
salad," said Delice dryly. "I see you're taking the ladies' lunch
approach, Mustang. You'd be better off with these," she added,
sinking her teeth into a large, meaty barbecued rib.

Sally had some of the poached salmon; a pile of salad made
from sliced-up iceberg lettuce, shredded carrots, and radish
discs; a spoonful of green bean casserole with cornflakes on
top—so far, so good. And then the ambrosia and a piece of a
cherry pie that could only have been baked by Maude Stark.
Maybe there would be some ribs left if she got up for seconds.
Buffets were insidious.

"So," said Delice, eyes glittering, lips smacking, "what's this in the morning paper about an unlawful entry at your house Tuesday night?"

Sally had her story all ready. "Dickie figured it was probably lowlifes from the rodeo. They came in and messed things up some, looking for valuables I guess, but they must have gotten scared off and left before they found my jewelry. No big thing."

Maude knew something about attempted burglaries, and she knew Sally. Her face registered her skepticism. "In my experience, having an uninvited stranger in your house is always a big thing."

Delice was scowling over her ribs. "Dickie asked me if there'd been anybody hanging around my house. What the hell's going on in this town anyway?"

Charlene sighed. "We get our little crime wave every year during Jubilee Days. Down at the Lifeway, this time of year, we got more shoplifters than shoppers. With all the cowboys and carnies and transient scum, what do you expect? Three years ago a guy came to my door and said his car had broken down and his grandmother was sitting in it, and he'd lost his wallet, and could I give him a twenty for the tow truck? I fell for it, I swear. I bet he's still laughing.

"Burglars busted into my sister's place last year and stole her TV and stereo. Jeez, even the tourist families think they're entitled to steal everything in the motel room that isn't bolted down. My niece works at the Reata motel, and she said she'd cleaned one room where the people had not only taken the towels, but even the toilet paper holder. One of the waitresses at the Holiday Inn restaurant told me they'd lost forty-six coffee cups during Jubilee week last year, and this year they're going to serve the coffee in Styrofoam cups."

Delice laughed mirthlessly. "It's a pain in the ass, but I figure rip-offs are part of the cost of doing business. Not that it's any fun. I can't tell you how many times the most wholesome-looking people try to beat the check and get out the door before we can nab 'em."

Brit chimed in. "It's like people who are mondo-respectable in some other town turn into criminals when they go on vacation. Last night at the Yippie I O, we caught a guy trying to stuff a candlestick into his sportcoat pocket. The guy said Burt better not mess with him, because he was a trial lawyer and a close personal friend of the vice president of the United States . . ."

"And what exactly was it about this fool that made you imagine he was respectable?" Maude asked.

Sally's strategy had worked—they'd moved off the subject of her and onto themselves. Now was the time to really change the subject. "So what's the story on the parade Saturday?"

"I've got a neighbor out in Albany who does a lot of haying, and he said we could borrow his tractor-trailer flatbed. I figure anybody who wants to ride on it could make any kind of sign they want, in support of equality and the idea that women have a right to feel safe and in charge of their bodies," said Maude, taking command.

Sally looked at Brit. "This was your idea in the first place. What do you think?"

Brit considered. "The flatbed's great, and we've gotten calls from people who want to do signs and banners. So what Maude said is fine with me, although I think people might need a little, like, help with the sign-making thing. Some of them might not be exactly clear on the concept when it comes to 'equality,' you know?"

Sally could easily imagine. Lots of Wyoming people carried their equalizers in holsters. If they weren't careful, the memorial display for Monette could turn into an NRA rally.

They ended up deciding that everyone who was interested could gather in the parking lot behind the Wrangler Friday afternoon to make signs and banners. "Do you think we could get the paint donated?" Delice asked Brit.

Brit made a face. "I already talked to the guy at Gem City Paint. He said he'd given a bunch of money to the rodeo committee, and didn't have any to spare for 'political causes.'"

Maude snorted. "I'll give him 'political causes.' From now on I'm buying all my paint at Wal-Mart, and telling all my friends to do the same. It's cheaper there anyway. Matter of fact, I'll be down there this afternoon, picking up whatever you think we need for the signs and banners. My treat."

"God, Maude, that's really generous of you," said Sally.

"No big deal," she said. "I might even ask the manager there if they want some free advertising as backers of Wyoming's long tradition of equality for women, and the home of one-stop shopping."

Charlene took a big bite of cherry pie, drummed her long nails (same color as the pie!) on the table, chewed, looked thoughtful. "You know, I'm all for controlling your own body and all that, but this being equal thing . . . I don't know. Take Monette. I don't think she was spending a lot of her time worrying about equality. When she got promoted, I asked her what she planned to do with her first big paycheck, and she said, 'Go to the fanciest beauty shop in town and get a makeover. Then go to the bar and make some dude beg.' "

They all shook their heads. "Give me a break, you guys!" said Charlene. She looked straight at Maude. "Do you really want to be *equal* to other people, Maude? I mean, do you want people saying, 'That cherry pie was just as good as every other cherry pie I ever had'? I doubt it. And how about you, Delice? I never have heard that you run your business by taking a vote every morning about who to hire and who to fire and how many pounds of potatoes to order. Then there's you," she said, turning to Brit. "When you get done with school and go out there and hang up your shingle as a lawyer, you want them saying they choose who gets to be a partner in the firm by lottery?"

"Come on, Charlene. That's not what we're talking about," Maude replied. "Women have always had to prove we were twice as good to get half as far. We don't want to be victims, we don't want special favors. We just want the chance to compete for the good things in life, and to make the world a little better."

"A nice sentiment," said Delice, "but you gotta admit, Maude, sometimes women who want that chance to compete couldn't care less about making the world a better place. They're just looking out for ol' number one. Hell, I sure am. I guess I'm already equal in one way—I pretty much want the same things men want."

"For instance?" Sally asked, finishing off her piece of that unequaled cherry pie.

"Oh, I don't know," said Delice. "How about money and sex for starters?"

Everyone laughed.

Charlene gave Sally a knowing look. "That sound good to

you? From what I hear, with the deal you got with that Dunwoodie Center, you won't be suing the university for 'equal pay' anytime soon."

"Point taken, Charlene," Sally said dryly. "Flog me for my pious hypocrisy." Sally's endowed chair came with a salary and a basket of perks that dwarfed the average college professor's take-home. She was paid at the level of rocket scientists with big federal grants, and engineers who got hired by corporations to consult on new ways to breed genetic monsters or turn planet Earth into a big round ball of waste. Most of them were men, and Sally figured that her research in women's history was at least as worthy as building a bigger nuclear reactor or finding a new way to freeze bull semen. She didn't lose a lot of sleep over getting what she had. Why shouldn't women finally get a piece of the pie?

"I wonder which corrupts us more," Delice mused, "money or sex? I mean, I've probably done some despicable things to get my bottom line where I think it ought to be, but then maybe I've done even worse stuff when I'm thinking with my ya-ya."

Charlene cocked her head, absently wetting a finger and wiping up the last crumbs on her plate, the nail clicking faintly against the paper plate. She licked the finger, then nodded, her poodle hair bouncing back and forth. "I definitely think sex is harder than money. I mean, I was a real idiot when it came to that damn ex-husband of mine. Haven't any of you just had those times when you were really really stupid, just because of something in a pair of pants that got you juiced?"

Charlene was staring at a spot behind Sally's head. Sally twisted in her chair and saw the backside of Scotty Atkins. Right on cue, Scotty turned and looked right at her, smiled a little, and beckoned to her with a forefinger. She knew she was blushing.

"I think Hawk *will* have to shoot him," Delice muttered.

"Police business," said Sally, rising, giving them all a brisk nod. "I'll see you guys at the paint-a-thon tomorrow afternoon."

How many pairs of eyes scrutinized Sally as she threaded her way between tables to the walkway where Detective Atkins stood waiting? She felt like a hologram at Disneyland, something visible and moving but not solid, the center of attention. Dickie Langham was looking at her with an expression of polite interest. And she knew Hawk was watching, not simply because she could feel his eyes boring into her, but because she knew exactly what spot they bore in on. He'd commented in the past on how well the black skirt she was wearing fit across her hips. She looked over her shoulder and saw that she was right about where he'd been glaring. Even as pissed as he was, a hip man to the end.

"Detective," she said, looking up into Atkins's pale eyes. "You want to talk to me?"

"As I believe I indicated last night," Atkins answered, in as noncommittal a tone as she'd used on him. "This obviously isn't the place. I'm hoping that you're free later this afternoon. I've got some things to do right now, but I'd like to come by your place in an hour. Would that be convenient for you?"

Courteous, professional, and . . . something else. What else did she see in his face? Anger? Worry? Heterosexuality? Not that!

Stick with courteous and professional. "An hour from now would be fine," Sally replied in her best scheduling-a-meeting voice.

"Good. That should give you time to change," he said, looking at his watch and shuffling his feet, a man getting ready to take his leave. Why did talking to Scotty Atkins always feel like interrupting somebody hurrying between much more important things?

"Change?" she asked. "What difference does it make what I'm wearing?"

Atkins's eyes traveled down, slowly, lingering on the skirt and then lighting on her high-heeled shoes. "I don't think those are a good idea."

"Gosh, Scotty. I hadn't realized you doubled as a fashion consultant."

"I'm a man of hidden talents," he said ambiguously. "But in this instance I'm just making a practical suggestion. You and I are going for a ride. And I think you'll find pants and hiking boots more comfortable where we're going."

CHAPTER 15
FALLEN ANGELS

SALLY AND HAWK sat side by side on their bed, tightening up the laces on their hiking boots. "So did Atkins tell you where you're going?" he asked her, finishing up with a double knot.

"He didn't say. But I've got a bad feeling," she answered, not meeting Hawk's eyes.

"Are you sure you can handle this?" he wanted to know.

"No. But I don't see that I've got much choice. For whatever sadistic reason of his own, Scotty must have decided he wants to drag me back up there and give me the third degree. Without you being present," she added unnecessarily, looking up from her shoelaces to see his reaction.

Hawk shrugged. "He called this morning while you were running. We went over everything that's happened, again. Looks to me like Atkins will keep after both of us to see if we remember anything about that scene that the police might have missed. But he wants to talk to us separately. Scotty told me he thinks you're an egotistical busybody with a bad reputation you've undoubtedly earned, but that you're also a smart woman who might be able to tell him something he couldn't figure out on his own."

Hawk paused, obviously considering how to phrase what he was going to say next. "I think Scotty's decided you need a little reminding of what some asshole is doing to women in this town, so that maybe you'll stop trying like hell to make yourself a target." He put a hand on her arm. "I have some sympathy for that point of view."

She looked at him, blank-faced. "I'm well aware of what somebody did to Monette, not to mention one or two things that have happened to me. What kind of cretin do you take me for?"

Hawk squeezed her arm. "My kind," he said. "I worry. I mean, I'm even to the point where I like the idea of you going off to the mountains with some stud who clearly wants to jump your bones. At least you won't be home alone."

She looked at him incredulously. "Oh yeah, Hawk. Let me tell you, my idea of a perfect setup for wicked sex is to put on my boots and go straight to the place I saw a dead body three days ago. And I especially love it when a guy calls me an 'egotistical busybody.' Boy, that really gets me hot."

He tossed her a half grin. "So I suppose there's no cause for jealousy."

She tossed the other half of the grin back. "I didn't say that."

He frowned.

"Hey," she said. "I have the strength of ten because my heart is pure."

"And I have the intelligence of a gnat if I believe that," he countered.

"Okay then," she said. "Pure enough for the foreseeable future."

"Guess it'll have to do," he allowed, shouldering his daypack and giving her a kiss sweet enough to push the foreseeable a little further into the future.

Hawk took off, and ten minutes later Scotty Atkins showed up in a dusty brown Toyota 4runner. He'd changed into Dockers and sneakers and one of those trademark polo shirts, bright green this time. "Hard to believe you're a Wyoming boy, Scotty," she told him as she climbed into the truck. "You always look like somebody who's heading out to Forest Hills to watch a tennis match."

"We Wyoming boys don't have to dress up to cowboy up," he said flatly. "We can leave that to the tourists."

"Speaking of tourists," she asked, "what's with the Natrona County plates on this thing?" The Toyota was sporting a license plate that began with the number one, indicating that it had been registered in the state's most populous county (certainly an irony; perhaps an oxymoron).

"I just moved back down here from Casper at the end of last year," he answered. "I'll reregister the truck when the plates expire. Let's remember, I'm a police officer. We're famous for being cheap," he explained as they buckled in and drove away.

"What were you doing up in Casper?" she asked.

"Living. Working. Getting divorced. My wife's from there," he answered shortly.

Presumably he meant ex-wife. The scars still showed. "Were you there long?" Sally didn't know why she was pressing the point—maybe to postpone other subjects? Acting, uh, like a busybody?

"Ever since I graduated from the law enforcement academy, over in Douglas." Again, not much elaboration.

"I thought you went to UW," she said.

"I did." He turned onto Grand Avenue, saying no more.

Sally searched. "What was your major?" she finally asked. This was beginning to feel like a first date. What next—hobbies?

"Biology. I was pre-med."

"How come you're not a doctor?"

He looked at her without expression. "I got sidetracked."

"Yeah," she conceded. "Me too." But not on the same path, and not by the same things. Boy, it was a lot of work dragging information out of Scotty Atkins.

They got onto the interstate, heading east, uphill into the pink granite and the pines, in silence. At last Scotty spoke. "Tell me," he said, "about honky-tonk angels."

She considered the question. "Are you asking me to answer as an expert on country music, or as a member of the species?"

"Either," he said.

"Okay," she said. "The music first. As it happens, I've performed the song '(It Wasn't God Who Made) Honky-Tonk Angels' probably two hundred times, here and there, in different versions. You're aware, I suppose, that it's a takeoff on a song called 'The Wild Side of Life.' "

"I wasn't," said Scotty, "until Dickie mentioned something about it. I'm not exactly a fan of hillbilly music."

"You're more the Mantovani type," Sally taunted.

"Pink Floyd," he retorted. Yeah, she could see it. Scotty was definitely "Dark Side of the Moon" material. All cynicism and attitude and undertow.

"To continue," she said. "The original song, 'Wild Side,' was a huge hit for Hank Thompson, back in 1952. One of the kings of country, that Hank. Famous for immortal songs like 'The Blackboard of My Heart' and 'A Six Pack to Go.' "

"How do you know this stuff?" he asked.

"I am a historian and a musician," she said haughtily, "a professional. Anyhow, 'Wild Side' is some old boy's lament to his wife, who's ditched him in favor of the glamour of going to bars and drinking and picking up men. Hank's real torn up about it—can't believe God would make an angel like her, who fell so far that she ended up in the honky-tonk life."

"Think about it," Scotty said. "Dude had a point."

"Believe me, I have," said Sally, wondering if Scotty's divorced-off Casper wife had opted for rowdy barrooms over his patented long silences. "I had years to think about it. And of course, I feel Hank's pain, and that of all the men who've been laid low by honky-tonk angels."

"Laid low," said Scotty. "Nice choice of words."

"Just my stock in trade," Sally said. "Hank's too. He was a hell of a songwriter. But all in all, I'm more partial to the girls' reply. Kitty Wells recorded it in 1953—it was her breakthrough smash record, made Kitty the biggest thing in country music and proved women could make money in the business. The gist of the song was that God didn't have a damn thing to do with making honky-tonk angels. The culprits were all those men who cheated on their wives and forced the women to give tit for tat."

"Nice words, once again," said Scotty.

"You're enjoying this way too much," Sally replied. "But really, you need to hear the music to have a true appreciation for the songs." And as Scotty drove on up the mountain, Sally sang both versions. She felt vaguely perverse, singing merrily along toward a crime scene, but that was just the way she was and always had been. Put her in a motor vehicle, and pretty soon she was bursting into song.

When she stopped singing, he was nodding. "I get the picture," he said. "And it's just as I suspected. All country tunes fall under three headings: jail songs, dog songs, and cheatin' songs. These are in the third category."

And here she thought she'd given a virtuoso performance. "That's totally unfair to country music. You forgot mother, moonshine, and car wrecks," she said. But then a thought struck her. "It's strange. I mean, if the guy who raped and murdered Monette was the one who busted into my house and wrote on the mirror, why quote the girls' version?"

"Not everybody has your exhaustive command of country music trivia," Scotty observed. "People get confused and mix up quotes. Especially people who are, shall we say, somewhat disoriented to begin with."

"Or maybe the guy's just gone into Hank Thompson overdrive, and he's decided that God might have made honky-tonk angels, but they're working for the devil now. Which makes your murderer the avenging angel with the flaming sword." It made sense to Sally.

Scotty considered her theory as they crested the top of Sherman Hill, the highest spot on the interstate, 8,870 feet above sea level on what had once been known as the Lincoln Highway. The summit was marked by a huge bust of Abraham Lincoln, mounted on a thick pillar of pink granite blocks surrounded by a split-rail snow fence. Sally and her friends thought the monument looked like Lincoln had stepped into an outhouse that was sturdy enough to protect those urinating from Wyoming's famous wind, but built a little too short. Even the slope of Lincoln's shoulders was right.

At last the detective spoke. "So our killer has a problem with fallen angels. That's certainly a possibility. But it's not the only one. It's also conceivable that the guy who did Monette isn't the same person who's been harassing you." He darted a narrow glance at Sally. "Why do you suppose somebody cut up your underwear and pushed you into that bucking chute?"

Sally's eyes must have shown the bafflement, and the fear. "I don't have a clue. I mean, let's face it, I've given plenty of people reason to be pissed at me over the years. At least a few may even hate me. But that stuff . . ." She shook her head.

"So we have to go with the little we do know. Somebody wrote that message on your mirror, and it makes sense to assume that they weren't addressing your vast knowledge of musical history. What about the personal experience part?" Scotty asked her. "What does make honky-tonk angels?"

The seriousness of his tone steadied her enough to think, and to answer. "Music. Dancing. Booze. Company. Sex. Up here, maybe just getting the hell out of the house on a slow night in a long winter. Or celebrating the fact that it isn't winter at the moment. In Monette's case, it seems like she was looking for any old kind of human contact. From all she'd learned growing up, a girl like her couldn't be real choosy about what kind of attention she got. There are probably a lot of girls who end up in bars for similar reasons.

"Then again, try to see it from her point of view. The guys she picked up could have made her feel like she was at least getting treated better than her mother. Plus, in a strange way, Monette was ambitious. She wasn't satisfied with just being promoted from shelf stocker to checker. I had the feeling, from what she said to me at the Lifeway Monday morning, that she was aiming a lot higher. You probably can't imagine how anybody would believe that going to bars is some kind of self-help strategy, but I bet plenty of people think that's exactly the case."

Scotty reflected on what she'd said. "So how about you? Why would a woman who obviously has as much on the ball as you do waste her nights closing down the honky-tonks?"

Sally gave him the easiest explanation. "In my case, the music was the main attraction. I was getting paid to spend my time in bars. I figured that sooner or later I'd get discovered as the song-writing genius and charismatic performer I was, and then the golden doors would open."

Scotty snorted.

"Come on, Scotty. You must have had a dream or two. Every gym rat who ever shot a thousand free throws at a time, and kept score, thought he was headed for Michael Jordanville."

"I got over it," he said.

Mr. Conversation strikes again. Sally carried on. "I also did my share of just hanging out, listening to bands I liked, and plenty I didn't like. Plus, remember, the bars were the places I got together with my girlfriends. Delice and I have been known to have a few beverages and laugh until our stomachs hurt."

She dug a bottle of water out of her backpack, twisted the top, took a drink, and slanted a glance at him. Now it was time for a little harder story. "I'd be a liar if I said the whiskey and the boys had nothing to do with it. And the music was a part of that too. I said Monette wanted the attention. Hell, so did I." She fiddled with the bottle cap. "At some point, you get to where there's nothing left to prove. If you're lucky, sooner or later you figure out there's something better you could be doing. For my part, I've come to prefer spending my time in silent rooms, reading and writing about the dead. When I get tired of that, I go into big noisy rooms full of college kids and talk about the dead. It's my calling."

She took another swig of water and looked him over, wondering. "You're a Laramie boy. Didn't you ever indulge in party time?"

"Only when my friends dragged me out. Even heard you sing a time or two," he admitted. "But I was a jock and a grind. I was a fanatic about staying in shape, and keeping up with my studies. I didn't even know what scotch was until I was thirty-five."

"It's a thirty-fivish kind of drink," said Sally, who only ordered scotch when she felt both jaded and snobbish. "As you can probably figure, I've heard people talking about what a jock you were. And I heard about your knee. It's kind of surprising that you're still playing basketball," she offered in sympathy.

"What Hawk and I play," Scotty said, "isn't basketball. Half court. No D. If we took on the scrubs from the UW women's team we might not score a point. Granny hoops."

"Beats eatin' donuts and smokin' cigarettes," said Sally. "I worry about Dickie."

"So do I," said Scotty.

"Maybe you could get him to consider working out a little," Sally told him.

"That's not what I'm talking about," Scotty answered. "You and the sheriff have been buddies a long time. I just started working with him."

"You grew up here. You must have known the Langhams."

"Knew who they were. Especially Delice," he said, the shadow of a grin ghosting across his mouth and disappearing. "I probably bought a beer or two from Dickie. But we didn't have much in common, considering the other line of work he was in, and the fact that I was a real straight arrow."

Sally was defensive on Dickie's behalf. "Don't dump on my buddy Dickie. He's been to hell and back and still has more than most people's share of wits. Not to mention a sense of humor and a giant heart."

"Relax. I'm one of the boss's biggest fans," said Scotty. "He's remarkable. It's not everybody who could sell drugs to half the people in town, take it on the lam, live some secret life for years and come back and get elected sheriff, and then turn out to be both honest and competent."

"Yeah. A lot of people would assume that he won that election because he had the goods on all those voters who'd scored dope from him. Law enforcement pros like you don't expect much from the politicians you work for, do you?" Sally challenged.

"Why should we?" Scotty countered. And then, at last, "Sheriff Langham's a good guy."

"Got that right," said Sally.

"But, admit it. He's pretty close to this case," Scotty said.

"Sure. He feels for Mary. And after all, he'd do anything to solve it for her. How many wives would take back some cokehead who'd been on the run for twelve years and then showed up one day hollering, 'Hi honey, I'm home'? You'd have to be either nuts or desperate or some kind of saint. Or maybe just loyal—if there's one thing about those Langhams, they're practically zealots when it comes to family."

Scotty looked at her again, and for a change said nothing. They'd gotten off the highway, onto the dirt road that would take them past Vedauwoo Glen and on to their destination. Gripping her thighs with hands that had begun to shake, Sally knew the literal meaning of the word "dreadful."

"You didn't come this way on Monday," Scotty said, beginning the process of taking her through that miserable experience all over again.

She took a breath. "That's right. We parked up by Abe Lincoln and then walked along the back side of the climbing rocks, following Middle Crow Creek. We did some meanders, here and there, across meadows." She felt her temper rising. "Hawk and I were just out for an afternoon stroll, Scotty. I mean, we weren't looking for the shortest route to Monette Bandy's body, now were we?"

"Settle down, there, princess," Scotty told her, his own patience visibly stretching. "Just tell me all about it, as carefully as you can."

And so she did, as they bumped over earth and rocks, churning up red dust, in that majestic beautiful place. She had no idea whether what she was saying to him now told him anything new, or beamed light into any dark corner. It all sounded to her like something she'd rehearsed and rehashed until she was seeing it in her dreams. Scotty Atkins drove on, past hikers and climbers and picnicking families, all those strangers blissfully unaware of the fact that willful, cerebral Sally Alder, telling her story along that road, wanted nothing so much as to start screaming, and not stop.

By the time they got to the Devil's Playground, the talking and the struggle against panic had pretty much emptied her out. Scotty pulled the 4runner over and parked at the bottom of the hill she'd watched him walk up, only those few days before. He got out of the truck, but Sally didn't move. He walked around, opened up her door, took her by the hand, and said, "Let's go."

She let him lead her up the hill, conscious of his warm, dry hand holding hers, of the thirsty, uneven ground, red dirt, and pink pebbles she could feel through the thick Vibram soles of her boots.

The words popped into her head—the devil is in the details—and she giggled like an idiot at the notion.

But for the life of her, as they came on the ring of blackened stones, where so many Wyoming party animals had built their fires and drunk their beers and sucked at their smokes, she couldn't make her brain do more than flit around the scene, and leap, like a flea, from one bit of trivia to the next. Oh look, she thought, this is good: The police have cleaned up all the litter. Now that's what I like in my public servants. But oh, see how all those heavy cop shoes have stomped all over this place. Not a blade of grass longer than an eyelash. It would be next summer, at least, before those ants she'd seen toting that piece of straw would have anything to practice their collective carrying instincts on.

Sally was a flea brain and Scotty was relentless. Dragging her along by the hand, he strode past the fire ring and on toward the outcrop. A sudden, too-vivid mental image of the jumble of rocks, that arm sticking out with the rope around the wrist, made Sally stagger and pull Scotty back. "I can't," she said. "I just can't do it, Scotty. Please don't make me. I keep seeing her arm and that rope."

Scotty let go of Sally's hand, grabbed both her arms above the elbow, shook her. "Get a grip, Sally. I want you to see it. When Dickie and I watched the autopsy, we saw rope abrasions on both her wrists. But she hadn't been dragged. She let somebody tie her up. And then whoever she was with led her over there, had intercourse with her, shot her, and tried to hide the body. We're saying it looked like rape, but maybe it was just some rough game that got a little out of hand. We've just gotten the results of the blood tests, and it looks like they had some beers and smoked a little weed. One thing led to another, but somebody lost control. And then, when he'd killed her, he couldn't get her down in that crack with her hands bound like that. So he cut the rope, and he just left it dangling off the one hand while he pushed her body down."

"Please," she pleaded, heart pumping, breath coming hard. "Why are you telling me all this?"

"Think about it, Sally. Why would he go to all that trouble and leave her hand sticking out?"

Hmph. The question brought her up short, cut through the

horror, made her . . . reason. She took a deep breath, straightened her shoulders, removed Scotty's hands from her arms and looked him in the eye. "I can imagine two explanations. One, the crack turned out to be too small for her body, but by the time he'd gotten her wedged in there, it was too hard to get her out. It took you guys a long time pulling her body up—she was stuck pretty tight."

Scotty stood silent and motionless, still looking at her.

"The other explanation is that he heard somebody coming as he was pushing her down, and he ran off. Maybe he heard Hawk and me. Christ, maybe he saw us." She was nearly too numb to be unnerved by that possibility.

"And maybe he knew you. Maybe that's why he turned his attention from Monette to you. Of course, this is all wild speculation, isn't it, Sally? In my business we try not to jump to conclusions." Scotty was forcing the issue, retreating, then forcing it a little further.

"Knew me?" she whispered. "How could he know me?"

"Lots of people do, ma'am," said Scotty, sounding like a man who wore a Stetson instead of a shirt with a little pony guy on it. "But there is one piece of evidence I'd like to share with you. It's something the sheriff is having trouble considering, because, as I said, he could be just a mite too close to this case. As you know, that rope around Monette Bandy's wrists was a calf roper's piggin' string."

"I know," said Sally, a sick foreboding feeling welling up inside.

"And as I believe the sheriff mentioned, only two such ropes were purchased here in town recently, both by local cowboys."

"Yes. He did mention that."

"What I don't believe he told you," Scotty persisted, "was that one of those cowboys was Jerry Jeff Walker Davis. Your friend Delice's boy."

CHAPTER 16
SENTIMENT, LOGIC,
AND DAMNED LIES

"DID YOU HEAR ME?" he said. "Jerry Jeff Davis. The sheriff's nephew. Your friend's son."

The cool pale eyes held her. She had to fight to look away.

Two things about Scotty Atkins pissed Sally off. First, that he was such a coldhearted bastard. Second, that he was such a fascinating coldhearted bastard. The man was perfectly willing to believe that a kid not even fifteen, who mowed lawns and took in stray kittens and whose mother loved him, could have done what had been done to Monette. And by now the detective had Sally doubting the people she cared about most. Scotty made Sally feel like a mouse facing a snake, cornered, mesmerized.

Jerry Jeff was big and strong, and you never could tell about teenagers these (or any other) days, but he was still in some ways a little boy. You didn't need any better evidence of that fact than the lame explanation JJ had come up with when the detective had asked him about buying a new piggin' string.

"He told me, 'Oh, yeah. I was out at the fairgrounds last week, checking out the stock, and I left my gear on the tailgate of somebody's pickup. When I came back, my piggin' string was gone.'" Scotty shook his head in disgust. "Jerry Jeff couldn't remember exactly whose pickup it was, or precisely when he'd left his stuff. He was even fuzzy about what day it was. Dickie was willing to cut the boy some slack—way too much, if you ask me. He said sometimes, kids were sketchy like that, and told me to back off. If you ask me, the sheriff just couldn't bring himself to question his sister's son about a story that sounded like the calf roper's version of 'the dog ate my homework.'"

Sally glared at Scotty. "This interview is over, Detective," she said, turning and taking off down the hill. "I've got a band practice tonight, and things to do before then. I need to get back."

"Look, Sally," Scotty said, striding up beside her. "I'm sorry this has to be unpleasant. Do you really think that browbeating traumatized people is my favorite part of this job?" He started to reach out to touch her, but then put his hands in his pockets.

Best he keep those hands to himself. "I don't think you enjoy hammering away at the bereaved, no. And though I hesitate, at this point, to be nice to you, I will say that I admire your dedication. You believe in justice. You're just trying to get to the bottom of this. But you know, Scotty, you could use a little lesson in finesse. You might want to think about who you're hurting when you push to the limit."

The air around him seemed to crackle as his patience snapped. "I won't take that crap. Murder hurts everybody it touches. And even if the attacks on you have nothing to do with Monette, you're a crime victim yourself. Sometimes justice is cruel. If you can't handle the idea that my inquiries are liable to turn up dirt on people you know, or even on you, for that matter, you might think about moving to another state."

"Thanks for the advice. Don't worry about me getting scared off by gossip. I've had plenty of experience with that." She wished she had a dollar for every rumor about her. Hell, wished she had five dollars just for the ones that had been true.

"It's not just the gossip. Face it, Sally, this case is about more than words. Dickie and Mary and all the rest of the Langhams, and you yourself, want to think that some crazed transient predator killed Monette Bandy. That remains one possibility. We've spent more time than we probably should have grilling guys out at the fairgrounds and down in the bars. Nothing I've turned up so far points to a stranger, and experience tells me to look closer to home. Most crimes are committed by somebody the victim knows."

"I'm aware of that," she said. "And up until this morning, my money would have been on Monette's father. But after he tackled me in Washington Park—"

"Tackled you." Scotty made it a declarative statement, not a question. "In Washington Park?"

"I don't think that was his plan. He grabbed me by the arm and tried to pull me into his truck, and I kind of slugged him, and the next thing I knew, we were down on the ground."

"Right," said Scotty. "This happen to you a lot?"

"Hardly," she answered.

"You're taking it in stride. Weren't you afraid?"

"Of course! I was terrified! That's why I wasn't about to let him drag me to his truck. Forget about it. Bone's a drunk and a shithead, but I've changed my mind about him. I don't think he killed her. We sat on a bench in the park and talked. He thinks Monette was blackmailing somebody, a cowboy maybe, and it sounded like he wanted a piece of whatever action she thought she had."

"Tell me what happened this morning, and what he said to you, and what you told him. No fooling around, Sally. Every little bit. Beginning to end. Every gesture, including the tackle. The exact words."

She told him, right down to Monette saying she'd "roped a good one" and planned to ride it down and get out of town. And the sad part, about how Monette had always thought she'd find a cowboy and ride away.

Scotty grimaced. "I'd better get back and pay a call on Bone. I need to hear what he's got to say, today. Before I visit with Jerry Jeff again."

"And I'm telling you, I don't think JJ is capable of murder. He's a kid, Scotty."

"And you're his mother's best friend. Kids aren't always innocent. Leave criminal investigation to the pros, Sally. They know how to separate sentiment and logic."

She stopped walking and turned to face him. "I would never dream of accusing you of possessing sentiment." He winced. "But in this instance, there's also a serious flaw in your logic. Whoever killed Monette had to get her up here somehow. She could have driven herself, of course—I assume she had a car?"

"She did," Scotty said. "An old beater Pontiac. According to several of her neighbors, it's been parked out in front of her apartment building for the past couple of weeks, with a dead battery. She's been walking to work or getting rides."

"Fine. However she got up here, whoever killed her had to drive out of here, back down the hill or on down the road or wherever. Jerry Jeff isn't driving yet. It's not just that he's too young for a license—he and his mother have a running battle over how soon she'll take him out and start teaching him. He never stops pushing, and she never stops stalling." Delice wasn't eager to get into the passenger's seat of her Explorer with JJ at the wheel, and lately she'd even started hinting to Sally about giving him a lesson or two.

"At the risk of pointing out the obvious," said Scotty, "there might have been a third party along. Or maybe he's covering for somebody. How much do you know about Jerry Jeff's friends?"

Sally pursed her lips. "How much does any adult know about a teenager's friends? Have you talked to Delice?"

He shook his head. "The sheriff said he'd handle that."

"As he should. But I assume you've at least gotten some names from JJ, or whoever, and you're checking them out. Kids at the high school. Rodeo pals."

"Yeah. We're running them down. And tomorrow we'll be getting the medical examiner's report on the autopsy, along with the physical evidence. I'm going to ask Jerry Jeff to come down to the courthouse and have a look at that piggin' string."

"And while he's doing that, you watch his reaction, and then use whatever you decide will work to push him into telling you everything you're so sure he knows. Tell me, Scotty, do you always treat people like biology class dissection projects? You make me feel like a pithed frog or a cow's eye."

"One more time you force me to apologize," Atkins said softly. "I'm hoping that when this is all over, we can be friends."

Reluctantly she looked up at him. For reasons that he hadn't divulged and she couldn't even guess at, Scotty Atkins preferred to show the world a blank face. But this time, for an instant, he failed, and she was drawn to a flickering glimpse of something raw and shredded, somewhere deep beneath the green ice in his eyes.

Sally was not a woman who hid emotion well, but experience had taught her how to tamp it down some, and use those frontal lobes, when the feelings she harbored were so riotously conflicting that exhibiting them might bring the boys with the straitjacket. "Yeah. Well. Let's get this over with, and then we'll see about friends."

Plenty left to think about, but nothing more to say. By the time Detective Atkins dropped her off back at the house, she was really wondering. What was this thing she had for pain lately? Except in her very darkest days (when the Vietnam war had poisoned everything she'd once held holy, when tequila and rootlessness had weighed her down), she considered herself a happy person. She was, usually, attracted to the light.

To the light. Like a moth. Flitting from flame to flame. God, she'd had a rough week. And it was only Thursday.

It would have been nice if Hawk had been there when she got back. She could have used a little welcome home. But she knew he was planning to stay up in the mountains until it got dark, tramping around the land swap parcel, getting to know the property and its surroundings. He knew how to read land the way Sally read words on paper, alert to subtle signs, faint shades of meaning, traces of past presence. He'd be taking his time.

The light on the answering machine was going batshit. She listened to the messages.

"Sally, it's Maude. I don't believe for a minute that the break-in at your place was 'no big thing.' You're up to something. Call me."

And she thought she'd been so clever. She should have known she couldn't fool Maude. Now Sally would have to figure out how much, if anything, to tell her. At this point she couldn't avoid having Maude in her face, but Sally knew it might not be a bad thing to have Maude watching her back.

"Hey Mustang. Bone Bandy informs me that you and he had a little tête-à-tête this morning in Washington Park. I'd be real interested in hearing your thoughts. There's a good band at the Torch tonight, and I thought I'd swing by at some point. If you can't make that, how about breakfast at the Wrangler tomorrow?"

Dickie Langham, laid back and thinking, like Winnie the Pooh, about breakfast. As usual. But it sounded like he was a step ahead of Scotty on at least one front. Whatever the detective might think, the sheriff, in his own way, was very much on the job. The next message confirmed it.

Barroom noise—conversational hum, clinking glasses, Willie Nelson on the jukebox. And the distinctive jingle of silver bracelets. "Hey Sal, my brother was just in here acting casual and asking nosy-ass questions about Jerry Jeff. What do you know about all this? What really happened at your house Tuesday night? Goddamn it, I want some answers. It's already a madhouse in here, but call me at the Wrangler as soon as you can." A hard hang-up.

Delice was pissed. Sally couldn't blame her.

And now the third Langham sibling, weighing in. "Hey Mustang, Dwayne here. I've got some business to take care of, so we're going to have to do a short practice tonight. Eight instead of seven at my place." The band would survive, and the Saturday night gig would be fine. It wasn't as if they were working up a lot of new material. If a song had been written after 1985, the Millionaires didn't play it.

The last message was for Hawk. "This is Molly Wood, calling for Josiah Green. I just want to thank you for offering to take a look at that property in the Laramies. I'm eager to hear what you think. I'll be at home this afternoon and evening, and will hope to hear from you soon. Thanks again."

"Eager," eh? From what little she'd seen of Molly Wood, Sally didn't think that the woman would use the word loosely. If Molly was eager, somebody might be putting on the real estate blitz. Was that the business Dwayne had mentioned? Or were Molly's kids pushing? That weekend deal-breaker deadline was closing in. For Molly's sake, Sally hoped Hawk was finding a mountain paradise, more than up to his exacting aesthetic and scientific standards.

But she doubted that would be the case. As any decent researcher knew, one look at something was only the prelude to a lot more digging. Even if the property that Dwayne and Nattie's investors wanted to trade for Molly's Centennial ranch was the prettiest bit of high woodland on the planet, Hawk wouldn't be close to knowing everything he'd want to learn about the place.

She looked at the clock. Since they were pushing practice back, she had time for a bath, the chance to relax for the first time in what had turned out to be another seemingly endless day. Lots of hot water, lots of bubbles, maybe a nice glass of Chardonnay, a spot of dinner. Sounded real good. But instead of heading for the tub, she went over to the desk and switched on the computer. She didn't feel like soaking just yet. She felt like surfing.

She did, after all, owe Edna McCaffrey a tin of pâté.

The modem went through its paces, dinging, beeping, screeching like a monkey, and there she was on the information superhighway, speeding along in an alternative universe.

First, out of habit, she checked her email. She'd sent word to Edna about the problems with the house and the arrival of Sheldon Stover, but as yet, no reply. Edna was probably in some village literally on top of the world, looking at breathtaking mountains, talking to kids with no shoes and L.A. Lakers T-shirts. Sooner or later, however, she'd check in.

And then Sally hopped onto the web. No matter what she'd just been doing, it was always like this, cruising the Net—a strange sense of timelessness settled over her as she set out on her journey in the land of lies, damn lies, astounding discoveries, and excess of everything.

She started out searching on the keyword "pâté de foie gras" and turned up a couple hundred vegetarian and animal rights websites that detailed the horrific force-feeding of ducks and geese, along with several listings for "the last dinner on the *Titanic*." So much for her own appetite, but then she'd never been that big a fan of organ meats anyhow. Next she tried "gourmet food," and this time the results were more appetizing. Somewhere in the first dozen screens among the hundred thousand sites the search engine fetched up, she found the entry for alicesrestaurant.com.

Slowly the home page revealed itself. The designers were obviously going for the same effect you could find in those organic/fancy supermarkets that were popping up around the country faster than homegrown alfalfa sprouts: spacious but folksy, healthy but luxurious. Purslane and lambsquarters weren't weeds, they were *salad*! Olive oil was *good* for you! Ice cream was even better if the cows who gave the milk had scenic surroundings and stayed off the needle.

In one corner of the home page screen was an icon of a smiling, postmillennial middle-aged babe (she looked like Sela Ward in a jogging suit, holding a spatula) and the caption, "Go Ask Alice!" Sally clicked, and was treated to advice about how to find nonsulfited red wines (answer: Go to California), what to do with salmon roe (Eat them and don't feel guilty; farmed salmon are a dime a dozen), and what new food products were HOT (would you believe that the industry was pushing the idea of gourmet salt?). If they could make salt expensive, what next, water? Oops.

Pâté was obviously pricey, but at least it had the excuse of having been forced, by hand, into and then out of some hapless goose or luckless duck. Sally clicked on a picture of a stylized cornucopia, captioned "Alice's Restaurant Emporium," thinking maybe she'd order some of the costly, grayish-brown stuff Edna loved so much, and Sheldon Stover had gobbled so gauchely

That was when her screen turned mostly white, with nothing more than the boringly typed note: URL not located on this server. And then the "fatal error message" and the stern warnings that her computer had done something not simply illegal but immoral, and she was being kicked off the Net and sent to the principal's office.

Huh. Must have done something wrong. She powered up the browser again, got as far as the Alice's Restaurant home page, tried the shopping link again, and once again found herself, cyberspace-speaking, out on the sidewalk with the saloon doors swinging. As they said in pâté land, *qu'est-ce que c'est?*

Alice's place headed for Chapter 11, *peut-être*?

Then again, having found that she couldn't get anything she wanted at Alice's Restaurant, it might just be a bad day for Alice Wood's website, or a good one for Sally Alder's technophobia. When Hawk got home she'd see if he could get the site to work. Meanwhile, she found another gourmet website that promised, on a stack of Bibles, that if Sally ordered fancy French delicacies and gave them her credit card number, she'd get what she'd paid for within the week. Easy as one-two-three. Doing business with them would not enable some lurker to steal her identity, empty out Fort Knox, and pin the rap on her. At least it was improbable. Not that she was paranoid about Internet shopping or anything.

Shopping, she thought as she shut down the machine, was the least of her worries.

CHAPTER 17
SAVOIR-FAIRE

SALLY REGRETTED the foreshortening of the Millionaires' practice that evening. For a change, the band was really on. The drummer was hitting his marks, the fiddler had light in his fingers, and Sally and Sam were singing like their voices wanted to run off and get married. Maybe it was just time to click into gear for the Saturday gig. But whatever it was, they were cooking, in spite of the fact that Dwayne was playing in a trance. He always went into something of an altered state under the influence of music, but tonight he was plain distracted. Still, even with only half his head in the game, Dwayne was solid where the music rocked, and liquid where it rolled.

There was no small talk, about the real estate deal or anything else. There wasn't time. They went through a dozen songs and called it a night. Consider it the last light workout before the big game—keep loose, and avoid injury. All things considered, Sally was on schedule.

The stars were out when she left Dwayne's house, blankety thick to brighten the black, moonless sky. The air was just cool enough to make Sally's skin tingle. Out there where Dwayne and Nattie lived, on the fat edge of town, dust still swirled and saplings were still working on growing up to be trees. But when she pulled into the garage of the house on Eighth Street and got her guitar out of the trunk, she paused on the lawn, green grass soft and cool under her feet, to listen to the bleating of the crickets and the murmur of the wind through the canopy of cottonwoods. Hawk had parked his truck out front, instead of in the driveway, so that he wouldn't be blocking the garage. He thought of stuff like that.

But she didn't have much time to contemplate Hawk's thoughtfulness. A car came screeching around the corner, zoomed down the street, and just as it sped around the next bend, something exploded next to his truck.

BANG!

The smell of smoke filled her nostrils. She realized she'd hit the dirt and was crouched behind her guitar case. Yeah, that'd give her a lot of protection from a bullet or a bomb. Maybe she should have taken up the double bass.

Next thing she knew Hawk had come running out of the house, barefoot, damp hair streaming out behind him, wearing nothing but his jeans. He saw her getting to her feet and hollered, "Hey, are you okay?" When she nodded he sniffed at the smoky air and edged toward the street.

"Don't!" she yelled. "Get back in the house!"

But by now he was walking normally, out into the street, bending down, picking up something—two things. One was an empty beer can. The other, smoldering cardboard and paper, the remains of an M-80, the kind of incendiary device sold at any of the hundred fireworks stands that opened up across the state every summer. And every summer Wyoming kids went crazy buying every conceivable device that could blow their fingers off, assail their eyesight, start fires in the forests, disturb the peace. Business was especially brisk around the Fourth of July, of course, but also during rodeo week. Goddamn kids.

The pounding of her heart felt like it would crack her chest right open. A firecracker could launch her this close to a coronary? Please.

Hawk had asked her if she was all right. Yes, damn it, she was. This was ridiculous. She couldn't say why—maybe it had been the music, or the starry night, or possibly even Scotty Atkins's callous insistence that she go back up to the mountains and face the devil on his home field. Stupidly, perhaps, she just wasn't afraid anymore.

Consider, she told herself, the mighty John Elway. For all those years he'd leaned down to take snaps from center, knowing full well that the game he was playing was designed to send fully a ton of raging, steroid-crazed meat down on him the moment he said, "Hike!" And most of the time he either stood in the pocket and got the pass off, or scrambled out and avoided dismemberment. Elway had lived to win the big one, ride off into the sunset, play golf, cash checks. It was fucking inspirational.

Whoever was trying to scare the hell out of her had nothing on the Oakland Raiders. She owed it to the Langhams, and Monette, and herself to get a grip.

Hawk clearly wasn't standing around, waiting to comfort her in her hour of weakness. He'd headed straight back inside. After a minute she picked up the guitar, squared her shoulders, and followed. Already seated at the desk, he was evidently resuming what he'd been doing before the blast in the street, frowning at the computer, a mug of chicken noodle soup cooling on the desk, a short Jim Beam in one hand and the mouse in the other. "Damn," he said. "I can't get this mother to serve up."

URL not found.

And the address in the window was alicesrestaurant.com, with a bunch of circles and arrows on the end of it.

With all that she'd been through that day, wasn't it nice that they were ending up on the same page? "I tried it earlier—nothing doing. I thought I might give them some business with the pâté for Edna, but they lost my sale. What do you think is going on?"

Hawk took a sip of his whiskey. "Maybe there's a glitch in their code. Maybe it's a problem for their webmaster to solve. Or maybe you couldn't get them to sell you anything because they aren't selling things at the moment, due to some cash flow difficulty. As I understand it, that happens a lot in the dot.com world. Think about it—you have access to a potentially infinite pool of clients. All you have to do is write up some clever copy and put some pretty pictures up on the web. Next thing you know, you're a household name. You don't have to do anything as tawdry as buy actual inventory, deliver the things the people buy, collect the money that your customers owe you, or pay suppliers for the goods. Not to mention cutting paychecks for the tech support people who keep it running, the shipping clerks, the number crunchers. It wouldn't take much heat at any point to make a cash-poor web business go up in flames."

"You think Alice Wood is running a scam?" Sally asked.

"I don't know. Whatever she's up to, she's not doing business today," said Hawk. "It could easily be a technical screw-up. At worst, maybe she just got in a tight place. From what Molly said, her daughter wouldn't shed any tears if she turned Wood's Hole into cold cash. If she needs money, Alice probably figures that she might as well have her inheritance now as later."

He set the whiskey down, logged off the web, and picked up the mug of soup. "It adds up, but maybe my arithmetic's too simple," he said, spooning limp noodles and salty yellow broth into his mouth. "After all, if I really had any idea how people got to be Internet millionaires, I wouldn't be in Laramie, toting rocks and eating canned soup. I'd be sitting on my yacht in Biscayne Bay, trying to decide whether to buy a major league baseball team or take over the lingerie industry."

He had a point. Sally and Hawk were doing pretty well for themselves, but with all the education they'd had, as smart as they were, as hard as they worked, it had occurred to them once or twice that it was a real shame they'd never figured out how to get rich.

"So," said Sally, picking up Hawk's glass, leaning against the desk. "Tell me about what you do know. How was your afternoon?"

Hawk ate some more soup as he thought about it. "Annoying and interesting. It was no problem getting up to the property—the road in is in decent shape. And Molly's right—it's a damn pretty place. A little shady and full of trees for my taste, but she's got a perfect building site, up on a slope with a view of the red rocks out one side and the beaver pond out another. I saw a couple of deer, some black bear scat, and maybe a dozen beavers building lodges."

He finished his soup, set down the mug, and leaned back in his chair. "Just as I was getting ready to do a thorough walk-over of the place, company showed up."

"Let me guess," said Sally. "Marsh Carhart."

"For one," Hawk said. "Sheldon Stover was with him." Hawk chuckled and shook his head. "That guy cracks me up."

"What were they doing there?" Sally asked.

"Carhart said he's going to deliver his report to Nattie and Dwayne tomorrow. He hired Stover as a human resources consultant, or something like that. They were doing a final survey of the property."

"Final?" said Sally. "Sheldon's barely figured out that he's not in New Jersey. What could he have to contribute?"

Hawk tilted his head. "It's worth wondering about that. One way or another, they didn't seem terribly surprised to see me, so I had a feeling they might have followed me up. Carhart saw me talking to Molly at the memorial for Monette—in fact, he was hovering over our table so close I thought about asking him to quit breathing all over my Frito pie. He clearly didn't want me poking around up there, but when I told him Molly had asked me to take a look at the place, he couldn't very well kick me off. So he offered to show me around. I wasn't in a position to refuse.

"Not surprisingly, he made a point of emphasizing what was so great about the place. Of course he wasn't showing me anything I hadn't already noticed, but I couldn't concentrate. Stover didn't stop talking. Not even to take a breath. I think he has gills."

"I hate to ask," said Sally, taking the last swallow of whiskey. "What was he talking about?"

"Oh, some total crap about the impossibility of doing a study of anything except human impact on any place, because once the investigator arrived, the site was hopelessly tainted with something he called 'ethnographic subjectivity.' I asked him if it was contagious."

"And what did Carhart have to say during all this?"

"Very little. Occasionally he'd nod at Stover and say something like 'Very interesting.' I can't imagine what he found interesting, except maybe that trick about not breathing. Mostly Carhart just stared thoughtfully into the blue. Every once in a while he'd make some remark about what a great thing it was that there were still pockets of 'intact ecosystems' in the Rockies. Did you finish my drink?" he asked, scowling.

"I'll get you a refill," said Sally, and he followed her to the kitchen. "So, 'intact ecosystems?' Guess that lets us know what his impartial resource survey will reveal about the property, huh? Nattie and Dwayne must be thrilled."

He got out another glass for her. "I can see why they would be. All you have to do is look at that beaver pond. The place appears to be thriving."

"Appears?" she said, catching something in his voice as she dropped ice into both glasses.

Hawk smiled at her, just enough to get one dimple showing. When he smiled like that, it meant that he was entertaining ideas, often of the carnal variety. But this time it was his Mr. Science smile. She knew he was revving up for one of his famous detailed explanations. He was a reticent man by nature, but once he started in on an explanation, he talked it all the way to the finish. She poured the drinks with a lavish hand.

"It's not that big a place," Hawk began when they were back in the living room, sharing the couch. "We walked the perimeter in an hour and a half. As I said, it's gorgeous, and evidently flourishing. But I kept wondering why, if the place was as good as it looked, they were leading me around. I figured there must be something they didn't want me to see."

"And what was it?" Sally had to ask, although she knew she'd never get Hawk to cut to the chase. For him, every explanation had its own rhythms and meanders, and there was no point being an impatient listener.

"Well," Hawk drawled, dragging the word out for all it was worth, "it wasn't actually on the property. But getting to it took some savoir-faire."

"Savoir-faire?" Sally said. Make that *Monsieur* Science.

"French for 'sneakiness.' I decided when I first laid eyes on that beaver pond that I wanted to check out the creek they'd dammed to make the pond. I meant to follow it upstream as far as I could, off the private parcel and onto the national forest. I'd planned to hike right up the bank, but I couldn't shake your buddies. So I decided to just play dumb, tag along with them until I got tired of it, and then announce that I was leaving. Which is what I did."

"But of course you weren't leaving?"

The dimpling smile again. "Nope. I got in my truck and drove back out, and then took off down a side spur and parked my truck out of sight of the main road. I hid in some bushes until I saw them drive out. And then I went back in on foot, and hiked up the creek."

"And what," she asked, "did you find?"

He put his glass down on the coffee table, leaned back against the arm of the couch, and hauled his legs into her lap. "About two miles upstream, the creek had been ditched. It wasn't that much of a ditch, and it must have been a long time ago. It wasn't a whole lot more than a kind of groove, all overgrown with grass and cluttered up with rocks and weeds, but if you know what you're looking for, you wouldn't miss it."

"I would."

"Not if you were with me," he said. "Had to do some tough bushwhacking to follow the ditch, but finally I got to a place where there was an abandoned rail spur, and the remains of a building—the corner of an old stone foundation, some busted timbers. I walked around there for a while, trying to figure out what it was."

"The Union Pacific Railroad was all over that country," Sally said. "Still is."

"Yeah, I know, but this is national forest now, and there's no road to it. Some people have even talked about making it a wilderness area. Whatever got built came before the feds took over. I thought I'd go over to Cheyenne tomorrow and see if the state Revenue Department has any records of what might have been up there."

The historian in Sally was intrigued. "I've got a little time tomorrow. I could do some digging in the archives here, see if there's anything interesting in the railroad collections."

"That's my girl," he said. "You know, what first attracted me to you was your research skills."

"Oh yeah?" she said. "Well then, I have to confess that the thing I like best about you is your penchant for detailed explanations."

"I thought it was my enormous . . ." he said, closing his eyes as she took his legs off her and stretched out next to him on the couch.

"Whatever," said Sally.

"So how was your trip to Vedauwoo?" he asked.

It took her a minute to answer. "You may not believe this, but it was just what I needed. Scotty was a big pain in the ass, and I didn't like being up there, but it got me thinking."

"You're great when you're thinking," he said, eyes still closed as her palm made circles on his chest.

"Yeah. I need to do it more. So he started out by asking me about honky-tonk angels, and I gave him a little lesson in country music history. Then, when we got up there, he kind of took me through Monday afternoon all over again. That wasn't so much fun."

He squeezed the hand rubbing his chest. "I can imagine."

"The hardest part was going up to the outcrop. I kept seeing her arm . . ."

"I keep seeing it myself," Hawk said.

"Yeah, with the rope dangling," she said, sitting up suddenly. "But listen to this. Scotty told me that her hands had been tied together. They've got the first autopsy report, and it looks like she and the killer got loaded together, then had sex—Scotty called it a 'rough game that got out of hand'—and she ended up shot dead. The guy had a hell of a time getting her down in the crack, had to cut the rope."

Hawk was on it. "So why would he leave an arm sticking out if he was trying to hide her?" Now he sat up too. "Heard us coming."

"It's a reasonable assumption," she said. "And Scotty has decided that the troubles I've been having are because whoever killed Monette and saw us up there, recognized us. His number one candidate is Jerry Jeff."

"Oh yeah, right," said Hawk. "How insane is that? He's just a boneheaded kid."

"So you and Delice and I think. Scotty has other ideas. He mentioned that Monette was bound with a piggin' string, and JJ just bought a new one. I allowed as how I didn't really find his Jerry Jeff the Killer theory all that compelling, because JJ can't drive yet. I oughta know. Delice keeps pressuring me to take him out in the Mustang, like that's gonna happen."

"But maybe it's somebody who had access to JJ's rodeo gear," said Hawk. "That's a troubling thought."

"Your pal Atkins just takes this stuff in stride. He's going to interrogate Jerry Jeff again tomorrow."

"Don't blame Scotty for doing his job."

Hell, everybody was on this job. And now Sally remembered all the phone calls she hadn't returned. Maude and Delice could wait. "Oh shit—I forgot to tell you. Molly Wood left a message—she wants you to call back. I wrote the number down there, on the pad. And Dickie wants me to meet him at the Torch. Do you feel like going out?"

Hawk yawned. "I'm ready to go to bed right now. But this is Jubilee Days. Let me try Molly, and then we can go."

He picked up the phone, dialed the number in Centennial. He listened briefly, then left a message. "I guess it can't be too urgent if she's letting her machine pick up."

"Do you think we should stay here and wait for her to call back?" Sally asked.

Hawk gave it a moment's thought. "I don't see the point. I'll call again tomorrow when I've had the chance to look some stuff up. As for tonight, if the sheriff thinks we need to go downtown to purchase intoxicating beverages and see if some band can do anything new with 'San Antonio Rose,' I suppose it's just our patriotic duty."

CHAPTER 18
THE NIGHTLIFE

THE TORCH TAVERN was packed with drinking, hat-wearing revelers, squeezed in hip to ass. They were inhaling first- and secondhand smoke, spilling drinks on one another, and trying to holler over a band that believed that if a little amplification was good, putting the needle into the red zone was spectacular. Sally saw Hawk slip some earplugs out of the change pocket of his jeans and twist them into his ears. He offered her a pair, and she took them, but stuck them in her own pocket. She'd decided to take the place on its own terms, even if the noise level made her brain buzz in her skull.

Sally had never been a fan of audio terrorism as an entertainment gambit. She thought bands that played too loud were competing with the crowd, not courting it. For her, playing had always been about tasty licks, heartfelt vocals, the band and the audience coming together and riding the mood, crest to crest, to some point of abandon where everybody was rocking. The right mix of tempo and volume, instruments and voices, not the wall of deafening distortion these guys were cranking out.

On the other hand, nobody else much seemed to mind. The bartenders were flying, setting up shots and pulling beers and making change for a throng that stood three deep behind the stools. Out on the jammed dance floor she spotted Brit Langham and Herman Schwink, putting on a Western swing clinic, and Sheldon Stover, hauling Nattie Langham around, elbows and knees flailing in something that looked more like a high school wrestling match than a country pas de deux. Down among the tables, Dwayne huddled with Marsh Carhart, apparently carrying on a conversation just as if they'd been sitting in Dwayne's office down at the bank. Not far away she caught sight of Adolph Schwink, hustling a waitress whose indomitable platinum-blond beehive warred with the deep lines of exhaustion around her eyes.

Sally recognized the song, a rocked-up take on "Move It on Over," the Hank Williams classic. That could explain why Dickie was recommending the band. He loved all Hank Williams tunes, but this one especially. As a young loadhead, he'd always dropped whatever he was doing when a band started up that song. He'd run out on the dance floor, shimmying like Josephine Baker and hollering an obscenely personal version of the lyrics, in which little Dick was expected to move over, "'cause the big Dick's movin' in."

In so many ways the old days were not gentle days. Now, when she found him, he was simply leaning against the wall, eyes closed, drinking a Coke, tapping a finger against the can in time with the music. At six-four he'd have been visible anyway, but his girth and his badge cleared a space around him roughly the circumference of a beer keg. She left Hawk at the bar ordering drinks and snaked her way through the crush, noting in passing a waft of smoke that smelled like mangoes, a number of people with red eyes or very runny noses, at least one small packet of white powder changing hands, and several guys who took the opportunity to grab a handful of her as she squeezed by. More alarming, she bumped against various hard objects that had to be sidearms.

Heat and crowding and dope and booze and guns were not

that good a combination. Sally really hoped that nobody would take a fancy to anybody else's hat.

The Torch Tavern wasn't her cup of hemlock anyway. She'd played there a few times over the years, but the Torch didn't generally book live music. Most of the year the management relied on the type of trade that brought the police on a regular basis and elicited frequent visits from the Ivinson Memorial Hospital emergency medical technicians. The regular clientele ran to bikers with their own pool cues, insane meth heads looking to get wired back up, johns hoping to hook up with moonlighting cocktail waitresses, junkies trying to act cool while sweating and shaking through a score, fast-aging daytime drinkers with noses like walnuts and brown teeth. And, of course, the vultures who fed their habits, and the cops who kept stopping by, learning enough for their troubles to make the occasional bust, but never enough to close down the Torch or dam the poisonous stream that wound through and out of it.

Tonight, between her morning with Bone, her afternoon with Scotty, and the nasty sensation that somebody she couldn't name was in the bar and way too aware of her presence, the Torch was really putting her on edge. But at least her timing was good. Just as she reached Dickie, the band was shuffling up a little instrumental—break time. People were heading for the door to go out and cool off in the street, getting their hands stamped so that they could come back in and obliterate their eardrums when the music started up again. She looked around and said, "I never liked this joint."

"No, you always preferred higher-class places like the Gallery," he said, lighting a Marlboro.

"At least you could wade through the bathrooms there," she told him. "Here you couldn't even get in, because the stalls were always full of people hitting up."

Dickie looked at the glowing end of his cigarette. "Too bad some things don't change."

"Can't you do anything about that?" she asked.

Now he looked at Sally. "You'd be amazed how much ingenuity and strength of purpose some people will put into getting fucked up. When we come in, they go away. When we go away, they come back. If we hang around, they scatter, but they don't go far. They need the shit that much. And every time we arrest a dealer, five more show up to take over the turf. There's so goddamn much money to be made."

"Doesn't the owner of this place object?"

"The owner," Dickie explained, "isn't a person. It's a corporation, headquartered down in Denver. The Torch has had thirty-two different managers in the last twenty-three years—every time we close in on one, he or she skips and we're dealing with some new scumbag. They all say they want to cooperate with us and run a clean operation, but these people aren't what you'd call long-term thinkers. Somebody pays them off, and they're on to the next hole."

"But you keep at it." She was trying to make him feel a little better.

"What the hell else would I be doing here tonight, besides indulging in my well-known masochistic urge to hang around watching other people drink? I had this brilliant idea of coming down here and waiting for somebody to waltz up to me and tell me who killed Monette. But unfortunately that hasn't happened, so I thought I'd play cop. You missed all the fun. I was compelled to bust one cowboy who came in here with a sheet of blotter acid in his hatband and started handing around squares of Mr. Natural like it was Pez. I'm thinking about dropping the hammer on that little old gal over there at the bar, the one with the glitter all over her face. She's gone out to the parking lot with half a dozen guys, fifteen minutes each. I'm beginning to worry that she's starting an epidemic."

Dickie's summary of the nightlife made Sally feel smug about trading the bar stool for her endowed chair. But then it occurred to her that his description of the sleazy gypsy bar managers could, with very little alteration, apply to a certain class of itinerant university administrator: moving in, moving on, and leaving the place (at best) as big a mess as it had been before. She silently repeated the mantra that had stood her in excellent stead throughout both her musical and academic careers: There are assholes everywhere.

"So what else have you been up to today?" she asked Dickie as

Hawk arrived with their beers and a fresh can of Coke for the sheriff.

"Well, let's see. After the memorial thing, I went down to the Lifeway and had a word with young Schwink over there," he said, pointing with his Marlboro. "Damn stupid little twerp started out with the same old song and dance about not having known Monette very well, just working in the same store and all, but I finally told him that several people had suggested that he had a somewhat more intimate relationship with her than that. He kept on lying for a while, but finally admitted that he'd—hmm, how did he put it? oh yes—gotten his rocks off with her a time or two, but that was it. He insisted that whatever was between them had been 'all her fault' because she was such a pathetic little skag and she kept on begging him, and after a while, well, he just felt so sorry for her that he had to oblige."

"Mr. Good Samaritan," said Hawk.

"Mr. Full of Horse Crap. Once I'd dragged that much out of him, I knew he was the kind who'd keep holding out on us and make us have to work for every single crumb of the true story. Took me another half hour to get him to admit that he'd driven her home after her shift, when he was on his lunch break. Christ, I wish I could pin this one on the little worm, but he only had a forty-five-minute break, and evidently after he took her home, he did come back to work."

"Why would he take her home?" Sally asked.

"Said he was just being nice," Dickie answered.

"Uh-huh. That Adolph is such a considerate guy. Couldn't be that she'd invited him over, maybe to smoke a reefer or have a quick one," Sally said.

"Adolph says he didn't even go in, just dropped her in front. Who the hell knows? I didn't have another hour to spend working on him. Places to go. People to see."

"The life of a busy public official," said Hawk.

"Ain't no good life, but it's my life," said Dickie, draining the first Coke and popping the tab on the one Hawk had brought. "Bone Bandy was next on my list—thought I'd go look him up out at the campground. We have a couple of witnesses who said they'd seen him hanging around the Kum 'n' Go mini-mart, across from the Lifeway, and one person who put him at the supermarket last weekend. His alibi for Monday has never been rock-hard, and I guess I've sort of been hoping we'd pull on a string that would eventually lead to him." Carefully he crushed out his cigarette on the top of the empty can and pushed the butt inside. "I was being a bad police officer. I wanted to be able to arrest him for Monette's murder because Mary's always blamed Bone for her sister's death. Couldn't nail him for that one, but maybe we'd get him for this."

"Can you get him for assaulting my girlfriend?" Hawk asked.

Dickie scowled at Sally. "Bone mentioned he'd talked to you, but he didn't say anything about getting physical."

"He tackled her," Hawk explained. "But then they ended up being best friends or something. Ticks me off, but what can you do?"

"With her, not a damn thing," said Dickie, and then asked Sally, "Do you want to file charges?"

She drank some beer and gave it some thought. You could consider a guy like Bone a public menace. Getting him off the street would be doing everyone a favor. Then again, was it worth her time, and Bone's continuing resentment, to make a big fuss about a tackle? "Why bother?" said Sally. "He didn't hurt me. And he didn't kill Monette. He's looking for the bastard who did. He's of the opinion that she was shaking somebody down."

Dickie had been leaning against the wall, but now he pushed off and stood upright, looking down at Sally from his highest height. "What makes you think that?"

"Because he told me so. He's been following me around, and he has this idea that I've been taking an unusual interest in the matter, and he thought I might know something he didn't know."

"Following you around? Has he got some kind of grudge against you personally?" Dickie stared a minute, craned his neck to look around, and then slumped back against the wall, slugging down some more soda, hauling his cigarette pack out of his shirt pocket. The gold foil on top glittered briefly in the barroom light. "Well, he doesn't seem to have tagged along tonight, but he did indicate this afternoon that he'd, uh, run into you this morning. He left out the part about grabbing you, and didn't say a word about Monette being involved in any kind of shakedown."

Sally watched as Dickie took out a Marlboro, put the pack back in his pocket, and lit up. "Maybe he thought it reflected badly on him. I couldn't tell exactly whether Bone was hoping to collect the blackmail himself, or if he wanted revenge. He was being as coy as he could, but hell, the guy isn't exactly a model of self-control and rationality. Maybe he figured he'd said more than he meant to with me, and decided to tail back on his story with you."

Dickie rolled his eyes. "Why should he be any different from anybody else? Seems like everybody I talk to lately has the idea that everything they say to me can and will be used against them."

"You're the law," Hawk said gently. "They're supposed to think that."

"Yeah yeah, I know," Dickie said. "It sucks. Days like this, I end up just wanting to crawl into a bed with a nice bottle of Joe the Crow and never wake up."

Hawk and Sally exchanged a look. The last thing Dickie Langham needed, after all his years of climbing up out of the pit one day at a time, was a tumble off the wagon and back into the dark abyss.

"Jose Cuervo is not a friend of yours," said Sally, "but we are. Come on, boy. Let's go over to the Wrangler and I'll buy you a burger. If we leave now, before the band starts up again, I might have some chance of saving what's left of my hearing."

"Nah," said Dickie, adding, to her amazement, "I'm not hungry."

She put her hand up to his forehead. "Are you feeling okay?"

"I been better. But really, it's just that I don't feel like running into my sister right now."

Sally thought of the phone message from Delice. When Dee was storming, people tended to go to the northeast corner of the basement. "She said you'd been over there asking questions."

"Yeah. For, like, fifteen minutes before she booted my ass out and told me that I better not come in there aggravating her again, or she'd file a police harassment complaint."

"You were down there asking about JJ, weren't you?" Sally asked.

"I just wanted to let her know that I'd have to have some time for a serious talk with him about this case. You can imagine how she reacted."

Hawk looked Dickie up and down. "You don't look to be leaking from anyplace new."

"I'm a spartan," said Dickie. "Carrion birds could be ripping my guts out and I'd be whistling 'Big Chief Got a Golden Crown.'"

"You're a hoss," Hawk agreed.

Dickie seemed to be cheering up a little. That was good. Sally and Hawk wouldn't leave him alone until they'd convinced him that the wall of the Torch Tavern wasn't the only thing he could lean on. She put her beer down on a table and put her arms around him and gave him back one of the hugs he'd given her, over the years. Those hugs had sometimes been all there was pulling Sally back toward the light.

"You think you've failed Mary because her sister died, and now Monette's been killed. And you think you're letting Delice down because you have to question JJ. But you're not a failure, sweetie. We all love you. You'll find the killer."

He sighed heavily, his big bulky body shifting in her arms, leaning his chin on her head. "Yeah, one way or the other, between Scotty and me, we'll run this fucker down. But it feels bad right now."

"Sure it does," Hawk nodded, his version of hugging.

"The worst part," Dickie said, as the band, back on stage, began tuning up for the next set, "is that Jerry Jeff's one of the ones who's lying to me."

FRIDAY

CHAPTER 19
SWINGING INTO ACTION

"ALL TEENAGERS LIE," said Delice the next morning, setting a poached egg on an English muffin in front of Sally, pulling a bottle of Tabasco out of her pocket, plopping down into a chair, and planting her elbows on the table with a clattering of silver bracelets. "They have to. It's in their code of conduct. If they're caught telling the truth to an adult, their friends break their skateboards and exile them to the geek table in the lunchroom. Jesus probably lied to Mary."

Sally shook Tabasco all over the rubbery white and hard, graying yolk, wishing that she'd just forsaken the path of righteousness and ordered a couple over easy with a side of hash browns. When it came to nutrition, the Wrangler was built for cholesterol, not for need.

"You're his mother. Can't you threaten him?" she asked Delice.

"With what? A whipping? He's got six inches and fifty pounds on me. Should I ground him? He'd just sneak out while I was at work." She took a sip from Sally's coffee mug, grimacing involuntarily. Sally wondered if, after all, Delice had gotten used to the superior brew at the Yippie I O.

Sally searched for a device. "You could take away his allowance, I guess."

Delice snorted. "JJ's been mowing lawns and walking dogs and washing windows since he was eight. He's earned all his own spending money, and for the past three years he's been working his ass off trying to save up for a roping horse. Allowance-schmowance."

Sally gave up on her egg and opened a plastic packet of grape jelly to spread on the other half of the muffin. She'd asked for it dry, but the cook had scorned the request. Whatever they'd squirted on it, Sally could easily believe it wasn't butter. "Isn't it supposed to be one of the warning signals of the end of the American family when parents can't control their children anymore?"

"Only according to people who've never had children. You can't control teenagers. You can only hope to keep them alive until their hormones settle down and their brains kick back in," Delice explained, finishing the coffee.

Sally looked at her empty cup. "Do you think I could get some OJ?"

"Not today. We had a product recall," Delice said.

"A product recall on orange juice?" Sally asked.

"Trust me," said Delice, "you don't want it."

Sally wasn't inclined to give that too much thought. "But you've got to get him to tell the truth. This is about murder, Delice."

Delice was the Vince Lombardi of Laramie—all offense. "Don't lecture me, Mustang. I do crack down on him now and then, and I can reduce him to tears when the situation calls for it. If I thought his lying about the piggin' string meant he killed Monette, I promise you, he wouldn't have a chance. I'd take him down to the courthouse myself and show old Scotty Atkins exactly how to work him over until he confessed."

Now Delice sat back in her chair and put her hands in the pockets of her jeans: jingle jangle. "But Jerry Jeff didn't kill Monette Bandy. He just plain couldn't do it. I know mothers are always the last to admit that their kids are psycho, but I'm telling you, mine isn't."

"They've got some of the evidence back from the state crime lab," Sally told her. "Scotty's going to make JJ go down to the courthouse today and look at the piggin' string."

"I know that. Dickie told me yesterday. I can't stop them from taking him in. In fact, I'm glad they're doing it. It's barely possible he'll have something useful to say. But my guess is that, short of torture, JJ won't tell even that pigheaded Atkins anything he doesn't want to tell him. He's not ready. Dickie already tried the good-old-uncle-sheriff approach; I doubt Scotty's tough talk will be more effective if he doesn't have anything more to hold over my kid than a stupid piece of rope.

"Look, I don't doubt that Jerry Jeff's done brainless things—fooled around with girls, maybe done some dope—things I've probably threatened to kill him for. Whatever he's hiding, he figures it's serious enough that it's easier for him to keep quiet than deal with the consequences of spilling it, but not so bad that if he doesn't tell, somebody might get hurt. That balance could change any time. For now I think we're going to have to keep reminding him that whatever he's covering up isn't going to get him thrown in jail, but it might help Dickie find out something important."

"Maybe I could talk to him," said Sally. "I mean, it's not like I'm his mother or a cop. I'm not really an authority figure in his life. We get along great."

Delice considered it. "Hmm. And of course, he does realize that you haven't exactly been a perfect little angel all your life."

Sally narrowed her eyes. "What have you been telling him about me?"

Delice laughed. "Let's put it this way. As his mother, I am forced to admit that I myself might have done one or two things that I would prefer he not feel compelled to try out. We've had those conversations about sex and drugs and borrowing the neighbors' car to enter in the demolition derby. But it would undermine me with him to own up to everything, so some of the time, when I'm giving him an example of the kind of stuff he's not supposed to do, I generally borrow a little from your life story."

"Borrow!" Sally exploded. "You didn't tell him it was me who drove up on Dickie and Mary's lawn that time we smoked all that hash and decided to deliver that pizza right to their door!"

Delice hung her head.

"You didn't tell him about the time I busted that jug of Almaden at the midnight movie at the Nixon Theater?"

"It could have happened to anybody," Delice said, charitably.

"You didn't suggest that I was the one who got kicked out of that hippie restaurant on Ivinson for spitting out my dinner and accusing the cook of making phlegm burritos?"

"No!" Delice exclaimed. "I told him that was Hawk."

They looked at each other. "It *was* Hawk, come to think of it," Sally admitted.

"Maybe you could talk to JJ at that," Delice agreed. "It's bound to make me look good, anyway."

Then, abruptly, Delice changed the subject and began bullying Sally about the events of Tuesday night. Sally reflected that it was probably true that if Delice hadn't been able to get anything out of Jerry Jeff, Scotty Atkins wouldn't do much better. Delice could have had a great career in the Spanish Inquisition. Reluctantly Sally gave up the whole story, down to the shredded teddy and the message on the mirror. She went on and told her about the unpleasantness out at the rodeo, and figuring that Delice would eventually find out about her tussle with Bone, she threw that in too.

Delice's dark eyes flashed. "Shit!" she exclaimed. "There go another pair of salt and pepper shakers!"

Sally turned to follow her gaze, and saw a very nice-looking family getting up to leave, the mother pausing to add a sugar dispenser to her bag.

"Excuse me, ma'am!" Delice yelled. "Could I have a minute?" The family froze. And then, in a much softer voice, Delice told Sally, "If she just hands them back and tells me they crawled into her purse, I'll let her off. If she doesn't, I'm going to spoil their vacation." She leaned over and clasped Sally's hand. "You've got problems, girlfriend," she said. "I'd be your bodyguard if I could find somebody who'd keep the customers and the help from walking off with everything in the place. Hawk'll have to handle it. Do you want to borrow a gun?"

"Sure," said Sally. "I want to shoot everybody in town. NO, I don't want to borrow a gun. I don't need a gun." And if she did, of course, Hawk had several on hand. But she didn't, because Sally would not, under any circumstances, use one.

"Talk to JJ," Delice told her as she hurried off. "He's working this morning, and supposed to go to the cop shop after that, but he'll be home later in the afternoon."

In truth, Sally was mortally sick of talk. Ever since Monette's murder, it seemed as if she'd done nothing but react to other people and yak about the latest crazy events. At the moment all she could do about Monette was to show up later in the afternoon to help paint signs for the parade. It was one more form of talking and reacting.

Enough. The time had come to swing into action. For a historian like her, that could mean only one thing: going to the library. She couldn't raise Monette from the dead, but she could do Molly Wood a favor (and help Hawk out, and distract herself from the matter of murder) by finding out what she could about the land upstream of Molly's potential new home in the Laramie Range.

For Professor Sally Alder, a good research library was church, stadium, theater, and battlefield all rolled into one. She particularly loved libraries in the summer, when the only people around were unlucky students, dedicated diggers, and a staff much less hassled than usual. She planned to put in a couple of hours in Coe, the university's main library, do a little background reading and then head up to the archives to root among the railroad documents. She figured she could find out a hell of a lot with maybe five hours' work. That would be five hours she wasn't thinking about honky-tonk angels.

She began with the catalogues, online and card (aesthetically she preferred the latter), looking up books on the Laramie Mountains and on the railroad in southern Wyoming. Finding what she wanted, she took the stairs. Up on the third floor the stacks stood dark and full, waiting for her. There were a few students studying at tables in open areas, but other than that, the place appeared to be hers. Seeking solitude, she headed for a desk in the shadowy far corner of the stacks, and then went to gather books. Soon she returned, piled the books on the desk, and went silently to work.

Hunched over her books and papers in the silver-gray fluorescent gloom, so lost in the past was Sally that when she looked up an hour later, she didn't at first comprehend the sensation that gripped her. Clenched muscles in the middle of her body, tight jaw, chills running shoulder to fingertips. Three seconds later the feeling had a name: terror. She was absolutely certain that somebody had followed her, was watching, lying in wait.

Once again room tone tipped her off. The breathy aspirations of library quiet had shifted, just a bit, just the fraction of one more soul, inhaling, exhaling.

Slowly she raised her eyes from a memoir by a woman who'd found a job with the Union Pacific during World War II, a book titled *I've Been Workin' on the Railroad.* She'd just gotten to a chapter where the woman joined an all-female crew that was working in a newly constructed railroad tie plant in the Laramie Mountains. Sally knew she was on to something, but the awareness of somebody else, prowling close by, held her fast. Trying to make as little noise as possible, she marked her place, closed the book, took off her reading glasses, and rose half out of her chair to peer over the high back of the library desk. And then she heard it, the faint sound of a book being slipped back into place on a stack shelf, sliding with a soft *ssh* between other books and then hitting the back of the shelf with a muffled thump.

She shot up and ran around the corner of the stack row. And plowed right into Sheldon Stover. "You flaming idiot!" she screamed, heedless of library etiquette. "You scared the bejesus out of me! What in the holy hell are you doing skulking around here?"

Sheldon, as was his wont, sighed. "I'd hoped not to introduce this disturbance into my methodology, but I suppose, as a subject, you have the right to know," he said. "I'm doing a brief experimental ethnography for Marsh's project, and I've been observing you. See, by taking this book off the shelf"—he selected a thick red-bound volume—"I had a clear view of you sitting there, working."

Sally leaned over and peered through the opening to see the desk where she'd been sitting. "You've been lying on the floor here spying on me? For your experimental ethnography? I don't get this, Sheldon. Why me?"

"Isn't it obvious?" he asked.

She had to think about that. "I sincerely hope not," she told him. "Let's assume there's a reason besides the fact that you're a potentially homicidal Peeping Tom."

Sheldon chuckled. "Not at all. I guess I'll have to explain. You see, my job is to theorize the endless signature of human presence on that apparently wild tract of land that Marsh Carhart is evaluating, up there in the mountains. Now, I'm no historian . . ." he admitted.

"That much I've figured out," Sally said.

"So I don't pretend to concern myself with the kinds of matters that must be well detailed in written documents," he continued without acknowledging her interruption. "What I contribute to Marsh's project is a kind of provisional cut at representing the perpetuity of human engagement with this so-called wild place."

Sally grabbed the red book and shoved it back onto the shelf. "I still don't get this. I haven't even been there. Why are you frigging stalking me?"

"I'm not! Pay attention here, Sally. I'm merely following a thread. Yesterday your boyfriend, with whom you appear to have something of an intellectual as well as a sexual partnership—"

"Sheldon!" she screamed again.

"It's just sex then? I doubt that. In any case, Marsh and I encountered this boyfriend at the site yesterday, obviously engaged in his own brand of scientistic observation."

"Scientistic?" asked Sally.

"As in, 'the kind of thing scientists do.' "

"Don't you mean scientific?"

"No. That has too much of the ring of empiricism," he said.

"Oh." How in hell could you take this guy seriously?

"As I was saying, we walked the property with your friend. His interest in the place put him in the category of a subject for my study. Being a scientist, he is presumably following up his observations from yesterday with more research of the sort that people in his field regard as useful. In other words, he's carrying the consequences of his presence yesterday in the mountains into other times and places, performing activities related to and impinging upon the Happy Jack location. It's called time-space distanciation."

"Oh yeah? Gosh, Hawk calls it 'going around looking stuff up.' "

But Sheldon, on a roll, missed the mockery in her tone. "I had planned, today, to discreetly follow him and see where his work led. But when I went to your house this morning, his truck was already gone. I decided I'd head back home, but then I happened to see you through the window of the Wrangler café. I believe in pursuing spontaneous contingencies, and it seemed to me at that moment that by following you, I was merely tracking the chaotic web of human relations that spins out of any place. And I was right. Why else would you be sitting here reading books about the history of the very area in question?"

Her bad luck. Hawk had left early for Cheyenne, so Sheldon had tailed her. Was every jerk in town following her around? The image of being snagged on some strand of a web that both Sheldon Stover and Bone Bandy, and God knew who else, were creeping along didn't improve her mood. She ignored his question and looked him right in the eye. "I want you to listen to me very carefully. I do not give my consent to be a subject in your experimental ethnography. Should you choose, in any way, to represent me, I will haul you in front of the Supreme Research Ethics Court, or whatever agency handles these things, and by the time I'm done with you, they'll be talking about your case the same way they talk about those psychologists who give people electric shocks for the hell of it."

Now it was Sally on a roll. "You are to go away this instant, and stop following me, and don't even think about bugging Hawk." She could just imagine Mr. More-Than-Sex-Partner's hilarity at the prospect, but she thought another threat might be useful. "If he catches you, I promise, Hawk will turn you into dog food. Furthermore, you are to move out of Edna McCaffrey's house today. I don't give a damn where you go. I don't care if you have to drive to South Dakota to find a motel room. This is it, Sheldon. *Capisce?*"

"I do have a contract for this project, Sally." Sheldon sniffed.

"It's unfortunate that you're taking a hostile attitude here, but I've got a professional reputation to maintain."

She couldn't help it; she laughed. "Then go follow Dwayne, or Nattie, or your buddy Marsh Carhart. They're the ones putting the human impact on the place. Just do me a favor, and get out of my sight and get out of Edna's house!"

Sheldon was crushed. "I'm sorry you feel this way," he said, turning to walk toward the stairs. "I'd thought you might comprehend."

Now he had her feeling guilty. "Hold on," she called. "Look, I know you think you've got a job to do, and God knows, Sheldon, I don't want to get in the way of you actually doing some work. Did your fellowship check arrive?"

Hangdog look. "Not yet. Maybe tomorrow." He brightened. "I'm not too worried. My prospects are good."

God took care of babies and guys like Sheldon Stover. "Okay. But please, just try to look at it from my point of view. I'm having a tough week, and I don't need you popping up like the White Rabbit."

"All right," he said, shoulders slumping, turning once again toward the stairs. Then he looked back over his shoulder. "Could I ask just one favor?"

No, she thought. "What?" she said.

"Can I just stay at Edna's for tonight? I really need to finish this report. I promise I'll pack up and leave first thing tomorrow morning."

What could she say?

And so Sheldon went away, presumably back to Edna's to raid the larder, assault the plumbing, and write his bullshit report. Satisfied, now, that she was really alone, Sally spent another hour reading and making notes, and then packed up her pads and pens to move on to the archives. She knew, now, what she was looking for.

The memoir had offered up the first clue: the railroad had hired a bunch of people to work in the Laramies during World War II, doing a number of things, including producing the wood ties that went between the steel rails. The tie plant would have had to be close to wood, water, and the railroad itself. As long as Sally had been in Wyoming, there hadn't been any kind of industrial production facilities operating in the Laramies, so the plant must have closed down sometime between the war and the early eighties. Could the ruins Hawk had found be the remains of the tie plant? Why had it closed?

Two hours later, with the help of an archivist who knew the railroad collections cold and dearly loved his job, Sally had what Sheldon Stover would have called "provisional cuts" at some answers, and as usual, more questions. She couldn't wait to compare notes, tonight at dinner, with the man she had learned to adore for his really big . . . brain.

CHAPTER 20
INTO THE PIT

SOMETIMES, living in Laramie made Sally feel like she was in the middle of an old movie. Just now the feature film seemed to be *Paint Your Wagon*. People were working, chattering, flirting, enjoying themselves, getting into the swing of the community activity. Of course, there were some signs that these were no longer the days when a smooth-faced Clint Eastwood could be found warbling onscreen. Fatigue-clad lesbians with shaved heads mingled with rodeo cowboys in Grateful Dead T-shirts, sorority girls with pierced navels, senior citizens wearing Birkenstocks. In the flatbed of the tractor-trailer, Brit, Herman Schwink, and an assortment of young people were building some kind of elaborate structure out of chicken wire, plywood, and two-by-fours. Paint, Magic Markers, paper, wood, and sheets lay everywhere. Maude, dressed in her usual faded jeans and sloganeering T-shirt, was supervising a couple dozen men, women, and children in the art of sign painting, nodding her approval as each sign was finished, stapled to wooden stakes, and stacked against the wall. Delice dashed in and out the back door of the café, shouting encouragement, and even bringing out a cooler full of cold soda and bottled water.

"Delice giving out free drinks?" said Sally. "There's one for the history books."

"Yeah," Brit agreed, jumping down from the truck bed, "and it's, like, not for the glory. We already put the Wrangler on our banner thanking our sponsors and volunteers, for letting us use the parking lot."

As Brit bent over the cooler to inspect the beverage selection, Sally watched Herman's eyes zero in on the back pockets of Brit's little cutoffs, then travel down her legs and all the way back up. Sally thought she might have heard him whimper. When Brit pulled out two Dr Peppers and took one over to him, you could practically see the twittering lovebirds circling his head. That boy had it bad.

"Hey Brit," Sally whispered, after Herman had gone back to work. "Do you think you could see if your buddy Herman can find out if his little brother knows more about Monette than he's been admitting so far?"

"Why?" Brit asked.

"It seems Monette and young Adolph had some kind of thing going."

"Gag me," said Brit.

"Fine," said Sally, "but could you get Herman to lean on Adolph a little?"

Brit put a hand on her hip. "I think," she said, "that I could get Herman to lean on a prickly pear cactus if I asked nicely." And then she too went back to work.

Sally walked over to check out the signs. They varied from the spunky and unobjectionable ("Wyoming Women Rule") to the straightforwardly memorial (Mary Langham painting one that said "Remember Monette") to the in-your-face feminist ("WIMMIN-POWER!!!") to the marginally commercial ("Wyoming Women Thank Wal-Mart"—presumably Maude's gesture). Coalition politics, Laramie style, although Sally noticed that Maude did remind some of the volunteers to stay on message ("Sorry, Sukie, I know we're all here to protest a killing, but I think you'd better save 'Abortion Is Murder' for another time").

"Looks like you don't really need me," Sally told Maude. "You got a great turnout."

Maude pulled a bandana from her pocket and wiped her face. "They've done a good job. We'll probably have forty or fifty people marching all told, and that thing on the float sure is big, anyhow."

"What is it supposed to be?" Sally asked.

"Don't know. Brit and her friends are in charge. They've been looking at a drawing and making modifications in the structure, but they're keeping it a secret from us old people."

Sally squinted up. "It doesn't look like anything in particular at this point."

"They're not done. They said they wouldn't put the finishing touches on until tomorrow, when they cover the whole thing in wadded-up crepe paper. I figure, if they want to treat this like they're building the homecoming float, that's okay. I trust Brit's taste."

"No one," Sally told Maude, "has a more finely tuned sense of the tacky than Brit. It'll be fine."

"Speaking of fine," Maude said, drinking from a water bottle, "are you? You never returned my call. And you'd better tell me the truth about what's been going on, because I'll find out one way or another. For instance, I already know that you and Hawk found Monette. Now tell me about what happened at your house Tuesday night."

Sally didn't ask how she knew. It didn't really matter. This was Laramie, and sooner or later, anyone who put her mind to finding out anything, would. "A little vandalism. Forget about it."

"Not a chance," Maude replied. "And that business about you fainting at the rodeo? Rumor has it you're hypoglycemic."

"That's right," said Sally. "The doctors are prescribing one of your oatmeal raisin cookies every two hours. Better start baking, Maude."

"You worry me, Sally." Maude frowned.

"My blood sugar's fine," Sally tried.

Maude gave her the steely glare. "Is there any chance that break-in had anything to do with Monette's murder?"

"Maude!" Sally said, then lowered her voice. "Why don't you just take out a full-page ad in the *Boomerang*?"

"Sorry," she said. "Maybe this isn't the time. But I just want you to know I'm on to you. And you surely understand how things are around here—I'm generally among the first to know what's going on, and I'm never the last. Let me know if you need my help with anything. Anything," she said.

The second "anything" presumably meant that Sally should make sure to contact Maude if anybody needed intimidating. Maude actually was pretty good at that. She never flaunted her money, but Maude made it a point of womanly honor to use her height, fitness, stubbornness, and firearms ownership when the occasion suited.

"Come to think of it," Sally said, "maybe you could help me with a different matter. What do you know about an old tie plant up in the Laramies?"

Maude poured some water on her bandana, then tied it around her neck. "It wasn't a very big operation. I'm not sure when they opened it up, but it closed down in the mid-sixties sometime. You know, when they finished the interstate, the railroads lost a lot of business and they started cutting back. One more Wyoming boom busting, I guess," Maude said, and then squinted at Sally. "My brother worked there a few summers. Why do you ask?"

"Just doing some research for a friend," Sally answered.

"Yeah, I bet," Maude said suspiciously. "You do a lot of this sort of friendly research?"

"I do all kinds of research, as you know," Sally said genially. "So was your brother a railroad guy?"

"Nope. He just worked up there as a summer job. Sometimes he did construction, but the tie plant paid more. Put him through the engineering program at UW. He was a lifer at IBM—retired five years ago."

"Any chance I could call him up and ask him a few questions?" Sally said.

"No. He died October before last. Lung cancer," Maude answered flatly.

"Oh. I'm sorry," Sally said.

"So am I. You'd think a brilliant scientist would have had a few brains. But he was a two-pack-a-day man for damn near fifty years." Her gaze sharpened. "You know, I've wondered sometimes about that tie plant job. From what I've read, those kinds of places are just chock-full of toxic chemicals. I wonder how many of the other workers have turned up with cancer?"

Sally should have known better than to raise the subject with Maude Stark, a woman whose bleeding heart often bled green. So devoted to the earth was Maude that she lived off the power grid, generating power from a small wind farm, and often modestly boasting that her solar panels collected enough energy to heat her own house and half of West Laramie. From the moment Sally had first learned about the tie plant, she'd had her own thoughts about pollution problems. Naturally, Maude would make the connection.

But she wasn't about to let Maude stare her down. Sally went for nonchalance. "I haven't really thought about it. I was just doing some reading, and happened to run across a mention of the plant. I'd never heard about it, that's all."

"With you, 'that' is never all. Why in the world are you researching the Happy Jack tie plant?" Maude thought a minute. "It can't be connected to Monette—too far from the Devil's Playground. This wouldn't have anything to do with that Wood's Hole land deal, would it? Is that why Hawk was hanging around Molly Wood at the memorial?"

"Damn it, Maude, would you give it a rest?" Sally sputtered.

"Don't ever try to bamboozle a nosy old lady," Maude said.

"If you were just a nosy old lady, you'd be a lot easier to bamboozle. But for the time being, I'd appreciate your backing off. I swear I don't know a bloody thing about any pollution from that plant. If I learn something, I'll let you know."

That much was true. The papers Sally had seen referred only to the period during which the plant had been in operation, from 1942, when it opened as a temporary facility meeting the war emergency, to 1963, by which time production had fallen way off, and the place shut down. For something that had turned trees into industrial equipment for a good twenty-one years, it hadn't left much of a paper trail, at least in the documents Sally had seen.

Mostly she'd found ledger sheets with columns of figures, showing board feet of timber ripped from the forest and prices and profits and overall outputs. There had been letters between the plant superintendent and railroad executives, talking about production quotas and employee turnover, now and again mentioning the odd accident where somebody sawed off a finger, or dropped a log on somebody else. But those were, in the parlance of industrial safety, operator errors, not environmental hazards. So Sally hadn't learned what she'd hoped. Maybe Hawk had found more in state records.

Maude finished her water and shook her head. "You'll let me know when you're good and ready, I reckon. But don't ever think you can put one over on me, or anybody else for that matter, Sally Alder. You're clever enough, but you lack guile."

Sally sighed. Maude was right. Sally had developed a measure of professional discretion over the years, but in her heart lurked the rash youngster whose idea of indirection was to wait fifteen seconds to barrel full-steam ahead. Since the beginning of the week, she thought she'd been slipping quietly around, making subtle inquiries, sly, cunning, artful, careful. Uh-huh. Cunning as a stack of railroad ties, and careful? The returns were in. Even goons like Bone Bandy and Sheldon Stover had gotten the drop on her.

And of course, she was not hypoglycemic.

Just now she wasn't even feeling very clever. If she had any sense at all, she'd leave the busy parade crew to its work and go directly home. Do not hang around trying to pick up information; do not attempt to question Jerry Jeff Davis. But hell, she'd flogged things this far, she might as well go for it. She might not be crafty, but at least she was persistent.

Sally sidled over to the flatbed. Herman Schwink, in pressed cowboy jeans and a sweaty cotton shirt, was banging a nail into a board on the side of the structure (did it look like a space capsule? A Coke bottle?) Brit was helping him by standing close by, holding the thing steady. By the time he finished nailing, the poor cowpoke was panting, and not just from the exertion of swinging a hammer. "Hey Herman," Sally said, "are you riding tonight?"

Obviously grateful for an excuse to take a breather, he picked up his can of soda and walked over to sit down, dangling his long legs off the back of the truck. "Yep," he said. "Gotta stay in the saddle to win the big purse for the week and rack up points for the year. Understand you missed the show the other night."

"Unfortunately I did."

"Sorry to hear it. We came in second. Well, if you can't come tonight, maybe you could catch us tomorrow. We rodeo in the afternoon, so we can all go party Saturday night. I'd be glad to leave a pass for you at the gate."

"Thanks. I'm not sure I'll get there, but I'd appreciate it."

"Pleasure's all mine," said Herman, stealing a glance at Brit.

He was such a nice guy. And also distracted—a perfect time to pump. "So your parents live in town, right?"

"Sure do. And my grandparents and about thirty assorted uncles and aunts and cousins." He grinned. "It's always great to come back home. When I'm out there in Tulsa or Tucumcari, the stands aren't exactly filled with people yelling, 'Herman Schwink is the Bomb!' "

Now for her very wily move. "So when you're here, do you keep all your gear at home, or what?"

Herman looked puzzled. Justifiably. She plunged on. "I mean, when I've been out in the stands, and seen everybody milling around, I've just always wondered about the life of a rodeo cowboy. How do you organize your stuff for living on the road?"

"Ohhh, I see what you're talking about, now. For a minute there, I wasn't following. You mean, like, do I have some specially equipped van or something to haul all my tack and ropes and saddles and stuff. But there's nothing as elaborate as all that. The horse trailer does just fine for some things, and of course a cowboy's horse is his most important piece of gear, not to mention his traveling buddy. Some other filly bucks me off, I always go home to McGuinn," he said.

Sally enjoyed a moment of unexpected glee. However much she overpacked when she traveled, she would never, ever be compelled to include a horse in her baggage. Especially not that snorting evil-eyed mare.

"For everything else," Herman continued, "I've got a camper

on the back of my pickup. Everything has its place. I don't need much." Another quick peek at Brit, who noticed and smiled at him, and then shot a quizzical look at Sally.

"Sounds like a lot to drag around," said Sally. "So have you been rodeoing since you were a kid?"

"Sure have. I was goat ropin' when even the pygmy goats outweighed me. By the time I was in high school, I went to the nationals they have every summer over to Douglas. Started out teamin' with my brother, but once Adolph found out it was gonna be work followin' the rodeo around, he gave it up quick."

"So who hauled the gear when you were young? Did your parents go along?"

"Aw, we didn't need hardly anything then. I mean, we mostly rode around here, or competed with the high school team. When we had to travel we borrowed horses, sometimes even saddles. We could pretty much fit everything we needed for a weekend into a duffel bag. Even the rope case."

Now they were getting somewhere. "Rope case?" she asked.

"On the professional circuit, team ropers, calf ropers, guys like that keep their ropes in a special case, a kind of round leather thing. You can buy 'em in a good ranch supply store, but some people get fancy designer ones."

"I bet you guys take pretty good care of your stuff."

Herman laughed. "Some do, some don't. Me, for instance, I can't stand anything out of order. Every jump—that is, every time I have to move to another town—I have this list I keep, and I inventory my stuff before I leave. But then, of course, some guys, for whatever reasons, couldn't find their boots if their feet weren't in 'em. And even then, some of those ones have problems with the feet!"

Sally laughed with him. She could think of one Montana cowboy whose feet had parted company with his boots one night long ago, over a hand of poker.

Herman smiled at her, and his damaged face took on a gentle glow that gave Sally a glimpse of what Brit saw in him, and reminded her, once more, of the power of cowboy sex voodoo. "For some of 'em it's drinking or drugs makes 'em careless, but I guess some of it's just human nature. My mom always said that if she went into a coma for twenty years and came out, and somebody took her to my house and Adolph's, she'd be able to tell which was which by whether or not she had to use a shovel to get in the front door."

"So can you tell when a cowboy's young whether he'll be more like you or more like Adolph?" Sally asked, abandoning the pretense of subtlety.

Herman finished his soda, crushed the can, looked Sally in the eye as he rose to go back to work. His eyes were still friendly, but now shrewd too. "Yeah. Can't you?"

He nodded a farewell, the gesture of a man so used to a hat that even when he wasn't wearing one, you had the impression he was tipping it. Gazing up at him, Sally was just trying to make up her mind whether to pursue him when she heard someone at her back say, "Hey, teacher!"

Of course it was Scotty Atkins, Pink Floyd aficionado, fresh from a day of putting the heat on young Jerry Jeff Davis. "So are you following your own advice, Scotty?" she said. "Shall we leave the kids alone?"

"Looks like everybody around here has something to do but you, Sally," he said. "Want to go inside and get a beer?"

"That depends. When I leave here, I'm on my way over to pay a call on a kitten I rescued from an imbecile a couple of days ago. My friend Jerry Jeff is taking care of him. Do I want to be cold sober so I can take care of JJ?"

"If it were me," Scotty said wearily, "I'd drink a fifth of something brown right about now. Then again, doesn't matter if you're knee-crawling or straight, he's still a little squirrel, so why don't we settle on beer?"

"Fine with me," said Sally, "but given what you've presumably been doing to her boy, are you sure Delice will serve you?"

"I never heard of a businessperson who thought it was a good idea to refuse service to a cop," Scotty answered.

"All the Langhams are unorthodox thinkers," Sally countered, but he was already headed around the building, toward the front door.

Coming in from bright sun and heat and fresh air, Sally took some time adjusting to the dim bar light and the smell of old smoke and spilled beer. Some people liked the sensation of plunging fast into a cold dank pit, but that was one of the things that had always made her an indifferent afternoon drinker, even in her worst days. Scotty was standing at the bar, ordering for them. She found a tiny table in a corner past the dance floor, surrounded by empty tables, where there wouldn't be any chance of anyone listening in on their conversation. Lucky for the detective, Delice was nowhere in sight.

When Scotty arrived with two Budweisers, she raised her eyebrows. "I'm taking the night off," he explained. "I'm not the smartest guy in the world, but I know when I've hit a brick wall. My brain needs to go off the clock."

"So your interview with JJ wasn't quite as productive as you anticipated?" Sally asked disingenuously.

For an answer, Scotty raised the bottle and drank half the beer in one swallow. "Well, I did learn one thing. That is his piggin' string. Took him two hours to open up at all, but finally he allowed as how, yeah, his old one was missing, and actually, yeah, he had marked his rope with some red nail polish so he could identify it, and he had to admit that there was some red nail polish in the same pattern on the rope we had, so he guessed it made sense to suppose that thing probably did belong to him. But of course, he had no idea how it had come to be used in a murder. Said he'd had it with him when he went out to the fairground last weekend, but he explained in great detail that he doesn't always keep an eagle eye on his gear. Claimed he didn't check his stuff until Monday morning, when he discovered it was gone, and bought a new one."

"Sounds reasonable to me. It's not like he was in an airport or something, with somebody hollering over a loudspeaker every five minutes that you're supposed to tightly control your belongings or else they'll be taken off to a bulletproof chamber and incinerated."

Scotty pounded down the rest of his beer, slammed the bottle on the table, and glared at her. "Don't bait me. I'm doing the best I can. And you can quit protecting Jerry Jeff. After spending so much quality time with him, I confess I have a hard time imagining him doing what somebody did to Monette Bandy. You were right—

he's too much of an airheaded kid. But I'm telling you, he's hiding something."

"Did you have to spend extra time at police interrogation class to unearth that startling revelation?" Sally asked, ignoring his plea about baiting. "His mother told me as much this morning. That's why I'm going over there to see him. Maybe he'll talk to me."

Scotty laughed bitterly. "Oh, definitely. I bet he'll tell you all his secrets, right down to where he keeps his condoms and what girls at the high school he thinks might give him reason to use one. I wonder what it is about you that makes closemouthed people want to reveal their deepest hopes and fears and dreams. Your sensitivity? Your sweet temperament? Your global reputation for sitting quietly and listening to what other people have to say? Why, I myself can hardly control the urge to confess everything I've never told anybody, just in the hope of basking in your famous warmth and empathy."

"Do you hate me?" Sally said softly.

"Hell no!" Scotty shot back, emphatic but turning the volume down. "You drive me nuts, that's all. You seem to have this insane desire to do exactly what's likely to get you in the most trouble. For instance, if JJ does know something the killer thinks might lead to him, and you make a big point of going over there and dragging it out of the kid, don't you think it's in the bad guy's interest to stop you from pursuing things further? Or maybe just to stop Jerry Jeff from talking? Have you noticed that wherever you go, somebody else is at least a step behind you—sometimes a step ahead? Get out of my case, Sally. You're going to get yourself hurt." He tipped back his chair, stuck out his legs, dropped his chin on his chest, and blew out a big hard breath.

Sally gave him a long, long look. "You're worried about me. That's very sweet."

"Shit," said Scotty, closing his eyes.

"You can have my beer," she told him, pushing the bottle over to his side of the table. "You look like you need it more than I do."

He took it, drank.

And now she pressed her advantage. "So along with the piggin' string, you got the rest of the state's preliminary report, right?"

"You don't exactly work your way up to things, do you?" His eyes were still closed.

"Not when there's something I want. And I want you to tell me what's going on, Scotty. I've got a right to know."

"That's debatable."

"Don't debate. Just tell me."

He opened one eye. "Haven't I seen you somewhere before? Were you the one holding the rubber hose?" He put the bottle to his lips.

She leaned forward on her elbows, clasped her hands together, and for once, said nothing.

He put the bottle down and imitated her posture. "Okay. We got some prints off the Skoal can, very distinctive prints—the middle finger is missing the tip. Our print specialist happened to remember a similar set from a bull rider who got arrested here last year for firing his gun down on Ivinson Avenue after getting fueled up at the Buckhorn. We've been leaning on him, but he didn't get into town until Monday morning, and he's alibied for the afternoon. Had an early lunch right here at the Wrangler—the waitress remembered him because he stiffed her—and then checked into a motel, where he had to wait in the lobby while they cleaned a room. When they finally got a room ready for him, he went in and took a nap. The motel manager reported that his truck was in the parking lot the entire afternoon."

Weird. "So how'd the can get up to the Devil's Playground?"

"Interesting question. We also got some prints off that Marlboro package you put in your pocket. Some are yours, of course."

"So how do you trace my prints?" Big Brother was watching.

"You have a Wyoming driver's license?" Scotty replied.

"Ah." Wyoming highways could use a little bit of Big Brother. "What about the others?"

He sighed, and leaned still further forward. And said in a low voice, "Belonged to Sheriff Dickie Langham."

Sally just stared.

"We should have known, of course. You saw yourself how that foil top had been shredded. I've seen him do that a hundred times or more." And now he polished off the second beer.

"You couldn't possibly think . . ." Her head was spinning.

"I don't. The sheriff and I have talked. Like our bull rider, Dickie also had lunch at the Wrangler about eleven o'clock on Monday—his usual Double Roundup Platter—and then came back to work. Our best guess is that our perp raided the garbage cans out back, left us a nice messy bogus trail to slow us down."

"A litterbug!" said Sally. She hated that.

"Right. And if we find this joker, we'll charge him with that too. Throw the book at him." Scotty was almost smiling. Cops were great humorists.

"So . . . what about the autopsy report?" They were practically nose to nose.

"I really shouldn't tell you any more, Sally," he said. "This is the ugly part."

"Tell me," she said. "I can deal with it."

He took a deep breath. "All right. I've gone this far down the road with you, God knows why. Must be that empathetic demeanor I mentioned before. Maybe it's the brown eyes."

Silent thunder rumbled. "Maybe that's the beer. Go on, Detective."

"Monette was shot with a .22 caliber pistol. In this state we'd call it a children's gun."

Sally shook her head.

"There was alcohol and marijuana in her bloodstream. The medical examiner determined that she had, indeed, had unprotected sexual intercourse sometime around the time of death. Not to put too fine a point on it, there was sperm in her vagina. But the physical evidence doesn't tell us whether it was forced contact or not. There were rope abrasions on her wrists, but they weren't bad enough that it appeared she struggled."

"I don't understand." Sally was puzzled.

"It looks like the sex, anyway, could have been consensual. Some people don't mind being tied up."

"But you said before that it appeared she'd been assaulted," Sally told him, pulling back.

"Most of us would consider getting shot to death an assault," Atkins said, leaning back himself.

"You know what I'm talking about, Scotty. I don't have to spell it out." Acting brave, but dreading what he'd say next.

"No. But I bet you don't really want to hear this," he said.

"No, I don't. Just say whatever you've got to say and let me worry about that."

"You asked for it." His eyes were almost transparent, frozen. "It's impossible to tell whether the deposition of semen occurred before or after she was shot."

"Oh. God."

"That's not all. Somebody—presumably the bastard who shot her—also penetrated her with some other object. The examiner found paint chips."

Sally wished she had the beer Scotty had just finished. "Paint chips?" she echoed faintly.

"Like from a broomstick, or maybe a shovel. The medical examiner's report can't tell us jack about the time sequence of events. But one thing is pretty clear. We're not dealing with a gentleman here. Now, does that give you some idea of why I wish to Christ you'd get a clue and leave this thing alone?"

CHAPTER 21
MAD MUNCHIES

SHE DIDN'T RECALL walking to her car. She was barely aware of sitting, for a long time, in the driver's seat, her forehead on the steering wheel. After a while somebody knocked on the window—a stranger, a passerby, mouthing the words, "Are you all right?"

Sally nodded, mouthed back, "I'm fine," though she was, it seemed, not up to actually speaking the words. The stranger looked concerned for a moment, then moved on.

If she'd been a Christian, she'd have headed for a church. If she'd been any kind of decent Jew, she'd have sought out a temple (not an easy thing in Wyoming). But being who she was, Sally took a deep, deep breath, closed her eyes, sent a fervent hope out to the cosmos, and turned on the radio.

The cosmos answered, in the gentle, wayward voice of Jerry Garcia. The guitar work was simple, lilting, reliable. The words offered solace, images of still water, invitations to reach out her hand and have her empty cup filled. Garcia, gone too soon across the Great Divide, had never in life known Sally Alder, but even now, he was wishing he could show her the way home. God knew he hadn't died pretty. Almost nobody did. But here was his beautiful music. It was enough. It had to be enough.

By now, she thought, she'd heard the worst of what Scotty Atkins could tell. How could anything else she found be much more horrible than what she'd just learned? She was scared. Borderline petrified. But at the moment it was just as easy to worry about Jerry Jeff.

When she got to the house, Delice's Explorer was parked in the driveway. Sally pulled the Mustang up behind. The front door was open, and through the screen she could hear screeching rock music, and even louder, Delice yelling at her son.

"You damn bonehead! What in holy hell makes you think burning something that smells like a cross between geranium death bomb and a junkyard fire will cover up the smell of weed? Goddamn it, JJ, talk to me!"

As she let herself in, Sally's nose confirmed Delice's impression. Jerry Jeff had indeed been burning quite a lot of extremely cloying incense. Of course, incense was nearly as old as fire, but in Sally's youth, when millions of Americans had first begun to discover the pleasures of the recreational use of burning aromatics, there hadn't been the varieties of incense there were now. You had your sandalwood, your jasmine, and your patchouli. Then as now, kids had thought incense burning a great device for masking the aroma of marijuana, which, of course, it had never been. Nowadays incense came in zillions of smells—everything from coconut to bat guano. JJ had chosen a fruity bouquet—wild strawberry? harvest peach? Sometimes consumerism wasn't a good thing.

One look at Jerry Jeff told her that he was indeed good and stoned. He lay on the living room couch, red-eyed and giggling at his livid mother, stroking Mr. Skittles with one hand, eating a Kit Kat bar with the other. A music video blared from the television, and wadded-up candy wrappers lay heaped and scattered on the floor next to him. "You're supposed to be at work, Ma," he managed between bites and guffaws.

"And you're supposed to have half a brain, goofball! Is this something you do all the time, or do you use illegal drugs only on occasions when the police already have you under suspicion?"

She picked up a magazine and whacked him upside the head. "Get up and get this mess cleaned up. Then go take a shower while I air the house out. Try to get a foot on the ground, boy. You've got some explaining to do."

Sally could almost see the wheels turn in his skull as Jerry Jeff got to his feet, still cradling the cat. Pot paranoia warred with marijuana euphoria, and then the giggles were gone and he'd moved into sulky teen mode. "Give me a break, Mom. I mean, didn't you and Sally and all your friends smoke pot? Didn't Uncle Dickie do stuff that was even worse? What kind of hypocrite are you?"

"The kind that can kick your ass. Don't start that shit with me, Jerry Jeff Walker Davis. Just because I killed a lot of brain cells, that doesn't mean I have to like it when you start obliterating the few you've apparently got. I'm not taking the blame—I don't buy your 'Mamas, Don't Let Your Babies Grow Up to Be Potheads' crap. Now go get in the damn shower. Your taste in incense sucks."

He slouched off then, but as he trudged up the stairs, Sally heard a chuckle escape him. It suddenly occurred to her that it might be a lot easier to get answers out of him stoned than straight. Whatever he'd been smoking, it looked as if it had been strong enough that a shower wouldn't sober him up. If she could get Delice to cool down, he might say a lot more than he meant to.

Delice was slamming around, cussing and throwing windows open. Sally went over to the couch and began picking up candy wrappers. Did kids these days still call the stoner's sugar binges "mad munchies"?

She wondered if what Jerry Jeff was hiding had anything to do with the fact that he was smoking dope.

"So is this the first time you've caught him getting loaded?" she asked gently.

"How could you tell?" Delice snapped back.

"Hey, I'd be pissed too. Especially given his situation with the cops."

Delice stomped into the kitchen to open more windows. Sally followed. "So what are you going to do about it?"

"Oh, for starters, rip his room apart, find his stash, flush it, and then tear him limb from limb," said Delice.

Sally nodded. "Sounds reasonable to me. Do you suppose he figured you'd be this furious if you found out?"

Delice pulled open a cupboard, found a glass, filled it with water, and drank it down. "No. I *suppose* he thought I'd be a hell of a lot madder even than I am. He knows what it's like when I'm really in orbit." And then she looked at Sally with misery in her eyes. "He's all I've got."

Sally'd never had kids, of course, but at that moment, looking at her dear old friend, she knew how children could shatter your heart. "He's a good boy, Dee. A hard worker. He goes after what he cares about. He loves you."

Delice was not one for crying, and as the tears came into her eyes, she flung them away with the sleeve of her satin cowboy shirt. "I know. I just don't get this. What's wrong with him?"

Sally didn't want to upset her more by being too nice. Then again, the woman obviously needed comforting. Sally obliged, and for a long moment they stood in the kitchen clinging to each other. "Maybe," Sally said softly, "it's just this. Just the reefer. If he expected you to go nuclear on him, maybe that's what he's been hiding from you, from the cops. As you so kindly pointed out to him, doing dope is illegal. He's only fourteen. It probably looks like a pretty big deal to him. Maybe that's all there is to it. It's a place to start, anyhow."

The hug had helped. They sat down at the kitchen table. "Think back, Dee. Remember when we were getting wasted? I seem to recall stoned conversations that went in a hundred different directions. Maybe they were a little light on coherence, but we covered a lot of ground. Put him at ease. Make him feel like you're on his side. If you don't holler him deaf and dumb, I bet he'll talk."

Delice put her elbows on the table, and rested her chin in her hands. "Are you suggesting that I take advantage of his intoxicated state to worm information out of him?"

"Exactly," said Sally.

"Well, in that case, maybe you'd better stick around and help him relax. He does think you're cool."

"Of course he does," Sally said. "I am cool."

"For someone old," Delice added.

Sally gave her a baleful stare.

Ten minutes later Jerry Jeff walked into the kitchen, hair wet and shoulders damp under his white T-shirt, handsome, vulnerable, spacy, and contrite. "I'm sorry, Ma," he said. "Really, really sorry. I don't want to make you mad or sad."

That was all it took. Now they were on his side.

"Oh God, Jaje," Delice said, rising and wrapping her arms around him, heedless of more dark water spots spattering her shiny shirt. "Just tell me what's going on. Let me help."

"You know, JJ," Sally put in softly, "nobody's going to lock you up for smoking marijuana. Your uncle's got lots better things to do with his time and his jail. Just for the moment, let's not worry about what doing drugs is doing to you, and talk about something a little different."

Jerry Jeff looked relieved and confused. "Yeah. What do you mean?" He sat down. There was a bowl of fruit on the table. He couldn't help himself; he reached out and snagged a banana.

Delice started right in. "How long," she began, working very hard at keeping her voice steady, "have you been getting high?"

Thickly, through a mouthful of banana, he replied, "I just started in the spring. I haven't done it that often, Mom, I swear. This is the first time I've ever bought it myself."

Before Delice could push further, Sally kicked her under the table. "Okay, JJ—so you're telling us this isn't a habit with you."

He finished the banana in three bites. "No. It's just kind of something I've done for fun now and then. Lots of kids at Laramie High get stoned every morning before school, but I never did anything like that. Just weekends and stuff. It relaxes me."

"What the hell do you need relaxing from?" Delice exclaimed. "You've got a roof over your head, all you can eat—"

"Mom, please," he said.

"Yes, Delice, please," Sally added, then turned back to Jerry Jeff. "I can understand. You've spent the week working and rodeo-ing. There's been a death in the family, and everybody's upset. The police have been hassling you. It's Friday afternoon. I can see why you'd feel like doing a number and kicking back."

Jerry Jeff rolled his eyes. "Doing a number?"

"Old," Delice told Sally. "Not cool."

"Okay. Anyhow, JJ, what I'm trying to say is that we've got some notion of how you're feeling. And even if your mom busted you, she's not going to make a federal case out of it."

"No," Delice agreed, "but I am going to ask you to hand over all your stuff, and I'm going to get rid of it."

"I know," Jerry Jeff said, reaching in his back pocket, pulling out a rolled baggie full of dried green vegetation and setting it on the table. "I figured you would. This is all there is, I swear it."

Delice picked up the bag, opened it, took a whiff, nodded. "You haven't been doing any other drugs?" she asked.

JJ shook his head. "Just weed. I know people who do all kinds of stuff, but I'm not into it. Seriously, Mom, you've gotta believe me." Mr. Skittles, toenails clicking on the kitchen floor, approached Jerry Jeff and then sprang into his lap. Kitten sympathy.

"What other drugs do they do?" Delice pursued.

The boy looked troubled. "Probably anything you can think of, and some things you never heard of."

"How do they get it?" Sally wanted to know.

He looked at her as if she were an idiot. "How do you think? Look, I don't want to get anybody in trouble. Let's just leave it at me, okay Sally? I gave my mom everything I have, and I promise not to do it again. Isn't that enough?"

"All right. We'll leave it at you. Where'd you buy this lid?" Delice zipped the baggie closed and put it back on the table.

And now, for the first time, the boy looked like he was thinking about crying. "Do I really have to say?"

His mother took his hands. "Yes, honey, you do. I need to know."

He looked at the table, struggled with his composure, and ultimately lost. One choked sob. Silence. They waited. When he raised his eyes, Sally thought she'd never seen anybody look that unhappy. "I bought it from Monette."

Sally and Delice exchanged anxious glances. Neither was surprised, but it wasn't reassuring news. "When?" Sally asked.

"Last weekend. She met me out at the fairgrounds."

Too far to walk. And Scotty had said that Monette's car wasn't
working. "How did she get out there?"

"A guy drove her."

Sally had some sympathy for Scotty Atkins—JJ wasn't giving
up any more than he had to, one morsel at a time. Then again, Scotty himself wasn't exactly Mr. Tell-all. "Who, Jerry Jeff? Who drove
her?"

"Come on, it doesn't matter . . ." he tried.

"Forget it, JJ. It does. I've had just about enough teenager crap.
Who was with Monette at the fairgrounds?" Delice said.

He mumbled the name.

"I'm not sure I heard you right. Speak so I can understand."
His mother was beyond cutting him an iota of slack.

"Adolph, Adolph Schwink, okay? I've roped with his brother
Herman."

As Sally had expected. "Do you think she was getting her drugs
from him?" Sally asked.

Jerry Jeff shrugged. "She didn't say. I didn't ask. He was just
there, kind of hanging around."

"Tell us exactly what happened Everything, Jerry Jeff. And
don't make me have to drag it out of you one piece at a time."

He peeled another banana. "Okay. Exactly what happened."
He chewed a large chunk of banana, swallowed. "Could I get
something to drink, Ma?"

Delice poured a glass of milk and set it in front of him,
scowling.

"Thanks. So let's see . . ." He looked down at the kitten, at his
hand caressing its fur.

"Stay on track, kid," said Sally, sensing that his brain might
be slipping out of gear. She gritted her teeth and pushed on.
"What happened when Monette and Adolph came to the fairgrounds?"

"Oh. Oh yeah. Well, it was last Saturday. I was out there getting some practice in, and checking out the stock. They showed up
just as I was finishing. That guy Adolph was driving, a little red
Japanese car of some kind—I didn't pay too much attention. We
went out to the parking lot out front, and sat in the car. Monette

rolled a joint, and we smoked it. We got pretty wasted." The milk had disappeared. Two banana peels lay flat on the table. Mr. Skittles was asleep. Jerry Jeff eyed an apple in the fruit bowl.

"Keep going," said Delice, handing him the apple.

He took a bite, chewed, swallowed. "Well, then they wanted me to show them around, so we kind of wandered around the stock pens and the arena and the waiting areas and all that. I don't remember, exactly. We were pretty messed up."

Sally was getting hungry watching him power through every edible item in sight. "All right. I want you to think hard, JJ. Where was your gear while you were showing them around?"

He closed his eyes, concentrating.

"Think!" his mother snarled. "Don't just zone out on us!"

He squinched his eyes shut tighter as he worked the apple down to the core. "Let me see. Okay, when they got there, I was sitting on the tailgate of some guy's pickup. I had my duffel bag with me. When I went with them, I took it with me. Then we sat in the car. I was in front with Adolph, and Monette sat in back. At first I had the duffel on my lap, but after a while I put it on the backseat next to her."

"Was the bag zipped?"

Jerry Jeff looked sheepish. "Er, actually, the zipper's been broken for a while. I've been kind of shoving it together with safety pins. When I remember. It works okay."

"So Monette could easily have taken something out of the bag, yes?" Sally asked.

"I guess so."

"Like your piggin' string," Delice added.

"Uh-huh."

"And she could have just stuck it under the seat while you weren't looking?" Sally's turn.

"She could have." Apple finished.

"And then, when you all finished smoking the joint, you picked up your bag and took it where?"

"Hmm. Give me a second. Oh yeah, since they wanted to look around, I went to put it in the contestants' locker room, but it was all locked up. So I ended up sticking it inside the VIP lounge."

"The lounge wasn't locked?"

JJ thought about it. "Nope. Usually it is, but sometimes, when there's a lot of traffic in and out, they leave it open. There were a bunch of committee guys out there that afternoon, doing stuff to get ready for Jubilee Days."

"Do you usually leave your things in the lounge?" Sally asked.

"No. Generally I put everything in the locker room, but I already told you it was locked. But Uncle Dwayne was there, and he told me it was okay for me to leave the bag in the lounge, and pick it up later."

CHAPTER 22
FABULOUS FOOD AND
TOXIC WASTE

SALLY WAS JUST DYING to tell him everything she'd learned that day, but when Hawk got home from Cheyenne, he had to call Molly Wood. Once again, no answer. Sally heard him leave the message: "This is Josiah Green. Molly, please call me as soon as you can." Josiah. It made Sally grin.

But Hawk wasn't smiling. "I wonder what the hell's going on out there," he said.

"She's probably out by her pond, looking at ducks," Sally said, trying to reassure him, but a little concerned herself. "Or maybe she's visiting a friend, or buying groceries in town. Don't worry. I'm sure you'll hear back from her."

"Yeah, I guess," he said, getting a can of club soda out of the refrigerator. "I'm going to go take a bath. I need to think."

Think. Okay. When absolutely necessary, Sally could manage

patience. Living in such a small house, they'd learned, after quite a number of snarling exchanges, that there was wisdom in claiming and ceding each other as much domestic space as they could find. He sloshed in the tub. She sat in the backyard and played her guitar and gave her voice the kind of workout she knew it needed, getting ready for the gig the next night. Then the bath was hers. He weeded the garden. Both thought. She had to admit, it helped.

And so they passed the time until they dressed to go out for the first decent meal they'd had all week. She wore a slinky black dress, high-heeled sandals, the gold drop earrings he'd bought her for her birthday, the emerald ring her mother had left her. He wore a black silk shirt, black jeans, polished boots. They gave each other the once-over and smiled. Tonight we're settin' the woods on fire.

Downtown Laramie looked like the governor had declared Wyoming Pedestrian Day. Most of the strollers wore cowboy hats, and many were a little unsteady on their stacked-up, slope-heeled boots. The bars were hopping with people hanging on after happy hour, and the restaurants had lines out the doors. Out on Old Ivinson Street, Sally and Hawk picked their way among revelers carrying plastic to-go cups that smelled like Coors Light and Southern Comfort.

Most people navigated pretty well, but there were those who didn't, with mixed results. A compactly built blond staggered into a chunky baldy with his name burned into the back of his belt, and it was true love. A tourist in shorts and fanny pack stumbled against a Harley, and the owner, in sleeveless leather vest and greasy jeans, objected. But before the objections became too strenuous, one of Laramie's finest intervened, reminding the motorcyclist that Jubilee Days was a lot more fun for people who weren't incarcerated.

The crowd at the Yippie I O café was short on hats and long on attitude. It was the best restaurant within a two-hundred-mile-radius—farther, if you didn't count Denver, and maybe farther even if you did. The decor was pure nouveau cowboy glam—original pressed-tin ceiling, tall walls painted to resemble blue sky with puffy clouds, dark gleaming floor, and in between, a color scheme that Delice had once described as "a cross between a Hereford steer and the Castro District." The showpiece decorating touch was the bar, a crimson resin swoosh mounted on a museum display of cowboy boots embedded in Lucite. In the open kitchen, the brick chimney of a wood-burning oven was festooned with a cow skull wearing a fez. The philanthropic owner, Burt Langham, and his genius chef partner, Frank "John Boy" Walton, had recently been inducted into the local lodge of the Shriners, for civic generosity that evidently overbalanced any uptight homophobic tendencies among the boosters. Rumor had it that Burt and John Boy would even be piloting mini-Corvettes in the Jubilee Days parade.

Brit was at the host podium tonight, looking luscious as always but glowering at a couple who appeared to be leaving in a huff. "Assholes!" she hissed to Sally.

"Aren't you supposed to greet us with 'Good evening. Welcome to the café'?" asked Hawk.

"Yeah yeah. Those idiots claimed we lost their reservation. Said they made one a week ago—said 'some young woman' answered the phone. I guess it's possible, but, like, the only young woman who even bothers to pick up the phone here is me, and I sure as hell don't screw up reservations!" Brit fumed

"Temper, temper, now darlin'," said Sally. "You're in the hospitality industry."

"Hospitality, shit!" Brit pronounced through her teeth, snagging menus and stomping toward a small corner table, private but with the best view of the action. "I swore I'd never set foot in a restaurant again, but Burt kept upping the ante. If it weren't for a month of free meals and double overtime, I'd be kickin' back at the rodeo watching somebody else work."

"Don't forget to ask Herman about Adolph," Sally reminded her.

"We're going dancing later," Brit murmured. "Leave him in my hands." Then she pulled out chairs upholstered in brown and white cowhide and stood back, squared her shoulders, smoothed her silk skirt and blouse, and shot them a smile so dazzling that Sally wondered briefly if Brit had manic tendencies, or just a great game face. "Time to please the people," Brit said. "Enjoy your dinner."

For such a nouvy-groovy place, the table setting was classic—

white linen tablecloth, cut-glass vase with fresh flowers, creamy candles, silver and crystal. Their waiter, clad in Levi's, well-worn boots, a crisp white shirt, and a wide tie decorated with a hand-painted giant saguaro cactus, appeared to understand the hospitality concept rather better than Brit. He said his name was Mike, and the special was a huckleberry duck breast, and they had some very nice sushi-grade tuna that the chef did with a wasabi butter and a bouquetiere of Asian vegetables, but personally he'd always been partial to the steaks. There were a few other things he'd be happy to tell them about, but first they'd probably want something to drink, right?

Boy howdy.

When Hawk ordered two Jim Beams, Mike the waiter allowed as how Burt Langham made the best highballs this side of New York City, and maybe they'd like to try something a little more uptown. "Okay," Hawk said. "Tell Burt we're in his hands. Just make sure it's mainly something brown."

Shortly, they were sipping Manhattans out of martini glasses. Sally felt her heart rate begin, finally, to slow down. Hawk was savoring his cocktail, torturing her. Finally he said, "So honey, how was your day?"

Lucky for her, Burt Langham and John Boy Walton believed that restaurant diners should be far enough apart that people wouldn't be listening in on seductions in progress at neighboring tables. The high tin ceiling made the place just noisy enough that she could fill Hawk in on everything she'd learned since her unappetizing breakfast at the Wrangler that morning, without fear of setting the rumor mill whirring. She talked all the way through the ordering phase and well into their salads (*insalate caprese* for her, romaine and Roquefort for him).

Hawk listened. He had the gift of sitting in repose, utterly focused, eyes wide and intense behind his spectacles, taking in everything. Eating didn't seem to break his concentration, although from time to time he put down his fork and rested his beautiful hands on the table, barely clasped. Watching Hawk listen as she talked produced an effect on Sally that some people got from reading erotic poetry.

He finished the last of his salad and spoke. "It doesn't really surprise me that Monette was tied up with JJ's piggin' string, or that she sold him dope, or that he's smoking it. What they found out at the autopsy is horrible, of course. But it's not astonishing news. The part about the garbage from the Wrangler ending up at the crime scene is a little puzzling, isn't it? Why would somebody haul litter all the way out there?"

Sally shrugged. "Trying to make it look like she'd been partying with lowlifes, I guess. Figure it this way—imagine if we hadn't found the body when we did. It's possible that she wouldn't have been discovered until the next morning, at the earliest—we got a late start, and from what I saw, we were the last people up there Monday afternoon. Overnight, the litter would have blown around, but it might still look like a party scene. One way or another, it was meant to leave a false trail and confuse the cops."

"A false trail, left by somebody who somehow managed to snag Jerry Jeff's piggin' string," said Hawk.

"Maybe. Maybe not. Maybe Monette had it with her. After all, she'd had the chance to lift it last Saturday when she and Adolph Schwink and the kid were getting high. Of course, Adolph could have taken it, but we know he didn't go up to the Devil's Playground that afternoon. So if he stole the piggin' string, somebody else would have had to get it from him. I asked Brit to get Herman to lean on Adolph a little."

Hawk pressed his lips together. "What about the brother?" he asked.

"Herman? No!" Sally exclaimed. "I just don't see it. He seems way too wholesome."

"So did Ted Bundy," said Hawk. They'd moved on from the Manhattans to a decent Merlot. He swirled the wine in his glass, tasted it, and said, "From what you've told me, Dwayne had a chance at the piggin' string too, when JJ left his bag in the VIP lounge."

"So did anybody else who went in or out of there. Scotty ought to have fun questioning the rodeo committee this weekend, huh?"

"Scotty. Yeah. Hmph," said Hawk.

Mike the waiter arrived to take their salad plates. The pause in the conversation gave Hawk an opening to change the subject. "I'm not sure I'm comfortable with the idea of old Sheldon Stover chasing you around. Ridiculous as he is, it bugs me."

"For God's sake, Hawk, of all things to worry about! I mean, let's face it, Sheldon's experimental ethnography is pretty low priority at the moment."

"It's not that, Mustang." He held the wine to the candlelight, gazing at the glass. "What bothers me most is that even that moron could get close enough to hurt you without your even noticing. The events of the past week don't seem to have had a good effect on your powers of observation."

No point being defensive. "Okay. I might be a little rattled. But I'm paying attention. And after all, I did manage to dig up some interesting stuff in the library and the archives today. Seems that ruin you found up at Happy Jack is an old railroad tie plant—"

"My turn," he interrupted. "Let me tell you what I found in Cheyenne, and then we can compare notes."

He knew what she knew, and more. The tie plant, closed down in 1963, had been operating on leased federal land, not by the railroad itself, but by a contractor called Golden Eagle Enterprises. It wasn't entirely clear why the plant had closed—the interstate hadn't yet been completed, so the rail lines were still the main conduits for freight, in and out of Wyoming. "I found that much in the state Revenue Department records," Hawk said. "That took me a while. I was looking for tax records on the railroad's holdings in Albany County. This Golden Eagle outfit was buried pretty deep, and there wasn't much documentation there. They paid their bills, as far as I can tell, and then just folded their tent and melted off into the shifting sands.

"That seemed a little drifty to me. So I decided to play a hunch and went over to the Department of Environmental Quality. Are you enjoying your steak?" he asked.

Sally gently sliced off another morsel of succulent tenderloin *persillade*. She nodded enthusiastically, mouth full.

Hawk looked down at his two-inch-thick New York strip. "Me too. Maybe I shouldn't go on with this story."

"No problem. My stomach is plenty strong enough for fabulous food and tales of toxic waste," Sally insisted.

"You asked for it," he answered. "All right. When I asked the clerk at the DEQ for anything he had on the tie plant, he hemmed and hawed and talked about 'proprietary information' and stuff like that, but I kept reminding him that he was supposed to be in the business of providing access to public records. Finally he went behind a door and came out with a nice, thick file.

"Looks like for thirty-five years, the old plant just sat there decaying, dust to dust and all that. But then two years ago the state geological survey happened to hire a new graduate of the UW program in groundwater hydrology, who happened also to be an amateur photographer who had a thing for industrial ruins. He followed one of the dried-up wastewater ditches downhill, snapping away, and came to a spot where the grass was dead all around the ditch. And then, lo and behold, he found the carcass of a deer that had evidently been grazing by the brown patch. He called up the game warden, who came and looked at the deer, and noticed that there were blisters on its mouth."

Sally put her fork down. "Maybe you were right."

"Okay. I'll leave out the dead animal stuff. One thing led to another, and by last year, the Environmental Quality Department had started doing soil and water sampling downstream of the mill."

"Water sampling? In the beaver pond on that swap property, for instance?" Sally was pretty sure she knew where this was going.

"Yeah. The pond and the creek checked out clean." Hawk carved off a big bite of his steak and chewed with relish.

"Clean! Well, hell. I mean, that's good news, but I have a feeling that's not the end of the story," Sally said.

"Right. The surface water is fine, but there's a bit of a soil and groundwater contamination plume spreading underground, downstream from the old plant."

"You're kidding! How come it hasn't been in the newspapers? How come they haven't declared it a toxic site or something?" This was outrageous.

Hawk gave her a long, tender look. "You know, Sal, in some ways you're so naive. It's kind of sweet."

Sally glared. "Thanks. Spare me the condescension and get to the point."

He laughed. "The point is that the soil sampling found enough creosote, dioxin, and PCBs to suggest that any wise stockman would think three or four times before letting his herd loose on the national forest up there. More importantly for our purposes, I'd guess that Molly Wood ought to be very wary of buying a piece of property where it would be, to say the least, imprudent to dig a well."

"Why? What would drinking the water do to a human?"

Now Hawk put his own fork down. "How many ways are there for a person to get cancer?"

She thought that over. Too much to get her head around, so she ate some steak and focused on the details. "Is it clear that the toxic stuff came from the tie plant?"

"What do you think, Sally? Beavers make dioxin? You sound like Ronald Reagan announcing that trees cause pollution."

Poor Hawk. He was working on ironic detachment, but stuff like this killed him. She leaned over, touched a finger to his cheek, left it there, stroking lightly. "So back to my original naive question," she said. "Why aren't the newspapers all over this?"

They were sharing an order of fresh asparagus. He selected a spear, ate it tip first. "Let's see. At a guess, how many toxic waste sites do you think there are in the state of Wyoming?"

"Absolutely no idea," she answered, sipping wine.

"Well, let's put it this way. There are a shitload more of them than are identified, and out of the ones they've listed, only a few are likely to get cleaned up. It costs an ungodly fortune to remediate even one site, and the agencies in charge have to set priorities. A site that looks like it could poison, say, the entire city of Casper will get attention first. One that might affect a major ranch, or some endangered wildlife, or what have you, will be considered a long time before some mess that might be nasty, but doesn't mess up the scenery and doesn't appear to be having a direct effect on people or any crucial resources. It takes a ton of time and money to clean up these sites. This one isn't even on the screen."

"But if somebody were to build on contaminated ground, and think about drinking the groundwater, wouldn't that give the state or the EPA or whoever cause for action?" Sally asked.

"Hard to say. My guess is that the Wyoming DEQ is pretty overburdened. And just think about the costs. Not only would they have to do the science, but they'd also have to put people to work tracking down the polluters. As far as I can tell, this Golden Eagle Enterprises just closed up shop and disappeared after 1963. And you haven't even started the job of cleaning the place up."

Hawk shivered a little. "If you think this one site sounds like a gigantic job, consider the whole state. Wyoming's been strip-mined, oil-pumped, dug up, and flushed out for the last hundred years. Some of the dirtiest industries in the world have paid a lot of bills around here. Not to mention the fact that our agricultural brethren have used their share of powerful fertilizers and pesticides." Now he took a big slug of wine. "Prosperity ain't pretty.

"Then, of course, there's the fact that enforcement of even the fairly loose laws on the books depends, as always, on the will of our splendid public officials—the ones appointed to clean things up and, of course, the ones we elect to provide the money for the job."

Great. Happy Jack was turning into Love Canal, and when it came down to it, the only ones who could save the day were . . . bureaucrats and legislators. People dependent on the will and the generosity of a Wyoming electorate famous for believing that the government worked best when it hardly ever worked. "What about the feds? Shouldn't they be called in?"

"Be assured, they're on the job. That DEQ file was full of correspondence with the EPA regional office in Denver. EPA promised to 'maintain oversight.' "

"Uh-huh. The same way a doctor says, 'Let's keep an eye on that cough,' as if he were going to be sitting around fixing cups of hot tea and listening to you wheeze instead of cashing HMO checks and heading for the golf course." Sally grabbed Hawk's hand. "You've got to get hold of Molly. This is really important, Hawk."

"I know." He took a deep breath. A sip of wine. "I'm wondering why she hasn't returned my calls. Maybe I should head out to Wood's Hole tomorrow morning and make sure she's okay."

And that was when they both noticed a loud cheerful party, barreling from the front door of the restaurant toward the bar.

"Bust out the Dom Perignon, Burt!" shouted Nattie Langham, one arm around Dwayne's neck, the other around Marsh Carhart's waist, Sheldon Stover at their heels. "We just made the deal of the century!"

Sally and Hawk exchanged stricken stares. "Maybe not tomorrow," he said. "Maybe it wouldn't be a bad thing to head on out to Centennial tonight."

CHAPTER 23
AN APPRECIATION
FOR AVOCETS

GOD BLESS JUBILEE DAYS. Law enforcement personnel who might ordinarily be patrolling the Centennial road were otherwise occupied. The speedometer on the Mustang went up to 140, and before the night was over, Hawk might use all of it. The front end was shuddering, and so was Sally.

A distinct clunk, followed by a clanging, rapidly fading off behind them.

"That noise," said Sally, "was some part of the car falling off. It tends to happen at high speeds."

"Car's still running," said Hawk. "Guess it was nothing too crucial."

Hawk was in a hurry. He had, however, insisted on stopping off at home, just long enough to grab his daypack. It sat on the console between them, top flap flipped back, drawstring opening loose enough for him to get a hand in and out with ease. It hadn't occurred to Sally to wonder why, until they were hauling ass across the prairie.

"What's with the daypack?" she asked.

"I copied some of the documents from the DEQ," he told her. "I want Molly to see for herself."

"Really?" Sally had a bad feeling. "That's it?"

"I just like to be prepared," he said lamely.

"Prepared? What the hell do you have in there that you could possibly imagine Molly wouldn't have?" Sally asked testily.

"Er, the cell phone?" Hawk tried.

"It would've been a good idea. We could phone ahead from the road. But it's not in there, unless you took it out of my pack. We all know what a big fan you are of those things," she said. "Unless, that is, Smith and Wesson is now making cellular telephones."

Hawk grinned weakly.

"So what are you going to do, Hawk? If there's somebody out there holding a gun to Molly's head and making her sign away her ranch, are you going to walk in, yank open your backpack, whip out your pistol, and shoot the fucker? Or are you going to go in there with your gun drawn, and maybe she's sitting around doing needlepoint, and you scare her to death? Or maybe she's lying in bed, like any good Wyoming matron, with her own loaded piece tucked under her pillow, and she's a quick-draw artist, and she shoots you right through the heart? This is a real estate deal, not a duel to the death. What's the point here?"

"Relax. I'm just being cautious," he told her.

"Cautious? A gun is cautious?" she persisted.

Hawk ignored the question. "In all likelihood, the worst that will happen is that we wake Molly up. It'll be embarrassing, but that's the chance we take. We've got to let her know about that underground plume. I hope to Christ she hasn't actually signed anything. Although if she has, she can probably get the document declared void, on account of bad faith on the part of the sellers."

Sally had to think about that. "Bad faith? Do you think the people Nattie and Dwayne are representing know about the contamination from the tie plant?"

A quick, sharp, sidewise glance: He was, thank God, keeping his eyes on the road. "Look—Marsh Carhart's supposed to be such an expert on everything. Either he's built his rep as a brilliant ecologist on the same kind of bullshit science as his hogwash about rape, or he's not quite that dumb and he's all too well aware of what's seeping down from upstream, but for his own corrupt reasons is pretending that the swap site is clean. Think about it. It took you and me exactly two days to dig up the information on the tie plant. He's supposedly been studying the site for weeks, at the least. Is it even remotely possible he wouldn't have spotted the problem?"

"He's not a geologist or a historian," Sally said. "And after all, his consultant on the human factor side of things is Sheldon. That alone would be enough to paralyze any possibility of knowing what the hell's going on."

Hawk couldn't help chuckling. The mention of Sheldon did that to him. "Well, even with the considerable handicap of Sheldon, my money's on Carhart orchestrating, or at least being involved in a cover-up."

Sally looked at him. "But he saw you up at Happy Jack. And Sheldon followed me to the library, so they know we're on to them. Do you think Marsh Carhart would follow us out here and try to stop us from talking to Molly?"

Hawk shrugged. "Who knows? One way or another, we've got to go tell her what we know. Either Molly's made her decision and signed off and we can't change her mind, or she hasn't, and Dwayne and them are jumping the gun before the paperwork's done, in which case we have a chance." He paused. "Just for the record, I don't mind at all getting you the hell out of town tonight. I don't like the way guys have been leaping out at you all week long."

She looked, again, at the backpack between them. "That's why you wanted a gun. You're worried that whoever's been following me, still is. You've decided I need a bodyguard."

"No. You need a keeper," he grumbled, standing on the accelerator and sending the car into a fit of Jesus shakes.

This, from a man who ordinarily drove with such maddening care that it made her think of rocking chairs and shuffleboard courts. "Please recall that you are driving *my* 1964 Mustang," she told him.

"Ninteen sixty-four and a half," he replied primly.

"Exactly. I want you to know that if you wreck this thing, and we end up as hamburger all over the highway, I will personally hunt you down, in heaven or hell or whatever rodent body you've been reincarnated into, and kill you all over again."

He flashed a grin. "This was supposed to be our romantic night. Sorry, baby."

Sally leaned back in her bucket seat, closed her eyes, and sighed. "Well, at least we had a couple of good steaks."

Hawk backed off the pedal, slowing the car to a manageably maniacal speed. High above, the sky was black and very clear, and this far from the lights of town, a million stars shone bright. He eased out a hand and stroked down the front of her body, chin to inside of her thigh. "The night is young."

For a time they drove on in silence. At last Sally said, "I wonder where Bone was today?"

Hawk grimaced. "No doubt pursuing his own inquiries in his engaging way," he said.

She took a breath. "You know, it's occurred to me that he knows who pushed me into the bucking chute."

"I thought he asked *you* who'd shoved you," Hawk said.

"Not exactly. He asked me if I knew anything about who had. As Bone himself pointed out to me, he's spent his share of time conversing with the cops. He's a maggot, but he's not stupid, and he knows a thing or two about getting information without giving any. The main thing he learned from our little encounter yesterday morning was that I didn't know anything he hadn't already found out. And the main thing I learned was that he thought Monette was blackmailing someone, and that he's looking for 'payback.' Whatever that means—maybe money. Maybe revenge."

"Maybe both," said Hawk, looking at the bruise on Sally's arm, the souvenir of her morning in the park with Bone. "Why not? You know, honey, I'll be just as glad if you don't run into him again. He's got his own agenda, he appears to be loaded most of the time, and I don't think he'd take kindly to anybody getting in his way. I think it's time we left the murder to the cops. You don't need to treat this as your own personal crusade on behalf of all honky-tonk angels, retired and active."

Hawk had a point. And for now, anyway, they were headed in another direction. The Mustang fairly flew down the dirt driveway to Wood's Hole. Molly's Expedition was parked in the turnaround, and next to it a late-model, dark green sedan with Colorado plates: rental car. A few lights were on in the house. Hawk slung his day-pack over his shoulder.

"Easy, big guy," Sally said to him. "If somebody besides Molly answers, what are you going to tell them?"

"Oh boy, glad you thought of that," he said. "We do need a cover story. I can just say I'm a friend who got worried when she didn't respond to any of my phone messages." With that he was out of the car and on the way to the front door. As cover stories went, Hawk's was at least a marvel of simplicity.

Sally caught up with him as a woman opened the door only as far as a chain lock permitted. She was about the same age as Sally and Hawk, petite, dark-haired. Her fierce, penetrating blue eyes told the rest of the story. Obviously this was Molly's daughter, Alice Wood, and she was clearly wondering what the hell two strangers were doing coming to her door, way out in the country, after ten o'clock on a Friday night. "Yes?" she said.

"I'm Josiah Green," Hawk told her, his voice muted, "I'm a geology professor at the university, a friend of Molly's. I've been trying to get in touch with her for a couple of days When she didn't return my calls, I started to worry, and thought I'd better come see if she was okay. This is my friend, Sally Alder."

"Oh," said Alice. "You're the one who's been leaving the phone messages." She shut the door, and they heard her take off the chain. She introduced herself. "Come in. I'm sorry, my mother isn't here. There's been an accident."

"Oh no!" Sally said. "I hope it's nothing serious."

"Too soon to tell," Alice answered, a little abruptly for Sally's taste. "I came into town yesterday—we have some pressing family business. And this afternoon my mother fell and broke her ankle. I took her to the hospital in Laramie. The doctors are doing tests. There's some fear that she might have had a stroke."

"A stroke? Why would they think that?" Sally asked.

"It's a pretty common cause of falls in older people. My mother likes to think she's immortal, but none of us is," Alice explained.

"So is she having trouble moving or speaking?" Hawk inquired.

"Obviously she's not moving very well, with a broken ankle," Alice said, "but I'm afraid it would take more than a small stroke to prevent my mother from speaking."

"I guess that's reassuring, but I'm so sorry," said Hawk. "Is there anything we can do?"

"Not at this point," said Alice. "They've made her as comfortable as possible, and we did, thank God, manage to get her a private room. I've been there most of the day, and my brother will be here tomorrow. We'll get by."

Why did Sally have the distinct feeling that Alice viewed her mother's medical problem as an inconvenience, rather than a personal and emotional trauma? "Is she conscious?" Sally asked.

Alice snorted. "She wants to be running the show. I'm sure she's in a lot of pain, but she won't let them give her anything. I've tried to convince her to take something, but she won't listen to me—never has." Alice shook her head, then looked at the ceiling, then sighed, shoulders heaving. "It's been an exhausting day, but there's nothing more to do, so I thought I'd come out here, catch some sleep, and pack up some of her things to take back in the morning."

Alice looked worn down, no doubt about it. But Sally knew that if it was her own mother lying in a hospital bed in agony, she sure wouldn't be way out at the ranch, complaining. She'd be sitting in a chair in the room, bothering the nurses for ice packs at the very least (and probably hassling Molly, as Alice evidently had, to quit being such a hero and take some painkillers).

"Listen," said Hawk. "We'd like to send her some flowers . . ."

Flowers! Sally's eyebrows went up. Hawk didn't send flowers. The thought just didn't occur to him. He installed computer software, changed her oil, surprised her, on special occasions, with things that made her life easier, and she'd even managed to persuade him that gifts of jewelry were never a bad idea. But not flowers. She'd hinted, tried the ploy of sending *him* flowers, even harangued him outright, but it didn't do a damn bit of good.

He tossed her a silencing look. ". . . and maybe we could visit Molly later in the week if she has to stay there," he continued. "Can you give us her room number?"

"Three twenty-eight," said Alice. "As I said, it's one of the few private rooms in that little motel you people call a hospital." And then she hesitated. "Say, Josiah. How do you happen to know my mother anyway?"

"Birdwatching," he answered smoothly. "We share an appreciation of avocets."

An appreciation of avocets. Great. What next, a suspicion of sapsuckers?

But Alice wasn't paying attention. "Oh," she said dully, and then yawned. "Listen, I really need to get some sleep."

"Of course!" Sally exclaimed. "We're sorry we bothered you. But please don't hesitate to call if there's anything we can do to help."

"Yeah, sure," Alice said, all but pushing them out the door, shutting it quickly behind them.

"She didn't even take our number!" Sally huffed as Hawk started the car.

"She has absolutely no interest in us, or anything about her mother's life. She acted like Molly was nothing but a hassle for her. If it were my mother who'd had a stroke . . ." said Hawk.

"I know. Me too. I'd be down there drinking crummy coffee and screaming at the nurses. You're right. Alice wasn't showing a whole lot of what I'd call family feeling. Maybe the brother will be better," Sally tried.

"I hope so," Hawk said, and fell silent. They were both pretty beat; they both knew it. But then, finally, he asked, "How would you feel about going to the hospital, right now, just to check on her?"

Tenderness for him spread warmth and new energy from her head to her toes. "I would feel," she said, "like telling you how much I love you."

It was closing in on midnight by the time they got to the Ivinson Memorial Hospital. Sally heard their heels clicking down the hallway, registered the bad lighting, the linoleum floors, the walls painted colors intended to cheer and soothe, overlaid with a grimy patina of sickness and worry and pain. Under ordinary circumstances Hawk set a comfortable walking pace, but tonight Sally was hustling to keep up. No one intercepted them to quibble about visiting hours. This was Wyoming.

Light and sound spilled into the dim hallway from room 328. Molly had her bed cranked up into a sitting position, her left foot propped up and swathed in a fiberglass cast. Her skin looked papery, pale and thin, and her blue eyes glittered with the pain she evidently refused to mask. She was gripping a remote control and staring at a television mounted high on the wall. David Letterman was laughing at one of his own jokes, but Molly's mouth was grim.

Until she realized that they'd come into the room. Then shock replaced discomfort and determination. Her eyes went wide and her mouth formed an O. "What in the world are you two doing here in the middle of the night?" she asked.

No slurred speech. No evidence that she was confused, no sign of change in the muscles of her handsome, tense face. Molly Wood wasn't showing any of the common signs of stroke. Thank God.

"We heard that you were in here and came to see how you were doing," said Hawk. "If you'd been asleep, we'd have come back in the morning."

"Sleep! With an ankle that feels like it's on fire, I hardly think sleep is a possibility," she snapped.

Amazingly, Hawk laughed. Molly glared. "I'm sorry, I'm not laughing at your affliction, believe me," he said. "But your daughter told us that you might have had a stroke, and from what I see, you're sharp as a tack and mad as hell. I find that reassuring, Molly."

"Perhaps you'd like to share your opinions with my doctor. The fool is putting me through all sorts of ridiculous tests. It seems my age is justification enough for assuming that my brain is going haywire and my body is breaking down."

"I'm sure they just want to be careful," said Sally. "Preventive medicine."

Molly offered up a withering stare. "That is the purest horse manure," she said. "When they X-rayed my ankle, they diagnosed the only thing wrong with me. I did not have a stroke. I was carrying a basket of laundry across the living room to the dining room to fold the clothes. I keep a tidy house, and I'm accustomed to everything being in its place. My daughter, Alice, left her laptop and briefcase in the middle of the floor, and I couldn't see them over the laundry basket. I fell. That's the whole story."

Hawk gave Molly a long look, and at last, to Sally's astonishment, took Molly's hand. "If that's it, and you don't have any obvious symptoms of stroke, why all the alarm?"

Molly grimaced, reminding them that she was suffering. "Alice has been insistent that they consider all possibilities. And the doctors are, as always, cautious. I don't blame them, but I rather wish they weren't quite so concerned that I might sue them somewhere down the line."

Alice had insisted. It occurred to Sally that the doctors might not be the only ones thinking in legal terms. Hawk shot her a glance that told her he'd had the same idea. "Maybe you should think about letting them give you something for that ankle. Wouldn't hurt you to sleep, Molly," Hawk said.

She took a moment to answer. "Josiah," she said, "I'm not opposed to painkillers. But I don't want to take anything that could interfere with my judgment just now. I have to be able to think clearly, as you're aware. The future of my ranch, and of my family, depends on it." Molly lay her head back on the pillows. "I am worn out, and I wish this thing didn't hurt so damn much."

It was hard to see her like that, aching, spent, aging by the minute. "Your judgment can wait until morning," said Sally. "Couldn't you just try to get some sleep tonight?"

A glint of tears flickered in the blue eyes, but her words were cool and even. "I don't think you quite understand the pressure I'm under," Molly told them. "Alice has been badgering me constantly for the last two days. My son, Philip, will be here in the morning. So will Nattie and Dwayne, and Alice is coming back, of course." Molly paused for a breath. "I've agreed in principle to the land swap."

"You haven't signed anything yet, have you?" Hawk asked.

"They're bringing the papers here tomorrow. I have to think about my grandchildren," she explained.

"Molly," Sally said, "we've found some information that could change your mind. Hawk—um, Josiah—will fill you in. It won't take long. Listen to what he has to say. I promise you, we have nothing to gain or lose personally from whatever you decide, but we do care about you. And then, if you want, we'll stay here with you tonight. After a while you could let them give you a shot and try to get a little rest."

Maybe they'd caught her at the point of utter exhaustion. Maybe, since they'd shown up at midnight, and she was alone and hurting, she'd decided to trust them. "As long as I don't have to talk," she said, closing her eyes a little too tightly.

So Hawk told the tale to the tired, gritty ranchwoman. When he finished, he asked if Molly understood what it all meant, and she nodded. "I'll have to think about it," she said. "I want to sleep."

Sally found a nurse, who arrived, presently, with a hypodermic. And then, in the dark and on into the dawn, they sat by the bed. Molly slept fitfully, reaching out, in wakeful moments, for a hand. Hawk never moved from her side.

SATURDAY

CHAPTER 24
MESSAGE IN A BOTTLE

AT SIX A.M. A NURSE came to take Molly's vital signs, and woke them all up. Sally had conked out in the chair in the room, a piece of furniture upholstered in avocado-green vinyl, a material engineered to stick to human flesh. The chair had proven not to be Posturepedic. Her back hurt, her knees ached, and every muscle in her neck and shoulders was knotted up dense as rock.

As she pried her eyes open, she saw Hawk raise his head from the edge of the bed and blink. He wore his glasses slightly askew—he hadn't meant to fall asleep. Now he took them off, rubbed his eyes and the bridge of his nose, wagged his head to loosen up his own neck.

Sally had done her share of all-nighters over the years, not a few during the high times of Jubilee Days. This was the first Jubilee Night she'd pulled in a hospital. Let the good times roll.

She caught Molly surveying Hawk with a hint of a fond smile on her face, but the minute Molly saw Sally looking at her, she replaced affection with dignity, as if she always woke up in hospital beds, in command.

"Well!" said Molly, looking at the two of them but addressing the nurse who was taking her blood pressure, "I nearly feel as if I've slept in my clothes myself. I wonder if you'd be kind enough to give me a sponge bath and to find my hairbrush before they bring my breakfast. I would also like to brush my teeth!" she concluded emphatically.

"We'll give you some privacy," said Sally, hauling the still half-asleep Hawk to his feet.

"Thank you," said Molly. "My foot still hurts, but I'm feeling better this morning. You might as well go on home. Philip is due in by nine, and I expect Alice will be here before long."

Sally stretched, felt and heard the muscles cracking in her back. "Whatever you say."

"Go home, go home," Molly insisted. "I'll be fine. I remember what you told me last night, Josiah, and I'll be thinking very seriously about what your news might mean for my plans. I am grateful to you both for staying the night, but there's nothing more you can do for me."

The nurse unwrapped the blood pressure cuff, told Molly, "I'll be right back with your bath," and walked out of the room.

"Now get out of here, I mean it!" Molly told them. "The last thing I want is for Alice to arrive and find you here. She'd never in a million years be able to understand why a couple of strangers would have spent the night here in the room with her mother."

Sally doubted if Alice could have understood why even a daughter would do such a thing.

"I've always heard," Hawk said as he drove them home, one hand kneading the back of his neck, "that people hate hospitals because they think they make you sick. Now I get it."

"I thought Molly looked a lot better this morning," Sally said. "She had some color in her face, and she was obviously well enough to boss people around."

"She looked better than I feel," Hawk said. "I need a bed real bad."

Sally didn't even have the strength to agree. Her lips felt as if they'd been glued together, and she was sure someone had come in during the night and thrown a bucket of rock salt into her eyes. "The parade doesn't start until noon," she muttered. "We could sleep until eleven forty-five."

After her sojourn in the green chair, she could have slept until September. But she woke up at ten that Saturday morning. Maybe she was just too wasted to realize how bad off she was, after only four hours' real sleep, but she felt refreshed and ready for the day. Perhaps it was one of those rare moments of instant karma: Spend a night in the hospital with somebody who needs you, and get back a little of what you need yourself. We all shine on.

She was careful not to wake Hawk as she slipped out to shower, performed her coffee sacrament, glanced at the *Boomerang*. Herman Schwink got some great coverage as a local hero contending for the team-roping title. No mention of the Monette Bandy case, but then what was new there? The paper that Saturday morning was predictably dominated by big photos of bucking animals and flying cowboys, and advertising for fast food, Western wear, automotive supplies, and weekend entertainment.

She had an hour and a half before heading off to join the parade contingent that was marching in memory of Monette, and in homage to Wyoming women. Plenty of time to check her email. She booted up her machine, and when the monkey had stopped screeching, she typed her password, logged into her mailbox, and was relieved to find a communique from Edna McCaffrey in Kathmandu.

A message in a bottle.

Edna, as always, was having amazing adventures, which she described in elegant, funny prose. Ordinarily Sally took time to relish Edna's exploits in faraway lands—hell, the most exotic place Sally had been in the last five years was, well, Laramie. But today Sally hurried through a hair-raising story about a day hike that turned into two arduous days' climbing, lost in the Himalayas, to find what she was looking for.

"So you say that the redoubtable Sheldon Stover has shown up in Laramie, and installed himself in my house," Edna wrote. "As I'm sure you've surmised, we weren't close friends at the institute.

But Sheldon has the appalling, yet somehow enviable gift of assuming, utterly without evidence, that he's welcome anywhere. By all means, disabuse him of the notion, and get him out of my house. He's craftier than he appears, so watch out—he'll do everything he can to convince you that he's harmless, and suddenly you'll find yourself doing him one favor after another."

Edna went on to say that once Sheldon was gone, the house might as well stay empty, since she and Tom planned to return in three weeks. She appreciated Sally's willingness to keep an eye on the place and to try to revive some of the plantings. And then she wrote, "It just occurred to me that you didn't say why Sheldon suddenly turned up in town. I remember that he mentioned, when we were at Princeton, that in the seventies he'd had a back-to-the-land period, and bought some undeveloped property up in the Laramie Range. I do hope he isn't entertaining some fantasy of building himself a little cabin and becoming a twenty-first-century Thoreau! The thought of Sheldon Stover camping out in our neighborhood inspires a dreadful image: an October blizzard howling, a banging on the front door, and a snow-crusted Sheldon, blowing in with the weather and a steamer trunk, asking if he can crash at our place until he gets the roof on . . . sometime next spring. Brr . . ."

Sheldon owned land in the Laramies?

Sally scowled.

What the hell *was* his game?

She answered Edna's message, saying she'd take care of everything, and inquiring whether Edna happened to know precisely where Sheldon's property was. It would be the next day at the earliest before she got the answer from Kathmandu, given the time change. But in her heart, Sally already knew.

Hawk had wondered aloud why Marsh Carhart would haul Sheldon in on the land swap job. The investment group Nattie and Dwayne and Marsh Carhart were working for obviously had money to burn. But for Molly Wood to give up Wood's Hole, it seemed money wouldn't be enough. The deal had to include a piece of land Molly could call home, in a place she loved. Sally'd be willing to bet her Mustang that Sheldon Stover owned the pretty spot at Happy Jack, where crossbills twittered, and the wind sighed in the pines, and beavers frolicked and labored in their thriving pond, and poison spread, inexorably and invisibly, deep beneath the whispering grass and the sparkling water.

The question, to paraphrase the Senate Select Committee questioning the Watergate conspirators, was this: What did Sheldon know, and when did he know it?

"That little bastard," said Hawk, when Sally woke him with a cup of coffee, a hard copy of Edna's email message, and her suspicions. "I'm getting out of this bed and going right over to Edna and Tom's house and nail him to the wall. It's time we found out exactly what's going on here."

"I just called over there," Sally told Hawk. "There was no answer. I let him know yesterday, in very clear terms, that he had to be out today—I wouldn't be surprised if he's split." And left them a huge mess to clean up, no doubt.

"But if he's a partner in this deal, don't you think he'd hang around at least long enough to make sure the ink was dry? What if you went over to Edna's and took a look, and I popped by the hospital?"

"Bad idea," Sally said. "What would you do—drag Sheldon out of there and thump on him until he pulled out of the swap? You'd embarrass Molly, and at this point, I don't think there's anything you could do if she's determined to sign off. She might well decide that the money's too good to pass up. She could just write off the Happy Jack parcel as a place to maybe build a little summer cabin, forget about living up there, get a big house in town."

"Or she could leave it as is, with the beavers in charge on the surface, and the toxins way down below. We can't tell her anything more that might change her mind. But what about Sheldon?" Hawk replied. "Even assuming that the Happy Jack parcel is Sheldon's land, it's still possible that he's not aware of the pollution from the tie plant. Maybe he's got a conscience."

Sally just looked at Hawk.

"You're right. I should just clobber him," Hawk said, swinging his legs out from under the covers.

"Hang on a second," Sally said. "Okay. It's possible he doesn't know about the groundwater contamination—after all, if the land is his, he hasn't ever done anything with it. He and Cahart go back a ways—maybe Marsh remembered that Sheldon had the land and Marsh brought him into the deal, but hasn't bothered to mention the tie plant. Suppose that's the case, and Sheldon has no idea that the land he's selling off is lousy with toxic waste. He just thinks he's gotten in on a good deal, and figures he stands to make out big as a partner in the Wood's Hole development. Or hey, maybe, since he's in the Insurgency, he thinks he can make toxic waste disappear simply by refusing to believe it's there. And in the meantime, gentleman scholar that he is, he rationalizes making out like a bandit by doing his participant-observer experimental ethnography. I bet he's got some really loopy ideas about the part he is or isn't playing in some complicated transaction between the global and the local. It makes you see land speculation in a whole new light."

"Please," said Hawk. "This is all getting a little postmodern for me. Recall that this is, after all, a real estate deal, and Nattie Langham will get her seven percent, or whatever. That ought to bring this conversation back down to earth."

Sally pressed her lips together, blew out a puff of air. "Do you think Dwayne and Nattie know about the tie plant?"

Hawk took a big swallow of his coffee. "It's not up to us to tell them. Molly asked me to look at the land—they didn't. How deep into this thing do you want to get?"

Sally put her hand to her forehead and closed her eyes. "How deep are we?"

"You've got me," said Hawk as the telephone rang, "but if that's Delice, and she's managed to find out that the deal's about to go down, then likely we're both in over our heads."

But it wasn't Delice. When Sally answered the phone, at first all she heard was silence. And then, faint and scratchy, music. Old-fashioned, twangy country guitar. Thumping percussion. A woman's voice, unmistakable. Kitty Wells. Singing "Honky-Tonk Angels."

The music faded. And then a whisper. "You better watch out, angel. Maybe you ought to stay home today."

Click. Dial tone.

Sally stared at the phone, frozen. Hawk took the receiver from her and hung up. "Who was that?" he asked quietly.

"I-I don't know," she stammered. "Kitty Wells."

Hawk grabbed her by the shoulders. "Did someone threaten you? What did they say?"

Sally swallowed. "I'd say it was a threat." As she explained, the phone rang again. Hawk snatched it up instantly. "Yeah. Oh hi, Maude. Yes, we'll be over there in a little while. We had a kind of a late night last night . . . No, we're fine . . . Yes, see you soon. Goodbye." He hung up. Then said, "Shit!"

"What's wrong now?" Sally asked, her voice shrill.

"If Maude hadn't called just then, we could have dialed star six-nine and found out where the previous call came from."

But Sally was already calling Dickie and Mary's house.

Mary answered, excitement in her voice. "Oh hey, Sally. I'm just on my way out the door, heading for the parade. Dickie's already down there. They've got him riding a golden palomino at the head of the memorial float group. Then after us come some twirlers with flaming batons, and then the Shriners. This is going to sound weird, but this way of remembering my niece seems right to me."

Somehow, Sally found her voice. "Could you tell Dickie I've got to talk to him right away? I'll be down there as soon as I can, looking for him. Tell him it's urgent."

"Yeah, sure. Are you okay?" Mary asked.

"I'm fine. Just a little shook. Listen, do you know if Scotty Atkins is down there too?"

"Couldn't say. I know Dickie's put a lot of his people on parade duty, but not everybody. Do you want Dickie's cell phone number?"

"No," said Sally. "I'll just look for him there."

CHAPTER 25
BIG ESTHER

SPECTATORS LINED Third Street, Laramie's main thoroughfare, waiting for the procession to commence. Early birds, many of them elderly, had set up lawn chairs in the gutters, and hundreds of people were gathering to jam the sidewalks. Small children sat on their parents' shoulders; teenagers and grown-ups jostled for the best view they could get. Boots and hats and shorts and fanny packs, everyone chattering excitedly. Vendors strolled in the blocked-off street, hawking keychains and T-shirts and ice cream bars, souvenir pins and hatbands and not-quite-hot pretzels.

The parade marchers, riders, floats, and bands were mustering in the big parking lot at the Lifeway, by now pure bedlam. Folks parading on foot: marching bands from the high school and the university, a passel of assorted drill teams (one of them composed of a dozen blinking six-year-olds made up to look like mini–Dolly Partons), the military color guard and three ROTC units (Army, Air Force, Marines), maybe twenty different banner-waving community organizations, from the Head Start program (more bewildered little kiddies) to the Lions Club (some of them looked a little sketchy too—evidently up early, celebrating) and the LDS church (new hat, big smiles). Maude Stark, in blue slacks, a white collared shirt, and a bright red blazer, was supervising the distribution of signs and banners to the marchers who were there to remember Monette.

People on horseback: the Jubilee Days Committee, of course, on matching mounts (Sally looked for Dwayne, but didn't see him yet). The Gem City Jewels equestrian team, teenage girls who'd been riding since they were old enough to get boosted into the saddle, pranced on gorgeously groomed and beribboned horses. The more adventurous politicians were riding too, not all of them looking exactly comfortable. And of course the rodeo cowboys and cowgirls sat their saddles and controlled their horses without making a big thing of it. A lot of milling, mixing, and shouting.

Add to that the automobile paraders. The rodeo queen and her court were arranging themselves up on the backs of classic convertibles. The nonequestrian politicians (the president of the university, for example) rode in vehicles ranging from stock trucks to spanking new SUVs: all American-made, Sally noticed. Then there were the classics, a contingent of antique autos sponsored by various Laramie businesses, and of course the Shriners in their miniature Corvettes. 'Check out Burt and John Boy," Hawk said to Sally, pointing at two exultant, fez-wearing figures practicing their figure-eights far down the parking lot, in front of a cell phone store.

The floats, maybe twenty strong, were lined up out on Third. It didn't take Sally long to pick out the float that Brit and her crew were still finishing. The big thing at the back end of the flatbed turned out to be a twelve-foot-high replica of the figure of Esther Hobart Morris, a Wyoming pioneer woman credited in the state's mythology as "the Mother of Women's Rights." In real life Mrs. Morris herself had been six feet tall—no shrimp, and certainly no trembling flower of the prairie. She was most famous as the first woman justice of the peace in American history (probably not true), and it was said that one of her earliest judicial acts was to slap her feckless husband in the clink for public drunkenness (that, apparently, was fact). This particular rendition of Mrs. Morris was modeled after bronze statues that stood in front of the state capitol in Cheyenne and in the U.S. Capitol building, neither of which approached the size of the present crepe-paper, two-by-four, and chicken-wire assemblage. Sally was compelled to admit that from where she stood, Brit's behemoth looked somewhat more like Mrs. Butterworth than the sainted Mrs. Morris.

Sally watched as Herman Schwink, clad in his best black Stetson, razor-creased jeans, and starched snap-button shirt, worked his way around the bottom of the creation, banging nails into the wooden platform. She sincerely hoped they weren't having terrible problems anchoring the thing down. It didn't look all that stable.

Delice, meanwhile, was helping attach a long banner to the side of the flatbed. "Welcome to Wyoming," it said, "Where the Men Are Strong, and the Women Are Equal."

Sally couldn't help smiling. And then she came to her senses, and with some desperation sought out Dickie Langham.

He was there in the parking lot, having a little trouble managing the palomino stallion that somebody—his wife, anyway—had decided would make him the image of the dashing Western lawman. Dickie had grown up in town, spent far too much of his wasted youth mounted not on animals but on bar stools. In short, he wasn't the world's best horseman (not that Sally was an expert!), but he was making a game effort. Jerry Jeff, aware of his uncle's limitations in the saddle, was holding the stallion's head, stroking its nose, and speaking sweet words into its twitching ear.

When Sally caught up with him, Dickie did his best to listen attentively, despite the fact that the horse was bouncing under him and JJ kept having to yank on the damn animal's head. The sheriff's mouth grew grim as she told him about the phone call. "This comes at an unfortunate time, Mustang," he said. "As you can see, most of my personnel are gonna have their hands full today. This parade route is crawling with cops, if that's any reassurance. I don't know if you'd feel safer going home, but in some ways you might be better off down here. That guy might have been trying to bluff you, and if he came after you at your place, we'd have a hard time getting people over there. You'll forgive me if I'm not inclined to approve of the idea of Hawk hanging around as an armed body-guard."

Dickie paused. "The guy who called presumably also did the number on your underwear. So as far as we know, he goes in for private harassment, not grand public gestures. I don't much like this, but I'm going to suggest that you go get a sign and march right along next to me. I've got a good seat up here on old Trigger," he said, patting the horse's neck in what he clearly hoped was a soothing manner, "and a good view of the crowd. I'll let my guys know to be on the lookout for anybody acting in a suspicious manner," he finished, slipping a radio off his belt.

"What do you think?" Sally asked Hawk.

"We're here now."

She went to get a sign from Maude, who gave her a piercing once-over and said, "You look terrible."

"Too much Jubilee Days," Sally said vaguely. "I heard Molly Wood had a fall. Have you talked with her?"

Maude looked at Sally with suspicion, but didn't ask how she'd heard. "Yes. When she didn't show up this morning to set up at the white elephant sale, I called her house, and her daughter told me she'd fallen. I spoke with her at the hospital. I'm going over to see her after the parade."

"The white elephant sale?" Sally asked. "I totally forgot. There was a captain's chair I wanted."

"Someone bought it—sorry."

Damn. "So how is Molly?"

"So far, they're saying she broke her ankle, but they're going to keep her in there a couple of days for tests. She's going stir-crazy. What are you up to anyway?" Maude asked, eyes narrowing.

"Oops. I'd better get in line," Sally said, grabbing a placard and escaping. Sounded like Molly had kept quiet about their night visit—good.

So Sally Alder was once again standing a little too near a horse, and with even more reason to be nervous than she'd had at the rodeo. This time she was holding a sign that said, "For Monette. For All Women," and waiting for the Jubilee Days parade to begin. Sally had a lifelong predilection for the ironic, and in that moment of anticipation, she reflected on the ironies of enshrining Monette Bandy as a martyr for women's rights.

Nobody could dispute that Monette had been a victim. She'd grown up in an unhappy, even brutal household, at the mercy of a rotten father and a terrorized mother. She'd fairly begged men to treat her like crap, and it looked as if they hadn't let her down. If Monette had ever had the chance to see herself as a valuable human being, not just a whipping post for men's anger or lust, things might have gone a lot better for her. A world in which women really were equal would have given her that chance.

But Monette had also been more than a victim. Even if Sally's own idea of a desirable career ladder didn't run to employment at the Lifeway, Monette had advanced from stocker to checker trainee: she was, in at least some measure, ambitious. If Bone Bandy had it right, his daughter was also unscrupulous and greedy (gee, wonder where she got that from?), possibly even a blackmailer. And say what you would about the possible causes of her aggressiveness about sex, there was no denying that Monette had lusted powerfully, and pushed hard to satisfy that lust. Ambition, greed, and lust—not exactly admirable traits, but not uncommon.

Monette was, in short, a highly flawed human being, whose faults were not solely matters of gender. She'd been murdered and violated in a way that reflected a hatred of women but also a grave offense against humans of all kinds. Maybe the sign ought to read: "For Monette. And for All Us Poor Sinners."

Not exactly an upbeat message for Jubilee Days.

And now it looked as if the parade was about to roll. Sally saw the color guard march out into the street and head south, followed by the first of the bands, then the Jubilee Days Committee. (Where the hell was Dwayne? Was he at that very moment shaking hands to seal the deadly deal?) Parade marshals made sure everybody went in the order they were supposed to go, trying hard to keep the various groups from tripping over each other, and yet close enough together that there wouldn't be gaps in the procession, a tricky task. At the edge of Sally's group, the twirlers were pulling out Bic lighters and touching them to the cloth wrapped ends of their batons, carefully wrapping fingers around the glinting chrome shafts between the flames.

At last it was time for Sheriff Dickie Langham to lead the Monette Bandy Memorial Marchers, and the Esther Morris float, out into the street to join the pageant. Sally looked back over her shoulder at the cheering, sign-waving marchers, at the sight of the lifelong radical Maude, the Sierra Club stalwart, Nature Conservancy board member, contributor to all things green and progressive, in her proper patriot's garb, waving her "Thank You Wal-Mart" sign. Herman Schwink, behind the wheel of the flatbed truck, was giving a thumbs-up, getting ready to put the big rig in gear. Brit stood next to the giant sculpture, one hand clenched in the wire and wood frame. Delice stood on the other side, her position mirroring Brit's, down to the clutching hand. Like Mary Langham and the twenty-odd other people standing and sitting on the float, Brit and Delice were smiling and waving, but unlike the others, they were not whooping. They weren't making any noise. Their smiles could pass for rictus grimaces, they were gritting their teeth so hard. The monstrous Mother of Women's Rights swayed slightly as Herman eased off the break, and the truck lumbered into motion.

Somewhere up ahead, the Laramie High School band was performing an out-of-kilter rendition of "Streets of Laredo." The old Model Ts and Stutz Bearcats, Chrysler Newporters and Ford Edsels were honking their horns. Along the sidewalks the crowds cheered as they passed, the sheriff waving his hat (and with JJ's help, appearing to be doing all right with that enormous horse), Sally brandishing her sign. Each group paused as it passed the reviewing stand in the center of town, right in front of the Wrangler Bar and Grill, and then marched on. Every time the parade halted, Sally shot a backward glance at the truck, where Delice and Brit were managing to keep Mrs. Morris erect, but clearly having a time of it. Indeed, three other people were also holding on to the sculpture's skirts. From the waist up, Big Esther shuddered a little with each slow start and stop.

As the Monette Bandy Memorial Marchers reached the reviewing stand, the parade announcer declared, "Ladies and gentlemen, please remove your hats and observe a moment of silence in honor of a young woman who recently fell victim to violent crime not far from our peaceful community. Let's all work together to prevent such terrible things from happening to our children, our friends, our parents, and our neighbors."

And the crowd, for just that instant, fell completely silent. Sally would never have been able to predict how that fleeting stillness would affect her. The tears came instantly, followed by a surge of warmth toward everyone there, friend or stranger, anyone capable of compassion, anyone who might reflect on Monette's death. She told herself she had to learn to be a little more generous and compassionate in the future.

Her vision was still blurred, her heart still full, when the moment was over, and Dickie began to lead them forward again. Thus blinded by sentiment, she didn't see the rock come whizzing toward her face, smack the sign next to her head, and ricochet off to hit the stallion right in the part of the anatomy that distinguished it from its gelded brethren.

The palomino whinnied and reared. Dickie dropped the reins and nearly fell off. As the horse plunged earthward again, JJ scrambled to snatch hold of the bridle. Hawk yanked Sally's arm and pulled her away from the irate animal. All around them, marchers scattered in panic.

A screech behind: Herman had slammed on the brakes. The next noise Sally heard was the sickening crack of breaking boards. As Hawk dragged her to the side of the street, she looked back to see people leaping off the sides of the flatbed as the enormous sculpture heaved and rocked, wobbled, and finally pitched over backward.

The twirlers, who'd only moments before been high-stepping gaily forward, saw the statue falling and dropped their batons, squealing in flight. Big Esther hit the ground right on top of the burning batons, and burst into flames. The Shriners, whizzing up from behind in their Corvettes, wrenched their little wheels to avoid crashing into the Mother of Women's Rights, now blazing brightly in the middle of Third Street. Their carefully choreographed driving routine obliterated, they veered around in crazy patterns, fezzes flying. Four Corvettes careened, fortunately at low speed, into one another. Sally was relieved to see that both Burt and

John Boy had avoided collision. It was probably all those years they'd spent driving California freeways.

Jerry Jeff finally managed to get the stallion under control. Dickie jumped off, ran to Sally, grabbed her by the shoulders, and said, "What the hell happened?"

"Somebody threw a rock at my head, but it hit my sign and bounced off and nailed your horse. I think it came from that direction!" Sally pointed toward the Wrangler's café entrance. The sheriff ran into the crowd, shoving people aside, his hand on the butt of his gun.

Now the sirens were sounding. Two fire engines came barreling down Grand Avenue, turned onto Third, and pulled up by the flaming Esther, firefighters leaping off the trucks. Several got busy hooking up hoses, while the rest worked to push back the surging crowd, many of whom were quite certain that this was absolutely the best Jubilee Days parade in history.

Esther was large, but crepe paper burned fast. Much to the disappointment of the crowd, the fire had soon been reduced to smoke and sodden ash, singed boards and blackened chicken wire. Now on the sidewalk in front of the Wrangler, Sally stood next to Brit, who was staring forlornly at the remains of Big Esther. "That was my most ambitious engineering project ever," she said.

"Happily, as a lawyer you'll be using other talents," Hawk told Brit, squeezing her shoulder.

Herman, who'd been busy pulling the flatbed out of range of the flames, got out of the cab of the truck, walked over to Brit, and put his arms around her. "Cowboy up, darlin'," he said.

Assured that Brit was in comforting hands, Hawk turned his attention to the dazed Sally. "Are you all right?" he asked, shaking her by the arm.

Sally looked down at the sign dangling from the hand on the arm he wasn't shaking, then looked back up at Hawk. "You're pinching me," she said. "Let go."

But as it turned out, Sally wasn't the only one getting pinched. "Comin' through!" somebody yelled. "Police! Clear out of here!"

Four sheriff's deputies came around the corner from behind the Wrangler, pushing the crowd back as they moved. They were followed by Dickie Langham, panting hard from his riding and running, but trying to jolly the crowd into dispersing. "No cause for alarm here, folks," he said, smiling and trying not to gasp. "Just a tiny bit of trouble with a fella who had a drop or two too much to drink this morning. You all get on home now, or have a bite of lunch, or go on out to the rodeo. Looks like the parade's about over. Enjoy the rest of your Jubilee Days."

Unaware of what she was doing, Sally watched, hypnotized, as an Albany County Sheriff's Department patrol car drove up in front of the café. Dickie walked past Sally and Hawk, over to the vehicle, put his hands on his hips, worked on catching his breath. And now, from around the corner of the building, here came Bone Bandy, weaving and reeking of whiskey, hands cuffed behind his back, held and prodded by an uncharacteristically disheveled Scotty Atkins. Bone certainly appeared a whole lot too piss-eyed to have the vaguest idea of where he was, or what was happening to him. But drunks, Sally knew, could go in and out of consciousness, in and out of memory. Just as Scotty pushed him past Sally and Hawk, Bone raised his head, on a neck that had seemed all but boneless only a second before. He looked Sally in the eye. "Hello, angel," he whispered.

CHAPTER 26
DAYTIME NIGHTMARES

"I DON'T WANT to go home," Sally insisted. "In fact, that's the last thing I want. I'd just sit there and brood about the fact that I have hardly any underwear. It'll be bad enough waiting around, wondering what that crazy bastard Bone's telling the police."

"But you're exhausted," said Hawk. "And if you're not, I am. Even without having your skull smashed with a rock, your brain must be fairly addled."

Not to mention another intimate moment with a frigging horse. "I am a little shaky," Sally admitted. Maybe I'm so mixed up, I think I'm fine."

"In that case, come in and have a cup of coffee, and tell me exactly what happened," Delice said firmly. She'd come jangling up just in time to see Bone bundled into the patrol car.

Hawk looked Sally over carefully. "Okay," he decided. "I could go for a burger."

It was noisy as hell in the Wrangler. Once the police took off, the parade-goers had flowed into the café and bar, jabbering about the thrilling surprise ending to the afternoon's entertainment. Delice commandeered a table in the restaurant, and soon Sally and Hawk were settling down to a late lunch.

Her heart was still hammering, but Sally figured that an order of Wrangler onion rings was just the thing to slow it down. Hawk had gone into brooding mode, saying nothing, barely looking up from the cheeseburger and fries he was demolishing, as if he hadn't consumed a full pound of aged American beef only the night before. Then again, dinner at the Yippie I O seemed awfully long ago.

Delice peppered Sally with questions. She mumbled answers while she crunched her way through four cheap paper napkins' worth of hot, sweet, greasy rings. "So it seems," Sally concluded, wiping the ketchup off her fingers with a fifth napkin, "that Bone Bandy is the one who visited our house Tuesday night, and called me up this morning, and just tried to bean me with a rock. Looks like it's up to Dickie and Scotty to find out whether he pushed me into the bucking chute. What I don't get is why? What's he got against me? I still can't quite believe that he was the one who killed Monette."

"That son of a bitch!" Delice spat. "Well, at least this'll probably be the last chance he gets to terrorize women for a while."

Sally looked up from the pile of soggy napkins, trouble in her eyes. "Yeah. I guess. But how could I have read him so wrong Thursday morning? I guess some part of me really wanted to believe that he was capable of at least a little fatherly grief. Boy, what a sap, huh?"

The burger was gone. Only a few hard, cold fries remained on Hawk's plate. He pursed his lips, staring at the ruins of his lunch, then looked up, expressionless, the round lenses of his glasses gleaming. "There's no evidence at this point that you were off-base. You said then you didn't think he'd killed his daughter—why change your mind about that now?"

Sally leaned on her elbows and put her head in her hands.

"He's no prince, but I don't think he killed her either," Delice told Sally. "Otherwise, why would he have been sitting at my bar at ten o'clock this morning, crying in his whiskey, telling everybody who could stand to listen that one way or another, he'd find the fucker who killed his little girl, and get all the bastards that ever did him wrong?"

Delice put a hand on Sally's arm. "Hey, I'm an expert on drunks. The ones who are bad off—and Bone's definitely in that category—get real confused. When they happen to be sober, they can have their sensible moments, but when they're loaded, they get wild hairs up their butts. Bone could have latched on to you because he's imagined up some diabolical connection between you and the murderer. Then again, he could just be obsessing about something you did a million years ago, that seems like only yesterday to him. Drunks are like that. People who deliberately lobotomize themselves have problems distinguishing between fantasy and reality, or for that matter twenty years back and this week."

You probably don't remember giving me a raft of shit one night when Tanya and me had a disagreement at the Gallery. You got me throwed right out of that place. I been a little annoyed with you ever since.

"Actually, he did mention something about me getting him kicked out of the Gallery bar, way back when," she said. "Maybe he has carried a grudge all these years, and this week's events have just set him off. But face it, guys, if Bone didn't murder Monette, then the killer is still on the loose. How reassuring is that?"

"At least we know the cops have the guy who's been bothering *you*. Take what you can get," Hawk advised.

She nodded reluctantly. "And there haven't been any more murders. I guess it's good news that it doesn't look like there's a serial killer, going around town stalking honky-tonky angels. So that leaves us back with Bone insisting that Monette was blackmailing somebody. Any theories as to who?"

All three sipped the ineffectual Wrangler coffee. When Dwayne Langham pulled a chair up to their table, Sally was grateful for the distraction.

"Hey guys! I hear I missed the parade of the century!" said Dwayne, with anomalous cheer.

"Yeah, Dwayne." Delice sneered at her brother. "Where were you? Down at the hospital, swindling crippled little old ladies out of their homesteads?"

Dwayne gave her his patented blank stare. "Something came up," he said mildly.

"How'd you know Molly was in the hospital?" Hawk asked Delice.

"It was the talk of the white elephant sale. By the way, Mustang, when you didn't show up this morning, I bought that captain's chair for you. Fifty bucks—figured you were good for it. I thought I'd better grab it before somebody else did."

"You're a pal," Sally told her.

"So what's going on with the land swap, Dwayne? Don't try to play dumb—Burt told me Nattie drank up half the Dom Perignon in the Yippie I O cellar last night, and then gave him grief about not getting a family discount. Like you two need a discount! Where is the Wicked Witch of the West anyhow?" Delice asked.

Dwayne ignored his sister's insult to his wife. "At the beauty parlor," he answered. "Or maybe getting a massage. Hair, nails, I don't know. Seems to me she just had it all done a couple of days ago, but you know Nattie. Pretty high maintenance. I can't keep her schedule straight."

Delice shot Dwayne an assessing glance. "Burt said you guys had closed the Wood's Hole deal."

Dwayne smiled faintly, sphinxlike.

"You're not going to tell me a damn thing," Delice said. "I know you."

Sally wasn't either. Even though it had been Delice's idea to get involved with the thing in the first place, Sally figured that what she and Hawk had discovered was Molly Wood's business. Discretion was admittedly not her strong point, but in this case, the fact that Dwayne was sitting there made restraint easier.

Dwayne changed the subject, addressing Sally. "I heard Dickie arrested Bone Bandy. Rumor has it that Bone burglarized your house and came at you with an axe. And he was the one who attacked you at the rodeo."

"Not exactly," said Hawk, answering for her. "As usual, the rumor mill is cranking up a somewhat faulty version of events."

Taking a page from Dwayne's book, Sally decided not to elaborate.

"So are you up to gigging tonight?" Dwayne asked her.

Was she? Was there anything she could do, with what remained of the day, about the tragedy of Monette Bandy or the displacement of Molly Wood? With Bone behind bars, Sally herself had nothing to worry about anymore. As for Monette, the police were, after all, in charge of the murder investigation. Scotty Atkins might have hit bottom, yesterday afternoon at a table not far from where they were sitting. But Sally knew, with a deep, not altogether comfortable certainty, that Scotty wouldn't let go of this case. He'd drive himself, and everybody else, hard, fast, and into the ground, looking for the answer.

And then there was the problem of the Happy Jack for Wood's Hole land swap. When it came to the future of Molly Wood's home on the range, Sally and Hawk had done pretty much everything they could. They had the carry-on-size eye bags to prove it.

Face it. Sally's Jubilee Days had so far been a bust (with the demise of Big Esther, a true flaming bust). But at last she was out of danger. She was entitled to seize a little pleasure, make a little music, blow off a little steam. The proceeds from Delice's benefit would go to the women's shelter. It would be partying with a purpose. "What the hell," said Sally.

"But first a nap," Hawk insisted.

Right as usual. She was beat enough to lie down in the gutter in front of the Wrangler, never mind the spilled drink cups and half-eaten pretzels, the drowned cigarette butts, the Slim Jim wrappers.

When he found out that they'd walked downtown, Dwayne considerately offered Sally and Hawk a ride home. In her demented state, she had to laugh. Riding in Dwayne's Beamer, the "little bitty" vehicle Nattie had complained about having to drive sometimes, was like sailing along in your own custom-made cloud. And Dwayne, unlike Nattie, kept his vehicle shipshape. Whatever emergency gear he might have stowed away, the interior of the BMW was immaculate, not marred by so much as a stray Post-it note. Sally wondered if some employee of the Centennial Bank was obliged to vacuum the boss's car every day.

"Nice car," she told him. "I remember a time when you were

driving a VW bus with a mattress instead of a backseat and the remains of a McCarthy daisy on the window."

"To everything, there is a season," Dwayne answered.

"Must drive you crazy, taking Nattie's Escalade fishing, the way she's got stuff piled up in the back," Sally went on.

Dwayne shrugged. "It's her car. The way business has been lately, I barely have time for fishing, much less organizing her gear. Here you go," he told them as he pulled up in front of their house, and leaned over her to open the passenger-side door. "Get some rest, and we'll rock 'n' roll." He took off the moment they were out of the car.

"Damn," Hawk muttered as they went inside. "Guess we missed our chance to grill him about the land swap."

"He sure split in a hurry," Sally said. "I don't think he was in the mood to answer questions."

And she did have questions, but not ones she could put into words. Something was tugging at the back of her brain, but at the moment there wasn't enough electricity firing inside her head to do more than pull her shoes off and fall on the bed. Hawk collapsed nearly on top of her.

She dreamed of a mountain brook, bubbling through a mountain meadow, and birds singing. But as it flowed on, the stream darkened and turned the grass the color of dried blood. Then there were ants, hauling the coated dead stalks away, groaning, and a woman lying in the grass, her hair and nails and lips the same deadly color, and no face.

And then Sally was dragged out of her daytime nightmare, in a tangle of jeans and T-shirts and Hawk's arms and legs, when the telephone rang. She put a pillow over her head, but Hawk sprawled over Sally's back to reach the bedside table and picked up the receiver. "It's Brit," he said, handing Sally the phone.

The sulky voice came through the wire, but for once Brit didn't sound bored out of her mind. "Hello, hello? Sally?"

"Gmmph," said Sally, trying hard to wake up.

"Listen. Herman just called me from the Lifeway. He went down there after the team roping this afternoon."

"Oh yeah? How'd they do?"

"Third. Hamburger money. But that's not why I called. Remember you asked me to get Herman to lean on his brother?" she said.

"Mmm-mmm," Sally murmured.

"He and Adolph are on their way down to the courthouse to talk to my dad. I don't know how, but somehow Herman, like, convinced Adolph that he had to come clean with the cops."

That woke her up. Sally shoved Hawk off her and pushed herself into a sitting position. "Yeah?"

"Uh-huh. I don't know what Herman did to him, but he managed to get Adolph to tell him that he didn't just drop Monette off Monday when he took her home."

"What happened?" Sally said.

"Adolph is a total worm," Brit observed.

"What happened, Brit?" Sally persisted.

"According to Herman, Adolph said he decided to stay for his whole lunch break. He 'just went in for a toke and a quickie,' " Brit answered. "At first he said Monette was 'her usual horny self,' and he was just doing her a favor."

"A favor. But then he changed his story?" Sally asked.

"When Herman leans on you, I guess he can get pretty heavy," Brit said.

"Get to the point, Brit," Sally said, fully alert and out of patience.

"Adolph finally admitted to Herman that he deals a little smoke now and then. Monette had made some connections for him, on a kind of barter basis, I guess—he'd give her a couple of joints if she found him buyers. And sometimes she'd trade sex for dope."

"And that's what she did Monday?" Sally asked.

"Yeah. This gets kind of gross, Sally." Brit hesitated.

"Don't worry about it, Brit. I've seen stuff that goes way beyond 'kind of gross,' " Sally prompted.

"She wanted something new. He went inside, and they got loaded, and then she pulled out a rope. Adolph used to ride with Herman, and he recognized it as a piggin' string."

"Go on," Sally said, wishing, with part of her heart, that Brit would just stop right there. Too late to stop now.

"She made Adolph let her tie him up before they had sex, Sally," Brit said.

"She tied him up?"

"Uh-huh." Sally heard Brit swallow, hard. "Then they did it, and then she wanted him to tie her up, and do it again, but he had to get back to work."

Sally had to ask. "Did Adolph say anything about how Monette was when he left her to go back to the store?"

She heard Brit take a breath. "He said she cussed him out for leaving her high and dry. And he pitied the next fool she got her hooks into, because, in Adolph's words, 'That bitch had a hole in her that nothing could ever fill up.'"

CHAPTER 27
DIRTY WORK

SHE HUNG UP THE PHONE and looked down at the bed. Hawk was gazing up at her, seeing through her, holding her with his eyes. "I'm afraid to ask," he said.

She told him what Brit had said. He took her hand, kept looking at her, said nothing.

"How in the world do the cops stand it?" she said, her voice rising. "You and I wandered into this hideousness completely by accident. All we wanted to do was take a walk in the mountains. It wasn't like we were looking for trouble. But guys like Dickie and Scotty Atkins have to live with every horrible, awful thing humans are capable of doing and thinking and saying. All the time. It comes with the job."

"Walk away," Hawk said simply. "Let them do what we pay them to do."

"That would be the sensible thing," Sally conceded.

"We both suffer from the delusion that there's something we

know, or can do, or have to do, to help," Hawk said. "For me it started with finding the body. That made this thing personal." He pulled Sally down next to him, put his arm around her, wrapping her close. "You know, Dickie amazes me. I don't know how he manages to stay on the wagon, living with what he's seen."

"Then again," Sally pointed out, "however tough it is staying clean, he sure knows the alternative. Imagine what he must have gone through, all those years he was on the run and at the end of his rope. And after all that, he came back sober and applied to the police academy. He looks cuddly but he's a tough mother."

"And how about Scotty?" Hawk asked her, his eyes very steady on hers.

"Tough. Not cuddly," said Sally shortly.

"Looks like his job cost him his marriage. Wonder what else it costs," Hawk mused.

"Too much," said Sally, kissing him and snuggling down into the curve of his arm.

Hawk's other hand slipped under her shirt. She felt the warmth of his palm, moving on her stomach, circling higher.

"You know, I really ought to get up and go over to Edna's, see if Sheldon's still around," Sally told Hawk, and then sighed as he unsnapped her bra.

"Be reasonable," he said. "If Sheldon's there, he'll just make you mad. If he's gone and left a mess, that'll piss you off too. There's no hurry about getting over there to clean it up."

"But maybe we should talk to him about the problem with his land," Sally insisted.

"We could tell Sheldon his hair was on fire," Hawk said, nibbling her neck, "and if he didn't feel like hearing it, he wouldn't pay any attention even when his head was burning."

His logic was persuasive. So was his hand, and his busy fingers, and the fact that he'd thrown a leg over one of hers and was pressed against her in a most intriguing and inviting way. She could feel the warmth spread from Hawk to her, and gave it back with a kiss, beginning slow and soft. She seduced his mouth with her mouth. She reveled in the sweet heat of kissing her lover.

After a time she wanted more. She wanted to look at him, and touch him, to enjoy him completely, in the golden light of the passing afternoon. Hawk seemed content with the lazy pace of the way she made love to him, encouraging her with his own gentle, persistent overtures. She could feel the hardness of him through his jeans. "You want to be inside me," she whispered.

"I want whatever you want," he murmured back, his breath warm in her ear, a finger rubbing over her lips. "Take your time. I'm loving this."

If she could have, she'd have stroked and kissed him for hours. One part of desire wanted just that. The other had claws, and no patience. "I need to see more of you," she told him. "Take off your shirt."

He did. And smiled slowly. "Aren't we supposed to be in the place where the women are strong, and the men are equal?" he teased. When he pulled her T-shirt over her head, peeled her out of her bra, pushed her back down on the pillows and bent his head to her breasts, nuzzling, suckling, she groaned and strained up against him.

"I know you're supposed to be doing me," he said softly, "but I'm having a hard time controlling my urges. You'll understand, won't you?" he asked, fingers working on the buttons of her jeans.

"I'll be very understanding," she said, her own hands shaking as he finished the job, and slid his fingers down.

"Conserving underwear," he said a moment later, "very sensible."

Sally was anything but sensible as she freed him from his jeans, as he dragged hers all the way off. She was too impatient to return the favor, but now she rolled on top of him, and had him where she wanted him. "I think you're going to like this," she said, kissing her way down his chest and belly, slow and deliberate.

"Oh man. Nice mouth," was all he could say when she reached her goal.

They were both shaking a little when she finally got his pants off, slid back up his body, and took him in. She remembered her resolution to go slow and gentle. Her intentions were noble, but soon it seemed that nothing could get in the way of a burgeoning desire to see if she could make him scream.

"There's a lot to be said for sexual escapism," Hawk said, after a while.

"Works for me," Sally agreed.

"I've been thinking about Sheldon," he allowed.

"You've got to be kidding," she told him.

"Not for long," he said, "just the past second or so."

"And what are you thinking?" she asked.

Hawk rolled onto his side and leaned on one arm, looking at her. "I should probably go over to Edna's with you, and if he's there, try to talk to him about the groundwater problem. The worst he can do is blow us off."

"Only a little while ago you thought Sheldon could wait." Sally smiled.

"Changed my mind," said Hawk.

She gave him a half smile. "A lot of women who'd just screwed a man halfway comatose would be insulted at the thought that he could switch from senselessness to contemplating the fate of the earth, in the space of just that second or so. But not me. I admire that kind of obsessive-compulsive move."

"You're my role model," he said, hauling himself out of bed and giving her a smacking kiss. "You've got great moves."

The good news: Sheldon was sitting in a lawn chair by the picnic table in Edna and Tom's backyard, staring up into the crown of the sheltering cottonwood. On the ground next to him was a packed duffel bag.

The bad news: He was guzzling wine out of a Mason jar, and Sally recognized the label on the bottle. Edna had a friend who ran a boutique winery in Napa Valley, a man who had made a quasi-religion of the mysterious California zinfandel grape. Edna had put down a bottle of the angelic inaugural 1989 vintage for a fitting occasion—say, the Second Coming. Not only had Sheldon cracked it open—he'd managed to shove the cork down in the bottle, and the jar he was just refilling had small, blasphemous pieces of cork floating a quarter of an inch below the screw-top.

Now *that* would be hard to find on the Net.

"I know you're eager to get me out of here, and as you can see, I'm packed and ready to go," Sheldon told Sally. "You'll be glad to hear that I've found a place to stay tonight. Dwayne and Nattie have kindly offered to put me up."

"Isn't that nice?" Sally said, too sweetly. "I thought you'd turned in your report to Carhart today. How come you're sticking around?"

Sheldon took a gulp of the zin, and then looked up with a weak smile. "Don't want to miss the big party of the week."

"Now which party would that be?" Sally asked. "The one for the benefit of the women's shelter, or the one you and your partners are going to throw in celebration of cheating an elderly woman out of her home?'

"Sal . . ." said Hawk, putting a hand on her arm.

"Lay off, Hawk. I want to know, right now, what the hell you're up to, Sheldon. We've found out some things that make us think you're not just here playing with yourself."

"There's no need for you to question the legitimacy of my ethnographic research project," Sheldon said, affront in every word.

"That's enough!" Hawk spat. "I refuse to listen to even one minute of horseshit. Just answer one question, Stover—yes or no, do you own the land up at Happy Jack that the investors' group is proposing to swap for Molly Wood's place in Centennial Valley?"

Sheldon ran his finger around the edge of his Mason jar. "For the moment," he finally answered.

Sally was ready to explode, but Hawk cut her off. "By that I take it to mean that the deal hasn't been finalized."

"In a world of uncertainty such as ours, nothing can truly be finalized," Sheldon pronounced.

"I said no horseshit." Hawk spoke slowly and quietly. "Facts here, Stover. You believe that the swap will go through, sometime soon, leaving you part owner of the ranch. And Molly comes out of the deal with the Happy Jack property and several millions of dollars in cash. Correct?"

Sheldon put a finger in his wine, chased a chunk of cork around, fished it out, and flicked it on the ground. "Understanding that knowledge is fractured and fragmented, and susceptible of reception according to innumerable contingencies, I see no reason why I should share any information on this matter with the two of you," he said, raising the jar to his lips.

Hawk's hand lashed out, slapping the jar out of Sheldon's hand and sending it flying, smashing against the trunk of the tree, dark purple wine and bits of glass cascading down. The next thing Sally knew, Hawk had him by the neck of his T-shirt, half out of his chair, and Sheldon appeared to be choking.

"Stop strangling him, Hawk," she said, batting at Hawk's fist, clenched tight in the fabric of the T-shirt. "No more postmodern fancy dancing here, Sheldon—in case you've missed the news, you live in a real world of real things, like land and water and beavers. And dioxin."

Sally watched his eyes. If Sheldon was surprised at her last word, it didn't show. "I don't deny the existence of real things, Sally." Hawk had released his hold only enough to permit Sheldon to breathe, and here he was lecturing. Priceless, in a way. "Only a fool would do that. I do, however, maintain that many of the things that have the appearance or the shadow or the trace or the imprint of the real are susceptible of interpretation, to an almost infinite degree. Most of what appears natural to us is, indeed, naturalized, conjecture masquerading as certainty."

"I know where this is going," Hawk hissed, teeth gritted, as he shoved Sheldon back into his chair. "Let me see if I can summarize. You do own the land, you're aware that the groundwater is polluted from the old tie plant up-aquifer, and you're fully willing to toss the potato, hot as it is, to the next poor slob in the game. Am I getting this straight?"

Sheldon shifted in his lawn chair, tugged his T-shirt back into place, settled his shoulders, rested his elbows on the arms of the chair, and steepled his fingers. "I'll attempt to be as precise as possible. In 1976 I received a bequest from a great-aunt I'd never met. I learned of my inheritance that summer, as I was traveling across the country, and I happened to be passing through this area. I saw the 'For Sale' sign while camping with friends, and the price was exactly the same as the amount I'd just inherited. At the time I was, like so many people, interested in the supernatural, the spiritual, the occult, and I had a little of the got-to-get-back-to-the-garden bug. It seemed more than coincidence."

Sally had heard much weirder stories. And like not a few people at the time, he'd probably been stoned to the eyeballs. "Okay. So you bought the property. What did you plan to do with it?"

"Nothing," said Sheldon equably. "Leave it to nature, for the time being, and if the occasion ever arose that I'd want to live on the land, I had my piece of the planet."

"But the occasion never came," Hawk said.

"Graduate school, postdocs, teaching positions, fellowships— the usual accoutrements of academic life. I got busy. Oh, I thought from time to time about retiring to a cabin in the wilderness somewhere, just to read and think, maybe do a little writing. It's everybody's fantasy, no?"

Guiltily, Sally and Hawk looked at each other. Of course it was their fantasy, or one of them, on days when they weren't too busy to fantasize.

"But after a while I stopped believing there was such a thing as wilderness, a place apart from human actions and intents, protected from global interpenetration. And, of course, I realized that I had no desire to live in Wyoming. Marsh called me up a couple of months ago and asked me if I still owned the property, and offered to bring me in on this deal. He said that the other partners had money to invest, but that the woman who owned the ranch insisted that there be some land involved. I found it intriguing, both financially and intellectually."

"Oh brother," groaned Hawk.

"Intriguing is a nice word," Sally said. "But I think juicy is more descriptive."

"I won't pretend to be immune to the profit motive," said Sheldon. "It is, after all, the dominant ideology of our time, pervading the entire world. But it must be equally clear that I am interested in a number of things here. This is more than just a land and money exchange—it is precisely the sort of cultural transaction I've studied for many years."

Hawk sighed. "What about the toxic plume, Sheldon?"

Sheldon turned his head, looking longingly at the spilled wine staining the cottonwood trunk. The bottle beside him was half full, but he didn't dare risk picking it up and swigging directly from it. "I'm aware that state scientists believe that they have identified certain problems. Marsh Carhart assures me that their computer models are flawed. I see no evidence to prove their contentions. Since I've owned that tract of land in the Laramies, there's been no industrial, commercial, or residential development anywhere in the vicinity. Ecologically speaking, my property gives every appearance of thriving—you've seen it for yourself, Green."

"And I've seen the state reports on the groundwater, Stover. That tie plant did its dirty work long before you showed up with your camping buddies. The effects of some of the compounds they were using could last hundreds of years. The state's hydrologists have mapped the polluted groundwater, and your property is on that map. If you *had* gone back to your little Eden, and dug yourself a well, chances are you'd be drinking a nice nasty chemical stew."

Hawk looked like he was about to grab Sheldon again. Sally put a warning hand on his shoulder.

He took a steadying breath. "If Molly buys the place, she'll be the one doing the drilling and drinking. And if the state does ever decide to do anything to clean up the mess, she'll be liable for at least part of the cost of the cleanup. The money your partners are paying her—well, that'll be a drop in the bucket, so to speak."

"Three things," said Sheldon, holding up three fingers as if Sally and Hawk were idiots or freshmen. "First, the state reports are certainly open to interpretation—they're models of nature, human creations, not things that exist in nature. Virtual reality, if you will, and a decidedly different virtual scenario from the one Marsh Carhart has constructed, using his own scientific methods. Scratch the surface of science, and you find—voilà!—scientists arguing."

"Where I come from," Hawk said quietly, "we resolve this kind of dispute by trying to figure out who's wrong. Or in some cases, who's lying."

Sheldon ignored the challenge. "Second, the money our group

has offered Molly Wood will leave her, and her descendants, extremely wealthy. Whatever the hydrologists may have reported, the state is unlikely to move any time soon, so even if there is a problem, which I doubt, the question of liability is unlikely to arise.

"Third, Molly Wood has lived a long, full life, but she is even now showing signs of failing health. Even if you grant the proposition that she will build a house up at Happy Jack, and that any well she digs up there might not provide optimal water, the effects on her health are unlikely to matter much."

Hawk gaped. He had gone far beyond angry, into astounded. "No liability? Health effects that don't matter?"

The devil wore a brown mustache, a wine-stained T-shirt, cut-off blue jeans, black socks, and walking shoes. Verbosity was his weapon of choice. "Let me put this as simply as possible," Sally said. "Don't you think you have an obligation to tell Molly about the problems with this land?"

For once Sheldon gave it to them straight. "No," he said. "And I'd suggest that the two of you stay out of what's not your business."

CHAPTER 28
JUBILEE SATURDAY
NIGHT

"I COMPLETELY underestimated the slimy little fucker," said Hawk, on the drive home.

"At the same time," Sally mused, "I wonder what Molly's thinking? She must suspect that the other guys know they're offering tainted goods."

"One way or the other, it seems she hasn't signed off on the deal yet. She's holding back," Hawk said.

Sally considered. "You know what really pisses me off?"

Hawk cocked an eyebrow. "How long is this going to take?"

"No, seriously. It's that Sheldon's not totally wrong about things. The world is an uncertain, mixed-up place. We do spend a lot of time and energy trying to make things that are, on some level, crazy, appear normal and natural and inevitable. Places and people are never what they appear to be," Sally reflected.

"But that doesn't mean that a guy like Sheldon has the right to go around acting like a smug, self-absorbed asshole, all the while hosing anybody he chooses," Hawk pointed out. "And he'd be just as much of an asshole if, instead of making everything as complicated as possible, he believed in idiotically simple causes. It's not what he *thinks*, or even the incredible crap that comes out of his mouth. It's what he *does*. He's venal and maybe criminally irresponsible."

Sally thought that one over. "Do you think Dwayne and Nattie know about the groundwater?" she asked.

"Impossible to tell. Hell, maybe they just don't care. Maybe it's all just money to them."

What a depressing thought. It wouldn't surprise Sally to find out that Nattie knew she was brokering a toxic deal—knew, and didn't give a good goddamn. Sally had been acquainted with Natalie Charlay Langham for twenty years. Nattie had proven, time and again, that her emotional range stretched from pure malice to mild self-interest, by way of lust. Nattie's callous response to Monette's murder was only the latest evidence of exactly how shallow Nattie's compassion ran. Sheldon Stover didn't seem to be worried about the prospect that an old lady, or anybody else, might end up drinking from a poisoned well. Why expect more from Nattie?

But what about Dwayne? Sally had never had reason to believe that Dwayne was dishonest, or fickle, or even irresponsible in any way. A little fussy—priggish, at times—and evasive, maybe, but not without scruple. Sure he was a banker, but that wasn't prima facie evidence of moral delinquency.

But Dwayne Langham, as Sally had known for years, was a puzzle. He wore his life like a suit with a dozen hidden pockets. She'd never know one-tenth of what went on behind his mild eyes, but she'd seen for herself how he could tuck his troubles away and turn himself into nothing more than a medium for music. Could he do that with money?

Memories flashed through her mind—a night when Nattie had followed Dwayne into the Wrangler, screaming and spitting and slapping at him, while he pleaded with her to calm down. Another night, when Branchwater had played a gig at the Medicine Bow

Lodge. Everybody else saw a blizzard coming, and decided to get a head start on the sixty-mile drive up into the mountains, but Dwayne had to close up the guitar shop and couldn't get out of town until almost dark. It had started to snow shortly after he'd left Laramie, and Dwayne had finally made it to Medicine Bow around ten-thirty, battling two broken tire chains and windshield wipers that had quit working somewhere around Bosler. Fighting a white-out, he'd spun off the road into the ditch, flagged down a passing truck, gotten himself towed out, and kept on driving.

And no matter what Dwayne had just been through, he stepped up on stage as if nothing had happened, and played his music as if nothing else in the world existed. In honky-tonks all over Wyoming, Sally Alder had heard what Dwayne Langham's fingers could do with the strings of a pedal steel guitar, and known what it must be like to hear the lifted voices of the heavenly host.

If she was really going to get up and sing tonight, she'd have to stand by Dwayne's side, and follow Dwayne's example, even as she was wondering whether he deserved to be behind bars. She'd need to leave herself behind and step into an alternative universe.

Sally had a trunk she used as a bedside table. She cleared off the lamp, the alarm clock, the clutter of books and paper, and opened the latches. Right on top, carefully wrapped in tissue and packed in plastic dry cleaner's bags, were the pieces of her Rose of Cimarron suit. Mid-calf red wool skirt with matching tight-waisted jacket, fringed at the sleeves and embroidered, on the lapels and skirt, with big blooming American Beauty roses. Stiff-collared white poplin blouse. High-button black boots. She'd bought the antique outfit long ago at a pricey vintage clothing store in Berkeley, blowing the whole paycheck she'd earned for a month-long stand at a shit-kicker joint in Hayward. She'd never spent that much on clothing in her entire life; she couldn't remember ever wanting anything more.

It was a costume, pure and simple. The kind of thing that every woman in country music, Kitty or Loretta or Dolly or Tanya, Emmylou, Reba, Mary Chapin, or Faith, would put on, step onstage, and feel like she was the Queen of the Opry.

But the prize of the collection was the hat—a flat-brimmed,

black felt number with a wide band and a slide chin strap, in nearly mint condition. She'd found it in its original Montgomery Ward
box, labeled "Our Cowboy Hat, 1907," one long-ago summer
when some lovesick South Dakota boy had taken her exploring
through the buildings of a ghost town that hadn't yet been discovered by historic preservation. Our Hat fit perfectly.

She hadn't put on the suit since the mid-eighties. It hadn't been
her style in an awfully long time. Since her golden heyday as a
honky-tonk woman. It was a little tighter in some places, a little
looser in others, and on the whole, absolutely over the top. In the
old days, her nearly black hair would have hung halfway down her
back. Tonight, silver threaded freely through the dark, and her hair
barely reached her shoulders. Her lips were a little thinner, her hips,
well. Her eyes were still brown, steady, and clear.

All in all, owning up to who she was and who'd she'd become,
older, to be sure, but not bad.

"So what do you wear under all that?" asked Hawk. "Silk
stockings and satin garters, one hopes."

"One may keep hoping," Sally said primly, adjusting the chin
strap so that her hat hung down her back, and admiring Hawk's
simple approach to cowboy dressing: Levi's, boots, a white shirt, a
belt with a Navajo silver buckle. "I've got a job to do."

By the time Sally and Hawk arrived at the Wrangler for the
Millionaires' sound check, there were already dozens of early
party-goers milling around. Technically, Delice's Jubilee Saturday
Night was a private party, admission by hundred-dollar ticket only.
The ticket entitled the holder to all the booze she cared to swill,
along with a barbecue buffet a notch above the Wrangler's usual
fare, not to mention the fabulous live music. Invitations to buy tickets had been sent out to pretty much everybody the Langhams
knew in town, which meant pretty much everybody. People who
weren't interested in partying in the bar (like Maude Stark, or
Molly Wood) didn't attend, but bought tickets anyway. Delice
donated the place and the food, covered her costs on the drinks,
and got her brother's aging but entertaining hobby band to play for
free. The rest of the proceeds from this year's party would benefit
the shelter. Hundreds of people would show up before the night

was over, bringing in thousands of dollars for women and children who needed all the help they could get.

It was a night, as they said in Wyoming, to get Western with it. Beginning with the band, everybody in the place had taken the occasion to dig out his cowboy finest. Dwayne, Sam, and the rest of the boys wore matching black and tan Western suits reminiscent of Bob Wills and the Texas Playboys—where they'd found the suits, Sally couldn't imagine. Delice wore a dress modeled on a frontier cavalry officer's uniform, midnight blue with a yellow neckerchief, a double row of brass buttons down the front, a silver concho belt three inches wide, and her usual subtreasury of bangles, dangles, and rings. Nattie had gone for the gunslinger look, black leather from head to toe and even a hip-slung holster, aiming at Johnny Cash but hitting a mark somewhere to the right of Joan Jett. When she made her entrance, Sally was talking to the bartender. Delice was on her way to the buffet table with a giant bowl of potato salad the exact color of her neckerchief, but she detoured, put the bowl down on the bar, and held out her hand. "No guns," she said shortly. "Give it here."

Nattie clucked her tongue. "Yeah, Delice. I'm a mortal danger to everybody here," she said, unsnapping the tooled leather cover and pulling her weapon, which turned out to be a chrome and plastic Mattel cap pistol of precisely the type Sally's brothers had begged for, and gotten, on a Christmas morning somewhere back in the Kennedy administration.

"Didn't anybody ever tell you that playing with guns is stupid?" Delice asked.

"You really want to make a big thing of this?" Nattie retorted, with what seemed to Sally more heat than the situation warranted.

"Jeez, Nattie, chill out," Sally said, wanting to ask about the land swap, but figuring that Nattie was too testy at the moment to talk real estate. Instead she turned to Delice. "Give her a break, Dee. If she wants to play with her toys, let her. You've got potato salad and baked beans to haul. Come on, I'll help."

"I don't like this," Delice grumbled. "If I let her keep her little popgun, what happens when some big yay-hoo with a .357 magnum comes in here and complains about unequal treatment?"

"Relax. People are here to eat and drink and dance, not shoot the place up. Take your boyfriend Marsh Carhart, for example," Sally said, sneering and inclining her head toward the other end of the bar, where Carhart stood with Sheldon, who was wearing a polo shirt with a red bandana tied around his neck, and pounding down whatever red wine the Wrangler, in its wisdom, was pouring. In a black slouch hat and a heavy canvas cowpuncher's duster, Carhart was smiling his most engaging, boy-screen-idol smile and sipping his Stoli. "He's gonna be hot as hell in that duster."

"He's not my boyfriend, but he did buy ten tickets," said Delice. "He can get as hot as he wants."

At last it was time for the music. Any other night of the year, the Millionaires liked to mix in lots of rock and blues, soul and jazz, and even a touch of salsa. On Jubilee Saturday Night, they kept it in the country vein. It wasn't monotonous—they did everything from Western swing to bluegrass, gospel, hillbilly music, and Southern California country-rock, Texas outlaw, Parrothead pop, and Nashville classics. They could swing it, rag it, stride it, or paint it blue, but whatever it was going to be, they were going to do it country. They fired right up with "Hey, Good Lookin'" and never looked back. Neither did the crowd. From the moment Dwayne counted them off and let a pedal steel lick fly, the dance floor was packed.

Halfway through the first set, Sally saw Brit push her way up to the stage, dragging Herman Schwink behind her. Both looked distraught. Brit was making it plain, over the music, that she needed to talk to Sally. "On the break," Sally mouthed, refocusing her concentration on Sam Branch, who was flat-picking the hell out of Doc Watson's "Tennessee Stud" and expecting her to come back in with a harmony on the chorus. Neither Brit nor Herman was dressed for the occasion—Brit wore shorts and a tank top, and Herman looked to be wearing the same clothes he'd roped in that day at the rodeo. Hmm.

Never had a set seemed so long to Sally. She sleep-sang her way through "Your Good Girl's Gonna Go Bad," managed to do her bit on four more songs, and sighed with relief when they finally polished off the last hell-bent note of "The Race Is On" and Sam announced, "Y'all come back in fifteen minutes."

"What what what, Brit?" Sally asked as she stepped off the stage. Brit grabbed her by the arm and hauled Sally away, Montgomery Ward hat bouncing against her back. "Can I at least get a drink on the way to hearing what you have to say?"

"This is important, Sally," Brit insisted, but Sally strode purposefully to the bar and made Brit and Herman wait while she got a whiskey. She spied Hawk by the pool table, leaning on a cue, a Budweiser longneck dangling from two fingers, and gave him a wave. He smiled.

Brit, out of patience, pulled her toward the back of the bar, shoving past Dwayne and Nattie, who were drinking shots of Cuervo, and Marsh Carhart, still in the duster but not sweating visibly—Joe Cool. Finally Brit pushed her through the swinging doors to the back, past a broom closet, and into Delice's office, Herman bringing up the rear. "We need privacy."

"This has to do with your brother Adolph, I assume?" Sally asked Herman.

"Yes, ma'am. He's still down at the sheriff's. Seems they want to take their time getting a statement from him."

Sally flopped down into Delice's desk chair, winced as she nearly crushed the hat, flung it out of harm's way, and leaned back again, taking a sip of her whiskey. "Did he kill Monette?" she asked, although she knew Adolph's alibi was tight.

"No ma'am!" Herman exclaimed, turning red. "The thing is, it looks like he knew her a whole lot better than he was letting on before," he admitted.

But Sally had been aware of that fact ever since she'd stood in the produce aisle, cradling an overloaded basket of fruit and eavesdropping on a conversation that was very much none of her business. "Brit told me about the day Monette was killed. And it appears she was with him at least one time when he was selling marijuana. I take it they had an ongoing thing of some kind?"

Herman swallowed. For a big, strong cowboy, he looked like he might cry any minute. "From what he told me this afternoon, they started up right after she came into town. She was lonesome, I guess, and, well, even though my brother likes to make out that he's some red-hot lover or something, he's never had all that much luck with the ladies. From the sound of it, they were both kind of ashamed of what they were doing, so they hid it. But I guess there was a lot to hide. They snuck off every chance they could."

Second oldest story in country music: cheatin' hearts. But was it really cheating if neither of them had anything else going? Or did the cheating start when Monette came on to every loser who walked through her checkout line? Or when Adolph said mean things about Monette to other people? Or not until the moment when Monette went off with some other guy?

"Did he say whether she was seeing anybody else?"

"I guess she tried right enough. Adolph said that one of the reasons he hated himself for going with her was the way she threw herself at every sorry old boy that came into the store. Of course, what with how he treated her, you kind of couldn't blame her. When it came down to it, they usually ended up with each other," Herman finished.

Some attachments, Sally reflected, didn't even qualify as third-rate romances. "Where did they go?" she asked.

"Anyplace. To Monette's apartment, of course, although her landlady lived downstairs, and she's the nosy type. Adolph didn't want anybody seeing him around there too much. Since he lives with our folks, they couldn't go to his place. So when they had time, they'd drive out of town and park," Herman explained.

Sally's stomach lurched. She set down the whiskey. "Where'd they park?"

Brit answered. "Everywhere you can imagine. Up Ninth Street Canyon a ways. Out past West Laramie. But mostly up east of town. Places in the Laramie Range. Vedauwoo. Happy Jack."

Double lurch. "Did Adolph say whether they ever went to the Devil's Playground?"

Herman, clearly incapable of speaking, nodded.

"And that was one of her preferred spots?" Sally continued. Another nod.

"It was Adolph who knew which places to go at first, but after a few weeks, she definitely had her favorites. From what Adolph told Herman, Monette could be fairly bossy about those kinds of things," Brit explained.

"So once Adolph had shown her the ropes, she could have taken somebody else to one of their places," Sally said, realizing too late how poorly she'd chosen her words.

"Reckon so," Herman managed.

Sally closed her eyes tight, thinking. "You know, this time of year there's a lot of traffic up in the Laramies. Doing it in your car would be pretty public."

"Yes ma'am. Adolph wasn't too crazy about that, but he said Monette got a kick out of the risk. In fact, it seemed to him like every time they went out, she was looking to take one more chance."

Sally picked up the whiskey, then put it down once again. "I'm still not seeing what's urgent here."

"Hey, this is hard for Herman—he's got to kind of run up on his point," Brit said defensively.

"I'm getting there," he told them. "Okay. Just last week, up at Happy Jack, they went down a dirt road and practically ran right into a parked truck with two people sitting in it. Adolph wanted to go home, but Monette made him keep driving until they were just around a corner, out of sight of the truck, and then she jumped him. He said she thought it was a big joke, and, well, she made a point of being extra noisy while they were going at it."

Talking about this subject was clearly embarrassing to the cowboy. Brit put a gentle hand on his shoulder and said softly, "Go on, Herman."

He took a breath, and continued. "After they were done she got out of the car—I guess to go to the restroom—and when she came back she was laughing her head off. Said the people in the truck had gotten out and been pretty near close enough to join in on what she and Adolph had just been doing in Adolph's car, but the people were so busy hollering at each other they never heard a thing. She'd even slipped up, through the trees, practically right on them, and they kept on arguing and never suspected there was somebody listening. And she said that some of the stuff those people were yelling about, they probably would have rather nobody had heard. Said she might be able to find a way to use it."

Sally stared.

"That Monette. She just had a way of looking for trouble," Brit said gravely.

"Did Adolph recognize . . ." Sally began.

The door to Delice's office opened, and Dwayne stuck his head in. He looked the three of them over with an unreadable expression in his eyes. 'Hey Mustang—we've been looking all over for you. Sam wants to change the order of the second set. Come on out."

"Can you give me just a minute here, Dwayne?" Sally asked, trying to act casual, and feeling sweat pooling between her shoulder blades, sliding down her backbone.

Now Sam Branch burst in. "Let's go, Sally. We need to make some changes in the next set, right now. I want to start out with a gospel tune . . ." he began, tugging her to her feet.

Helpless, she shot a look back at Brit and Herman as Sam pulled her out the door.

"The answer is, he didn't!" Brit shouted. "We'll talk more on the next break."

Was Sally Alder really standing on stage at the Wrangler Bar and Grill, shoulder to shoulder with the other members of the Millionaires band, formed in rank and singing in the choir? Were their voices really blending so perfectly that they sounded like one instrument, richly multitonal but a single device, nonetheless? On this one old gospel standard, "I'll Fly Away," everybody in the band sang, even Dwayne, putting in a deep bass line you'd never know, looking at him, that he possessed. Make a joyous noise for life after death.

And then they broke apart, taking up the acoustic instruments and hammering out a ripping fast bluegrass standard, "Don't Let Your Deal Go Down ('Til Your Last Dollar's Gone)." Sally almost laughed aloud. Money and death, cheatin' and prayin'. Welcome to my world.

She desperately wanted to collect Hawk, and get back with Brit and Herman. She just knew she was on the brink of making a connection that would lead to the murderer. There was something so close to the surface of her mind, it felt like a splinter in a finger, visible under a translucent layer of skin, poking deep and sharp.

Pulling it out would be bloody work, but leaving it to fester could spread poison.

And all this, just as the party was really starting to crank. As excruciatingly slowly as the time seemed to pass, the music whirled faster and faster, the fiddler sawing away like a maniac, the drummer's arms a blur. Sam had insisted on reworking the set so that it was nothing but up-tempo stuff, no ballads, no blues, building and building with nothing to stall the crazy climb. "We can give them a rest in the third set," he said. "They'll be drunk enough by then that they'll want to be holding each other up, swaying to 'Too Far Gone,' " Sam said.

Hotter. Sweatier. Smokier. Crazier. Ordinarily, by this point in a gig, Sally had drunk some bourbon, loosened up, given herself over to the gods of the night. But tonight the air was smothering, the demons, always close by, closing in. At the edge of her control, she made it, finally, to the last mad number in the set. A crash—somebody had dropped, or thrown, a beer bottle. The crowd was really whipped up now.

"That's the way to do it!" hollered Sam, barely audible over the screaming, surging, cheering throng. "See you in fifteen!" Sally fairly jumped off the stage this time, pushing through the crush, peering through the dim barroom light, searching for Hawk and Brit and Herman, and needing a bathroom. She nearly stepped on a cocktail waitress, crouched down with her hand on the throat of a dilapidated broom, sweeping up broken glass and spilled beer.

Sally froze. Wet broom straw. Tuesday morning, helping Nattie get that coffee urn out of the back of her Escalade. Monday afternoon, sitting on a rock, watching the ants carry off what she'd thought was a piece of dry grass, but what she knew, now, had been a broom straw. Yesterday afternoon, practically right where she was standing, Scotty talking about poor Monette, and some kind of penetration, and paint chips.

Monette was blackmailing somebody. People she'd overheard arguing somewhere up at Happy Jack. A couple of days later, Monette was dead, and Nattie had a wet broom in her Escalade.

Nattie said Dwayne had taken her truck on a fishing trip.

Dwayne, who liked things tidy. Dwayne, who'd been the one

by Sally's side when she'd been shoved into the bucking chute. Who had the kind of money Monette would covet.

Or Nattie, covetous in her own right, dead solid set on this Happy Jack land deal—had she been one of the people Monette had heard arguing? Who was the other?

Dwayne *and* Nattie?

Frantic, Sally searched for Hawk. Finally he materialized at her side, a bourbon in his hand. "Thought you'd need this," he said, spilling the drink on both of them as she yanked his arm and began to drag him toward the bar. "Dickie isn't here yet, is he?"

"No. Delice said he called a little while ago and said he and Scotty were wrapping up a few things and would be over soon. Why?"

"We've got to call him and get him here *now*. I'm not completely sure what's going on, but I think I'm about to figure out who killed Monette. And it won't be good news. Dwayne or Nattie might be involved."

Hawk pushed their way to the bar, told the bartender they had an emergency, got the phone, and made the call. Sally, meanwhile, scanned the place, looking for Dwayne and Nattie, and for that matter, Sheldon and Marsh Carhart. She caught sight of Nattie chatting with Carhart and Sheldon.

"I gotta talk to her," Sally said. "Can you try to find Dwayne, and keep an eye on Nattie while I take a pit stop?"

"Okay," Hawk said dubiously. "But if she's been going around killing people, how damn dumb is it to go chasing after her?"

"What's the choice, Hawk?" Sally snapped. "Besides, she's not armed. I just want to keep her occupied until Dickie gets here."

Knowing that the public restrooms at the Wrangler were no better than they should have been, Sally headed for the small, private bathroom in Delice's office. She performed her ablutions and was just about to head out when, fortuitously, Nattie blew into the office. "Thought I'd use Delice's bathroom," she explained.

"Just the woman I've been looking for," Sally said nonchalantly. "I'll wait for you."

Nattie did her business, and then opened the door between the bathroom and the office as she pulled a cosmetic bag out of her purse and went to work fixing her makeup. "So what's the story?" she asked warily, leaning toward the cloudy, cracked mirror, mascara wand in hand.

"Saw you celebrating last night," Sally told her. "Did you close the land deal?"

"Not that it's any business of yours," Nattie shot back, "but in fact, yes, we're signing the papers tomorrow morning." She finished the mascara, went for her lipstick.

"I'm a little surprised to hear that," Sally said. "What with Mrs. Wood being in Ivinson Memorial and all."

Nattie grimaced in the mirror, wiping orange lipstick off her teeth with a tissue. "We're meeting there, at her request. She's consulted with her family, and they've all agreed that this swap is for the best. A broken ankle doesn't affect her ability to sign her name."

Time to inch partway out on a limb. "I suppose not. But it's a little puzzling that she'd be so eager to sign, since it means trading off her ranch for a toxic waste dump."

"I beg your pardon?" Nattie aimed a cold eye at Sally.

"Are you aware of the fact that the old Golden Eagle tie plant, up the hill from the beaver pond property, spilled all kinds of nasty stuff for twenty years? And there's creosote and PCBs and dioxin in the groundwater where Molly would be digging her well?"

"Butt the hell out, Sally," said Nattie, tossing her makeup bag in her purse, closing the purse with a snap. "If you're half as smart as you claim to be, just leave it alone."

Nattie tried to walk out, but Delice's office was small and cluttered. Sally stood, blocking her way. "This isn't about who's smart, Nattie. It's about what's right. You can't go through with this deal, knowing that in all likelihood somebody's liable to get real sick drinking the water up there."

"It's not that simple," Nattie told her. "Get out of my way."

But now Sally was gripping her arm. "Just tell me one thing. Was Monette mixed up in this somehow?"

Nattie flinched. "Monette's dead," she said, turning her head, not meeting Sally's eyes.

"How?" Sally wouldn't let go. "Why? You know something

about this, damn it, Nattie. You've been covering up for days, but you've got to come clean."

Nattie's lips were trembling, even as she tried to get herself under control. "I don't know shit. Get out of my face, I mean it."

Sally would never have predicted that at this moment, she'd be feeling pity. "You're obviously miserable, Nattie. What in God's name happened?"

Her eyes filled with tears, spilled over, a plume of mascara cascading down her cheeks. "You're just like her. Nothing would have happened to her if she hadn't stuck her nose where it didn't belong. Listen to me, Sally, leave it alone."

She couldn't. She wouldn't. "Can't. Did you kill her, Nat? Did you hurt her with that broom in your truck?"

"No! No! All I wanted was to make sure the deal went through. You couldn't understand, Sally. You always had it easy. I've had to work for everything I've ever gotten, and people still think I'm just the greedy bitch who spends Dwayne Langham's money. This deal is my big chance to make something of my own."

"I know about work, Nattie," Sally said. "Don't patronize me."

"You don't know squat. You don't even know half of what Monette knew. You didn't have an old man who beat hell out of you and then thought he'd make it up to you in a way that hurt even worse."

Sally was stunned speechless.

"I've survived a lot, Sally. Monette did too. That much about her, I sure can understand." Nattie paused for a breath. "She called my office early Monday morning to say she heard me and Marsh arguing up at Happy Jack about what to do about that state groundwater report, and she thought we needed to talk. I've been worried that the report would cause trouble since I first heard about it, but Marsh kept insisting it was no big deal—if the state hasn't seen fit to do anything about it, why should we bother? Monette said she expected we'd be interested in doing all we could to keep the information confidential, and I thought, uh-oh, here it comes.

"I just wanted to buy her off and make her shut up. But Marsh said we had to meet with her. She took one look at him and decided she could make him pay more than one way. She had some bondage fantasy she wanted to play out with him. It was so fucking pathetic."

"What then, Nattie?" Sally whispered. "Tell me. I've already got some ideas, and it's just a matter of time until Dickie and Scotty figure it out. Maybe I can help you."

Nattie looked around, panic in her eyes. "We picked her up at her apartment, and drove up to Vedauwoo. I had five thousand dollars in cash. But she wanted Marsh too, and she had that damn rope, and . . ."

"Come on."

"We drank some beer, and she had some smoke, and then . . . he took her over to these rocks. She thought she could make him . . . she said it was part of the bargain. But I guess he couldn't get it up or something, or maybe he told her he wouldn't, I don't know. I was over by the fire ring. I heard her laughing, and crying, all at the same time, taunting him and yelling at him, and then I heard the shots. I didn't want to look. It was an accident. He told me so. He said she'd driven him to it, trying to force him to have sex with her."

This from the guy who'd written *Man, the Rapist*? "He had a gun?" Sally asked.

"My gun," said Nattie. "The little .22 pistol I keep in the glove box."

"If it was an accident, why'd he take the gun?" Sally asked.

"I don't, I don't know," Nattie moaned, mascara in flood. "I can't think."

"And he'd gone out back of the Wrangler and rooted through Delice's garbage. He took it up there, and scattered it around to make it look like drifters had been partying there. And then, of course, there was that business with the broom—what was that all about? After he shot her, did he come back for the broom, so he could make it look like rape? Was that it? The gun, the garbage, the broom—you're going to protect this guy?" Sally was relentless.

"Stop! She tried to force him to have sex with her! He didn't mean to kill her! It just happened! And I don't know, didn't see—he came and got the broom, but I wouldn't look. I can't think about it, I won't. Things just got out of control. That's the way it goes, sometimes, right?"

Oh God. "What did you expect when you let him have the gun, Nattie? What in hell were you thinking?"

"I couldn't imagine he'd do it. He'd been so sweet, all along. He said he just wanted an advantage. It was a complicated piece of business, and we worked so hard on it. Monette just, just . . . got in the way. I know, I know, it was horrible. I can't tell you . . . but he promised me that once we'd put the deal through, I could go see him in California. I'd have all the money I'd ever need, and he'd have a big finder's fee from his California friends who were putting up the cash. Once the deal went through, we could do anything we wanted. Maybe I could even move out there and be with him. You're not from here. You're from country clubs and fancy schools. You lived in Berkeley and L.A. How could you possibly imagine what it's like, growing up poor, and afraid, and your whole world being Laramie?"

"Is that why you haven't told Dickie what you know? Because you're hoping Marsh Carhart is your ticket out of here?" But then the truth struck Sally. "Or are you afraid he'll get rid of you the way he got rid of Monette?"

"She can't understand, Nattie. I told you," came a voice behind Sally's back. She turned. Marsh Carhart stood in the door of Delice's office, pistol in his hand. Cold blue steel in his grip and his eyes. But then he made the eyes go warm, looking at Nattie. "And I said I'd take care of you, didn't I, baby?"

"Marsh, what are you doing?" Nattie asked, staring at the gun.

"Solving a problem I should have finished off at the rodeo," he answered flatly.

"You pushed me in that bucking chute!" Sally exclaimed.

"Evidently not hard enough," he said.

"But tonight you brought the gun to make sure. That's what the duster is about," Sally told Carhart, her anger growing. "You're even more asinine than I thought. What are you going to do, Marsh, shoot me? Haven't you noticed that there are about five hundred people in this place?"

"You can shut up any time, Sally," Carhart said. "You always did have a big mouth."

"Not to mention," Sally continued, ignoring him, "that Hawk is undoubtedly looking for me at this very moment, and will probably show up here inside of two minutes."

Carhart laughed. "Imagine how that terrifies me. After what I saw of how the two of you reacted to finding that kid's body up in the mountains, puking and shaking, I'm not too worried about his quick wits or reflexes. He's a good match for you, I guess," he added, "not too challenging."

"You saw us?" Oddly, the thought of Carhart watching them cut, for a moment, through the fear and the fury, and embarrassed the hell out of her.

"My only regret," said Carhart, as if to himself, "is that you arrived too soon for me to do a decent job of stowing the body. It was almost comic, though—I thought I'd about gotten her stuffed down in that precipice, and suddenly Nattie here was right beside me, blubbering something about people coming across the meadow. She recognized you, of course. I probably should have just shot you both then and there. A simple answer to a simple problem."

"It won't do you any good to shoot me now," Sally told him, desperate to keep him talking. "The cops are on the way. And you want to know something? You didn't even have to kill Monette. It wouldn't have mattered if she'd told about the groundwater pollution."

"What are you talking about?" Nattie asked, eyes wide amid the ruins of her makeup.

"Who could she tell? The state? They aren't doing anything about it. Molly Wood?" Sally laughed bitterly. "She knows. Hawk told her last night. But from what you say, she's ready to go ahead with the deal, creosote and dioxin in her well and all. In other words, Monette didn't have anything on you that she could use. Isn't it ironic?"

For the first time in twenty years, Sally saw an emotion she'd never seen cross Nattie Langham's face: shame. Then Nattie collected herself. "This has gone far enough, Marsh. Would you please put my gun away?" Nattie said, trying for bravado, but achieving only pathos.

"Listen to me, honey." Carhart's voice was gentle, warm, as his eyes caressed Nattie, the .22 still pointed at Sally. "She's the only one who can mess us up now. Her boyfriend may have figured out the problem with the land, but hey, he solved it for us by blabbing to Mrs. Wood. That's good, very good, isn't it sweetheart?"

Now his eyes glittered. His forehead was beaded with sweat. He licked his lips and spoke to Nattie again. "I put the money guys together with my old friend Sheldon and his land, didn't I? I dealt with that little slut too. I can deal with Green later, but for now, we need to tie up this particular loose end. After I fire, I hand the gun to you. We'll say she found your pistol in your purse. She tried to take it away from you, and you struggled, and it went off. An accident. I came in here and found you hysterical. It fits in your purse, right? It's just a little gun, after all."

Sally whirled and ducked just as the gunshot exploded in the tiny room. She felt something jerk her back as she hit the floor, heard Nattie scream.

She shook her head. A surge of unadulterated joy went through her as she realized that whatever had happened, she hadn't been shot. She was shaking uncontrollably, but intact.

"That's right," said a voice. When she finally looked up, Hawk was kneeling in the doorway, inspecting the pistol on the floor. Carhart was still standing in the door, but there was an arm around his throat, the barrel of a 9-mm Glock up against his temple, the burning cold, clear eyes of Scotty Atkins just visible above the crown of Carhart's black slouch hat. "It's just a little gun," Scotty said. "Mine's bigger."

SUNDAY

CHAPTER 29
HEAVEN AND HELL

"BIG, LITTLE, medium, tiny, behemoth, whatever, I hate them all!" Sally said, whisking green chiles into eggs for breakfast burritos. "I never, ever want to see another gun again. Half of what's wrong with this country could be solved by banning guns. Look at my hat! It's ruined."

The 1907 Montgomery Ward hat sat in the middle of the kitchen table, a pair of matching bullet holes—entrance and exit—through the front and back of the crown.

"Oh, I don't know. If it were me, I might hang it on the living room wall as a souvenir. Sort of a Wordsworth motif—intimations of mortality and all that," said Hawk, sneaking up behind her to snitch some grated cheese. "And admit it, Sal, it's not guns that made honky-tonk angels. You could take every weapon in the world, dig a hole two thousand feet deep, drop them in, and seal it all off with cement, and you'd still have more than enough cruelty, rage, horror, and just plain meanness in the world—hell, in the state of Wyoming alone. From what Scotty told me last night, Bone Bandy's terrified of firearms, but what with his fists, and knives, and rocks, he's done his share of harm."

"Don't you think it would be worse if he worshipped guns, like most people around here?" Sally slapped his hand as he pinched more cheese.

"You're right, of course. Guns make bad things a lot worse. Look, can we stop having an argument where we both really agree, and just be relieved it's all over? I've never been so glad in my life to see the end of Jubilee Days." Hawk headed for the counter where they kept the coffee rig.

"All I want to do is sleep, cook real meals, take long walks, and read a million books, like a normal college professor," Sally said.

"You want another latte?" Hawk asked her.

"What normal college professor wouldn't?" she replied.

"Or even an abnormal one," Hawk said. "I keep expecting Sheldon to show up demanding cappuccino. I still can't believe you let him go back to Edna's last night, even if he did promise to clear out of town at dawn."

"As usual with him, there wasn't any choice," Sally said. "Obviously he couldn't go to Dwayne and Nattie's. He's a greedy, self-obsessed little scumbucket, but he clearly didn't know anything about the murder. He was really freaked about the whole thing."

"If you ask me, he was more concerned about the idea that he wouldn't be able to unload his land," Hawk observed. "I don't know why you cut him so much slack."

"The slack ends if I go over there this afternoon and find him microwaving Dinty Moore Beef Stew in one of Edna's pueblo pots," Sally said. As Hawk busied himself with the espresso machine, she checked the hash browns in the frying pan. Almost crispy enough. "Do you think Nattie will have to go to jail?"

"I'd bet against it," Hawk said. "The police will be needing her testimony against Carhart. The real estate deal is dead, and somehow I don't think Molly will want to press charges for the attempt at fraud."

"But Carhart's already claiming that it was Nattie who killed

Monette. It was her gun. Won't she have to defend herself?" Sally poured the eggs into the sizzling frying pan.

"After last night? He shot at you, in case you forgot."

"I didn't forget." Not even close.

"He's the one they're charging with the murder, and the assault on you at the rodeo, and last night. And can you imagine any Wyoming jury that would take the word of some slick-ass California ecologist over the local girl he done wrong? The author of *Man, the Rapist*? By the time it's all over, they'll probably award Nattie damages for pain and suffering." Hawk poured milk in the steel pitcher.

"Did you see how Dwayne swooped right in to take care of her? I mean, there Nattie was, explaining to Scotty Atkins about the things she and her lover had been doing for the past week, while they'd obviously been keeping Dwayne in the dark about the tie plant pollution, not to mention the murder! And the whole time Dwayne sat right by her side, holding her hand, and wouldn't let her open her mouth until he'd gotten that lawyer buddy of his in there, telling her exactly what to say."

"If you were being interrogated by the police," said Hawk, "I promise I'd get you an attorney."

"I appreciate your devotion," Sally said, scrambling eggs and chiles and cheese, warming tortillas on another burner. "But I wonder how you'd feel about listening to me talk about what a jerk I'd been while some other guy was seducing and deceiving me."

"Aren't you the one who sings a song called 'Love Has No Pride'?" asked Hawk. "Maybe that's Dwayne's theme song."

"And yours would be?" Sally inquired.

Hawk gave her a hard look. "I wouldn't want to have to listen to any song that captured how I'd be feeling under those circumstances."

"I'll keep that in mind," Sally said quietly. "I think these eggs are about done."

"Promise me something." Hawk walked across the kitchen, wrapped his arms around her waist as she heaped potatoes on plates and folded the eggs into the tortillas. "Promise you'll go back to being a normal college professor, and stop getting yourself into situations where guys pull guns on you."

Sally said, "Am I too much trouble for you?"

A sigh escaped him. "Just enough, I guess."

They were finishing their coffee and discussing whether they had the energy to go for a hike in the Snowy Range, or whether it would be more fun just hanging around the yard, reading novels and pulling weeds. It had, by any measure, been a taxing week. The phone rang. "Let the machine get it," Hawk said. "It's probably Delice wanting to rehash last night, or Maude, expecting the low-down. They can wait."

But when the answering machine clicked on, it was Molly Wood's voice they heard. Hawk rushed to pick up the phone before she hung up.

"No . . . that's not necessary. Really Molly, you don't have to . . . but you don't owe me anything. What you do with your land is your business . . . Yes, Sally and I can get over there, if you want. But it's really not . . . okay. I understand. We'll see you in about an hour."

Hawk hung up, scratched his chin, and sat back down with his coffee. "She wants to see us at the hospital. Said she owed me an explanation. Can't imagine why."

"You can't? I can," Sally told him. "At her request, you bust your ass digging up information on that mountain property and spend a night in the hospital, holding her hand, while her own grown children are snug in bed. I almost get shot over the deal, and in the meantime she announces that she's ready to trade away her big piece of paradise for a bunch of cash and a much smaller property she knows is poisoned. I'd say that calls for an explanation."

"I'm nothing to her," Hawk said shortly.

"It's funny how you keep saying that. It's almost as if you're trying to convince yourself," Sally told him.

"Oh yeah?" Hawk was on the defensive.

She took one of his hands in both of hers. "Okay, I'll level with you. I like Molly Wood—I even admire her—but the New England schoolmarm thing works differently on you than me. It's like she reminds you of some long-ago memory of your mother, and you're fighting it, working hard to remember that she's another person altogether. You're doing the right thing, but it's hard for you."

"Thanks, Dr. Alder. I didn't realize you were a psychiatrist as well as a historian," Hawk said.

"Hawk, missing your mother doesn't mean you love your father or your stepmother any less." Sally leaned over and kissed him. "There's enough to go around."

"You're making too much of this," he insisted. "I just think Molly Wood's business isn't mine."

"Then don't go to the hospital. I, for one, am curious about what she has to say. I can fill you in later," Sally said, picking up the empty plates and heading for the sink.

Hawk eyed her over his coffee cup. "I didn't say I wouldn't go. The last thing I want is you going up there to read her the riot act about dragging me into this thing."

Sally grinned. "Still think I'm just enough trouble?"

Hawk grunted, staring at the Montgomery Ward hat, still in the middle of the table. "It's one of those William Blake 'heaven and hell' things. You never know what's enough until you know what's more than enough."

She'd always wanted a man who'd quote poetry to her. But she'd had in mind love sonnets, Shakespeare, or maybe John Donne. Not Wordsworth's meditations on death or Blake's odes to excess.

Still, he'd do. As she watched Hawk head out to the backyard to water the garden, smart and strong and serious and so very solidly hers, she knew he'd more than do.

The flowers were, of course, her idea. Hawk had put plenty of work into growing the cosmos and zinnias and marigolds that had only just begun to bloom in their garden, but it would never have occurred to him to suggest that they take Molly Wood a bouquet. It was Sally who cut the first bright blossoms, wrapped the stems in a wet paper towel, and then in aluminum foil. When they arrived Molly was cranked way up in the bed, reading glasses perched on her nose, doing a crossword puzzle.

"I'm surprised to find you alone," Sally told Molly, putting the flowers into a water carafe on the bedside table. "I'd have thought your kids would be here."

"Alice flew back to New Jersey this morning," Molly said, taking her glasses off and letting them dangle. "Once she learned that the Centennial Bank had withdrawn financing for the land swap, she said she didn't see a need to be here, and she really had to get back to work. I agreed with her. Evidently she's having some problems with her business." Molly's blue eyes were very cool. "The orthopedist says I can go home tomorrow, and Philip is going to stay a couple of days and help me get settled. He's off at the drugstore and the grocery now, getting the things I need. Thank you again for staying with me Friday night."

"It's good to see you feeling better," Hawk told Molly.

Hawk really meant it. For reasons Sally couldn't yet explain, his concern infuriated her.

"And good to know you're being taken care of," Sally added, struggling for compassion—and failing. "Sorry to hear that your real estate deal went south."

Something flickered in Molly's eyes, and she smiled very slightly. "No sense wasting time on the niceties, eh Sally? Well then, all right." She aimed her gaze at Hawk. "Josiah, I think you have the right to know why, after all the trouble you took to warn me about the groundwater pollution on that land up at Happy Jack, I was willing to go through with the trade."

Hawk stared out the window. "I told you, it's none of my business. You asked me to check out the land, so I did. It wasn't up to me to tell you what to do."

Molly searched his face, finally managing to make him look at her (schoolmarm voodoo?) "No. And though you've no way of knowing it, I do know that country well, myself. I've been going up there to look at birds almost sixty years, after all."

"Birds?" Sally asked, something starting to hum in her brain.

"Yes. When Ezekiel and I were first married, we used to birdwatch up there all the time. It was even better than it is now. The eagles were especially abundant."

"Golden eagles," Sally said.

Hawk stared at Molly. "You knew about the tie plant," he said.

"We owned it," Molly told him. "That was Zeke's first big war contract. It was the beginning of his business. He named that company after the birds we saw. And of course, without it, we'd never have been able to dream of buying a place like Wood's Hole. He always had a sentimental attachment to Golden Eagle."

Hawk anticipated her. "But something happened to change that."

Molly lay her crossword puzzle and her pencil next to her on the bed, and folded her hands. "Yes. Back in June of 1962. I remember the day quite precisely. We'd taken a picnic up to Happy Jack, figuring the eagles would be nesting. We'd seen half a dozen nests in years past, so we knew where to look. We were right, but there was something terribly wrong."

The horror showed in Hawk's eyes. "The birds were there, I bet. But they were sick, weren't they?"

"Sick, stillborn, dying, dead. I've never seen anything like it. Absolutely horrible." Molly closed her eyes at the memory.

"Did you understand what you were seeing?" Hawk asked.

"Not then. But a couple of months later, I read this book. A bestseller of the time. *Silent Spring*, by Rachel Carson. Zeke read it too."

"Yes. We know the book," Sally said. Who didn't? *Silent Spring* was to the environmental movement what *Uncle Tom's Cabin* had been to abolitionism.

"We realized, instantly, what had happened. The tie plant must be poisoning the birds. My husband was horrified, of course. He shut the place down immediately, and not long after, gave the land back to the federal government, with the stipulation that there be no further industry on the site. In fact, he liquidated the entire Golden Eagle company. We told ourselves that we'd done absolutely everything we could do to set things right. Probably, in time, the chemicals would dissipate and nature's balance might be restored." Molly picked up the pencil. Put it down.

"But you worried, didn't you?" Hawk asked.

"Yes. But only intermittently, and less and less. As time went on, and nothing happened, we pretty much forgot about it. In fact, I didn't really think of it again, until just a few weeks ago, when Nattie came to me with the proposition for the swap. Then, of course, I began to wonder.

"Please understand," Molly continued, "in the last forty years there have been plenty of other things to occupy our minds—Ezekiel's other business interests, our ranch, and the fact that our children were growing up in the sixties and seventies. Those were not easy times for parents."

"What times are?" Sally asked, thinking of Delice's recent bout with Jerry Jeff.

"Some are worse even than most," Molly retorted, holding her ground. "Alice was the uncomplicated one—she merely hated us. But Philip almost didn't make it out alive. To have endured those times, and with grandchildren to boot, has felt like a notable accomplishment."

"And so," said Hawk, "you've been thinking about that legacy question."

"I could hardly help it," Molly said dryly. "Alice has made a particular point of bringing it up."

Sally and Hawk exchanged a look: no big surprise there.

"So what do you leave behind?" Sally prodded.

"Progeny, of course, and land. But from what Josiah tells me, other things. Creosote." She held up an index finger. "PCBs." A middle finger. "And dioxin." Ring finger. "What to do about that was the question. I had several options."

They waited.

"First," Molly began, "refuse the land swap, hang on to Wood's Hole, and sound the alarm about the groundwater pollution. In that case, the state might be forced to consider cleaning up the site."

"But if you'd done that," Hawk said, "as an owner of the site when the contamination occurred, you might end up having to pay at least part of the cost of the cleanup. I don't know the federal environmental regs, chapter and verse, but I do know that whenever they can find the original polluters, they try to make them pay."

"Correct," Molly told him, as if he'd just been sent to the blackboard to perform long division, and had not only gotten the answer, but had shown his work. "Although, of course, in this case, the tie plant is now on U.S. Forest Service land, so the government would bear substantial responsibility. But it's possible that between the lawsuits and the ultimate damages, I'd be bankrupted, and have to sell Wood's Hole to pay the costs."

"So why not sell now, getting the best price you could?" Hawk said. "I begin to see. And you were willing to risk your own health in the bargain. Why?"

Molly smiled faintly. "There is such a thing as bottled water, Josiah. Even in Wyoming."

"That's just one scenario," Sally interjected.

Molly pierced her with a look, and continued. "Right again. A second possibility: agree to the swap, get the money, but say nothing about the contamination. Put all my assets in trusts for my grandchildren, and live out my days in modest comfort, watching the seasons and the beavers and the birds."

"And then, even if the government did decide to act, the money wouldn't be yours. You'd have managed very neatly to sidestep liability," Sally said. "A Yankee solution if ever there was one. Diabolical, though."

"Practical," Molly retorted.

"Which were you going to do?" Hawk asked, his voice low.

Molly looked into his eyes, and sighed. "I hadn't decided."

Neither devil nor angel. Like most people. "But now the deal's off. So what do you do, Molly?" Sally pressed.

Molly smiled. "I made two calls before I rang you this morning. The first was to my attorney, setting up an appointment for later this afternoon. The second was to a friend of mine who works with the Nature Conservancy. I told her that I wished to make a substantial bequest."

Again they waited.

"My grandchildren will be taken care of—at least they'll get what they need to go to college. After that, they're on their own."

"What about your kids?" Sally couldn't help asking.

"Philip says God is providing for him—who am I to quibble with that logic? And Alice has never made any secret of despising Wood's Hole, so I can't imagine that she'd feel justified profiting from it."

"No," said Hawk, eyes on his hands, mouth quirking, "of

course not. You wouldn't want to trouble her conscience that way."

"So you're going to give the ranch to the Conservancy?" Sally asked.

"Right away. With the provision that I will be able to live there, just as I have, for the rest of my life, as steward of the land I've been trying to restore. I've also agreed to donate the remainder of my financial holdings to the Conservancy, and in return they'll pay me a reasonable salary for taking care of Wood's Hole."

Hawk looked up, his mouth still wry. "And what about the land up at Happy Jack?" he said.

"It wouldn't be a bad thing," Molly said, "if somebody decided to call up the Sierra Club, or perhaps *High Country News*, and drop a hint or two about a story involving an old tie plant in the Laramie Range."

"Somebody probably will," Hawk told her.

"And if anything comes of it," Sally said, "at that point, since you'll have given away pretty much all of your assets, it'll be the United States government's problem. Very nicely done, Molly."

"It's only fair," Molly replied. "This is Wyoming, Sally. Out here, there's one thing we know for certain. If there's a problem, it is undoubtedly the government's fault."

CHAPTER 30
IMAGINE THE REST

"WELL, THAT'S DONE," Hawk said, staring at the telephone he'd just hung up. "I told that guy everything including where to park when he goes to Cheyenne to look at the state report. Now it's up to the intrepid fourth estate to find out most of the facts, and imagine the rest."

"Amazing that you'd actually find a reporter working this late on a Sunday night," said Sally.

"Yeah, it is. Makes me think we ought to give a contribution to that *High Country News* investigative reporting fund. Those people must stay up nights praying for a tip like this."

Hawk had been going nuts all afternoon, having promised Molly that he wouldn't make the call until she phoned to say that her lawyer had the trusts in the works. He could have waited until Monday morning, but he was worried that things would go haywire again. It had been a harrowing week, and Hawk was up past his bedtime, rubbing his eyes and fighting off crankiness. "Molly's going to get some bad press out of this," he said.

Sally leaned over his back and put her arms around him. "I don't think she gives a rat's ass. Looked to me like she worked things out according to a combination of New England logic and Wyoming government blaming. And in the meantime she'll be out there in Centennial, nurturing her grass and enjoying her avocets. What could be more satisfying?"

Crankiness won. "You do realize that Sheldon will probably be able to hold up the feds for twenty times what that property of his is actually worth?" Hawk asked her, looking over his shoulder and peering into her face. "Any way you cut it, he ends up making out."

"Hey—out here in the Wild West, we believe everybody deserves a little slurp at the federal trough," Sally said. "Especially when we can revile those bastards in Washington at the same time. Pure bliss."

The telephone rang again. "You answer it!" Hawk said, tossing her arms off him and jumping up. "I hate the goddamn phone."

It was Scotty Atkins. "Hey, teacher."

"You sound bloody cheerful," Sally said.

"My life is beautiful. I've had five solid hours of sleep, and thought you'd like to know that our friends in South Dakota have some outstanding warrants against Pettibone Bandy for assaults and burglaries in Rapid City, back in 1997. Guess he went on a bit of a bender there, and they're happy to catch up with him. What with this and that, he's liable to do enough time to keep him out of trouble."

"Now I feel more cheerful," said Sally. "How's Nattie?"

"Sleeping, I hope. We sent her home with Dwayne an hour before I left the office. Dickie and I managed to persuade the D.A. to agree to immunity, in return for everything she's got against Carhart. She's going to need a good shrink and a new line of work."

Therapy, okay. But Nattie without real estate? Unthinkable. Ruthless drive, and the willingness of most businesspeople to overlook past trespasses in the face of present wealth, would heal Nattie's reputation, slicker than elk snot. "How about Dwayne?" Sally asked.

"He blows my mind. If it were me, I'd be kicking her butt all the way to Rawlins, but for now, anyway, he says his main job is to help his wife through her crisis. The man's a mystery."

"So I've thought for twenty years. What does Dickie say?"

"Dickie's busy. When I left he was in the interview room. He'd gone through two packs of cigarettes and a gallon of coffee, questioning Marsh Carhart. When I got back neither one of them had moved, but he'd smoked most of another pack, filled up a wastebasket with fast-food trash, and was talking about sending a deputy down to the Wrangler for refreshments. He didn't even look tired." There was admiration in the detective's voice.

"What about Carhart?"

"He looked tired."

Sally chuckled. An awkward pause.

"Well," said Atkins, "I just called to bring you up to date, and to tell you that you're a big pain in the ass."

"Nice mouth," said Sally.

"Coming from you, that means something," he replied. "I want you to promise me that I'll never again find myself slamming a chokehold on some shithead who's getting ready to put a bullet hole in you. I will admit that you were smart enough to figure it all out, but from this second forward, you're officially out of the crime-fighting business. Go back to your books."

"You're the second man today who's given me those instructions," Sally said. "Lucky for all of us, school starts soon."

"Put Hawk on the phone," he told her.

"Hey Hawk!" He'd stalked off to the bedroom, but now he came back. She handed over the receiver, but stayed right there, leaning against him, close enough to hear Scotty through the wire.

"Hoops tomorrow?" Scotty asked.

"Why not?" Hawk said.

"I just told your woman she's a giant pain in the ass," said Scotty.

"Was she shocked?" Hawk asked, one arm stealing around Sally.

"She acted like she'd heard it all before," Scotty said.

"At her age, she's not likely to change," said Hawk, yawning. "But she's got her good points."

"I don't want to hear about it," Scotty said.

"Fine," Hawk answered, grinning sleepily when she kissed him. "We'll leave it to your imagination."